The Ethical Hitman

Steve Dewey

An original publication of watwo

The Ethical Hitman

Copyright © 2017
Steve Dewey

ISBN-13: 9780993222245
ISBN-10: 0993222242

http://cometodereham.co.uk
http://www.watwo.me.uk

Cover design: Paul Vought

watwo, marlborough, wiltshire, uk

Steve again thanks Lizzie for her eyes and ears

Prologue

He liked to smoke some pot before a job – a hit for a hit – in memory of his crazy Muslim antecedents. He knew the meaning of the word *assassin*, and its derivation. Unlike those antecedents, he wouldn't see the Garden of Paradise, but the pot would help him relax – always useful in his profession.

Sometimes, on days like today, it could make him too relaxed. Even he saw his job as something that should happen among grey concrete and dirty back streets in London or Newcastle or Bristol. So now when he found himself sitting on a quiet hill in Hampshire, looking down on a pleasant country house with quiet fields around him, skylarks twittering somewhere above him, and a pale but still warm autumn sun beating down, he wanted to put the gun down, turn over on his back, and let the light bathe his face. If he missed the mark today, he could always come back.

But he was a professional. If he felt proud about anything in his life, it was his attention to detail, his Zen-like detachment, and his belief that the important thing was the work. He had, as always, planned this job meticulously. He knew the mark was at home, and would go out to his car somewhen in the next hour, and that this hill was the perfect location. This was as close to the mark as he wanted to be. The house was in view of the main road, and other cottages pressed up close to the house. Postal deliveries were erratic out here, and bored village housewives walked their dogs down the road at unpredictable times.

He had decided, therefore, that a rifle was the best tool for this job. He had brought with him the trusty old Mannlicher-Carcano that he used in honour of Lee Harvey Oswald, the man who had shown how quickly three rounds could be fired from this rifle. He only intended one shot to the head. He was confident that he could hit the centre of the mark's forehead from this range. He had one of the rare variants of the rifle, produced for the German army, that had been fitted with a telescopic sight. The rifle was unsilenced. Anybody who heard it would simply assume a local farmer was out shooting rabbits in the fields.

He stood about half a mile from the driveway in which the car waited. He had watched this hill for days, and knew people rarely came here – he had seen only one person in that time, walking a black Labrador across it. The slope of the hill had a ditch cut into it, the perfect hiding place. He lay in the ditch, his rifle resting on the top of the bank. The ditch had its own microclimate. The sun warmed air that hardly moved. He felt relaxed, comfortable, and slightly stoned. He hoped the mark would put in the expected appearance soon, before he fell asleep.

He needed to keep himself alert. He raised his head and looked through the telescopic sight of the rifle. He studied the large, red-brick Georgian manse. It had large bay windows on the ground floor, and a porch covered in the same grey slates as the steeply pitched roof. On the upper floor, the dormer windows of the bedrooms cut into the roofline. Ivy and roses climbed the side of the building. There was a double garage, and other outbuildings scattered about the large rear garden. It was a nice house. In the drive was a Jensen FF. A nice car. Ground-breaking in many ways. Almost as ground-breaking as his own. The car and the house obviously belonged to somebody wealthy. That the mark had made the money illegitimately, the hitman had no doubt. Perhaps part of that money had come from whoever had hired him to make this hit. He never liked to know the reason for the hit, and only asked for the barest information about the mark. But, invariably, somebody had been double-crossed, an inviolable code had been broken, or money was chasing money.

He knew that he too was a criminal, but he was only interested in this job – not robbery, not cons, not security. He had done all of those things in his time, but they no longer held any appeal. After he'd quite heartlessly killed his brother and sister he realised he had a certain aptitude for this profession. He was cold, distant, and not really involved with the rest of humanity. He still felt sorry about the girl, though. Death, mutilation, blood, had never made him queasy. He had a stomach of iron – quite literally, as he worked out every day. He liked to exercise, knew that being fit helped even when using a rifle, as his breathing was easier. He knew how to relax without dope. He wasn't some over-muscled ape, not like the security he saw surrounding some of the crime lords he met, and he'd back himself hand-to-hand against any one of them.

If you're going to do a job, do it well, as his father used to say. Not that he'd ever liked his father much – if at all. Yet this simple catechism had stayed with him. Mr Miles, his careers master at school, had suggested he follow in his father's footsteps. And he had done well in the Army – pilfering from it until discovered. He had then done a good job of stealing from his boss at his next place of work. Nobody, however, could have foreseen *this* career choice. He imagined, for a moment, the quiet voice of Mr Miles. *Now, boy, I've noticed you have an interest in knives and you're a dab hand with an air rifle. Have you ever considered hitman as an occupation? The job is what you make of it really. Of course, there's a small chance you'll be caught by the police and end up in pokey for the rest of your life, or that you'll be hit by a hitman in turn. But it's a lucrative business and the hours are flexible.* He began to giggle. The dope was talking.

He had enjoyed handling weapons when young. His so-called father, a military man, had encouraged it. He joined the army, where he could follow his interests legitimately. He became a marksman, and learned hand-to-hand combat. He liked the discipline, but not the orders, ranks, and saluting. The money he had illegitimately attempted to make was recompense, he thought, for all the effort he'd expended in complying with military strictures. The Army, however, had thought otherwise, and discharged him. Some time had passed after that, a couple of years, before he'd found his true métier. And now he'd found it, his father's saying made sense.

He glanced at his Rolex. It was time, surely? He looked through the telescopic sight again. A robin flew into the ivy at the side of the house. The bird must be young, he thought, perhaps coming up to its first moult. Its breast was brown rather than red. The robin's head twisted from side to side warily, and then, alarmed, it flew away. Darkness momentarily obscured the sights, a darkness he knew to be the favoured blue sports jacket of his mark. He tilted the gun quickly, found the head, and waited. *If you're going to do a job, do it well.* He knew that it would be best to fire just... now, as a hand reached out to the chrome door-handle of the Jensen. He absorbed the recoil of the rifle in his shoulder. A startled bird fluttered from the long grass in front of him. A skylark. The mark remained standing for a moment, although he could see through the sights that a blood-rose had blossomed on the mark's forehead. He quickly worked the bolt, chambered another round, just in case. But, as expected, the mark slowly buckled and fell onto the gravel beside the burgundy car.

He continued watching the body through the sights for a moment. The body remained still. He put the rifle into a golf bag he had with him. The shell the rifle had ejected he left in the grass on the chalk bank. It was his signature – and also a joke on the conspiracy theorists. Some said that the dented shell casing, found in the schoolbook depository from where Oswald had shot Kennedy, suggested a conspiracy, since it could not have been fired from Oswald's gun. However, *his* Mannlicher-Carcano often dented the ejected cartridge cases. He glanced down at the case in the grass, and could see the damage to it. Ammunition was becoming scarce, however. He would soon have to rely on another of his rifles – probably the L42A1 that somebody had pilfered from a military warehouse somewhere.

He walked along the bottom of the ditch, the golf bag over his shoulder, the dope wearing off, feeling relaxed and happy. He had done his job, and done it well. He wouldn't enter the Garden of Paradise with its abundant drink and beautiful virgins. But he would be well paid.

Love

1

This Wednesday morning is like my life, Nick thought. Dull, drizzly, grey and autumnal. Of course, he wasn't really in the autumn of his life. He was, after all, only twenty-one. Yet sometimes he felt as if he were. *I was neither at the hot gates*, he thought, *nor fought in the warm rain.* He'd left his teenage years behind him, years not crowned in glory. Somehow, though, part of him remained in those years – nostalgic at only twenty-one for years that were inglorious. *I was neither at the hot gates*, he thought again. The day was warm and close, although the warmth was nothing in comparison to the heat of the summer just gone. The trees unscorched by the hot sun of that summer still carried green leaves, but they were turning. He wanted to do something, but he wasn't sure what. Instead of fighting at the hot gates, he found himself fighting tourists looking for the hot-baths, as he wandered the streets of Bath, looking into second-hand bookshops. A gust of wind tugged at Nick's jacket.

At least he was free. He didn't miss the job he'd left last week, unable to push paper around any longer. His mother and father had been incredulous at the time, and wondered what he would do for money now. Nick had shrugged, and continued to eat his lamb chop, boiled cabbage and mashed potatoes in silence. His father had read the paper while he ate, but Nick had been aware of the occasional disapproving glance from his mother. Still, he had saved a little money, and had come to Bath this morning not only to look in the shops but also to get away from his mother, who didn't leave for her job cleaning at the school until the afternoon. Nick carried, in a brown paper bag under his arm, a couple of second-hand books he'd already bought.

He wondered if he should get another job. His savings wouldn't last forever. He still had another year of study before he could get a university grant and leave town. At least the evening classes were free. He knew his chances of getting decent references were receding with every job he left. He could sign-on, he supposed. That would provide enough money to hand over to his mother for his keep. There might be enough left over for drinks down The White Lion, and the odd second-hand book, or album. Did he really need much money? Drinks with his friends, books and albums were his only vices. He didn't smoke. He didn't drink much, really. What was that drink Simon always had in the pub? A *Bugger Me*. Lemonade, lime, soda water and ice. It was incredibly cheap. Perhaps he'd join Simon in drinking that. They could be the Bugger Me Boys. Well, perhaps not.

The wet, brown pavements of Bath were quiet. Summer was over. Nick passed beneath the arch from Stall Street into the square in front of the Abbey. He walked towards the large wooden doors, set into the grey Bath stone, at the west of the building. He was fleetingly tempted to enter and sit quietly on one of the pews. Although he was an atheist, he liked the quiet of churches. He passed on by, however, around the side of the Abbey, across the High Street and into the Guildhall Market, where he made for the second-hand bookstall, and its towers of books. He wasn't looking for anything in particular, he was just browsing and killing time before he returned home. If he arrived after one o'clock, his mother would have left for work. His father was at the factory. He could have a peaceful afternoon.

His parents would be back in the evening. They'd ask if he'd been looking for work. He might lie and say he had, that he'd checking out the agencies in Bath. Perhaps that wasn't such a bad idea. There might be something temporary he could do. He hoped an agency would ask fewer questions than a permanent employer would. He wouldn't then have to explain why he kept leaving perfectly good jobs. He knew that, in his book-browsing perambulations, he would pass one or two agencies. He might even sign up with them. Even if he only looked at the cards in the windows, he could say to his parents in all honesty that he'd been to Bath to look for a job.

Now he returned to far more pleasant business – looking for a book. He enjoyed browsing in second-hand bookshops. He could only afford cheap books anyway, titles he wouldn't necessarily buy full price. He had, of course, read all the authors associated with the A-level English he had done at evening class last year, and particularly liked William Golding and Arthur Miller. He also liked some of the authors that still seemed hip but were now, really, quite passé, like Kesey and Kerouac. He would buy books by these and other writers if he found them. But on the shelves he would find blue Pelicans, light green Penguins, and Picadors that intrigued him, authors and books about which he knew nothing, or had been referenced in other books, and he would buy them because they were only 10p or 20p. He was buying books faster than he could read them.

Two hours later, the drizzle had turned to rain. Nick was wet, and had in his pocket only two pound notes and some change. He had bought a couple more books, and a scarf, and was now standing on the outskirts of Bath, his arm outstretched, his thumb raised. He had walked out of town, along the main road towards Dereham, and then stopped next to a bus stop in Bathampton. He had been standing there for half an hour now. He could have caught the bus that had pulled into the stop earlier, but he wanted to keep the last of his money for the pub tonight. There was little he could do but stick out his thumb, wait, hope, and get wet.

And he was getting very wet. All he wanted now was get home. That was the thought that repeatedly sprang to mind. Tea. Mother's food. Warmth. He despised himself for thinking this. He was desperate for independence, and desperate to get away from Dereham. Yet here he was, eager to return to the loathed house, and to his mother's tea and food. He was indulged at home. Everything washed for him. Food ready for him. How easy to sleep in such an environment. Perhaps he had slept. Perhaps he had spent the last two years sleepwalking around Dereham. Now, he wanted freedom. But he had no money, and no inclination to make it.

A car sped past his outstretched arm, trailing a fine spray that tickled his face. He closed his eyes for a moment, and then opened them again. The grey, wet, shining ribbon of road stretched away into a haze between the houses. Fat, black clouds, heavy with rain, clumped low over the hills. Another car came towards him. Nick stuck out his thumb. The car slowed. Nick turned expectantly, hopefully, but the car accelerated again. "Bastard!" he shouted at it. Then he shrugged. You became accustomed to people's little jokes if you were a hitchhiker.

After a brief lull in the traffic, Nick noticed a rather fancy-looking car coming towards him. He stuck out his thumb again. To his surprise, the car pulled into the bus stop. Nick jogged over to the car and opened the door.

"Where are you heading?" Alan asked.

"Dereham," Nick said.

"I'm going to Bournemouth."

Nick couldn't have hoped for a more direct lift home. It was almost to the door – he could get out at the crossroads at the top of the housing estate where he lived.

The road wound out of Bath. The windscreen wipers tracked across Nick's line of vision.

"What a foul day, eh?" the driver said.

He was a salesman. Nick didn't need to ask; he'd done a lot of hitching in his time. The car. The suit. The manner. They said everything – symbolic eloquence. He'll glance at me, Nick thought, see the way I dress, my wet brown paper bag of books, and make his own assumptions, all of which will also be correct. "Yeah. The weather's terrible. I apologise for being so wet myself. I hope I don't make a mess of the seat."

"No problem," the driver said.

Nick looked at the landscape around him. Something moved in him, barely felt, at an unconscious level. Nick knew it, could feel it – it was autumn, he was certain. Dull, wet, but beautiful.

The earth was arraigned in perfect colours under the dull grey lid of the sky. Perfect greens, perfect browns, perfect greys. The world was a vision. Death had begun. The change of the world's tide. Life would fade, fall, and moulder in the damp brown earth. Nick responded to the unconscious prompt. "It does feel, sort of... well, autumnal today, don't you think?"

"I suppose so," the driver replied. He paused. "But it was a glorious summer, wasn't it?"

It *had* been a glorious summer. The summer of "76 would go down in the history books. Nick supposed he'd never experience another like it. Not only because it had been so hot, so sunny, so dry; but also because he had still been young enough, free enough, to experience it fully. And because of Heather.

"My name's Alan," the driver said.

Nick introduced himself.

"What do you do?" Alan asked.

"I'm unemployed. I left my job last week. I couldn't take it anymore."

"You look like you should be a student."

"I think I am. An eternal student."

"Are you returning to college, then?"

"I don't know."

"Do you mind if we listen to the radio?"

"Of course not."

Alan reached over and turned it on. It was a Blaupunkt, Nick noticed; he thought it must be expensive, like the car. He knew nothing about cars, but knew this had to be expensive. Classy. He glanced over at Alan. Classy, expensive. Like the suit. The sound from the radio was clear, full. Classical music. Nick knew nothing about classical music.

"Ah," Alan said quietly. "Britten's Violin Concerto. Do you like classical music?"

"I don't mind it. I don't have any myself, and I know little about it. I don't find it offensive. I wish I knew more about it, really."

"It's the second movement," Alan said. "I was like you, once. I didn't mind it, either, but also knew nothing about it. But one day... I listened to something for the first time. Really listened to it, closely. It was only a few years ago. I heard... what was it? Prokofiev, *Romeo and Juliet*. I loved it. I listen to it all the time now."

"No rock music?"

"Sometimes. Do you mind if I smoke?"

"Go ahead," Nick said. The man was polite. This was the first time, in all the years Nick had been hitching, that a driver had asked permission to smoke in his own car.

Alan took a packet of cigarettes from his pocket, and shook one out between his lips. "Do you want one?" Nick shook his head. Alan flipped open a silver lighter, and lit his cigarette. Nick had the impression the lighter was also expensive. Nick knew he would soon have to ask what Alan did, to keep the conversation alive, so that they did not travel to Dereham in awkward silence. Nick was already plotting the course of the conversation. *Oh, you're a salesman. What do you sell? Really? Is it difficult at this time of year?* Except this man – Alan – was probably not a salesman. Now he'd had time to consider, the car, the suit, the lighter, all spoke of something else. An executive, perhaps, or a manager. Some time had passed since they'd last spoken. Alan seemed untroubled by the silence. He was enjoying his Britten. Still, it would be... rude... not to ask what he did. Alan had asked Nick what he did, and now it was his turn to ask about Alan's job.

Nick was surprised to find that his stereotyping had been wrong. Very wrong. And he was now slightly frightened. Without preamble, without hesitation, Alan had said, "I kill people."

Nick had laughed. What else could he do? "Oh, good joke," he said. "You surprised me. Bravo. But what do you *really* do? Sell?"

"Really? I shoot people. Well, sometimes I shoot them. Other times, I garrotte them. I'm a contract killer. A hit man."

Nick laughed again. He didn't believe it. If he now felt anxious, it was because the conversation – the standard hitchhiking chit-chat – had taken a bizarre twist, and Nick wondered if he'd entered the car of a nutter. He tried to make light of it. "Yeah, right. Make a lot of money from it, do you?"

"Can't complain," Alan said.

Nick glanced over at Alan. Alan wasn't smiling. There wasn't even a merry little twinkle in his brown eyes. There was, rather, a clichéd, steely, cold, determination in them. Nick had never thought that brown eyes could be cold.

"I've killed scores of people," Alan continued. "I've forgotten how many. Mostly criminals. I'm hired by criminals to kill criminals. Survival of the fittest. I see it as a rather Malthusian attempt to keep the population and the productive capacity in balance."

"I see," said Nick, playing along. What else could he do? "So you think you perform a socially useful function?"

"Oh, yes." Alan paused to stub out his cigarette in the ashtray, and then turned a smile on Nick. The smile was, Nick thought, meant to be reassuring. "That's not to say I don't feel guilty about it. But somebody has to take on this onerous burden. I do so hate violence, don't you?"

"Well, sure, oh yeah, uh..." Nick stammered.

"It seems that–" Alan glanced over at Nick, before continuing, "God has chosen me to take this weight upon my shoulders." Alan suddenly turned and looked intently at Nick. "You... you do believe in God, don't you?"

"Uh, yes," Nick quickly spat out. He felt he'd betrayed his long-held atheism. There are no atheists in foxholes, he'd heard somebody once say.

Alan turned to look at the road again, his body relaxing slightly as he did so. "I'm glad. So many of you young people have turned your faces away from God. I don't see how you can do that. How can you live like that? To whom do you turn, if you cannot see God? Without God's benevolence, I would undoubtedly have gone mad by now, with the blood of so many deaths staining my hands. But God knows what I do, and hasn't intervened. He must see what I'm doing as right, don't you think?"

"Uh... I don't know. Don't you think that what you're doing might be morally wrong? That it might be a... mortal sin?"

"Oh, no. I take out other criminals. Criminals who have crossed other criminals. The unwritten codes and all that. Once or twice it's been a public official, somebody who seemed clean in his public life, but was really a part of the criminal world. I have morals. I couldn't, wouldn't have done Kennedy, for example. That was a political killing, you see. The Mafia and the Teamsters hand in hand. protecting themselves. Two dirty organisations."

"You know that?"

"Know what?"

"That it was the Mafia and the Teamsters? I mean... The Warren Commission, it..." Nick trailed off, wondering why this had suddenly intrigued him, when he should have been more worried that he was in the car of a hitman – or a nutter.

Alan nodded emphatically. "Of course it was."

Nick didn't know what to say next. He didn't want to say anything, really, for fear of restarting the crazy conversation about hitmen. Alan, too, was quiet for a while. Then he broke the silence. "And, of course, no women or children. Still, only one person shall judge me. I shall be judged in heaven. Nobody will judge me before I'm brought before the ultimate judge. *He* knows my life, *He* knows the crimes I'm guilty of. Only *He* can judge me."

"Aren't you worried that as soon as I get out the car I'll go to the police?" Nick asked.

Alan smiled. "Of course you'll consider it. You'll even get out of this car intent on it. Yet I often give lifts to hitchers, and I always tell them what I do. They always ask and I feel that lies are so immoral. Each reacts in a different way. Some are cool like you."

Nick smiled, knowing he didn't feel cool.

"Others begin to panic," Alan continued. "But I calm them down, tell them not to worry. I've never yet met a hitcher yet who I was contracted to kill." He laughed. "It would make my work easier if I did."

"Yes, I suppose it would," agreed Nick.

After this, the conversation became rather more pedestrian – weather, house and home, money, and, rather boringly for Nick, cars. Soon, they arrived at the crossroads in Dereham.

"Thanks for the lift, Alan," Nick said.

"No problem, Nick. Thanks for helping me pass some time."

Before he closed the door, Nick leaned back into the car. "You were pulling my leg, right?"

"Yes." Alan gave Nick a reassuring smile. "You're right. I don't know whether it was the Mafia and the Teamsters. That's simply a pet theory of mine."

Nick was confused for a moment. "No, not that. Your job, I mean. What you told me you did."

"Oh, that." The man's smile fell. "No."

"No what? You're not a hit man?"

"No, I wasn't pulling your leg. And my name is *not* Alan. Now close the door, and walk away."

The man was no longer smiling. Nick did as he was told. As the car pulled away and headed down the road, Alan – or whoever he was – gave two merry peeps on the horn. Nick could see him waving.

What the hell that all about, Nick wondered. *Have I just sat through an entire journey with a self-confessed hitman?* He resolutely began to stride home through the rain that was still falling. Of course, the man could simply be one of the oddballs you meet on the road. Yet, what if he were a hitman? Nick thought he should get to a telephone, and call the police. *What make of car was he driving? Shit. I've never been good with cars. He even told me what it was. He was so thrilled with it. What was the registration?* He looked down the road, but the car was already too far away, and soon rounded the corner towards Barton. *What did he look like?* Nick realised that he couldn't really remember anything about the man's appearance, except for the eyes. He tried to recall features, identifying marks. Nothing but the eyes returned to him. They were, he thought, blue. Steely grey-blue. Or bluey-grey. Or perhaps grey. *Fuck. The colour of the car?* He could remember nothing. How would he get the police to believe him? It was like a dream. A nightmare. Except that he wasn't scared, now he was here, on this familiar pavement. He was almost tempted to believe he'd never met the man. Yet here he was, now, back in Dereham.

Nick laughed. The whole thing was crazy. No wonder nobody had ever reported the man to the police. He was a blank canvas, upon which you could paint whatever vision you had of evil. Now that the canvas had been removed, he felt that all the elements that had made up the image of the hitman had been stripped away. How could he ring the police now? He'd sound madder than the hitman.

2

Simon wondered where Anna was. He scanned the faces that passed him in the corridor. Before the summer break, in May and June, about this time on a Wednesday, Anna would be walking along the corridor towards him, having finished her morning lectures at the same time as he had. Together, they would have then have walked under a blue, cloudless sky over to the park, or around the streets of Southleigh, or out into the fields that were but a few streets away.

He had been both excited and anxious when he'd walked into college this morning, and hadn't really concentrated at all during the first lecture of the day, had been eager for it to end. Now the corridor was a sea of unknown faces, more so given that many of his friends had left college at the end of last term. He and Anna had been so close then. Yet, because he was shy, because he didn't understand the girlfriend thing, because he thought he was odd looking, and for many other reasons, he had never said to her what he wanted to say. He wasn't sure what that was, but it was more than *thank you*. At the Summer Ball at the college, before the long summer holiday, just before she had left, Anna had unexpectedly reached up, run her fingers through Simon's hair and said, "You are nice, you know." Simon didn't know what to say. He couldn't speak. In the end, he managed to mumble some words. "Thank you." He smiled. She had smiled in turn, squeezed his hand, and then walked away. Simon's friend Mark had been playing bass in the band at the Ball. Simon knew everybody in Honeyhouse, and was getting a lift a lift back to Dereham in the band's Ford Transit. Simon told Mark and the rest of the band what had happened with Anna. Danny, the guitarist pointed, out the obvious. "She fancies you, Si." Danny had girlfriends - he knew about these things.

Simon realised then that Anna really did fancy him. She thought the same as he did. And now the summer break had arrived. He wouldn't see her for ten weeks. Their relationship had been so loose and free he'd never thought ask for her phone number, or for her address. He wasn't even sure of her surname. Simon knew for certain only what she had once written on his jeans. *Anna Lesley.* He thought she lived in one of the villages around Southleigh. Within a couple of days, Simon had looked through the Southleigh and district phone directories for Lesleys, and found none.

"Perhaps it was her middle name," Nick had pointed out.

Perhaps it was, Simon thought. How dumb was it that he hadn't even known that after four months?

Mark had a motorbike, and on some of the hot summer days they rode over to Southleigh, the breeze cooling them. They would ride around the town centre, then out to the villages, hoping to see Anna. To no avail. Having left college, she had effectively vanished.

Ten weeks is a long time when you're only eighteen. Perhaps because Anna had said she liked him, Simon was now ready to believe other girls could also like him. One warm evening, at a party Mark had arranged when his parents had gone away, Simon found himself kissing his friend Julie. The kissing went on into the night. Those kisses had been important. They were his first, proper, big kisses. He had been so shy, for so long, so unsure of himself. Yet, with Julie, it had been easy. No fuss, no bother. Simon had been dancing with her one moment, kissing the next. Subsequently, there had been a few sunny days of gentle, genial companionship. Julie was easy to be around. In the end, though, whatever that relationship had been had evaporated. Simon wasn't sure why, but as he didn't really understand relationships, that was no surprise. And Julie had said that he must get together with Anna, it was the only sensible thing to do. Julie was right. He trusted her. They were good friends. She knew how he felt. So he and Julie had drifted apart. But now he knew how to get close to Anna. All he needed to do was find her.

Simon now had some two hours of free time. He walked slowly towards the refectory, hoping that Anna would be there. Not that he knew what he would say if she was. He had planned so many times what he *should* say, but each time he reformulated his opening address. Often, the imaginary conversation began with him declaring his undying love in a strong clear voice that brooked no interruption. He would, however, most likely mumble a hello and then ask how her summer had been. The conversation would then ramble on from there, and they would start flirting and joking with each other. That's if she didn't say she'd met a *really* lovely man during the summer and that Simon *really, really* must meet him. After all, he had kissed Julie, and then taken rather a fancy to her during the summer. It was possible, then, that Anna had also met somebody. Given the beauty of the summer just gone – when love had, it seemed to him, always been in the sticky, sultry air – it was, surely, very likely that someone else had turned her head.

He couldn't imagine how he would feel if Anna started talking to him about her new, special someone, not after he had spent most of the summer regretting that *he* wasn't her special someone. He knew that their relationship would change, that she would no longer want to spend so much time -any time – with him. Simon wondered what he would do if she started writing bad poems about her new love, and reading them to him, asking what he thought.

He bought a cup of tea and sat alone at one of the refectory tables, ladled the tea out of and back into his cup absent-mindedly with a white, plastic spoon. He looked around him. *What if she's fallen for somebody here, somebody she's at college with?* He was surprised that he hadn't thought of this possibility before, and was suddenly aghast. He would have to watch them snuggling up to each other in the refectory. In the corridor, he would have to watch her run past with a curt hello before she fell into the arms of somebody else.

He felt, rather than saw, somebody sit next to him. He turned his head and found Warren smiling at him. "Penny for them."

"Just thinking about... stuff..." Simon said.

"You're sitting here, alone, without the lovely Anna beside you," Warren said. "Even I can guess what you're thinking about."

Of course, Warren could. The reason Simon had made so few friends in his first year was that, of course, he had spent most of the summer term at college with Anna. When he hadn't been with Anna, he'd been with Gaz and Mark, a year above him. He and Warren shared classes for two of the courses they were taking. Of his cohort, he knew Warren perhaps the best because they caught the same bus most days – but, even then, he didn't know Warren well.

"I'm just wondering why I haven't seen her yet," Simon said. How much could he say to Warren? He plunged on. "I've been thinking about her all summer. I had big speeches prepared. It's a bit of a let-down to find she isn't here."

"Perhaps she left," Warren said. "People do. Decide to find a job, give up."

Simon hadn't thought of that.

"Alternatively," Warren continued, "She's just starting a week later. Perhaps she's on a late holiday with her parents. Or perhaps her timetable has changed."

"Maybe." Simon hadn't thought of that, either. Warren, it seemed, had thought of more things than he had, and yet he hadn't been thinking about her all summer. Or perhaps he had? It was a thought Simon had no need to pursue further, because Warren said, *sotto voce*, "Now, *who* is *that*?"

Simon looked towards the doors of the refectory, which were just swinging shut as a bespectacled blonde girl walked slowly between the rows of tables towards the counter, looking around as if trying to recognise a familiar or friendly face. Warren smiled as her eyes momentarily met his, but she gave no response.

"She's new," Warren said, his gaze following her to the counter.

"Are you sure?" Simon said.

"As you only had eyes for Anna last term, I assume you noticed little else. Yes, she's new. She must be a fresher."

She was attractive, Simon noted, though a bottle-blonde for sure.

"Isn't there a Fresher's Ball on Saturday?" Simon asked. "She might go to that, and then you can chat her up. I think there'll be competition, though." Simon had noticed several pairs of male eyes follow her slow walk across the refectory. She bought a sandwich and cup of tea and walked to a table behind them.

"I don't want to appear obvious," Warren said. "So can you take a peek, and tell me if she's sitting with a bloke?"

Simon glanced over his shoulder.

"You needn't worry. Not yet, at least. She's sitting with three other girls."

"I wonder what courses she's doing?' Warren said. "She might be on one of mine."

"You'll find out soon enough," Simon said. Not that he really cared. Where was Anna?

Simon leaned against a wall in the corridor. Lectures had finished, and he waited for Warren. They would walk to the bus station together. He was lost in thought, wondering where Anna was, what she was doing. For a moment, he looked down at his baseball boots, and instead of wondering about Anna, wondered instead if it wasn't time he bought some Doc Martens.

"Mister Simon Darby, I believe?"

It was the voice he'd been longing to hear. He looked up into a broad smile, the oval face. The brown eyes twinkled as they so often had in the summer months, and later, in his imagination. She was eating a Kit Kat. The grand speeches he'd prepared, as he'd suspected they would, disappeared in an instant, melted away by her smile.

"Oh, all right, thanks." He couldn't help smiling. That wasn't what he'd wanted to say, but it was, at least, something. He glanced at her Kit Kat. "Can I have a bit?"

Anna looked up and down the corridor, then up at him. "What, here and now? It's a bit public, isn't it?" She gave him a cheeky smile, and then broke off a stick of the Kit Kat. "Open wide."

Simon laughed, and did so. She popped one end of the stick into Simon's mouth. They were already falling into the easy, bantering relationship they'd had before the summer break. He snapped the Kit Kat in half with his teeth, and chewed, smiling. He was idiotically happy to see Anna. "Where have you been?" She looked adorable, in her yellow tee-shirt, blue jeans, and denim jacket. He'd seen her often enough in these clothes before the summer – now they reminded him how fantastic she was, how great it was to see her again.

"New timetable. My first lecture wasn't until today."

Warren walked by, and winked at Simon. "Hi, guys," he said as he passed.

"I'll catch you later," Simon said to Warren.

"Oh no, catch him now," Anna said, "I'm going for a walk with Joan." Simon looked down the corridor, where he could see Anna's friend.

"Will I see you tomorrow?" Simon asked.

"No lectures tomorrow. Thursday?"

"No, I have no lectures on Thursday," Simon said. But I could come in, he thought. I'd come in to see you. *Ask me to come in, go on ask me.*

"Perhaps Friday then?" She sighed. "Mind you, first week of term is always a bit crazy, catching up with everybody, sorting the lectures out, wondering when the free time will be. Tell you what, if we miss each other Friday, I'll see you at the Fresher's Ball, on Saturday. Is that a deal?"

"It's a deal," Simon said.

She held out her hand. "Shake on it, then."

Her hand was soft and warm, and Simon held it longer than he needed, didn't want to let it go. When he did, Anna gave him one more mischievous look.

"Would you like a little bit more?"

"Of course, I would."

She broke off half of her last finger of Kit Kat. "Open wide again." She placed the Kit Kat on his tongue. "Don't chew it, just suck it." She winked at him and laughed, then popped her half into her mouth. She turned and skipped down the corridor, calling to Joan at the far end. Simon watched her slip through the door after Joan. Anna glanced back before the door closed, and gave him a wave.

It's a deal. It's a fucking deal, he thought. He ran down the corridor in the opposite direction, and through the doors into the daylight. The rain that had been falling had stopped, but the sky remained overcast. He still had time to catch the bus. He arrived at the bus station just as a dawdling Warren arrived there.

"I see you found her at last," Warren said as Simon ran up beside him.

"Yeah, yeah. It was cool. We've arranged to see each other at the Fresher's Ball if we don't see each other before."

Warren and Simon climbed into the waiting bus and walked to the back. They sprawled across the long bench seat. Warren took a packet of cigarettes from his pocket, and lit one.

"Doing anything tonight?" Warren asked.

"Not a sausage. Nowt. Nicht. Nothing. I might see Gaz or Mark, I suppose."

"So you're not writing a symphony? Or planning your assault on Everest by speedboat? Or declining a seat on the board of EMI?"

"Why do you talk such rubbish, Warren?"

"It's the effect of A-level Chemistry. There's far too many free ions in my brain, and they've given me an awful headache bumping around all the time."

"Poor boy. I just happen to have a spare covalent electron shell in my pocket. That should get rid of your headache."

"Thank you, but I think I'll lean out of the window instead and get a breath of fresh carbon dioxide." Warren stood up, and pulled open one of the ventilation windows. Simon slipped a book out of his jacket pocket, and began to read.

After a while, Warren sat down and said, "Phew."

"What?" asked Simon.

"Nothing. Just "Phew'." Warren said. He sat still for a while longer. Then he stood up again and looked out of the back window. After a while, Warren said "Phew" again, and Simon decided anything attracting so many *phews* demanded attention. He stood up and joined Warren at the back window.

"What?" Simon demanded.

Warren pointed through the dirt-encrusted glass. The bespectacled blonde they'd seen earlier in the day was chatting to a friend behind the bus next to them. The blonde looked up, and Warren smiled. She smiled back.

"Phew," Warren said again.

Warren took another cigarette from his packet, and put it between his lips. The blonde girl looked up again. Warren performed some frantic gesticulations, which Simon realised were an attempt to interest the girl in a cigarette. The girl looked puzzled. Again, Warren indicated that he was offering her a cigarette. She continued to look puzzled. Simon then tried with some mime that would, he considered, have done Marcel Marceau proud. The girl nodded her head, at which point Warren turned and happily bounded down the bus and out of the doors. Simon shrugged, and followed laconically.

The girl took the offered cigarette. Warren looked at her with slightly too much interest, Simon thought. Warren flicked his lighter for her. "I haven't seen you at this classy joint before," he said.

"It's my first year," said the girl. "And I catch a different bus to you guys, it seems. I live in Foxton. I catch this one." She pointed to the bus. "It's supposed to leave ten minutes earlier than yours. Where do you guys get off?"

Simon immediately thought of half a dozen rude answers. He caught the smirk on Warren's face. "Dereham," Simon said.

"What's your name?" Warren asked.

"Jill. Who are you?"

Warren and Simon introduced themselves.

"I have to get on the bus now," Jill said. "See you guys around college."

Simon and Warren got back on their bus. More students had now crowded into the back seats – it would soon be time for the bus to begin the journey back to Dereham.

"Jill," Warren sighed as he sat down.

"Yeah. Jill," Simon said.

The driver arrived and sat behind the wheel. The passengers who had already boarded the bus went down the front and paid their fares. When they had all finished, the driver looked expectantly in his rear view mirror.

Warren noticed. "The driver wants to see our passes, chaps," he said.

He took his bus pass out and held it up. Following his lead, the other students did the same. The bus driver continued to stare into his mirror for a few more seconds, then shouted: "You lot have got bloody legs haven't you? You're all young enough to walk! So get yourselves down here! You're not special just because you're *students*!"

The other passengers applauded, and, shame-faced, the dozen or so students marched down to the driver, who laboriously checked every pass. Warren and Simon were last. As they returned to their seats, the driver started the engine, crashed the bus into gear, and let the clutch out with a jerk. Warren stumbled into the back of Simon, and they both fell over, much to the amusement of the passengers. Even the other students cheered, glad that they were no longer the centre of attention. Simon stood quickly, and brushed himself down, glanced towards the driver, who, he could see, was looking in his rear-view mirror. Simon made it back to his seat, and Warren arrived just as the driver turned a bend sharply, causing Warren to fall into Simon's lap. Simon could see that the driver was smiling.

"The bastard did that on purpose," Warren said.

"Obviously," Simon replied. "We probably deserved it."

"I'll get my own back," Warren snarled.

Simon wondered, how, and when, Warren intended wreaking his revenge, but decided he was only blustering, and that he would have forgotten about it by the time he was back in Dereham and smoking a fag on the pavements.

Simon took his book from his pocket again, and began to read. He wasn't really reading, however, and was glad Warren appeared to be plotting some revenge against the bus driver or the Bristol bus company. All he could think about was Anna's warm hand in his.

It's a deal, he remembered. A *deal!*

3

So this is Dereham? Molly Shepherd stood on the platform at the station, where the train clanked and roared away into the distance, towards Salisbury. Black smoke from its exhaust still drifted around the station, mingling with the light rain that fell on this dull Wednesday afternoon. She was the only person to have alighted from the train. She had seen two people board the train. They were running away, Molly thought. The station was small, a bit grubby. Baskets hung from joists that held up the station roof. A few pathetic pansy heads, red, yellow and blue, danced in the breeze.

Molly picked up her bag, and walked over the green iron footbridge, spotted with rust, that crossed the tracks. On top of the bridge, she stopped, and turned to look behind her. The wooded slopes of a large hill overlooked the town. Ramparts followed the contours near the summit. On the train ride from Bristol, she had studied the Ordnance Survey map she carried in her bag. The hill was, she knew, Derebury Hill. The cloud was low, and touched the summit, shrouding a barrow on the top. She left the station through the dark Victorian booking office.

She had booked a room for a few nights at The White Lion hotel. She didn't know how long she'd stay. On this dull, September afternoon, Dereham didn't look inviting. She knew the town was small; she'd looked it up in a gazetteer before her journey. Her sister had so loved this place, though. Molly wanted to know what had kept Peta here. Of course, one reason had been the UFOs, but, to Molly, that was all so much nonsense. Harry had loved the place, too. Poor Harry. She missed him.

The White Lion was in the Market Place, and she guessed the town centre would be at the end of the road from the station. She would have asked somebody for directions, but the ticket booth in the station had been empty, there had been no taxis at the taxi rank, and, on this dull day, there was nobody else around. Her work had brought her to a few towns like this. The Victorian railway stations were often at the edge of town, and connected to it by a road, usually called Station Road, which inevitably led to a High Street, or a Market Place, or sometimes a New Road. If she followed this road, she would end up somewhere near the town centre. She shifted her canvas bag from one shoulder to the other, wondering how far she'd have to walk. She could see shops at the end of Station Road – it wouldn't be far. She looked around her as she walked. Empty car parks. A drab and dark stone police station. The town seemed dull, hardly worth a visit. She knew she shouldn't judge the town just yet. Station Roads tended to be semi-industrial. Still, she couldn't imagine what she'd do with herself in the evenings. There would be a small cinema, she guessed, and plenty of pubs. She might walk up Copsehill one night, follow in the footsteps of Harry and Peta, and relive something of what they'd felt. She doubted she would feel it. Harry had always said, though, that the view was beautiful.

Station Road gave out onto a street full of shops. Here, there were a few more people on the damp pavements, their heads bowed against the wind and drizzle. She stopped a woman and asked for directions to The White Lion. It was only a hundred yards away. This was the High Street, she learned. She turned and walked towards the Market Place. The shop fronts were bland. She looked above them. She could see Tudor jetties, Bath stone, and hipped roofs. As town centres became increasingly uniform and bland, with their Top Shops and Woolworths and Smiths, she knew the only place to find the real old town was above the plate glass, infill bricks, and steel columns. Somebody had written, she remembered – was it Cobbett, Priestley? – that

36

Dereham was a solid, unpretentious town, blessed by its setting beneath the Plain.

She walked up the steps into The White Lion. In her room, she took off her leather jacket, and unpacked her bag. There were few clothes in it. She hung up the one decent dress, now creased, that she had brought with her in case she felt the need to pretty herself up for something, and folded two pairs of jeans on the top shelf of the small wardrobe. Her underwear she put in the drawer at the bottom, and her one pair of going-out shoes she threw on the bed. She unlaced her cherry-red Doc Martens and flopped beside her shoes. The single bed felt comfortable, at least. She looked at the phone beside the bed. She wished there was somebody she could call. The only people she wanted to talk to were gone. She could talk to her friend, Len Stone, but at this time of day he would be setting up the club in London for the night. Len might be appalled to know she was in Dereham. He was one of those who had inadvertently set Molly on this course. Molly wasn't sure where this course was leading.

Molly had joined MI5 because of Harry, long gone. Now, she was on a fortnight's leave. The draw of Dereham, which she had spent so long resisting, had finally broken her. She might be here for a couple of days, or for the rest of her leave. It didn't matter. She had been drawn here. She had succumbed to temptation. Now she would see what Dereham could offer. She might find help here. There might be clues. What help she was looking for, what clues she was seeking, she didn't know. She only knew she was looking for something, anything, that would help her forget her loneliness. Dereham was but one stop on a journey that might yet take years.

Molly took her diary from her bag. She would shower later, but now she wanted to capture her impressions of the day, the journey, the town. Writing was therapy for her. As she wrote, images of Peta and Harry came to her. She was writing about Dereham, after all, and their ghosts were bound to haunt her here. Peta, Harry, and the town were intertwined. Then the other name came to her – the name that weaved them all together, including Molly – the real ghost, the name she'd heard from Harry, and she'd heard again at MI5, the name of the man who had once lived in Dereham with Peta, the man who now appeared to live a quiet life in Cheltenham. Archibald Franklin Conn.

4

Nick sat at a table alone, waiting for Simon, Mark and Gaz. Unusually for a Wednesday night, the saloon bar of the The White Lion was packed. Hot, humid, full of cigarette smoke, the bar smelled of sweat, rain, patchouli, sandalwood, Havoc, Tramp and Charlie. The tables and chairs were occupied by friends, soon to leave for university and polytechnic, making the most of their last days together before everything changed for them.

Nick had left his house, where his mother and father sat in front of the television, as soon as he could. He had first done the washing-up to mollify them. He had also told them he had gone to Bath to look for work. That had ensured there were no arguments before he left for the evening. By the time he arrived home tonight, they would both be in bed.

Nobody had sat at Nick's table, nobody had even asked if they could have a stool. Everybody in the bar knew he was waiting for his friends. As usual, he had picked a table next to the members of Honeyhouse, the band for which Mark played bass and rhythm guitar. Nick had said hello to them all, and chatted with them while he waited. Mark and Simon knew them better than he did; Mark was, after all, in the band. The Honeyhouse table was less crowded than it would normally have been. Steve and John had already left for university. Danny would go next, and then Kate, leaving only James, Imogen and Stuart in Dereham.

Nick knew all about the changes they would soon face. The friends from his age group had left town, drifted away, two or three years ago, when they had completed their studies. Some had joined the forces, or taken jobs in other towns, or gone on to higher education. When they'd gone, the people he had most in common with – who shared his interests in music, books, film, whatever – had been Simon, Gaz and Mark, two years younger than him. At the time, Nick had thought he was too mature to hang around with a bunch of sixteen-year olds. It turned out he wasn't.

Nick had come to know Simon through the wide network of friends and acquaintances they all seemed share at that age. Simon knew the younger brother of one of Nick's friends. Nick's friend had gone to university, and Simon was no longer particularly close to that brother. Then, one evening, Nick had been mooching around town after splitting up with a girlfriend and had bumped into Simon. They had chatted for a while, then Simon said he was heading to The White Lion for a spot of under-age drinking. Nick was welcome to join him. Of course, Gaz and Mark had also been there. Also there had been the amorphous groupings that constituted the fluctuating milieu of their next few years. Steve, John and Danny, the other members of Honeyhouse, in which Mark played bass. James, the band's lyricist, and his girlfriend Imogen, and their friends, Stuart, Charlie, and Kate. Then there was the girl that Mark had met on his first day at Southleigh College and now, two years later, couldn't stop thinking about, Chrissie, and all her friends. They all drank in the saloon bar of the Lion, the meeting place for the local freaks, hippies and students. The smooths – as they called the people not like them – drank in the public bar, or in other pubs in town. The saloon bar of The White Lion was *their* place, their club. What would happen to it when this particular cohort went on their way, Nick already knew. The vacuum would be filled, and the empty tables and chairs would be occupied by new freaks, students, hippies or whatever came next.

It would be different for Nick this time, though. This September saw no changes to his inventory of friends. Simon was a year behind at college, having had to resit some O-levels. Mark, who had intended going to university to study architecture, had surprisingly failed his A-level Art. So astounded had he been by this he hadn't even tried to find a university that would accept his two rather good A-levels. His self-image had been disturbed. If he couldn't get into the university he wanted, on the course he desired, he'd rather not go at all. As for Gaz... Gaz had been studious rather than academic, bright rather than intellectual. Gaz was unusual among the people Nick knew in that he desired money. He *wanted* to work. His A-levels had enabled him to find a good job at a bank. He was the polar opposite to Nick. Gaz considered this job to be the first step towards inevitable riches.

Nick had spent another hour talking to Imo, Stuart, Danny and James about poetry and UFOs before Gaz, Simon and Mark arrived. They seated themselves around the table. Mark looked at Nick's glass. "Sorry, should have offered to top you up."

"Don't worry about it," Nick said. "I have to make it last." He had nursed the same half of shandy for the last hour, anyway.

Mark leaned back in his chair and chatted to Danny and James on the other table. Mark was worried that, as the other band members one by one left Dereham, the band would collapse. Danny reassured Mark again, saying that of course the band would continue, that they would all return at weekends for rehearsals.

Nick envied them all and wanted to leave with them. He wanted to get away from this town. Yet, he still didn't know what he wanted to do. Simon and Nick would leave Dereham at the same time, because Simon was a year behind the others. Simon was philosophical about it. Like Nick, he hadn't known, really, what he had wanted to do when he left school, and had spent his last year there mucking about, taking nothing seriously, skiving a little, and forgetting his homework. Then, during that summer, two years ago, he had been hanging out with Mark a lot, Mark who already knew that he wanted to go to university and study architecture. And Mark had been hanging out with the band, who all intended doing A-levels and going to university. They talked about books, art, and poets Simon had never heard of, and then, suddenly, Simon had also wanted to know, and he had borrowed books, and then he knew, too, that he wanted to do A-levels and go on and study *something*, although hadn't known what. He knew, however, that to study *something*, he would have to resit some of the O-levels he had failed, and though it was by then late in the summer, he'd managed to get a place at Salisbury College. Now that he actively desired education, his grades had been good, and he'd started A-levels at Southleigh Sixth-Form College. Simon's new-found enthusiasm had rubbed off on Nick, who had started doing A-levels at evening classes.

"Any idea what you're going to do yet?" Simon said to Nick.

"Get out of town for certain," Nick said.

Simon already knew that, of course. They all did. Nick wondered if he sounded monomaniacal.

"Is it so bad, living here? Among your friends, in lovely countryside?"

"No, of course it isn't," Nick said. "Even the town's not that ugly."

Dereham had buildings of Bath stone and Georgian townhouses, streets where medieval jetties hung over the pavements. Nick could do worse. Milton Keynes. Bracknell. Nick was restless, though, for something. He just didn't know *what* that something was. He knew he didn't want to live with his parents. He was twenty-one, after all. It was simply the cheapest option. Granted, they *all* still lived with their parents. But as they began to earn more, they would soon move on. Nick knew that Gaz was already saving money, ready to buy a house as soon as he could. James was too. Even Mark intended saving money from his job, the job he'd taken instead of going to the university of his dreams, ready for a deposit on a flat. Mark and James had talked about pooling their money and renting or buying a house together. Gaz could joined them – the offer was there – but Nick couldn't imagine Gaz sharing a house with the two boys. But then, neither could he imagine Gaz sharing a house with a girl. Gaz was definitely a loner.

"Where would you go, though," Simon said.

Nick whiled away idle hours looking at university prospectuses. "York, possibly."

"That's a long way away," Mark said.

"Far enough that I don't have to come back too often, and just close enough to make a monthly rail-trip tolerable."

"What about Aberdeen?" Simon suggested. "Isn't that about as far as you can go? Have you thought of that?"

Nick hadn't considered Aberdeen. "No, I haven't. That would be *madness*. Wouldn't it?" Yet, now he thought about it, the distance between it and Dereham seemed tempting, pleasing in some way.

"It *is* a long way. We'd never see you again," Simon noted.

"Of course you would," Nick replied. But perhaps they wouldn't. He wasn't Gaz, that was for sure. Nick would miss his friends and want to see them, but then there were the long academic holidays during which he could visit. Yet if he did come home, Nick would have to stay with his parents, and one reason for getting out of town was to cut the apron strings. Perhaps Simon was right. If he went as far as Aberdeen, they might never see him again. "Oh well," Nick sighed. "Plenty of time to make my mind up. I don't have to start making choices until next year."

Nick wanted to change the subject. He'd been waiting eagerly for his friends to arrive so he could tell them the mad tale of the hitman. He hadn't wanted to digress into *the problem of Nick*, as Mark once called it, even though it was a recurring topic of conversation – almost as regular as *the problem of Anna*, and *the mystery of Chrissie*. "There's something I need to tell you chaps," Nick said.

"Is it serious?" Mark said.

"It is," Nick said. "I went to Bath this morning, and I've been waiting to tell you the fascinating story of my ride home."

"You hitched?" Simon asked.

"Of course, I'm not made of money. Not like Gaz. Go on, ask me what the hitch was like."

"Wet, I'd imagine."

"Oh, yes. Bloody wet. But there was more to it than that."

The others could tell, by the tone of Nick's voice, that there was a story to be told. "What was the journey like, Nick?" Mark dutifully asked.

"I got a lift back to Dereham with a contract killer."

Gaz's broad face cracked into a smile. "Oh yeah, right."

"No, honestly," Nick insisted. "He said he was a *hitman*."

Simon laughed. "And you believed him?"

"Of course I did – eventually. I mean, you ask someone what they do, they say they're an accountant. You believe them. Or, they say they're an architect, right? You believe them, right?"

"Not if it's Mark," Simon said.

"Low blow, man," Mark said, and punched Simon's arm.

"Careful. I know kung fu. I could have your arm off with one swift move."

"*Anyway*," Nick butted in. "So I have to believe that this guy was what he said he was."

"Sounds like he's off his trolley to me," Gaz said.

"He did to me at first."

"Have you reported it to the police?" asked Mark.

"No."

A few seconds passed before anyone said anything. "But you should," continued Mark. "He might be really dangerous."

"Hit men usually are," Simon noted.

"Ah, but as he said," Nick offered, "he's only dangerous to other criminals. Not to you or me. He implied that he has a very moral code."

"The ethical hit-man," Simon said.

"Good title for an album," Mark said. He called across to the other table. "Hey, James! The first album. Let's call it *The Ethical Hitman*."

James nodded. "Right on!" He took out the notebook he always carried in the pocket of his coat – as the lyricist for Honeyhouse, he needed a ready supply of paper for moments of inspiration – and scribbled in the back of it. "Cool," he said.

Gaz shook his head. "A *hitman*? What did he look like?"

"Well, it's difficult to remember exactly. Sort of cold-eyed, square-jawed, handsome, I suppose; completely typical, really, of the sort you see in films being cold-blooded killers."

"A cross between Lee Marvin, Clint Eastwood, and Lee Van Cleef, then?" Mark pointed out.

"Yes, sort of, I suppose."

"I still think you should have told someone," Mark said.

"Now, here's the weird thing," Nick began.

The others all sat forward, smiling. Nick laughed at their unconsciously orchestrated ironic eagerness.

"You mean there's something... even weirder?" Mark said.

"Okay, okay," Nick said. "Look, here's what's weird. He said that he always told the truth, and so had told loads of hitch-hikers what he did. And yet he's never been arrested."

"Perhaps no-one ever did tell the police," Mark pointed out.

"He said that everybody thinks they'll report him, but he knows they won't. Because they won't remember either him or the car. And he's right." Nick paused, allowing this strange, almost supernatural, information to register before saying, "It's all down to God, really, you see."

"God?" Simon snorted. "Where does God come into this?"

"Ah, well – you're a non-believer. So many of today's youths are non-believers, won't let God come into their lives. That man believes God chose him to do that work, and that God therefore looks after him. So he never worries about anything. He thinks he'll go straight to the Pearly Gates, and there'll be St Peter saying, *Oh yeah – the Hitman. C'mon in, you been doin' a great job for God.*"

Ever the pragmatist, Mark still thought Nick should report the event to the police.

"Well, I would, if I could remember anything about him."

"So, it's just as he predicted, then?" Simon asked. "You remember nothing?"

"Nope. Yeah. No. Oh, I remember some vague things, like the cold eyes and the granite jaw. But no definite features."

"What about his car?" Mark asked. "You must remember that."

"Of course not. He told me I'd forget that too. And I did. Immediately. I remember it was a nice car. He was very proud of it. We even talked about it. But you know me..." Nick paused. "I'm just not interested in cars, so I switched off."

Simon frowned. "Yep. God is looking after his own."

"Perhaps I could draw him!" Mark said. "I need paper." He leaned over to James, who retrieved his notepad again, and ripped out several sheets of paper and handed them and his pen to Mark. "So," Mark continued, looking up eagerly at Nick, "A bit of Clint, and a bit of the two Lees?"

"Perhaps," Nick said, suddenly doubtful, as Mark began scribbling.

They were all silent for a while as they watched a face forming on the paper. Mark sketched quickly. "This is only from memory of some late night films, of course. So..." He turned the paper around towards Nick. "Anything like that?"

There were hints of the three actors in the drawing; it had Clint's eyes, Lee Marvin's chin and Lee van Cleef's cheekbones. Nick raised his eyes and found Mark looking at him expectantly. "Hmm. Something's... wrong. Try Van Cleef's eyes, Marvin's chin and Clint's cheekbones."

Mark began scrawling again.

"You're not doing Marvin in *Paint Your Wagon*, are you?" Simon wondered. "Wouldn't *Point Blank* be better?"

"And should it be Clint's hair from *Play Misty for Me*? Or *Rawhide*?" Gaz said.

"Shut up, shut up," Mark said, scribbling frantically.

He turned the paper towards Nick again. "Is that him?"

Nick thought for a moment. "Not unless he looks like Jack Nicholson, no."

Mark turned the paper back towards himself. "Oh shit, shit." He started scribbling again.

"Hey, that's Henry Fonda's chin!" Nick said.

"No way, that's Kirk Douglas," Simon suggested.

"No, there's no dimple," Nick said.

"Warren Beatty," Simon said.

"Same problem," Nick replied.

"Shirley Maclaine!"

"Shut the fuck up, you two," Mark said. He spun the paper around again.

"Jack Lemmon?" Nick wondered.

Mark sighed, and began again.

Gaz sipped at his drink. "Red Buttons!"

"Shirley Temple!" Nick offered.

They all laughed, and Mark scrawled a bonnet of curls across his portrait.

"That's the man," Nick said, trying to look serious. "You've got him to a tee."

Mark screwed up the paper and threw it at Nick. It bounced into Simon's lap. "Oh well, I tried."

"I thought you said the hitman was scary?" Gaz said. "Who'd be scared of Shirley Temple?"

Simon picked up the ball of paper, unravelled it, smoothed out the creases, and looked at Mark's drawing again. He handed the drawing back to Mark, who added it to the other drawings. Simon then looked at Nick. "Did he tell you his name?"

"Yes, he said his name was Alan. Then when I got out of the car, he laughed and said it wasn't his real name."

"Shirley Temple," Gaz said. "Shirley bloody Temple." He pointed to the piece of paper. "There's the evidence."

Mark smiled. "No wonder I failed A-level art."

"I suppose I'd better buy another round," Gaz said, reluctance in his voice. He slowly stood, and went to the bar.

"Guess who I saw today?" Simon said.

Mark lit a cigarette. "If this doesn't have something to do with Anna, I'm a Dutchman."

Nick smiled. "How could we have forgotten to ask about that? And on the first day of term, too!"

"She was there," Simon said. "She talked to me."

Mark laughed. "I'm amazed. It's a bloody miracle we do."

"Yes, but you haven't finally opened up to me, run your fingers through my hair, looked deep into my eyes and told me I was nice and very lovely. I'd be worried if you did. You aren't thinking of doing so, are you?"

Mark smiled. "If I did, I hope you'd think of something better to say than "Thank you'. How useless was that?"

"So," Nick said. "After ten weeks you finally met up again. What did she say? Did she declare her undying love?"

"She said she might not see me much this week, because of the new term. But we should meet up on Saturday."

"What's happening on Saturday?"

"The Fresher's Ball."

"Oh, yes," Mark said. "Of course." He lit another cigarette. "I suppose you'd like a lift?"

"If you could," Simon said.

"You treat me to a ticket, and I'll give you a lift."

"Fair enough." Simon fiddled with a beermat. "You know what worries me? She wants to meet up at the Ball to tell me she's met somebody far more handsome and amusing."

"While he might be more handsome and amusing than you," Nick said, "will he have lovely long hair like yours?"

"Or your... what is it... your *sartorial eloquence?*" Mark added.

"Hah! Good one," Nick said. "Or how about your *manly* physique?"

"You guys are beginning to worry me," Simon said. "You sound a bit homo. Is there something you haven't told me? Something you want to *share?*"

"No, no. You misread us," Nick said. "We're merely close friends who appreciate your finer points and can thus address them in good faith, man-to-man. I think it's *your* misreading of our comments that is indicative of... *something.* Is there anything *you'd* like to share?"

"All this talk of sharing," Mark said, "strikes me as a bit... how shall we say... feminine? It's not something you'd catch me wanting to do, sharing my inner feelings like this. I therefore conclude that there is something... *effeminate* ... about you two..."

"Well, you might say that, but... Oh, we could be here all day," Simon laughed.

"Where's Gaz?" Nick wondered. "He's been ages."

Mark looked over towards the bar. "Oh, he's chatting to Danny."

Nick looked over his shoulder and caught Gaz's eye. He waved Gaz over. "Come on!"

Gaz arrived with a pint of 6X, half a shandy for Nick, a vodka and Coke for Mark, and an orange juice and lemonade for Simon. "Make room on the table, you lazy bastards." He sat down and looked around the table. "Have you been talking about me?"

"Don't be ridiculous," Nick said. "You're of so little consequence we'd forgotten about you until Mark started gasping."

"What's been happening?"

"Simon saw Anna yesterday." Nick said.

Gaz sipped his 6X and smirked at Simon. "Still mooning over her, are you? Pah! Either you shag them, or you don't. If you don't, what's there to think about?

"All this relationship stuff is alien to you, isn't it?" Nick said.

"No, it's not that. I just don't fancy anybody."

"Well, that not quite true, is it?" Mark said. He nodded towards Imogen at the Honeyhouse table.

"Well, okay," Gaz said quietly, "Imogen is attractive, but she's with James."

And there was Chrissie, too, Nick thought. Gaz had said, a few months back, that he had fancied Chrissie. But she had Jake, of course, and then there was the whole situation with Mark.

"When I fancy somebody," Gaz said, "when I really, really

fancy somebody, and it's not just some stupid infatuation like some people sitting at this table seem to suffer-" Gaz looked meaningfully at Mark and Simon. "I'll go for it, I'll go in for the kill."

"But what if you're rejected?" Nick asked.

"I wouldn't give a fuck. And I wouldn't be as stupid as Simon and not say anything at all until it was too late."

As yet, though, there was nobody, and there had been nobody. Nearly every girl about whom Gaz showed the slightest interest was already hooked up. About any other girl, he seemed indifferent. But then... Perhaps if Imogen weren't with James, she wouldn't be so attractive. Perhaps it was only through her relationship with James that Gaz was able to *imagine* a relationship. Perhaps it was only because he knew how Mark felt about Chrissie that he could see Chrissie as attractive.

"Sometimes, though, " Gaz continued, after another sip of his 6X, "I think relationships are just too difficult. Too complex. I'm not really sure I understand them at all. Perhaps I'll stay celibate."

Mark laughed. "Hah! Fat chance." He looked at Simon. "Hey, is this thing with Anna *a date?*"

Nick smiled as confusion momentarily crossed Simon's face.

"Uh, I don't know," Simon said. "I just thought it was some kind of loose arrangement thing."

"It sounds like *a date,*" Mark said.

"I know, it just struck me. It *does* sound like *a date.*"

"It'll be the first time you've seen each other outside of college hours, won't it?"

"Well, we saw each other after college sometimes, but that just felt like any other bit of the day, you know, part of the college day. We went to the pub for a quick drink sometimes before catching later buses."

"So this must be *a date,*" Mark said, and smiled. "How does it feel to have a date with the lovely Anna?"

"Uh, the more you say, *it's a date,* the more nervous I feel."

"Why should *a date* make you nervous? I mean, a *date's* a *date*, you should think yourself lucky. Why, there must be loads of students who would like to *date* Anna, and here *you* are, going on *a date* with her."

"Stop it, Mark, you're killing me!"

He was smoking one of the joints he rarely smoked at home, and listening to Prokofiev. He had been able to spend some time with his son, and Peter's mother – the ex, The Cow – had been tolerable, friendly rather than the sniping, carping harpy she normally was. Okay, he had to admit, she hated what he did. And why not? She had never been stupid enough to carry out the threats she had shouted at him when she had left him. He sucked on the joint. Mind you, what would he have done had she carried out the threats? No women, no children. And, in this case, the woman was his child's mother. He liked to think he would have just gone down, taken his punishment like a man. He'd done it once before, for GBH; he'd accepted it then, because he had to. He could do it again. She knew this, of course. If she hadn't said anything, it wasn't through fear of him, but because whatever she thought of him, of his work, he was still their son's father.

The music had stopped playing. He walked over to the Linn Sondek, and put on Ravel's *Bolero*. He actually preferred *La Valse*, which was at the end of this side of the LP. He turned up the volume on the Marantz a notch or two, to better hear the quiet rat-a-tat-tats at the beginning. He looked around him at the opulent furnishings. He had good taste. The room lacked something, though. He returned to his black leather sofa and toked at the joint. Yes, it had been a good day. He'd seen his kid. And he'd had a laugh with the freak he'd picked up. The freak had been cooler than most. He had enjoyed spinning out the God yarn. He was an atheist. *No, an agnostic. No, an atheist.* The God-fearing persona he'd created for himself amused him. The hit man judged in heaven. *And not found wanting. Hah!* He did wonder if the freak would ever recognise his car again. He did drive through Dereham often. But the freak had appeared bored by his car talk, and probably couldn't tell an Alfa Romeo from an Austin Princess. He would recognise the freak if he saw him again. He wouldn't pick him up a second time. He wasn't that careless. Once was always fun, twice was just gambling, and he didn't gamble.

He patted his stomach, tapping out the snare beat. His stomach felt a bit fleshy, he thought. He lifted his head up, and looked down at his belly. *Am I putting on weight?* He decided he was, and thought he'd better start eating less, and working out again. He didn't want to become soft and middle-aged. He couldn't help the latter, but intended doing something about the former. Not now, though. Now, he was too laid back to do anything. Tomorrow, he thought, he would start a new exercise regime. He sucked on the joint. *That's if God doesn't call me to judgment first, of course.* He spluttered blue smoke out from between his lips.

5

Molly woke on the bed in her room, confused for a moment about where she was. She had been dreaming, she knew, but the content had flown from her when she had opened her eyes. Images returned, but they weren't coherent – Peta and Harry, hills and UFOs. And a handsome man, a man she had never seen. She had called out to him. She didn't know what he looked like, but he would sometimes appear in her dreams. Archibald Franklin Conn.

Molly looked at her watch, then picked up the thin booklet on the bedside table. She checked the restaurant opening times. It was still open. She hadn't eaten for a while, but didn't feel very hungry. The bar sold sandwiches. That would do.

She pulled on her leather jacket, took the book she was reading from her bag, picked up her purse, and left the room. She locked her door and made her way down the dimly lit stairs. She wasn't sure whether the hotel was trying to create ambience, or whether the landlord was saving money with sixty-watt bulbs. At the bottom of the stairs was a better-lit foyer, the one she had entered when she had first arrived. On one side was a door marked 'Public Bar'; on the other side was a door marked 'Saloon'. She opened the door to the public bar, and looked in. There were some locals playing darts. A grey-haired barman looked up expectantly. She could hear music from a jukebox through the other door. She turned, and walked across the foyer. When she opened the door to the saloon bar, she was hit by the smell of smoke, the din of music and raised voices. This bar had more people in it, and they were younger. This was more her scene.

Molly went to the bar, put her book on top of it, and sat on one of the red-topped stools. She ordered her drink and a sandwich. When she received her vodka and coke, she turned on her stool and looked around, taking in the positions of doors and windows. She checked out the people in the bar. Two tables particularly interested her. They were close together. One had four young men sitting at it; the other had four young men and two young women. One table, the one with the two girls, was very... hippie. The other less so. The girls at the hippie table were very attractive. One was particularly striking, with her long, hennaed, curly hair, and her stripy blazer. Occasionally, somebody from one table would lean across to talk to somebody at the other table. She recognised the movement from when she had been younger. Each table contained a group of best friends. Through some linkage, however, some friendship, everyone on each table knew each other. They all went to the same parties, went to gigs together. She smiled to herself. Not that she was old. She just felt old, sometimes. She sipped at her drink, sucked up an ice cube and let it melt in her mouth. One of the blokes at the hippie table was tapping along to the music on the table top. She watched. He kept rhythm very well. She thought he might be a musician. A drummer? Perhaps, she surmised, this was the link between the two tables: some of them were in a band together.

At the four-bloke table, one of them leaned back in his chair and looked across to another table, where a girl with long black hair sat. She knew that look. She had noticed one or two men giving her the eye. She was used to that. She knew what she looked like. The people around those two tables interested her, though. If she stayed in town for a while, she thought she'd like to get know them.

She picked up her book and began to read it. It was this book that had so impressed Peta, the book that had led her into all the flying saucer nonsense, the book that had, in the end, led her here, to this town. *Panlyrae – A Message for Mankind*. Molly didn't believe in UFOs. She knew that Dereham was the centre of a UFO flap – that had been the attraction of this town for Peta, and for many like her. She glanced over at the tables with the hippies again. She wondered if any of them believed in UFOs. They looked the sort. And they would also be interested in the occult, and ecology, and Marxism. Poor babes, she thought cynically. She looked at four-bloke-table. So far, two of them had given her the glad eye. The one with dark, short, curly hair – his look was rather leering. And the well-built one, with long, fair hair; he had looked at her, while pretending not to. There was something rather shy about him. Of the other two, one had his back to her, and the other one was far too interested in the girl at the other table.

The guy with the long, fair hair stood up, and drained his drink. She pretended to read her book again. More people had drifted into the saloon bar. The fair-haired lad had walked to the bar, at which the only space was next to her.

"Nice Doc Martens," he said.

She looked up. "I like to take care of them."

She saw him glance at the cover of her book.

"Have you read it?"

"No. It sounds like one of those crazy UFO books, by one of those crazy contactees."

"I don't usually read this sort of thing," Molly said.

"Don't worry, we're used to seeing that type of book around here."

Molly laughed. "You make it sound like porn."

"Well, Dereham is a bit like a red light district, I suppose. The town attracts people who want to read *that* sort of thing without fear of *censure*. They want to talk to each other about it, too. And stand on hills together discussing the things they've... *seen*. You can read a book like that quite openly around here, don't worry."

"I take it you're not a believer then?"

"I'm an agnostic, I suppose." The youth pointed back towards the hippie table. "They're the people to talk to. They're sceptical too, but they actually do go on skywatches. I can't understand it, myself."

"Oh, I don't believe in any of it, either. I'm here... Well, I'm here because my sister used to live here. She loved the town. I decided to see what all the fuss was about." She looked Simon up and down. "You look like a student."

"Very astute. You could be a spy or something."

Molly leaned over, close enough to smell patchouli. "Don't tell anybody, but I am." She winked.

She could see that the bloke didn't know whether to believe her or not. Surely, he would be thinking, a spy wouldn't simply blurt it out. She always played this game. She was sure nobody ever believed her.

"Can I buy you a drink?" the youth said.

"I'll buy you one," the woman said. "You're a poor student. I doubt you can afford what I'm drinking."

The youth looked at his glass. "I must admit, I've been nursing this drink for ages. I've already skipped two rounds. I can't afford to buy a round myself."

"Your friends must love you."

The lad turned his head to look at his friends, at the table he'd left. He smiled. "They know it. They accept." He laughed. "Well, Gaz moans like buggery, but you know..."

"What's your name?"

"Simon. And you are?"

"Margaret. Maggie, Margie, or Molly. I prefer Molly, and it's the name I go by. Pleased to meet you." She shook Simon's hand.

Simon took his orange juice. "Would I have known your sister?"

"I doubt it." Molly sipped at her vodka and coke. "She lived here back in 1972. You would have been, what, fifteen?"

"Fourteen. You *are* very good at this," Simon said.

"Peta was... nineteen at the time."

"Yes, well out of my age range. She would be, what, twenty-three now?"

"Yes, she should be going on twenty-four." Molly turned away for a moment, to hide what might be showing on her face. "Peta was only here for a few months. She used to live in a place called White Street, in one of the cottages."

"My friend Nick is twenty-one, but he's never mentioned anybody called Peta."

"She only knew the skywatchers, I think. She knew Richard Patterson."

"Ah yes, our font of ufological wisdom."

"She knew a couple of people her own age, though. Miles and Reese. I don't know their surnames."

"Miles and Reese? Those two? They're a laugh."

"So I heard." She had heard that from Harry, not from Peta. She had never heard enough from Peta.

"They're at Uni. One of them is the brother of a friend of my friend Nick's."

"I think I followed that."

"I should hope so. You *are* a spy, after all."

They drank in silence for a moment, then Simon said, "How long will you be in town?"

"I don't know. I've got a couple of weeks leave from MI5." She fashioned a smile for Simon that she hoped was both charming and mysterious. "I might be here a couple of days. Perhaps more. It depends what I find."

"Why, what are you looking for?"

"Peta, I suppose."

"I thought she wasn't here anymore?"

"She isn't. We... lost touch... for a long time." When it came to Peta, she always danced around the truth. "As I said, she loved this town. If I can understand that, it'll be one more thing I understand about her. I have to get to know her again."

"Have you been up Copsehill yet?"

"No, not yet. I only arrived this afternoon."

"You don't have to be a skywatcher, a UFO nut, to understand everything about Dereham. Go up to Copsehill. Stand on the hill. Look out over the downs. You'll understand part of what your sister loved about this town."

"You love it too?"

"I've never thought about *loving* it. I've grown up here. It's part of my life. It *is* beautiful around here, I know that."

"So they say. I'll go up there. I will. I know it was important to Peta."

There was silence again while they sipped at their drinks. Molly was in control of herself, and this conversation. She knew she had a certain power, some of which came from how she looked. She was surprised, therefore, by what she next asked. "Can I have your phone number?"

"Uh, yeah, of course," Simon stuttered.

Molly took a pen from her purse and handed it to Simon. She held out her hand. Simon wrote his number on the back it, near her slim wrist. "If I do hang around for a couple of weeks, I might like somebody to talk to. I'll let you get back to your friends." She looked around at them. "Your friend, the one talking to the petite girl with long dark hair?" Simon looked back at his friends. "You might like to tell him he has absolutely no chance with her."

"He knows. We all know. It's just one of *those* things."

"Ah yes, one of *those* things. I know about them."

"Have you been watching us?"

"I watch everybody."

"Are you really a spy?"

Molly only smiled, and sipped her drink. Simon turned to go, but Molly gently held him back by the arm. "If I get bored, I can phone, right?"

"Do you want to join us?" Simon nodded towards his friends.

"No, not tonight. If I only stay a couple of days, well... you know."

Simon nodded, but Molly knew that he didn't understand. How could he? How could he know what it was like to be always in different towns, among new people, looking for clues, identities, ideas. She knew now why she had so peremptorily asked for Simon's number. She liked the look of him, and his friends.

If she stayed for longer than two days, she wanted to feel like she belonged, especially here, in Peta's town.

Simon began to move away again, but Molly was overwhelmed by the need to ask one last question. "Peta. She had a boyfriend while she lived here. The bastard dumped her and ran off. You haven't heard of him by any chance?"

"What was his name?"

"Archibald Franklin Conn. Archie."

Her control had slipped as she said that name. She sounded bitter. She wondered if Simon had noticed. "No, sorry, it means nothing to me."

Molly gave him a tight smile. "Just a long shot."

6

Simon sat down at the table with Mark, Gaz and Nick. He looked back towards Molly. She gave him a little wave.

"You're on fire," Gaz said.

Simon was baffled. "What?"

Gaz nodded back towards the bar, towards Molly. "Her. What were you writing on her hand? Your number?"

"Uh, yeah."

"Can't imagine why she'd want your number."

Neither could Simon. He'd given Molly his number because she'd asked for it, not because he had any designs on her. He had enough on his plate trying to understand the Anna situation. He had no desire to become involved with somebody who would be here today and gone tomorrow. If she did stay longer than a couple of days, though, and needed an escort around the town, he'd be happy to oblige.

Gaz said quietly, "I'd give *her* one."

"I haven't seen her before," Nick said. "She's not," he leaned in conspiratorially, and spoke quietly, "from these parts."

"She might be staying *here*," Mark said. "After all, the Lion isn't just a hang-out for hippies, it's also a hotel."

"She's a bit of a looker, though, isn't she?" Gaz said.

Nick nodded. "She is." He studied her for a moment. "She's different to the girls we know. She looks... *hard* is the wrong word. Tough. I wouldn't want to mess with her."

Simon looked over at Molly again. She looked up at that moment and winked, then smiled and returned to her book. She was a pretty woman, but she was more Mark's sort. Although Mark wouldn't give her a glance now - not, at least, while Chrissie sat at a table near them with Jake and his mates. Bloody Jake."

Simon followed his gaze. Chrissie and Jake were now kissing.

"He only does that to annoy me," Mark said.

"Hey, keep your cool, man," Simon said. "He might actually be kissing her because he enjoys it." He remembered Julie. "I would."

Mark smiled grimly. "I don't care, most of the time," he said. "So surely I can be forgiven the odd outburst of frustrated desire?"

"I suppose," Simon conceded.

"I don't intend doing a Charlie, if that's what you're worried about," Mark whispered.

Nick tutted, "It's wicked to mock the afflicted," he whispered.

They were all talking quietly now. Charlie had been a friend of James and Stuart and they were, after all, at the next table. Simon spoke softly. "*Doing a Charlie*. Is that what we'll call it? When you finally lose it? Will I have to phone Nick and say, guess what, Mark's finally *done a Charlie*?"

Nick watched Chrissie and Jake. "Do you really believe," he said to Mark, "that Jake is actually thinking about you now? I mean he's with this attractive girl, who he's been going out with for six months. Do you really suppose he's thinking, oh, I know, I'll only kiss her when Mark's around, just to upset him?"

"With a sinister little giggle at the end for added emphasis?" Gaz said. He did a sinister little giggle, to show Mark what he meant.

"I bet they kiss all the time," Simon said. "When you're not looking. Did you ever think of that?"

"I bet they do other things while you're not around as well." Nick added.

"Yeah, like buttock fondling..." Simon said.

Nick nodded. "And mimple wompling..."

"And teetee rimpling..."

"And he'll gander her nimbles..."

Simon smiled. "Oh, and he'll nurdle her crannies during their erastic pindlings."

Nick, who had taken a sip of his vodka and orange, spat it back into his glass and burst out laughing. "Well, who wouldn't?"

Mark laughed as well. "Stop, stop, you bastards. Now you're just twisting the knife like the fucking sadistic torturers you are." He lit a cigarette. "Call this friendship? I don't need you, you know. I could always go and hang out with the rest of Honeyhouse."

Mark turned to his friends on the next table and caught Imogen's eye. He gave her an exaggerated wink. Imogen waved at him. Mark waved back. "See, they like me. They're nice."

"Yeah, but they're a bunch of fucking freaks," Nick said.

It was true. Simon again wondered at a band that consisted entirely of freaks with long hair and beards but for Mark, who was an oddity with his clean-shaven face, short, if messy, hair, and whose clothes sense was relatively conservative. He wasn't a smooth, in his collarless shirt, waistcoat, flared jeans and Doc Martens. But he didn't sport ripped and patched jeans, had never been near a desert wellie, would most likely run from the sight of a Jesus boot, and would almost certainly use a cheesecloth shirt to clean his motorbike.

"Who wants a drink?" Gaz said.

"Molly has already bought me one," Simon said.

Gaz nodded towards the bar. "Is that Molly?"

"Indeed it is."

"So you've given her your number and she bought you a drink. You're in, there."

Mark and Nick said they'd have another. Gaz went to the bar.

"I bet he heads straight for Molly," Simon said.

Molly was still reading her book. There were other bodies in the way, though, and chance set Gaz on a different course.

Mark lit a cigarette. Simon wafted the smoke away. "Hey, my body is a temple," he said.

Nick leaned back in his chair. "I'm definitely thinking of going to York. It has a psychology department." He sighed. "Although I'm still not really sure psychology is what I want to do."

Simon shrugged. "When will you ever be sure?"

"Oh, I don't know."

"It's two hundred miles away."

"That is an advantage."

"So not Aberdeen, then?" Simon said.

Nick shook his head. "One has to take into account factors other than distance. Like it's bloody cold in Aberdeen. And full of Scottish people."

Mark tipped ash into the ashtray. "Won't you miss us?"

"Yes. I suppose I will," Nick said. "But I'll make new friends."

Mark laughed smoke out into the bar. "You make me feel really wanted."

"Oh, I'm sure I'll pop back occasionally. And you guys could come up and see me. It would get you out of town for the weekend."

Simon couldn't imagine Gaz missing Nick, or anybody else, when they all left. Gaz would find something else to occupy him, to fill the gap. Poker schools. Share analysis. Or women. Perhaps.

Simon sipped at his orange juice. He looked around the bar, then at Nick. "Won't you miss all this?"

Nick laughed. "Don't be ridiculous. I won't miss this. There'll be other bars full of freaks. You know..." He paused, almost shyly. "I can see myself sharing a house with other students, full of stripped pine and bright red teapots, earthenware mugs, oddly assorted chairs from second-hand shops, art on the walls, posters."

"But not Che Guevara, I hope." Mark stubbed out his cigarette in the thick glass ashtray on the drink-ringed, dark brown table between them. "That would be too much of a cliché."

"Okay, then. Perhaps a rug on the wall."

"A rug on the wall! How decadent," Mark said.

"I know," Nick said. "My parents would think I was mad. That I'd gone all.... *oriental*." He paused. "And that's one reason I want to get away. Because my parents would never understand *rugs* on the walls."

Simon supposed that it wouldn't *really* matter if Nick left Dereham. They were all changing. Friends were moving away, into their first jobs, or to universities and polytechnics. The ever-shifting groupings that linked them all as friends were breaking up. Everybody was drifting apart as they grew older. The only glue was Honeyhouse, Simon noted.

Contributing to his sense of change was the passing of the long, hot summer that had seemed so splendidly idyllic. The summer of 1976 had been a record-breaker. Evenings had been warm and cloudless. They had often found themselves in the beer garden at the back of The White Lion, all of them in the knots of their closest friends, but always on the move between these groups, drinking, chatting, smoking, and flirting. After the pub, they had taken many star-lit, moonlit, night-time walks across the local hills – Red Post, Copsehill, Derebury. After the heat of the day, the nights had been a balm; warm but not hot, filled with gentle breezes that rustled the parched leaves on Copsehill and cooled their hot bodies.

Simon had spent much of the summer thinking about Anna, of course, and Nick had hooked up with Heather for a few weeks. The heat and the light had limned everything into his memory. Simon, Nick and Mark had lazed on the grass. Julie had also been there, Simon remembered, she had been hanging out with him then. Heather and a friend had come into the park. Her friend sat on a swing, and pushed her self backwards and forwards with a black espadrille, smoking. Heather had been singing a Genesis song – *I'm counting out time, hoping it goes like I planned it...* The sun above them dazzled, and baked warmth into the soil beneath them. Mark had been complaining about a heat-induced headache, and Heather's blonde hair had glittered in the afternoon sun. Simon had talked about something with Julie and made Nick laugh, then Mark and Nick walked over to the swings to flirt with the girls. Nick was particularly attracted to Heather. She wore, over jeans and a white tee-shirt, and despite the heat, an old red velvet dressing gown so long it swept dust from the grass.

"Remember Heather?" Simon said.

Nick smiled. "Of course. We had a good time. Short but sweet."

The passing of the summer and that idyll had been thrown into sharp relief by what had happened to James, which had only reinforced Simon's sense of the changes to come as they moved from adolescence to adulthood, as relationships became more grown-up: serious or stormy, permanent or transitory. For, at the end of the summer, before the Bank Holiday and the storms afterwards, James had been attacked, stabbed, by his best friend Charlie. Simon wasn't sure about the details. Nobody was, outside of Honeyhouse; and then not even Mark knew everything. Something to do with jealousy about Imogen, and UFOs, and zombies. It all sounded, frankly, crazy. And perhaps Charlie was crazy - he was now in a mental hospital. The stabbing had created a sombre end to the summer holidays, and it had affected everybody connected with James, Mark and Honeyhouse in some way. Simon hadn't been close to Charlie, but knew him well enough, and had liked him. He'd been saddened to hear that Charlie was mentally unstable, couldn't now lead a normal life, couldn't be out in the world drinking, chasing girls, smoking weed as he always had. Change was coming. The adult world was coming. Simon wanted to put it off for as long as he possibly could.

Anna was part of a dream world Simon wanted to maintain.

Simon glanced over at Molly. She still sat at the bar, undisturbed, engrossed in her book. Gaz arrived back with the drinks.

"You never quite made it to your destination," Simon said.

"Bah! Those ruffians at the bar forced me to one side. I'm sure I could have had her, if I'd been able to work my charms on her."

Mark smiled sweetly at Gaz. "What charms?"

"You're one to talk, Mr I-Can't-Have-Chrissie-Because-She'd-Rather-Go-Out-With-a-Grease-Monkey-Than-a-Failed-Artist."

"Well, I might be a failed artist, but at least I have charm. The only artistry you are au fait with is piss."

Nick smiled at Gaz. "Touché. Enough of this ribaldry. How's work?"

Gaz rubbed his hands together. "It's good. Money, money, money at last. I've already opened a savings account."

"No wonder you play badminton," Simon said.

"Yes, I'm middle class," Gaz said. "I come from the middle classes, and I shall probably die in the middle classes. In Middle England, somewhere. But I intend to be a very rich middle class."

Simon studied Gaz for a moment. He was wearing his combat jacket, a collarless shirt, jeans, and baseball boots. "Will you continue to be a weekend hippie?" Simon said.

Gaz looked down at himself. "Oh, I expect so. Although, if I was rolling in it, I might wear a suit even at weekends." He looked Simon up and down. "I don't know if I'll hang around with you lot as I make my way up the corporate ladder. I might drop you all like hot bricks."

"What, and do us all a favour?" Mark said.

Gaz glanced over at Danny and Steve on the next table. "Mind you, if Honeyhouse ever take off they might end up richer than even I intend to be. Then, of course, I'll continue to hang around with you, hoping that their glamour will rub off on me, by... err... proxy." Gaz looked at Mark. "Hey, perhaps I should be your manager. Do you think Honeyhouse will ever get anywhere?"

"I don't know," Mark said. "We've invested a lot of time in the band. But with the rest of them moving away, I can imagine it all falling apart."

"They wouldn't if I was their manager."

"How long have you been thinking about being their manager?" Simon asked.

Gaz grinned. "About two minutes. But if they made it, I could get wealthy without working."

"I think if you *were* their manager they'd expect you to do *some* work."

"I'd delegate," Gaz said.

Nick laughed. "I don't think they'd be paying you to do that."

Gaz sighed. "Oh well, I suppose I shall just have to keep on clerking for the bank."

"Excellent pension scheme, though," Nick said; then he frowned. "Did I really just say that? I must be getting old."

"Fuck that," Gaz said. "I'll get some of their excellent management courses under my belt, then I'll leave for pastures new. The computer industry is expanding."

"If there's a computer bureau on the Dereham Industrial Estate, it must be expanding." Simon mused. Otherwise, why would something as exotic as the computing industry come to grey old Dereham? "Why didn't you get a job there?"

"There was only one job available," Mark said, "And that was the one I got, remember?" He looked at Gaz, and smiled acidly. "Because I had charm."

Gaz frowned. "Bastard. And it pays a lot more than my job."

"I'd prefer to be going to University. I'm still disappointed I'm not."

Simon knew that Mark thought himself a failure.

Gaz grimaced. "Huh. You'll be getting paid five hundred pounds more a year than I will for doing the same thing, pushing paper. Some disappointment. Lucky git."

"Rankles, eh?" Nick said.

Gaz clattered his glass back on the table, laughing. "Hey, I'm the middle-class, badminton-playing, money-grabbing, capitalist, Tory-voting, scum-bag around here. That job should have been mine!"

Simon was surprised. "I didn't know you were a closet Tory."

"Well, I haven't been old enough to vote before, but while I was being educated for free, I would have voted Labour. Now, however, I want my taxes reduced."

Simon was sure that, in their past political conversations – of which there had been few, as they were all mainly a-political – Gaz had been as nominally left wing as any them. Perhaps not as radically left-wing as James, who had read *Das Kapital* and liked to quote Marx occasionally, but Simon seemed to recall Gaz berating Conservative policies. He said as much to Gaz.

"I'm practical," Gaz said. "Labour, free education, good. Conservative party, lower taxes, good."

"Practical, or selfish?" Nick asked.

"Both, I suppose," Gaz said. "I just want the money. Lots and lots of it."

"And with that attitude, you'll probably succeed."

"Anything wrong with that?"

"Not at all, not at all," Nick said. "We're just different. If I can just get into Uni and stay there for the next ten years, I'd happily live on very little."

"You'll be a leech, sucking away all my money in taxes," Gaz said.

"No, you'll be investing in the life of the mind you can't be bothered with," Nick pointed out. "Somebody has to do your thinking for you. Man cannot live by money and badminton alone."

"Sounds like a blissful existence to me. Throw in a self-refilling cask of Wadworth's 6X and it sounds like some kind of utopia."

"What kind of utopia is that?" Nick said.

"What?" Gaz smiled across the table. "Money to pay for the 6X, blissful unconsciousness in the evening so I don't remember what I had to do at work during the day to earn my money, and badminton to fight off the beer belly? And you say this isn't utopia, you egg-head?"

"Point conceded. If you'll accept that my utopia is quiet university campuses, libraries, and lots of dreamy undergraduate girls. And, of course, being as far away from here as possible."

"Not even 6X?"

"Oh, yes, perhaps I'll allow that into my utopia."

"I wouldn't visit it otherwise, you know," Gaz said.

Simon smiled at the easy bantering between Nick and Gaz, and then drained down the last of the orange juice Molly had bought him. The rest of his friends still had half-full glasses. He decided to buy himself another drink. Everybody knew he was a poor student, and wouldn't be offended if he only bought himself one. He half-hoped Molly would still be at the bar, but she'd finally left. He'd have to pay for the drink himself. He did a paper round on Sundays, and earned £1.80 for carrying around a heavy bag stuffed full of the Sunday Times and Sunday Mail. Fifty pence went on the tai chi class, another fifty pence on the kung fu class. He'd heard there was a master teaching in Bristol, but the classes cost a pound each session, and he'd have to spend more money to get there. He was learning enough at the class in Trowbridge. When he went to Uni or Poly, he'd have a grant. Then he could afford a better teacher. *I might finally be able to kill somebody.* Simon smiled to himself.

The bar had become noisier, smokier. Julie and Sarah came in. Julie stopped behind Simon, put her arms around his neck, and kissed his cheek. Simon returned the kiss in kind, then she and Sarah went to another table. Somebody behind the bar had turned up the jukebox to overcome the babbling voices, but the conversations had, of course, in turn increased in volume to outdo the raucous sound of Family, and Roger Chapman singing *Burlesque*. It was a good jukebox, thought Simon, packed with well-chosen singles to please the clientele. As long as nobody used their last ten pence piece to play *Hi Ho, Silver Lining* again, and got half the pub singing drunkenly along, he would be happy. Simon decided he should put his last ten pence in the jukebox now, just to hear Suzi Quatro sing *Devil Gate Drive* and forestall for a while any reoccurrence of Jeff Beck. He walked to the jukebox, looking around him at the crowded tables as he went, and at the laughing, smiling faces that jostled around them. Simon nodded at Danny, who was walking back to the Honeyhouse table. He'd probably been out to score some dope. Danny stuck two fingers up at Simon and laughed. Julie blew him a kiss. He blew one back to her. They held each other's eyes for a moment and Julie gave him a secret smile. A pall of smoke hung across the room – illuminated by the dim wall-lights and a standard lamp that had not yet been broken in a brawl – a thick, blue, mist that moved slowly, forming waves, twisting and curling as people walked through it. Chrissie, the girl Mark loved, was kissing Jake, her boyfriend. Simon thought he could smell hash at one of the tables, but it might only have been the heady collision of ylang ylang, sandalwood and patchouli that drifted from Imogen as she wandered by, towards the toilets, touched his arm and smiled at him. Many of these people would be gone soon, he noted again. How would it be? If those leaving were moving into a new life, then they would leave behind them gaps, holes, spaces that would somehow have to be filled again. By leaving, by creating their new worlds away from this town, they would force a recreation here.

He reached the jukebox and slipped his last, shining, ten-pence piece into the slot, dancing gently to the jerky, fading rhythm of *Burlesque*. He punched the remembered code, A9, for *Devil Gate Drive* on the thick plastic buttons. He now had to choose two more singles. As he did so, by some fate of jukebox programming, Suzi and the band started playing. He swung backwards and forwards to the chugging rhythm as he looked at the singles listed in white on the thin strips of black card he could see through the Perspex cover of the jukebox. He chose his singles, and punched in the codes. Just as he turned back towards the table where Nick, Gaz and Mark sat, he caught the eye of Danny at the Honeyhouse table, and Nick smiling. He knew what he had to do. It was revenge on all those who sang *Hi Ho Silver Lining*. "So come alive!" he sang. He heard Nick,

Gaz, Mark and the rest of the Honeyhouse table join in. "Come alive! Down in Devil Gate Drive."

Imogen sang as she walked back past him. "So come alive!" She trailed sweet exotic scents along with her as she went.

Chrissie had stopped kissing Jake, and was looking over at Mark, smiling, singing along at the top of her voice. Simon laughed.

"Come alive!"

7

On Thursday morning, Molly woke in her room in The White Lion. The bed was comfortable, and she had slept well, although, as she had expected, there had been dreams of Peta during the night. She slipped out from between the white sheets, which contained at least some cotton, and no nylon. In the shower, she mapped out her day. She needed to visit Richard Patterson. She wondered where he lived. He was a celebrity in the town, so she was sure he would be easy to find. After she had brushed her teeth, she phoned Simon, but there was no answer. When she came downstairs, she was too late for breakfast, and there was nobody at the desk. She didn't mind missing breakfast; she ate little in the morning. She would buy a sandwich or a pie later.

For now though, she was eager to find Patterson. She didn't ring the bell on the desk. She walked out into the marketplace. There was watery sunshine through a thin layer of hazy cloud. At least it was dry, unlike yesterday. She turned right to walk along the curved pavement at the top of the Market Place. She recognised Simon's friend, standing by the bookshop, looking in the window. She approached him, quietly, stealthily, cautiously. Not that she needed to, but it was always good practice. As she arrived behind him, she could hear his voice. "We got to get out of this place," he quietly sang to himself.

He hadn't noticed her approach. He seemed to be lost in thought, peering through the window at the books on the shelves. Molly followed his gaze. The books closest to the window were about Dereham, and Wiltshire. Histories by local historians; folklore encyclopaedias; and, of course, Richard Patterson's books about the Dereham mystery, the flying saucers that so excited him. She became aware that the eyes of the man, reflected in the glass, had focused on her. He had seen her.

"Hello?" he said.

He turned to look at her. She knew he recognised her. "I don't know," she said, "if you recognise me, but weren't you with that guy Simon last night, in the bar?"

"You're the woman Simon was talking to in The White Lion. You're..." He thought for a moment. "Molly, is that right?"

"Yes, that's right. And you are?"

"I'm Nick."

"I tried phoning Simon, but nobody answered."

"Si's at college today, in Southleigh. He won't be back until later this afternoon."

Molly frowned. "Shame. Do you know where the UFO Centre is?"

"Patterson's place? You want to talk about UFOs?"

"Not really. Did Simon tell you anything of our conversation?"

"No. Nothing beyond your name."

"Ah. Okay. So, do you know where the UFO Centre is?"

He had nothing to do this morning. He shrugged. "Of course. Would you like me to lead you there?"

"That would be great, Nick. Thanks. I could do with some company."

"It's not far. Follow me. Do you know Patterson?"

"Only a little," Molly said. "I met him once about four years ago. I was younger. He might not remember me."

Nick turned, and led Molly out of the Market Place, towards the High Street.

"Were you looking for a book," Molly said.

"Not really. I like to look. But I blew my money in Bath yesterday, and in the Lion last night." Nick looked down and patted his scarf. "I bought this too."

Molly looked at the scarf. "Very nice. So you were window shopping."

"I suppose so. I like books. I suppose I could have stayed at home and actually read... I do have plenty to read. I have about *thirty* unread books

"But you came out."

"Well, yes." Nick looked at Molly. "There's a tale. Are you sure you want to be bored?"

"Either that or walk in silence, " Molly said.

"You could tell me about your life."

"You're in the groove. Carry on."

"Well, when I sat at the kitchen table this morning, drinking tea, before my mum had gone to work, the house seemed too small, you know? I had to get out."

She sensed dissatisfaction in Nick. He wanted, she thought, to get out of town. Was he bored? Stultified?

Molly was a tall girl, and easily kept pace with Nick. He was, she guessed, about six feet two. A bit skinny for her liking. She liked the look of Simon.

Nick glanced over at her. "So what do you do?"

"I'm a spy," Molly said.

"Oh yes, go on, pull the other one."

"No really, I am."

Nick looked at her, and she gave him her disarming smile. Nick smiled. "Oh no," Nick said, "two nutters in two days."

"Do what?" Molly said.

"Nothing. As you would say, you're in the groove. So tell me, what do you really do?"

"I'm a spy."

"You wouldn't just tell me if you were."

"Ah, but nobody ever believes me, so it's the perfect answer."

"You seem a bit young to be a spy."

"Young? I'm twenty-one. And a bit."

"Still, I thought you were all recruited from university?"

"I got into the service after A-levels. I *was* young, but I had a ... friend inside. He thought I had potential. I was fast-tracked. I've learned a lot, quickly."

"You're the same age as me, then."

"Are you twenty-one? You look a bit older."

Nick laughed. "Thanks. I'm care-worn."

"Oh, I didn't mean it like that. You look more experienced, I suppose. There's something in the eyes. You must be older than your other friends."

"Yes. Most friends of my age left to go to university or got work out of town. The few who stayed were... Well... Let's just say Simon and his friends were of more interest to me."

They passed a pub, *The Rising Sun*. It hadn't opened yet. "Do you guys ever go in there?" Molly asked.

"We never go to *The Rising Sun*. That's a smooth's pub."

"Smooth?"

"Ah. Yes. I forgot, you're not one of us. A smooth is... not one of us. Not a freak or a rocker or a greaser. They are..."

"Smooth," Molly said. "I get it. I see it."

She did see it. Nick saw everybody else as little pebbles, with no rough edges. The rough edges were where his interest lay.

"We turn here," Nick said. He led Molly into Five Chains Lane.

Molly looked at the sign screwed halfway up a wall. "Five Chains. Half a furlong."

"You know your ancient metrology, I see."

"I know a lot of things."

"I don't think I'll be in any pub tonight," Nick said. "I don't have any money."

"Neither has Simon, from what he said last night."

"We'll have to convince our other friends that we should go to somebody's house for coffee. Not *my* house, if I can help it. Simon's, or Mark's or Gaz's." Nick paused for a moment, and then took a different track. "Are you into the UFOs then?"

"Not really. I have other business with Patterson. Do you have an interest in them?"

"Vaguely," Nick said. "I was more interested when I was younger. I've been on skywatches with Mark and Simon's other friends. We call them the Honeyhouse gang. They're in a band, Honeyhouse.

"I thought so. The people at the table next to you, right? They had that look."

"Yeah. Our friend Mark, he's in the band. Bass player. The quiet one. So we tend to sit together, our gang, and the Honeyhouse gang. We do things together. Pubs, films, clubs. We go to the gigs." He smiled. "Which is just as well, because nobody else does."

"So, why do you go to these skywatches, if you only *vaguely* believe in UFOs?" She asked because she wondered what was so fascinating about the flying saucers, what had lured Peta to this town, and what had kept her here.

"I suppose I went, because... Well, when you live in Dereham, and you're young, and a bit of a freak, you just do. Skywatches are fun."

"If you were into it when you were younger, you might have met a girl there. She was called Peta."

Nick frowned. "No, I've never heard of a Peta."

"Did you ever see anything? A flying saucer?"

"No. And, really, I never expected to." He paused. "Well, I did expect to see a balloon with a torch attached it. I knew the brother of a notorious hoaxer, Terry Dyson. In the early days of the Dereham mystery, I used to read Patterson's reports in the *Dereham Gazette*. The reports were very exciting, you know, very... breathless. But I knew what people had seen. Graham, my friend, told me what Terry used to get up to, and when."

"Nobody else knew?"

"Oh, loads of people *know*, and knew back then. Yet that information became... buried... in all the excitement the UFOs generated. In fact, Terry Dyson even wrote to the *Gazette* a few years back, in '72 I think. He called Patterson a fool for thinking that one of his hoaxes had been a UFO. Patterson wrote a letter in reply, saying that hoaxers were a pain in the arse, and, anyway, there were more sightings than there were hoaxes. So there. Nah nah. Or something like that."

"So it was controversial."

"Very much so. There were letters in the local papers, pro and anti. Journalists everywhere. Public meetings. Television. And still it goes on. Sometimes I wonder if the madness will ever stop." Nick looked at Molly. "Have you ever read *Extraordinary Popular Delusions and the Madness of Crowds*?"

Molly shook her head. "No, I haven't."

"I sometimes wonder who else has. Well James has; he's read everything, it seems."

Molly wondered who James was, but guessed it was one of their friends in the Honeyhouse gang.

Nick carried on, musing. "Patterson's an intelligent man. He *should* read it."

"The trouble is," Molly said, "if you believe, well... you believe. I should know. I was brought up as a Catholic. Lapsed now, though. If you believe, you don't tend to read things that will undermine your faith."

Nick grunted. "But what about all the others? Those who come to Copsehill to watch the skies with Patterson, who wait and stare at the sky until they are converted? My favourite line in the book is something Men *think in herds; they go mad in herds, and only recover their senses slowly, and one by one*."

Molly nodded. "So perhaps in the next ten years the herd of ufologists will have recovered their senses, and Dereham will be mysterious no more."

"Perhaps," Nick said. He didn't sound convinced.

They had walked almost the entire five chains up the lane, and had arrived at the gate of a large, detached Victorian house.

"Here we are," Nick said. He stopped by the gate.

Molly also stopped, and looked at the house. A small plaque announced that this was *The UFO Centre*. The large house looked quite grand. A closer view, however, revealed it to be in need of repair. The garden also required attention; it was badly overgrown, a jungle. Patterson seemed to have no time for such mundane pursuits as gardening. He had the ineffable and mysterious to pursue.

Molly tentatively pushed open the black wrought-iron gate, blistered with rust. Nick held back as she began to walk up the path, carefully pushing aside overhanging branches of buddleias. She stopped and turned. "Aren't you coming with me?"

Nick shrugged. "I don't know what your business is with Patterson."

"Don't worry about that. It'll make little sense to you. Come on, be my wingman."

Nick followed Molly up the path. She stopped before the heavy red door. The paint was peeling from it. Nick rang the bell. After a few moments, Patterson opened the door. He was a sharp-featured man in his early forties, with blonde, thinning, hair.

"Good morning," Patterson said. He looked at Nick. "Why, young Nick." He smiled wryly. "We don't often see you down here. You're one of those sceptics." Patterson had a prodigious memory for faces and names; a useful trait in a journalist. "And you young lady, you're not from these parts." Molly did notice, however, that his gaze lingered on her longer than necessary.

"Hi, Richard," Nick said. "This is Molly. As you so expertly deduced, she is indeed not from these parts. She wanted to meet you, though."

"Ah, I see," Patterson said. He had a soft West Country accent, and the *a* in his "ah" was broad, and lingered. He opened the door. Nick allowed Molly to enter first.

"So," Patterson said, as Molly and Nick followed him down the hall. "Have you seen something you'd like to report? An unusual light in the sky?"

"No, nothing like that," Molly said.

"We'll go to my office," Patterson said. "There's a few skywatchers staying here this weekend, and they've occupied the kitchen and living room."

They walked along a passageway, past the stairs, and into a large, bright room. It had once been the dining room, Molly guessed, but now Patterson's desk, and shelves of books and magazines crowded the room.

Patterson went to the chair behind the desk. "Do sit down, Molly." He studied her carefully.

Molly sat in the only chair on the other side of the desk. Patterson looked up at Nick. "Oh, I'm sorry, Nick, would you like me to-"

Nick interrupted him. "No, it's alright, Richard, I'll stand." He leaned back against the bookshelves that lined the room.

Molly noticed that the typewriter on Patterson's desk was electric. An expensive looking machine. Molly knew that Patterson's UFO books had been published by reputable publishers; she wondered if he had recently received a royalty cheque. It was possible, though, that one of the many supporters of Patterson's work had donated the typewriter - that he had followers had been another thing she had learned about him.

Patterson picked up a pencil and fiddled with it. There was an open notepad on the desk in front of him. He looked at Molly. "So, what can I help you with?"

"Peta," Molly said.

Patterson studied her more closely. He smiled. "Of course. Molly Shepherd. I thought I recognized the face."

"Yes."

"We met."

"We did. That would have been four years ago, Mr Patterson."

"Please, call me Richard. You were younger then. But... you also do look like her."

"Do you remember what we talked about?"

"Not much of it. Yes, it was a few years back. But I *am* a reporter. Faces get logged in here." Patterson tapped his pencil against his temple. "We talked about Peta. You wanted to know what happened. How can I help you now?"

"I don't know really. I'm looking for Peta. I won't find her, of course..."

"No, you won't," Patterson said.

"But I'm following in her footsteps."

"She left a lot of footsteps here. We all liked Peta, she was a sweet girl."

"And Archie?"

"A smooth-talking conman, of course. Did you know him?"

"No, Peta and I had lost touch by then."

"I didn't like him much," Patterson said. "I didn't hate him or anything. He just wasn't my sort of lad. He had a roguish charm, though."

"So I've heard."

"Really?"

"There was somebody else who lived with Peta and Archie. I knew him quite well."

"Oh yes... that would be-" Patterson was lost in thought for a moment. "Colin? That was his name, wasn't it?"

"Yes. Colin."

"Now, he was a nice lad. I liked Colin. He believed in Peta, and in the UFOs. Archie never did. He was pretending, I think, to make Peta happy."

"You, Richard, are obviously an optimist with a rosy view of life. Archie never did anything to make Peta happy. Everything he did was to make himself happy. Which might include armed robbery, murder, and whatever else is held on file about him, suspected but never convicted of."

Patterson had leaned back in his chair, and rolled the pencil contemplatively between his fingers. "And you know all this, *how?*"

"Let's just say I have contacts."

"Then why are you asking *me* about Archie?" Patterson tapped the pencil on the notepad "I don't remember you asking about him when you visited with your mother."

"I didn't know then what I know now. Conn appears to lead an apparently blameless life in Cheltenham, buying and selling antiques, mainly books, first editions, some fine art, that sort of thing. Yet he seems to make much more money than I would think possible for somebody in that business. But his bloody accounts all check out."

Patterson looked at her gravely for a few moments. "Again, I have to ask, how do you know all this?"

"Ask Nick."

Patterson looked up at Nick, puzzled. Nick also looked puzzled for moment. "Me? What do I know?" Then he smiled and looked at Molly. "Oh yes. Molly is, apparently, a spy."

"Ah, good one," Patterson said.

"That's what I thought," Nick said.

"So," Patterson said. "You've gone to great lengths to learn all you can about Archie." He looked at Molly again, his face serious. "Is he *really* a murderer?"

"Oh, I don't know," Molly said. She shifted uncomfortably in her seat. There were things she knew about Archie, and things she didn't. And she didn't know herself why she would pursue him. "Shit happens, you know? Harry thought... I mean, Colin thought... that there was more to Archie than a simple conman. But the evidence is missing. Call it intuition, call it sixth sense. I think he's worse than you can possibly imagine. A charmer with a sociopathic streak, perhaps."

Patterson's pencil was in action again. He twirled it expertly between the fingers of one hand. "But what can I tell you?"

"What happened between Peta and Archie? Do you know? Colin told me some of it. I'm wondering if there's anything you can add. She hung around with you as well as with Archie and Colin."

"I can't tell you much about that. Archie simply disappeared one day. A bit like one of my UFOs." Patterson smiled. "At the time, I supposed it was a lover's tiff. Peta never really talked about it. I wasn't close to her in that way. We shared the UFOs, but we didn't talk about her private life. Colin is the one you want for that."

"Yes, I've talked to Colin."

"What happened to Colin?"

Molly shrugged, and looked down at the floor before continuing. "I don't see Colin anymore."

"Shame," Patterson said. "As I say, he was a nice lad. But Archie and Peta?' Patterson shrugged. "There was an argument, and he left. That's all I know. He never struck me as the murdering sort. A bruiser, yes. Didn't he work as a bouncer at some London nightclub?"

"Yes, the Purple Parrot it was called then."

Patterson nodded. "Ah, that's the one."

Molly pushed her chair back and stood up. "Thanks for talking to me, Richard."

Patterson stood slowly, still looking at her measuredly. "My pleasure, young lady. It was nice to meet you again. Come on a skywatch one night, and we can talk about the good old days."

"Perhaps I will."

Patterson quickly scribbled in his notepad, then ripped off the page and handed it to Molly. "That's the name and addresses of a couple other skywatchers who knew Peta. They might be able to tell you something."

As Molly and Nick left the room, two of Patterson's guests came out of the kitchen. One was stocky, with ginger hair and glasses, the other skinny with dark hair. "Hello," they said, to Molly and Nick, but Patterson was obviously the centre of their attention. The one with ginger hair spoke excitedly in a thick Black Country accent. "Richard, a local just came in with a sighting report. Him and his mates saw three shining spheres when they were travelling to Bath."

"Who was it?" Patterson asked

The other one piped up; his accent was milder. Middle class, Molly thought. "Stuart... somebody."

"Stuart Garland?"

Nick knew Stuart well – he was one of the Honeyhouse gang. Patterson obviously knew him too. "Ah, he's a sceptic. I expect he warned you they might be a gliders out of Keevil."

The two enthusiasts nodded.

"Oh well. It's good of him to report them, even if he does think they're something mundane."

"You two lads," Molly said. She pointed to the ginger-haired one. "You're from Stourbridge." She moved her finger to the other youth. "And you're from... Worcester." They nodded again. "Bostin' lads." Molly adopted her Midlands accent. "I'm from your way. Hagley." The lads had been reduced to mute nodding. Molly wasn't sure if her perspicacity had dumbfounded them. More likely, they had been rendered mute by the fact that an older woman was talking to them. She smiled at them, then turned to walk down the hall. Patterson opened the front door, and Molly stepped back onto the overgrown path. Nick followed her. "Thanks, again, Richard," Molly said.

"Sorry I couldn't be more help."

"No problem. I don't really know what I'm looking for, or expect to find."

"You're looking for something, though. Is it some intuition? Some sixth-sense?"

"I don't believe in them."

Patterson smiled enigmatically. "Perhaps you don't have to believe in them. Perhaps they're just *there*, inside you."

Nick and Molly began to walk down the path, but Patterson's voice stopped them.

"Do you know he's a murderer? Any evidence?"

Molly stopped and turned. She shook her head. "No, there isn't."

"Shame. There'd be a good story there. Some linage from the nationals, perhaps."

"Sorry, Richard. If I could help you, I would. In memory of Peta."

"Yes, in memory of Peta. Keep those memories close to you, Molly." Patterson waved, and closed the door.

Nick and Molly walked out of the gate, back into Five Chain Lane.

"Peta was your sister?"

"And you didn't know her?' Molly asked again.

"Peta... Shepherd? No, never heard the name."

83

They walked back towards the town. "Do you know these addresses?' Molly handed the paper from Patterson's notepad to Nick.

Nick looked at them. "I kind of know the people how live at this house. The other address... well, I at least know how to get there."

"Can you take me to them?"

"Of course," Nick said. "I can either mooch around all day, or spend some time with you. And you *are* rather exotic and interesting."

Molly let the last comment pass unremarked. She said, instead, "Why aren't you at work?"

"Why should I let the toad work squat on my life?"

She also knew the poem. "Have you used your wit as a pitchfork and driven the brute off?"

Nick looked at her, and raised an eyebrow. "You are most interesting. Are you really a *spy*?" He shook his head. "We'll go to the house in Crossleigh Road first," Nick said. He turned right at the end of Five Chain Lane.

They were quiet for a few moments before Molly spoke again.

"Were you listening to us? Or were you pretending to look at books? Did you know Archie?"

"I don't think so..."

"Archibald Franklin Conn? Archibald Conn. Archie Conn?"

Nick at least pretended to think, but she knew she was grasping at straws. Nick had said he didn't know Peta, why would be know Archie? "No, never heard of him. What is this all about? Your conversation didn't make much sense to me. I'd been expecting a conversation about UFOs, or the Golden Ram of Satan, or some such nonsense. What you said... It seemed very... serious, somehow, personal."

Molly walked beside Nick on the pavement, which was quiet at this time on an autumn Tuesday afternoon. "I don't know why I talked to Patterson. He didn't know what had happened between Peta and Archie, of course he didn't."

"Do you really look like her?"

"So I've been told." She could feel Nick glancing at her, studying her profile.

"I can't say I've noticed anybody looking like you. She'd only be a couple of years older than me, right?"

"Right. I got the impression, though, that she was really into this UFO stuff. I think she only hung around with the skywatchers."

"And Archie?"

"A few years older than her. Handsome, by all accounts. Tough." Molly looked at Nick. "Not as tall as you. But hard, definitely. You wouldn't want to mix it with him. He's ex-military. He was being groomed for special forces."

"SAS?"

"Possibly. Something like that. Anyway, he got kicked out of the Army for minor pilfering."

"All that stuff you told Patterson... You know, the murder? Is that true?"

"Nobody knows. A friend of mine, he had an... intuition. Archie did do time for GBH. I think he walked all over my sister, used her, treated her badly. I'm just very, very angry with him."

"So what do you hope to discover here?"

"Something that will make me angrier still."

"Can't Peta tell you anything?"

Molly spoke quietly. "That would be difficult." She didn't speak for a while afterwards.

The skywatchers weren't helpful. They had liked Peta, and distrusted Archie. They had no idea what had happened in the end.

"Nothing new there, then," Molly sadly said as they left the last house. The skywatchers had been friendly, and had talked about Peta. None of them had known her well, but they had all liked her. There as a theme developing, Molly noted. Of course everybody would like her, Peta had been lovely. Bright, open, friendly. And yet, the skywatchers hadn't known her well. She wondered if Peta had socialised much. Perhaps her life here had only been about the UFOs, and the voices of the aliens.

"Look, if you want to follow the trail of Peta," Nick said, "perhaps you should go to Copsehill."

"I'm beginning to realise that. Where is it?"

Nick nodded to his right. "That's White Street there." A few tens of yards away, a smaller road ran off to the right from the main road. "It's about a mile from here, up that hill."

"Let's do it."

"Are you sure? You've done a lot of walking today."

"Hey, what do you think I am, a mere girl?"

"That is one thing I already know you're not. Still, off we go."

"White Street was where Peta lived," Molly said, as they began to walk up the steeply inclined road.

They walked in silence. At the top of White Street, Molly paused and looked at a cottage.

"Is that it?' Nick said.

Molly nodded. It was a small house. "When she lived there with Archie, they were doing it up in lieu of rent. Somebody famous owned it. Uh... Lord Creighton, that was it. Philip Creighton."

"Ah, rocking Lord Creighton."

"You've heard of him?"

"He manages The Gentlemen Farmers, doesn't he?"

"Yeah, that's him. I've never listened to them. Too soft-rock for me."

The house was sweet, very English and rural. The only thing it lacked was a trail of roses around the front door.

"Come on, Molly," Nick said, softly. "You're, uh, beginning to frighten the current inhabitants."

Molly came out of her reverie. A face looked back at her from the window. She smiled at the face, which slowly smiled back. Reluctantly, she turned, and followed Nick.

"If you don't like soft-rock, what do you like?' Nick said.

"I'm from the Black Country. Black Sabbath, of course."

"You're a metal girl?"

She nodded. "I am. Sabbath Bloody Sabbath!"

They carried on down Lavington Road, under tall hedgerow trees from which leaves were falling, and past Red Post Farm. The day was bright, with small cumulus clouds drifting across the sky on a gusty breeze.

"Are you really a spy?"

"What do you think?"

Nick chuckled. "I really don't know what to think. I think it unlikely I'll get a straight answer."

"I am a *spy* I tell you."

Nick smiled as he shook his head.

They began the long climb up the road to Copsehill. The town quickly fell behind them, hidden by the large mass of Derebury Hill. They were only a half a mile or so from the last house, but already silence had fallen across the fields around them.

Molly broke that silence. "Why don't you work, Nick?"

"I haven't found what I want to do. I was clerking until last Friday. But I jacked it in."

"What do you really want to do?"

"I don't know. I think I want to be an academic. It sounds a bit pretentious when I say it."

"It's a dirty job but somebody has to do it."

Nick laughed. "I suppose I want to get a degree, then a PhD. Then teach and research."

"Subject?"

"That's the thing... I can't really decide. There are a number of options."

They reached the top of the road. White gates barred their way across Salisbury Plain. Molly turned and looked out across the countryside. The trees in the small copses dotted across the landscape were turning red, yellow and brown. The downs fell from the Plain like green and yellow waterfalls, and the grasses flowed across the fields, down into the valley, and then up across the rolling hills. Molly closed her eyes, and took some long slow breaths. "It smells good."

"I'm used to it," Nick said. "This is how it always smells. Grass, cow shit and mud."

"It's so different from the London air I usually breathe." Molly said. Then she opened her eyes wide and looked at the landscape around her. "Wow," she said.

"Pretty, isn't it?"

Molly smiled. "I know why Peta loved this place."

The landscape around them was a solace to Molly. Nick sat on a grass bank and remained silent while Molly looked around her. Finally she turned to Nick. "Lovely," she said.

Nick pointed behind him. "Think you can manage the last bit? The walk isn't complete until you've been to the copse."

"Of course I can." She climbed over the white, five-barred gate, and began to walk up the flinty track. Nick followed her. At first, the copse seemed to come no closer, but slowly the summit of the hill and its crown of trees came fully into view. The copse was dark, thick with branches and boughs. Molly walked off the path, and into the twilight beneath the trees. She moved slowly, one hand always on the rough bark of a tree trunk. Her feet kicked through the weeds and bracken that crawled across the ground. There was an uncanny silence deep in the copse; they could hear no birds, no sounds from the town, and the wind had been stilled. Nick had followed her into the copse, and walked a little way behind her. Molly turned to look at him. "Peta might be here," she said, thinking to explain something to him, the reason why she had walked between these trunks, under these boughs. "She might be a dryad, living in these trees."

Nick looked around him. "Do you believe that?"

"I wish I believed in that kind of thing, like my hippie friend, Len. It would be good to find Peta's tree and hug it tightly to me."

She hugged a tree anyway.

Nick walked quietly out of the trees, back to the path, leaving Molly alone.

And then, slowly, her tears came.

8

Simon and Warren sat next to each other in the refectory at Southleigh College, saying little. Warren idly watched the world go by, as students entered and left the bar. His main object of interest was, of course, the comings and goings of the female students. Simon distractedly spooned weak tea out of and into his cup. He was thinking about Anna. In a few days' time, it would be the *date*. No, not the *date*, Simon thought. The prospect of Saturday night became unbearable if he thought of it as a *date*.

Warren dragged Simon from his reverie. "I'll get that bloody bus driver."

Simon was confused for a moment. Then he remembered yesterday. "Oh, yes. Still annoyed about that, are we?"

"I bloody well am... Making me look like a tit."

"You always look like a tit."

"You do realise Sally was on the bus?"

"I didn't notice."

"Probably thinking about Anna."

Simon smiled. "Probably."

"I really like Sally, and that bloody bus driver made me look a tit."

"You're obsessed with tits."

"I am. Particularly Sally's."

"Particularly anybody's."

"Not yours."

Simon cupped a hand over his right breast. "Are you sure you wouldn't like a look?"

"Oh no, yuk, what are you saying, man? Let's not go down that road. Please."

"So what are you going to do about the bus driver? Set fire to his bus?"

"That's not a bad idea, actually."

"Arson? You'll go to jail."

"They'll never get me."

They lapsed into silence for a moment, before Warren drawled, "Well... helloooo."

Simon followed Warren's gaze. The glazed door to the refectory swung open, and Jill came in. She waved at Simon and Warren. Warren waved back. She went to the counter, bought herself a cup of tea, and came over to their table.

"Can I join you guys?" she asked.

"Of course you can, my dear," Warren said.

She smiled across at Simon, and then pouted. "You didn't wave at me."

"He has a lot on his mind," Warren said.

"Oh, what's that then?"

"Nothing important," Simon said.

Warren and Jill began talking to each other, while Simon's mind followed its usual course. *Anna Anna Anna. Date date date.* Calling the meeting with Anna *a date* had disoriented Simon, destabilised him. His previous meetings with Anna had always been casually arranged, or had happened by chance. He had, of course, consciously sought her out at lunch-times, or after lectures, but she didn't know that. At least, he thought she didn't know that. Perhaps she did. Perhaps that's why she'd finally arranged this meeting at the Summer Ball, something more than a casual arrangement, something more than a chance encounter. A *date. Damn Mark! Damn him!*

He was looking at Jill now, but wasn't listening to what she and Warren were saying. He could hear them talking, but any meaning was only at the edge of his consciousness. At this moment, he didn't really care what they were saying. It was student-y stuff, no doubt. He was vaguely aware that Warren was flirting. The skin around Jill's blue eyes creased as she smiled at something Warren said. The gold frames of her glasses moved as she talked. She pushed some of her blonde hair behind her ear. Then she turned and looked at Simon, directly into his eyes. Her eyes were extraordinarily blue, he suddenly noticed, a light blue, cornflower blue. He hadn't realised quite how striking they were until that moment. Julie's eyes were blue, a darker, deeper blue. If they too were compared to a flower, he wondered, what would that flower be? A peony, possibly. He remembered kissing Julie. That had been a lovely evening. But then nothing had happened afterwards. Some walks. Some hugging. A little bit more kissing. But Julie hadn't wanted to go out with him. Just like Anna, and all the rest of them had never wanted to.

"What are you looking at?" Jill said, interrupting his thoughts. Her voice was light, bantering.

"Yeah, are you looking at my bird?" Warren said.

Jill turned back to Warren for a moment, and raised an eyebrow, before looking at Simon again.

"I don't think I was really looking at anything," Simon said. "I was..."

"Wool-gathering?"

"Yes, I was wool-gathering."

"Did you come back with enough for a nice cable knit?"

"Possibly."

"That would be nice and snuggly."

"Well, I'd have to learn to knit first."

"Would you do that for me?"

"Perhaps. Mum could teach me."

Simon glanced over at Warren, who appeared to be wondering why the conversation had taken such an obscure turn, and no longer involved him.

"Is your mother good at knitting?"

"She can turn her hand to most things."

"Knit, purl, garter..."

"Box, basket weave, mock cable... ribbing... err..." Simon was surprised that even this many knitting terms had made it past his general indifference.

"Very good. That's a start."

"I'm sure I could shape something around your curves that would show them off most admirably. After the lessons, of course." Simon wondered at himself. Was he *flirting*? Was *this* flirting? Wasn't he simply messing around? And yet... this was what he had done with Anna. Talked nonsense, he had thought. But he had liked talking nonsense. He liked talking nonsense now.

Jill swigged down the last of her tea, and then stood up. "Right, I'm off. Don't you two have lectures to go to?"

"I suppose," Warren said.

"I don't think I really care," Simon said.

Jill shrugged. "Oh well. See you here tomorrow?"

"I hope so," Warren replied. Simon noticed a not unexpected eagerness in Warren's voice.

"See you then," Jill said. She looked at Simon, and then touched him on the arm. "Make sure you get enough wool for my jumper." She winked at him, then turned and left.

"Wow," Warren said, when the door had slowly closed behind her.

"I see you're still *Wow*-ing," Simon noted.

"She's a good looking girl. And she came and talked to me!"

"To us," Simon pointed out.

"To *me*," Warren emphasised. "I'm in there, I think. She said she'd see us tomorrow."

"*You*, surely?" Simon noted.

"Yes, me, me, me, lovely, lovely me."

Simon hoped Warren wasn't getting too full of himself. Simon knew little about the ways of love, but from what little he did know, Jill had seemed uninterested in Warren. In fact, she had seemed more interested in him. Then he remembered Molly. She, too, had wanted his number. *I am a sex-god.* Then Simon smiled to himself for thinking such nonsense. Then he remembered he had a *date* on Saturday, and returned to fretting.

*

Simon was practicing tai chi in the back garden of his parent's house. It was after six in the evening, and twilight was falling fast. The nights were definitely drawing in, Simon thought, as he began again at the first form. Mark sat on the brick dividing wall that separated Simon's father's vegetable patch from a small lawn that was surrounded by Simon's mother's flower borders. The lawn had been brown for a good part of the summer, but was now, after the thunderstorms, slowly returning to green.

Mark had a drawing pad on his knee, and was trying to sketch Simon with a heavy 3B pencil. Simon knew it must be difficult, as he was constantly moving. He glimpsed, as he moved, small, smudged sketches all over the pages of Mark's drawing pad.

Simon finished his forms and sat down next to Mark.

"What do you think?" Mark said, holding the pad at arm's length away from them. He had isolated Simon at different moment, drawing quickly, trying to capture only bare lines that represented a form. Mark's drawings were becoming more abstract, minimal, simply lines and shapes, forms reduced to pencil strokes.

"Cool," Simon said. "They're almost Chinese in their simplicity."

"Yes, that's what I thought." Mark looked at his Simon. "Is that it? Finished for the day?"

"I think so. I need to learn some new forms. I'm getting bored with the few I know."

"Are there many?"

"Hundreds. Actually, I suppose it's sacrilege to say I'm bored. I should be aiming to perfect the few moves I know, while learning some new ones. And then, as I keep practicing the old ones, even *you* would be astounded by their beauty."

Mark brought the pad down to his knee again and flicked back through the pages.

"They're good," Simon said. "You're good."

"So how did I fail A-level Art?"

"How would I know? I'm not arty at all." He paused to look at one of the sketches more closely. "I do think you're good, though."

The fact that he had failed still rankled Mark; particularly as he had passed A-level Maths. He often brought it up – when he wasn't talking about Chrissie, at least. *But then, I talk about Anna all the time.* They all needed other things to talk about.

Mark studied one of the drawings. "There's little I regret about my short life so far." He frowned down at the page. "But being labelled a failure at art really hurt me."

Simon took the drawing pad from Mark and flicked through the pages, studying the drawings. He stopped and held the pad away from him. "Hey, now that's a better subject." Mark looked at the pad. It was open at a charcoal of Chrissie. "When did you do that?" Simon said.

"Last night. She was upset about something, about Jake. He'd gone off to buy some pot. So I sketched her while she talked."

"So that's what you did after we left you at the door to the Lion last night?"

"Yes, she was upset pissed off at him and wanted to talk to me."

"But she's still *with* Jake, I suppose?" Simon shook his head. "There's no hope for you."

"I gave up hoping a long time ago. I'm resigned to the hopelessness of my situation."

"Well, it's a lovely drawing," Simon said. He handed the pad back to Mark. "Do you want a cuppa?"

Mark lit cigarette. "Have you got anything stronger?" he said, morosely. "I'm depressed,"

Simon squeezed Mark's shoulder as he stood. "Poor Mark. Tea is all you'll get in this house."

"Not even a coffee?"

"There might be some instant, if you're lucky."

"I must have helped Chrissie in some way, though. She was in a good mood before I left. She was *very* lovely. She danced around the dining room. She played *School Days*."

"Isn't that one of your favourite albums?"

"Of course. Stanley is a great bassist. I listen to it a lot."

"It's very funky. Did you dance with her?"

"Don't be a fool. Of course I didn't. I can't dance."

"Everybody can dance."

"No they can't."

"Yes they can. Look at me, I'm dancing now."

Simon moved through a series of forms.

"You practice a lot," Mark said. "And you're not trying to follow a beat."

"Hah!" Simon began singing the opening bass-line to *School Days*, moving through forms as he did so. Mark immediately opened his pad and sketched a few lines.

"You could dance too," Simon said, still moving. "You just need to feel the music, feel the beat, and allow yourself to follow it." Simon didn't lose the beat as he talked. "Don't think about the dancing. Don't think you have to *be* something, that you have to *be* a dancer."

"But you know these *forms*, you can look good when you dance."

"You've seen me dance at a parties. I don't do *this* all the time. I just let my legs and arms go where they want with the music." Simon started humming the bass-line to another track from the album, *The Dancer*.

"I'd love to be able to dance with Chrissie."

"Haven't you ever danced with her?"

Mark shook his head, and scrawled more quick lines across the paper.

"Man, that's sad," Simon said. "You really should, you know. Come here, we'll get you dancing."

"Nah."

"Bloody hell, Mark. Come here and dance. If you learn to let yourself go, you'll feel closer to Chrissie. Even if you are two feet apart, you'll be sharing something, a moment, an experience. Get over here, you lump of lard."

Mark reluctantly put his drawing pad, charcoals, and pencils on top of the low wall on which he sat, and walked over to Simon still executed forms and hummed *The Dancer*. He stood in front of Simon.

"So what do I do?"

"Start humming *The Dancer* with me. Actually, you do the bass line, and I'll do the melody."

Simon stopped moving, as they began to hum the tune together.

"You're out of tune," Mark laughed.

"I can't sing."

"Everybody can sing."

"Don't change the subject." Simon began singing again. "Now, just tap your foot," Simon said.

Mark did so. "I feel like a fool."

Mark looked tense. Simon walked over and shook Mark's shoulders. "Loosen up, man. Let your body be free. It wants to dance. Think of Chrissie. From the top... 1, 2, 3, 4..."

Mark began to tap his foot again.

"You've got the rhythm," Simon said. "Now, just swing your arms."

"Is there anybody watching us?" Mark said.

"Nobody cares about us. There's television to watch and pork chops to eat. Now move your feet. See, you *can* do it," Simon said.

"I feel like a berk."

"You look just fine. You go to any party, and see how most people dance.... They look as stupid as you."

Mark stopped moving. "So I look stupid?"

"No, not at all. That was badly put. What I mean is, this is how most of us dance. Apart from the ones who train themselves, or want to be disco dancers... You know the ones. We try to find the music and jig about a bit. But when you're into it, it feels good, even if it looks crap. It feels good to *you*, that's what it's about, not how it looks to other people."

"What I really want is to be able to slow dance with Chrissie."

Simon stopped dancing and singing. "You can do that, too. You won't even look stupid when you're doing it. Everybody looks the same when they do *that*."

Simon put his hands on Mark's shoulders, and smiled at him.

"Is that your reassuring smile?' Mark said.

"I suppose it is. Don't worry, I'm not getting any closer than I have to."

"I'm not reassured."

"Relax. Put your hands on my waist."

"Have you no shame? What *will* the neighbours say?"

"They're all at watching *Nationwide*. Don't worry about it."

Simon could see that Mark was uneasy. He was tensing up again.

"Now," Simon said, "you just sway with me. If I were Chrissie, you would be a lot closer, I hope. Anyway, feel the rhythm. Sway. 1, 2, 3, 4... No, more from your hips, not the shoulders... there, that's better... 1, 2, 3, 4... You're looking good..."

Simon heard Nick's voice. "Is there something you two haven't told me?"

Mark jumped away from Simon. He was blushing. Simon could see his red cheeks even in the twilight.

"Simon was just teaching me how to dance." Mark said. He quickly walked back to the wall, where he picked up his pad and charcoals and sat down looking sheepish.

"I knocked but nobody heard me," Nick said. "I thought I heard a noise back here."

"Can you believe he's never danced with Chrissie?' Simon said.

"Actually, yes I can."

Nick sat on the wall beside Mark, and took the drawing pad from him. He thumbed through it, studying the drawings. "I like them." He looked up at Mark. "You could sell them."

Mark shook his head. "Don't be ridiculous, man. Who'd buy these? Would you buy one?"

"I might." Nick paused, studying a drawing. "If I didn't know you'd give me one if I asked."

"I wouldn't give you one, no matter how much you asked."

Nick laughed. "But why don't you sell them?"

"I don't know if I'm ready. I need a bigger portfolio. And who do I sell them to? They might teach you how to draw at A-level, but they don't teach you to sell the results."

"There must be a way. Can't you have your own art exhibition or something?"

"I've thought about it. I can't afford it, though. Not yet. And who *would* want to buy it? That's what I keep asking myself."

Nick flipped back through the pages and stopped at an abstract of Simon. "How much do you want for this one?"

"Oh, you can have that."

"See, I knew you'd do that. No, come on, how much do you want for it?"

"No, I couldn't."

"Do it, Mark," Simon said. "Take the money. Sell it. Learn to value your art."

"Oh, I don't know," Mark said. "You're a mate. Fifty pee?"

"Done," Nick said.

Mark tore the page carefully from the pad, rolled it up and handed the drawing to Nick.

"Thanks," Nick said, and handed Mark a fifty pence piece.

Mark looked at the shiny coin in his hand.

"You've done it," Simon said. "You've sold your first work of art."

"But it's only to Nick."

"So?"

"Perhaps he's humouring me."

"I most certainly am not," Nick said.

"Everything has a value," Simon said. "If Nick is willing to buy one, perhaps somebody else might".

Mark slipped the coin into his trouser pocket. He nodded towards the picture. "What are you going to do with it?"

"Frame it, of course," Nick said.

"Really?'

Mark looked proud, Simon thought. So he should be. "You know what we should do?" Simon said. "*We* should have an exhibition. Let's exhibit your art."

"No, that's ridiculous."

"No, it's not. We could hire The Wool Hall. How much does it cost?"

"Not much for a day, for something like this," Nick said. "A fiver, I think."

"I'll go without my tai chi class for a week and put some money in," Simon said.

Nick nodded. "Yeah, let's do it. I'll scrape some money together. And Gaz is a moneybags. He'll put something towards it, I'm sure."

"But the pictures need to be framed or mounted," Mark said.

"Oh, we'll think of something," Nick said. "Dad has plenty of wood, and a mitre box. We can get a job lot of glass."

"Frame some of them, and charge more," Simon said. "The rest you could lay flat on tables."

"Yeah, yeah," Nick said. "You've got loads of these minimal pictures of Simon, and the drawings of Chrissie."

Simon could hear Mark's reluctance falling away. "Yes, and some still lifes. And the charcoals of Copsehill."

"Let's do it, then," Nick said. "Come on. The Wool Hall is never busy this time of year. We could get it sorted within a few weeks."

"Okay," Mark said. "Okay. We'll do it." Mark looked at Nick, then at Simon. "Thanks guys."

"I'll sort it," Nick said. "You select the pictures you want framed, and Simon and I will sort out the framing. I'll arrange the hall. We'll do it."

Gaz arrived in the back garden. "Hello kiddies."

"We were just talking about you," Nick said.

Gaz feigned worry, "Uh oh," he said.

"Indeed." Nick tapped Mark's drawing pad. "Have you seen Mark's drawings?"

"Well, yes. I don't really understand them."

"Do you think the drawings are pretentious, or something?" Mark asked.

"Oh, I don't know," Gaz said. "I'm not good at that art stuff. They're all right, I suppose."

"Good, I'm glad you said that," Nick said. "We've decided we're all going to stump up some money to help Mark exhibit his drawings." Nick smiled. "Including you."

Gaz shrugged. "Bastards." He looked up again at Nick, a mischievous smile creasing his face. "What's in it for me?"

"Nothing except a good feeling."

"Is that all? But... What if he sells one of them for a million?"

"That won't happen," Mark said.

"But what if you did?"

"Oh, I'd cut you all in somehow."

"How much?"

"What do you mean, how much? It's not going to happen."

"So, let's say if you make more than ten grand, then I want ten per cent," Gaz said.

Mark's laugh was incredulous. "But that's not going to happen."

"Ten per cent."

"That's ridiculous. It just won't happen."

"So you have nothing to worry about. Ten per cent."

"So have ten per cent. A thousand quid for you if I make more than ten thousand."

"No, ten per cent. Two grand if you make twenty thousand. Ten per cent."

Mark sighed. "Okay, ten per cent, you money-grubbing celibate madman."

Gaz thrust his hand out. "Shake on it."

Mark laughed, and shook Gaz's hand. "It'll never happen," he said.

Gaz looked puzzled for a moment. "Hang on. When did I become celibate?"

"Last night," Mark said. "In The White Lion."

"What? I gave that up when that bird with the leather jacket came in."

"Molly," Simon said.

"Oh yes, Molly," Nick said. "Interesting story. I bumped into her this morning. In fact I took her around to the UFO centre to see old man Patterson."

"Lucky you," Gaz said.

"Then I took her up Copsehill."

"Wahey!" Gaz said.

"Don't be irksome, Gaz. She wanted to talk to Patterson about something. Something about her sister."

"Ah," Simon said. "The sister thing. She mentioned that last night. Peta, was it?"

"Yes. I'm not sure, but I think she might be dead. Although nobody wanted to say that word."

"She said something about some bloke called Archie."

"Yes, she mentioned him too. A rum cove by all accounts. Big tough bastard."

"Did she say she was a spy?"

"Yes, she did."

Gaz laughed. "A fucking spy? First a hitman, then a spy. What is this, weirdo week in Dereham? Have they opened the doors to the loony-bins or something?"

Simon shrugged. "I was tempted to believe her."

"So was I," Nick said.

"She has a certain ... something," Simon said.

"Yeah," Gaz said. "She's hot. I'd be tempted to believe her if she said she was a chess grandmaster or a brain surgeon."

"I need a drink," Mark said.

Simon looked at Nick. "I'm broke," Simon said. "What about you?"

"Same here. I can't go to the Lion tonight."

"Oh, let's go back to mine for coffee then," Mark said.

"Well, we could stay here," Simon said.

"We could, but I have access to spirits at home."

That was true, Simon noted. His parents didn't keep drink at home. Mark's parents did, and as long as he eventually replaced what he drank, they didn't mind him drinking the odd glass or two, or sharing it with his friends.

Mark stood, and made for the garden gate. Gaz followed. Simon looked at Nick. "So what did you really think of Molly?"

Nick smiled. "As Gaz says, she's hot. An interesting person to be around. My morning certainly wasn't wasted. She asked for my number, too."

"So, do you really think she's a spy?"

"About as much as I think my hitman is a hitman. I have no idea. Perhaps they're both as mad as hatters. Perhaps Gaz is right, and they've unlocked the doors of the asylums."

9

Molly picked up the phone in her room at The White Lion, and dialled a London number. She was passed through two operators before she reached Mick Edge. She told him she would be staying in Dereham for a while longer. "I might use up the rest of leave here."

Edge's accent was, she was sure, getting more Scottish the longer he lived in London. "That's all right, lassie. You take as long as you like," he said. "You've no allowed y'self a real holiday for a couple of years."

"I don't like holidays, Mick."

"I know. But you should have taken this trip a while ago."

"I do like the town. I'd like to get more of a feel for why Peta liked it."

"Stay there a week or two, have a rest."

"Resting is not what I do."

Edge was silent for a moment. Then he said, "Well, if you do want to do something, you could do what Harry did when he was there."

"Spy?"

Edge had obviously been hatching a plan over the last few days. "Yes. Watch Patterson. See if he knows anything."

"Knows anything? Like what?"

"Something from..." Edge paused. "From the aliens."

"Have you gone mad while I've been away? I didn't think you believed in that nonsense."

"Aye, it's all shite, of that I'm sure. But Parker-Martens... you know?"

"He's one notch below director, right?"

"Yes, that's the one. It was all him, and he's still interested in all that... rubbish. If I could say you were working on that...

bollocks... he wouldn't care how long you were there, or that you're no longer working on the Bristol job."

"Do we know any more about that?"

"The local plod are looking into it at the moment. They're making some connections for us. You don't need to worry about that. Liz Carter has gone off to scrumpyland to work through some evidence. You'll be kept in the loop."

"So, I just cosy up to Patterson?"

"Harry said Patterson was pretty talkative."

"Yes. About flying saucers, about the Dereham mystery. Not about Peta, though."

Molly had made Edge momentarily uncomfortable, she could tell. Everything had started with Peta, that was certain. Peta, Harry, Len Stone, Panlyrae and everything else. Everything. Nearly all of it gone now, expect for Mick Edge and Len Stone.

"Perhaps Patterson will open up some more when you're on the hill with him."

"I doubt it."

"Well, you do what you do best. Get people talking. Listen what they say, and what they leave unsaid. You're good, Molly."

"So, I talk to Patterson, and find out what the aliens are telling him, right?"

"Right."

"It's bloody mad, Mick."

"Aye, it is that. What did Harry tell you about the first Dereham op?"

"Not much, we weren't together for very long. Sadly." She still missed Harry, even though she had only known him a short while.

"One other job is to check out the skywatchers. There might be interesting people in that crowd."

"As far as I can make out they're just the local hippies, and some middle-aged spiritual types."

"Well, you never know who might turn up. Dereham is on the edge of Salisbury Plain. Skywatching gives our friends from the

East a legitimate way to spy on whatever our armed forces are up to out there."

"And Harry did that too?"

"He did."

"Did he ever find another agent?"

"Only himself. And he found trouble in the shape of Conn. But nobody knew quite how much trouble Conn was going to be at the time."

This must be an odd situation for Mick, Molly thought. The first MI5 operation in Dereham had been a surveillance job for Harry. Here, four years ago, Harry had met Peta and Archibald Franklin Conn. Both she and Edge were having to confront again everything that had so unexpectedly spiralled out of that first operation; a seemingly simple task that had led to guns and bombs and death. Now, here she was – Peta's sister, Harry's ex, back where it had all started, trying to find memories of Peta, remembering Harry, talking to Mick Edge.

"I'll do my best, Mick."

"You always do."

She put the phone back in its cradle. At least if she were working, she could claim the room and phone calls on expenses. Perhaps even the food. What would Mick let her get away with?

Watching the people in the town wouldn't be such a bad job. She liked people. She liked listening and talking. All she had to do was insinuate herself with Patterson, and she would soon be on the hills, meeting the skywatchers. She had, after all, already met the man. She had only to show an interest in UFOs, she was sure, to be taken under his wing and introduced to the local UFO buffs. And then there was that guy Simon, and his friends. They seemed like an interesting bunch. And Simon was a good looking boy.

She decided to go down to the bar now, and have an evening meal, a plate of The White Lion's simple fare. There was no formal dining room; the food would be brought to wherever she was sitting. When she walked into the saloon, Pam Wallace was serving behind the bar. Pam and her husband Josh ran The White Lion. They seemed friendly enough. She sat at a bar stool, and ordered a vodka and coke, and asked Pam for a menu. There was little on it – scampi, chicken, simple breaded fish, peas, chips. She asked Pam for chicken and chips.

She liked Dereham. It would be no hardship to stay a little longer. It was a small town. Already she had seen the same faces at the same tables in the bar. The same faces on the street outside. The people in the bar all knew each other. There were tighter knots of friends at the tables, yes, but there was constant flow between the friends and acquaintances. This easy acquaintance with people, this community, was something she'd never had. There were a few friends in her home town, but she had been studious, seeing University as the ultimate escape from her father, rather than the streets as Peta had. That same father had also restricted her life in ways she didn't quite understand until she left. In London, she had been older, too old to develop a network like the ones she saw in this bar. She envied Simon, Nick and all their friends. Some of them came in now, the ones she thought might be in the band together, and sat at a table.

Pam came back down to end of the bar where Molly sat. "Are you alright, love?"

Molly smiled. "I am, thanks, Pam." She had a thought. "Have you been the landlady here for very long?" She wondered why she hadn't asked before. She knew Peta was no great drinker, but Conn surely liked a pint now and again.

"Four or five years," Pam said. She paused. "Where are we now... Late seventy-six. And we took over from Mr and Mrs Weeks in seventy-two. So, yes, four, four and half years or so."

"In seventy-two? When?" There was every chance then that Pam had met Peta or Archie.

"Oh, April or May time."

Peta hadn't arrived in Dereham with Archie until 1972. "You

might have known my sister," Molly said. She tried to disguise the eagerness in her voice. "Peta? Peta Shepherd? She was in town back then."

Pam looked thoughtful. Then she shook her head. "No, I didn't know any Petas, dear. Oh..." She paused for a moment. "There was that one who..." She stopped, and then shook her head. "No. No, love, I don't remember a Peta."

Molly noted the pause, and thought Pam had at least heard the name. But she didn't want to pursue that, not now. "How about an Archie? Archibald Franklin Conn."

"There was an Archie who frank here sometimes. Easy to remember." She looked around and then her voice dropped to a conspiratorial whisper. "He was a handsome fellah."

"Did he live around here?"

"He did. I saw him in town sometimes. Lots of women did I think."

Molly wasn't sure where this line of questioning would take her. She knew where Archie was now, anyway. Pam wasn't going to say anything about Peta. Molly knew she just wanted to hear somebody say, "He was a bastard, and treated Peta badly." If she stayed in Dereham long enough, she might finally hear somebody say it.

Her chicken and chips arrived. She didn't want to eat at the bar, surrounded by people eager to get a drink. She stood and looked at the tables. Simon and his friends were sitting at what she took to be their traditional table. They had come in while she had been talking to Pam. Simon and Nick looked at each other and said something. Molly was about to move towards a small, empty table when Simon called her name. She looked over.

Simon's smile was welcoming. "Come and sit with us."

She needed no further invitation. Edge had asked her to get involved in the town. So she would. She smiled in turn. After all, who knew what foreign agents might be hiding among Simon's group of friends.

The hitman was back in Cheltenham after another job. The hit had been quick and clean. He looked out of his lounge window. He liked Cheltenham. Its regal grandiosity fit well with how he saw himself. All right, the killing was messy, brutal, and, well, illegal. But aside from that, he thought himself restrained, polite, well-mannered, well-dressed, educated, disciplined, and cultured. He had been a spiv when younger, but had left that behind him when he'd come into the money his brother and sister had left him after their unfortunate deaths. He smiled at the memory.

He walked over to his shelves of LPs and pulled out Poulenc's *Gloria*. He had a penchant for religious music. Even as an atheist he could admire the passion that inspired it. Wasn't that passion as admirable as the passion for a naked woman? And what was wrong with that? He liked naked women. He liked passion. So what if the choir was crowing about God - it had passion. The *Gloria in Excelsis Deo* that began the piece made him think, for some reason, of large, brushed aluminium cubes being set down in a pattern and then being picked up again - by God, presumably - and then set down again in another pattern. It was something to do with all the brass and the fanfares, he thought.

He sat on the sofa with a glass of brandy in his hand, and leaned back, relaxing, deep into the soft cushions. He supposed he could get another job. But he liked the money he made from this. He had an aptitude for it. *And what work could I get that has the freedom of this one?* He could even turn hits down if he wanted. Nobody thought badly of him if he refused to do a hit, nobody got in touch with personnel and started disciplinary proceedings. He had enough money in the bank to take only the jobs he fancied, when he was willing to do them. Although hitmen weren't two a penny, there was always somebody ready and willing to do a contract he turned down. He was free - to work when he wanted, to earn what he wanted, to not work when he wanted. Oh, so there was a risk he wouldn't see his kid again - but, it seemed to him, a very small one. And the money he was making now was for his son's education, for the comfortable home life he provided, for fine clothes, expensive toys and day-care, the best in everything.

He'd never known he would feel this way. He had before seen children as a burden that prevented couples from having fun. But when it had finally happened with The Cow, having a child had been *so* different to how he had imagined it would be. He'd bonded the moment his son had popped out of The Cow, and he had seen the absolute helplessness and frailty of that baby. He knew, in that instant, that only love, nurture and protection, especially protection, could ensure his child entered into adulthood a strong, educated, handsome man.

To protect his son he would have to stay out of prison. to If the law got him, fair enough. If his wife squealed, well, fair enough again; that was a risk he had always taken with The Cow, and he couldn't hold her accountable should she finally break, carrying the secrets that she did. He didn't like to kill people outside of the business - outside of the criminal fraternity where most of his hits took place. But he would kill anybody else who came between him and his son.

10

Gaz, bustling quickly along the pavement, head down, thinking, almost bumped into Nick, who had bounced down the steps out of The Wool Hall. Nick was the last person Gaz wanted to see. He had intended to walk around the town park for a while. He had hoped for some time alone, walking around the boating lake, contemplating what he had done. He wouldn't be able to do this now.

"Gaz!" Nick exclaimed. He put his arm around Gaz's shoulder. "Just the man I was looking for."

"Must be some of that telepathy shit that James and Imogen believe in,£ Gaz said.

"Used to believe in, when they were young and naïve."

"Whatever. What are you doing?"

"Booking the Wool Hall, of course. Remember what we roped you into?"

"Yes, I do, unfortunately. How much will it be?"

"Only a couple of quid. We only need one of the rooms."

"I'm surprised they'd open up just for that."

"Have you never been to our illustrious Wool Hall?"

"Only to see Honeyhouse play upstairs. And what a waste of a night that was."

Nick pulled a face of mock alarm and looked furtively around him. "Shush. Don't let Mark hear you say that. The Wool Hall arranges small *évènements* in as many rooms as it can. We'll be showing Mark's work at the same time as..." He paused, thinking. "Ah, yes, local water-colourist, Wendy Price, and photographer Jimmy Roberts. They were very eager to get Mark into the remaining empty room. They even offered me a cheaper rate. It should have been three pounds."

"You haggled?"

"Not really. I think I just looked moderately startled at the price."

"You should have haggled, just for the hell of it."

"That's more your area, you skinflint."

"Of course. Do you think Mark will sell anything?"

Nick shrugged, and put his hands into his pockets. "Who knows. I like his stuff. If he does, it'll... you know... After failing the A-level... Boost his confidence."

"I fucking hope so," Gaz said. "It might stop him whining all the time."

"Don't be ridiculous," Nick said. "There'll always be Chrissie."

"That's true. There'll always be Chrissie. Unfortunately."

They had, by now, reached the steps up to The White Lion, as if it had always been their intended destination, although it had been Gaz's intention to avoid the pub this afternoon, and thus avoid his friends, particularly Nick. Nick was older, wiser than the others. Gaz feared Nick would sense his anxiety.

The saloon bar was quiet. Nick and Gaz sat on small cushioned stools, around one the bar's smallest tables. Jake sat in the corner with somebody they all knew to be a local dealer, scoring some grass. Jake and the dealer looked cool, despite the illegal transaction that was taking place. Gaz wondered if *he* looked cool. He was still thrilled by what he had done, and still felt the effect of the adrenaline. The walk to the Lion with Nick had calmed him somewhat. He hoped he looked cool, otherwise Nick would quickly notice that something was up.

Gaz didn't really know why he had started stealing. He'd always had money from his parents, and now he worked as well. He knew he wanted more money. He always wanted more money. He wanted to be seriously rich one day. But the few things he'd already stolen - the Sweet single from Benton's, Dereham's only department store, from under the nose of James, who worked there and would most likely have given it to him had he asked, the pack of batteries he'd stolen from a garage, the bottle of vodka he'd stolen from Gateways, and a few other knick-knacks now in a box beneath his bed – he'd not yet sold. He didn't know how to sell them. He'd need to find a fence, or whatever they were called.

Nick returned with the drinks, a pint of Wadworths 6X for Gaz, and what appeared to be half a shandy for himself.

"Are you still broke?" Gaz said.

"I'm okay for the moment," Nick said. "I saved a little before I chucked that job in. But it won't last forever. I'll have to eke it out."

They hadn't been to the pub since Monday night. Mark had said that he and Gaz shouldn't go too often, to save embarrassing Nick and Simon. Simon had visited Gaz during the week to play a few hands of canasta. Simon had laughed at the piles of ten pence pieces, ten to a pile, on the squares of Gaz's chessboard.

"What the hell is that?" Simon said.

"You may mock," Gaz said. "When the board is full, I'll have sixty-four quid. Which is sixty quid more than you." He was proud of his simple scheme. It provided discipline.

They had all visited Mark's house on Thursday evening. The talk then had, as usual, mainly been about Anna, Chrissie, and what Nick was, or wasn't going to do. Still, it had given Gaz the opportunity to take the piss out of them all; they in turn had made jokes about piles of gold. Simon had obviously said something.

Gaz never wanted to spend cautiously again, not now he worked. He would be careful, yes, but not cautious. And, from here, the only way was up. Up the corporate ladder, up the greasy pole, up to smart suits, BMWs, credit cards, and a classy bird. Perhaps that was why he stole – to provide insurance while he was still a lowly clerk.

"Are we coming down here again tonight?" Gaz said.

"Well, you and I might be, but not Mark and Simon. It's Simon's big night, remember? The date."

"Of course, *the date*." But Gaz had forgotten, even though they'd only been talking about it on Thursday night. He'd forgotten because of the bottle in his pocket, the bottle that seemed to become bigger and heavier the longer it remained there. Gaz surreptitiously slid a hand into the pocket of his battered combat jacket, and wrapped it around the bottle of aftershave.

Boots had been quiet earlier in the afternoon, despite today being Saturday. He'd gone there for shampoo and aspirin, but, with the shop nearly empty, he'd suddenly wondered whether he would have the confidence, bravery and temerity to lift something in a shop with such open aisles. There had been nobody else in the aisle containing the aftershave, and he could see that the counter staff were idly gossiping to each other. He knew them both anyway; Julie and Janet had said hello to him as he entered the shop, and then ignored him. He had once kissed Janet at a party, but he wasn't affronted by Janet's indifference. He could remember little of it. Glancing over the top of the shelf, keeping one eye on the two girls in their white uniforms, he had quickly pocketed the small green bottle. He had then picked up a bottle of Head and Shoulders and wandered over to Julie at the medicine counter, where he'd asked for the aspirin.

"I hope Si gets on all right tonight," Nick said.

"I'm sure he'll blow it," Gaz said. He sipped at his beer. "Then he'll whine for another six months."

"I'm afraid that if he *doesn't* get off with Anna tonight, he'll be moody, depressed, and write bad poems until he gets obsessed with somebody else."

"Huh. But then he'll simply turn into Mark."

"Not quite the same. Mark knows his obsession is hopeless. With Simon, there's always a happy optimism. He'll get it right in the end."

"And then he'll get some, hopefully, and shut up at last."

"You're one to talk. Not only have you not had a girlfriend,

114

you don't even talk about girls. There's been nothing apart from the odd dalliance at parties. And that's mainly with Janet. Always Janet."

At the sound of Janet's name, Gaz almost started. It was an odd coincidence that Nick should mention her. That Gaz had snogged Janet, more than once, was undoubtedly why Gaz had avoided her at the counter.

Nick smiled. "Do you fancy Janet?"

"Enough to snog."

"Don't you fancy anybody else?"

"Well, yes," Gaz said. "But they're all taken, or out of my league. I fancied Chrissie as well, you know."

"Yes, I know."

"And, of course, I fancied Imogen."

"Who hasn't?"

"Except, of course, I haven't stabbed anybody because of it."

Nick smiled grimly. "Poor Charlie."

"Yeah, poor Charlie," Gaz echoed. He made a passable attempt at sounding sincere, but he actually thought Charlie was where he belonged, in a mental hospital. Everybody said *Poor Charlie*, but what about poor James? And if somebody like Charlie could stab James, over what was rumoured to be Imogen, then who knew who would go bonkers next. It could be Mark bottling Jake, or Simon topping himself over Anna. Gaz intended to be careful with the women he chose; and when he did finally choose, he wanted nothing more than simple contentment and security while he made amassed great wealth.

"Can we come here late-ish tonight?" Nick asked. "Not that I would want to miss a minute of your scintillating conversation, of course. I just want to make the money last."

"Oh don't worry about that," Gaz said, grateful that Nick had not appeared to notice any guilt that had crossed his face or, indeed, the bottle that still seemed to be growing larger in his pocket.

The small bottle had been growing since he had stood at the counter. He had wondered if Janet would notice anything, say anything. But she only asked how he was, and how Simon was, put the shampoo and aspirin into a bag, and then taken his money. When he was back on the High Street, he was surprised to find how calm he felt. His heart rate had, he noticed, accelerated a little, and he could feel the thrill of what he'd done buzzing through his blood. But other than that he felt very little. If there was guilt, it lay far below the surface. Perhaps, then, it was no surprise that Nick hadn't noticed anything unusual. Perhaps, Gaz thought, I'm good at this.

Having stolen the aftershave, however, he didn't know what to do with it. He never used it himself, and he knew neither Nick nor Mark would buy it. They would want to know where it came from, anyway, and why he wanted to sell it. He didn't want his friends to know what he'd done. He did know, however, that a couple of the smooths that frequented The Swan might be interested in a cheap bottle of aftershave. They were tempted by anything hot or bent. They might be interested in the other items he'd stolen. Certainly, the vodka should be easy to dispose of. The problem was how to convince Nick to go to The Swan.

"Perhaps we could go somewhere different tonight," Gaz said.

Nick, for the first time, eyed him suspiciously. "Oh, really? Where?"

"I don't know. We always come here. We could go to... I don't know, The Swan?"

"*The Swan?*" Nick said, incredulously. "Have you taken leave of your senses? If you hurriedly learned to drive and suggested taking me to Southleigh, to The Vine Tree, then I might go along with you. But *The Swan?* We don't know anybody there. And much as I treasure your *witty* repartee, I might want to talk to somebody else. At least we know people here."

"I know people there."

"Who do you know at The Swan."

"Janet, for a start." Janet was actually the only person Gaz knew who frequented The Swan. He kind of knew Diane through Janet, and there were one or two other people he had met at parties through Janet and Diane. Julie went there some-times, but she had started coming to the Lion again after her fling with Simon in the summer. Luckily, Nick never pressed him for other names, otherwise he would begin floundering.

"Well, I'm sure Janet is a lovely girl," Nick said. "But if you want to go to The Swan, you'll have to go by yourself."

It had been worth trying, but Gaz knew Nick never went anywhere but The White Lion. Sometimes he would go to another pub for a birthday party, of if somebody was getting engaged, and sometimes they went to Bath or Salisbury for what Mark liked to call *a night out*. Gaz sometimes wondered how Nick would survive in another town. Nick had, though, inadvertently provided Gaz a reasonable excuse for visiting The Swan. He could tell Nick and the others that he was going to see Janet. Nick would like the idea that he was at last taking an interest in a woman. Nick liked being understanding and helpful, and talking about relationship shit.

There was no rush, anyway. Gaz knew he wouldn't make much money from the haul as it stood. But it would be money, and that was obviously better than putting the aftershave on a shelf, never to be used, or keeping the vodka in a box under the bed. He could go out alone during the week, and pop down The Swan and have a quiet word with Dodgy Len or Greaser, using Janet as an excuse to go without Nick, Simon or Mark.

The hitman had asked around. The shells he already had for the Mannlicher-Carcano were likely to be the last he'd find for a while, if ever. He decided to save the Mannlicher for special hits. He didn't know what those special hits would be, not now, but he'd know when he was assigned them. If he had to hit President Carter, he'd use the Mannlicher, of course he would. If he had to hit the Commissioner of the Met, he'd use it. But not for the Deputy Commissioner. He'd use the L42A1 for that.

The Army had been training him for Special Forces. He'd become a designated marksman and was being groomed as an officer before the unfortunate business with the NAAFI. Still, he was earning more now than he would ever have done in the SAS. And this line of work was a lot safer than hunting Charlie in the jungle. He didn't actually know if there were British special forces in Vietnam; he'd lost all contact with most of his friends from the army days. Not that he'd had many. He was a bit of a loner. He still had a drink sometimes with Jeff Briggs, the man with whom he'd run a scam in the army, and the man who'd first suggested his present line of work. It had been Jeff, indeed, who'd set up the first meetings with clients.

He pulled the case containing the L42A1 from under the sofa, opened it, and took out the rifle. He found the rag and began to clean the outside of the barrel. He liked rifles. He liked knives. He liked hand-to-hand combat, as long as it involved the element of surprise and a quick snap of the neck – otherwise there was always the chance he'd lose out in any ensuing fight. Some of those he was asked to kill were, after all, tough fuckers. Still, sometimes he wished he could do something a bit different. Hit a mark with a piece of pipe. Choke them on a cucumber. Drown them in orange juice. Or, perhaps, use some fancy piece of equipment, like in a spy film. A metal hat with a razor-sharp brim. Rockets in his car. Or use bazookas, or mortars, or some other form of artillery. He sometimes felt he wasn't using the full range of skills he had acquired in the army. He chuckled to himself, and began to polish the wooden stock of the rifle.

He looked out of the window of his house as he polished, through the net curtains and into the street. What would he do if, say, he was asked to take out that hippie Nick? It hardly seemed worth wasting a bullet on somebody like him; even breaking his neck seemed like hard work. He was a hippie. Peace, man. How do you kill a hippie? Say "Boo!" He laughed. It was like a joke. "How do kill a hippie?" Answer: "Steal his stash." Which reminded him that he *had* once done that. Len Stone, from whom the stash had been stolen, was not your average hippie. If he had hung around long enough to reap the consequences, he might have been killed. How far would Len have gone in retribution? He thought back to the days before the killing had started, when he had been a simple thief and bruiser. He'd stolen Len Stone's stash from the Purple Parrot – the nightclub in London where he worked as a bouncer – and then fled to Dereham with his girlfriend, Peta. She was into all that UFO stuff, so it seemed a natural place to go. He thought he might be able to con some money from the gullible idiots there. Peta had been in contact with aliens. At least, that's what she thought. He had seen an angle right there, charging people to watch Peta perform. But that had never happened. The people in Dereham, the ones who believed in UFOs, weren't as bat-shit crazy as the people Len Stone had collected around him at the Purple Parrot. Still, he had got a rent-free house out of the deal. Shame it had ended so sourly. She'd been a nice girl. What happened had been unfortunate. It still disturbed him a little, though. that somebody so young, so pretty, so smart, could do that. Her life was just opening up. If she could do that, anybody could.

He sat down on the sofa, and put the rifle barrel up between his knees. He reached down into the rifle case and found a chamber cleaning stick and some flannelette. He pushed a piece of the flannelette into the end of the stick, and then inserted the stick into the barrel. He idly twisted the stick, wondering if Nick and his hippie friends were into all that UFO shit. Were there still nutters in Dereham who thought they saw UFOs? Did Richard Patterson still live in the town, writing his crazy stories for the newspapers, and cranking out that tatty magazine? Okay, so he had never conned the cranky old ladies as he had intended, but he actually liked Dereham. It wasn't as grand as Cheltenham, which was his home now. Still, there was something about the town – an atmosphere, as Patterson would say. There were downs and copses, and birds sang out on the hills. He toyed for a moment with the idea of staying for a weekend in the town. But then he remembered Nick. He couldn't risk running into Nick, and questions being asked. Still, he drove through the town most weeks. He could watch the landscape around the town unfold as he passed through in his NSU. He headed towards to the kitchen to make a cup of tea, wiping down the stock of the rifle again as he went.

11

It was a sticky Saturday, not as hot as the summer had been, but warm nonetheless. Broken cloud tumbled across the pale afternoon sky, occasionally obscuring the sun. Simon hoped Anna would be at the Fresher's Ball this evening, just as she had said she would be. He turned away from the window. He composed grand speeches in his head. He couldn't stop himself. He had been doing it all summer long. It might take a while, it seemed, before the portentous voice ceased its random declamations and declarations. Perhaps if he finally kissed Anna, it would.

Part of him couldn't help thinking, however, that somewhere, somehow, he'd done something wrong. Something that his worldly-wise mates perhaps wouldn't have done. He couldn't put his finger on it. It was just a feeling. A sin of ... omission, rather than commission. He tapped his fingers on the radiogram. He had been about to put some music on, but had been distracted by the blue sky outside the window. Perhaps he was mistaken. Perhaps he had done nothing wrong. He was always foreseeing disaster for where Anna was concerned. Hadn't she been happy to see him in their brief five minutes? She had never mentioned anything about a lovely man she'd met over the summer. And she had said he must come to the Ball to see her. It was *like* a date. And surely she wouldn't make such a date if she didn't want to see him. He could say *date* to himself now without feeling the sudden light trembling in his belly. Everything would be fine tonight. They'd talk a bit, dance a bit, flirt with each other like they had done before the summer, and then, perhaps...

Anna, you are the most beautiful girl I've ever met. You make me laugh. I love the way your eyes twinkle in the sunlight. Your smile melts me... Shut up, shut up...

The inner voice that declaimed these speeches was always so meaningful that Simon thought of this voice as belonging to another self. Mr Meaningful, Simon called him. Mr Meaningful made him more nervous than he would otherwise feel. Anyway, unless he could get Anna away from the disco and out into the quiet somewhere, he knew his big speech, however it turned out, would be reduced to hollered fragments punctuated by *What? What was that? You want to what?*

Simon laughed to himself.

What? You want to boff me? Slap.

No, I want to love you.

Boff me? Slap.

Imagining the worst helped with the butterflies somewhat. Preparing for the worst was the only preparation Simon knew how to make.

Anna, I adore you.

What, you want to maul me? Slap.

The phone rang. He walked into the hallway and picked up the handset.

"Are we still on for tonight?" Mark asked.

"Yes, we are. I've got your ticket here. I didn't get our tickets until late in the day yesterday, just in case I saw Anna and she suddenly declared that I was the ugliest man in Dereham and that she'd been taken over by a mind parasite for the last six months."

"Well, it's good to know she didn't, and hasn't."

"How about you? You'll miss seeing Chrissie."

"Oh, I'm not expecting her to be down the Lion tonight, anyway. She's kissed and made up with Jake." Mark sighed. "No surprise there. I expect they'll be... what did you say the other day... teetee rimpling."

Simon laughed.

"Have you got any money to buy the girl a drink?" Mark asked.

"I've got a little bit. A couple of quid. Dad lent me a fiver to get the tickets."

"That might buy a couple of drinks, I suppose. I'll treat you to some. If you're not snogging Anna behind the bike sheds by then."

"I wish," Simon said.

"So do I," Mark said. "I'd love to see you two get together. Then I'd know that all was right with the world. That there is hope for some perfection." He paused. Simon could almost imagine Mark gazing wistfully out of the window. "Love will out, and all that shit," Mark finally added, attempting a cynicism that Simon knew he didn't really feel, that what he said was as much about him and Chrissie as it was about what might happen tonight.

"What time do you want to be picked up?" Mark asked.

"About eight, I suppose."

"I'll see you then. Splash on some Old Spice, old boy." Mark put down the phone.

Old Spice? Simon wondered. Mark had to be joking. Some sandalwood perhaps. Did Mark wear Old Spice? He'd never really thought about it before. Nick certainly one of those manly aftershaves around his neck before he went out for the evening. Gaz went as far as spraying some antiperspirant under his armpits. And Mark? Old Spice?

Simon twisted his wrist, looked at the watch that was strapped beneath it. There were still four hours to kill. *Old Spice?* He slowly walked towards the kitchen to make a cup of tea. He stopped in the hallway, and looked in the mirror there. He wasn't, he supposed, bad looking. His hair was long. Not as long as the boys in the band, but shoulder length, parted in the middle. He liked the colour of it, fair, almost blonde. Girls had always commented on his hair. It had become almost white this summer, in the incessant sun. Would Anna have still liked him with hair as white as snow?

*

123

Molly slowly drank her vodka and coke, looking over the rim of her glass at the occupants of the bar. It was Saturday evening. She should really visit Copsehill, as Edge had asked her to do. She couldn't face Richard Patterson alone. Nick and his friend entered the bar. Molly smiled at Nick and Gaz. She bought them both a drink. She knew Nick had been skywatching before. An evening on the hill with Nick would make the burden of spying less onerous. She wished it had been Simon with Nick, rather than Gaz, but she couldn't have everything.

She looked at Nick. "Do you fancy going to a skywatch?"

Nick looked at Gaz and raised an eyebrow. "Well," Nick said, "I'd sworn off them after witnessing too many over-excitable souls convincing themselves that distant car headlights were evidence of otherworldly manifestations... but... Well, you will need a guide."

Gaz looked at the door to the bar, as if he wanted to be somewhere else. Then a look of resignation crossed his face, a sigh almost heaved his shoulders. "Yes, I suppose I'd better come as well."

"Where's Simon tonight?" Molly said.

"Somebody's hot for our hippie friend," Gaz said.

Molly almost blushed. "Oh, well, yes, of course I am."

Nick smiled "Oh well, that's a pity. For tonight he is on a promise."

"That *is* a shame." Molly noticed that what she was already coming to recognise as *the Honeyhouse gang* was already sitting at its usual table. "And your other friend?"

"Mark," Nick said. "Yes, he's gone with Simon. They went on Mark's motorbike. It's the Fresher's Ball, over at Southleigh College. There's... well, there should be somebody there who Simon has missed over the summer. We're hoping that she has missed him too."

"Yes," Gaz said. "Then he might shut the fuck up about her."

Molly nodded towards the table. "Do you think your friends in the... Honeyhouse gang will want to come with us?"

Nick went over to the table and asked. When he returned, he shook his head. "They said thanks for asking, but another day perhaps. Stuart asked if we knew that thunder is forecast tonight. Do we?"

"Not me," Molly replied.

"Nor me," Gaz said. "Still, a bit of distant lightning should get the nutters over-excited, and that's always worth a laugh."

"Right then, boys," Molly said. "Finish your drinks. Let's get going before the rain arrives."

Nick and Gaz swigged down the last of their drinks, and Molly led them out on the street. At the end of the crescent, Gaz and Nick turned into a footpath Molly hadn't noticed before.

"Who's the lucky girl, then?" Molly asked.

"Anna," Nick said. "They almost hit it off before the holidays. But... well, I don't know... Confusion, star-crossed love, or something. He's been pining ever since."

"Apart from when he was snogging Julie," Gaz pointed out.

"Well, yes," Nick conceded. "But then eight weeks is a long time. And anyway, that dalliance with Julie helped clear his mind, helped him see straight. I think. So he says, anyway."

They reached the end of the lane, and Molly found she was near the station. The boys turned left and Molly followed. Nick explained the travails of Simon and Anna as they walked. They reached a junction and turned right. Molly glanced over the road, and saw a car park. The car park was almost empty apart from a Ford Cortina and an old white Vauxhall Viva that was, Molly could see in the faint single streetlamp, rusting at the sills. A street sign was screwed to the low wall at the entrance to the car park. Trowbridge Road. She recognised the road now. She had walked along it when she had come back from Copsehill with Nick.

She thought it was about time she bought a car. She fancied a sporty number. A Triumph TR6. Or a Stag. Or a TVR. It seemed a bit frivolous. What would she do with a car in London?

She always had access a pool car, if necessary. Still, it would be a nice way to define herself as young and carefree, and sporty and adventurous. She wondered if she were an advertiser's dream.

They were, Molly remembered, heading towards White Street, where Peta had lived. Peta must have walked this road many times when she went to town. Molly wondered if she had walked alone, or with Archie by her side. Most likely, alone. He didn't seem the romantic, sharing, caring sort. Peta would have struggled back up the hill to the cottage, carrying the heavy shopping bags by herself. Molly looked across at Nick. "So you never knew Peta?"

"No, sorry," Nick said.

Molly sighed. Picking up Peta's trail remained difficult. "What about you, Gaz?"

Gaz shook his head. "Never heard of her. Was she a tasty bird?"

"Yes, but too tasty for you."

Gaz sniffed. "As always."

"What about her boyfriend? Archie? You must have been going to the pubs by the time you were sixteen or seventeen, Nick. We all do."

"Yes, I was. But I don't remember any *Archie*. It's a pretty uncommon name around here, so I'm sure I'd remember it."

"What about you, Gaz?"

Gaz smiled. "I'm younger than Nick. I would've been... oh, fourteen in 1972. Even I wasn't drinking back then."

Molly turned back to Nick. "He was medium height, tough-looking, handsome, a charmer."

"Yes, you told me before." Nick said. "And that is *exactly* the kind of man I look for when I go to the pub."

Molly laughed.

Nick gave her a resigned look. "Give it up, Molly. I don't know your sister or this Archie."

"I should get a photo sent down to me," Molly said. "A photo of Archie. See if that jogs your memory."

"A photo?" Gaz said. "Sent down? From where?"

"From..." Molly paused. "From, uh, work."

"Oh yes. Simon told us. Because you're a spy."

"That's right. Because I'm a spy."

Gaz and Nick looked at each other, doubt in their faces. Molly smiled, enjoying their confusion. They began to walk up White Street. Molly dropped the topic of Peta and Archie. She couldn't learn anything from Simon and Nick. They were just too young. They walked the rest of the way to Copsehill talking about music, and Honeyhouse, and Simon and Anna, and London.

Simon watched Mark work his way back from the bar, clutching a bottle of beer for himself, and a bottle of Britvic orange for Simon. He bumped into a few dancing bodies on the way. There was nowhere to sit, the few tables around the edge of the common room being already occupied, and Simon and Mark had ended up as wallflowers. Elton John and Kiki Dee were singing *Don't Go Breaking My Heart*, and Simon was wondering where Anna was.

She might not be coming.

His heart skipped a beat.

She could be outside snogging somebody else.

She could be somewhere else snogging somebody else.

Simon was rather missing Mr Meaningful at this moment.

"Have you seen her yet?" Mark shouted.

"No. Would I be talking to you if I had?"

"What?"

"Would I be talking to you if I had?"

Mark shook his head. "No, I suppose not. Did you arrange a time?"

"No, just a date."

"Well, the night is yet young."

But then Simon saw her, through the crowd, dancing with Joan and some of her other friends. And then, she was all he could see. His heart was in his mouth. He heard Mark say, "I see her."

"Yes, so do I."

"This is your moment. Time to get off your horse and drink your milk."

"What?"

"Forget it. Just go and say something."

Simon was unable to move. He took the bottle of beer from Mark's hand and swallowed it down.

"Hey, two can play at that game!" Mark snatched Simon's Britvic and downed it all, wiped his mouth, then handed back the empty bottle. "Hah!" Simon smiled. "You've got to talk to her," Mark said. "You've been waiting for this all summer."

Mark was right, of course. It wasn't that it was now or never. But it had to be now, or else what had been the point of all that mooning, all that talking, all that speculation, during the holidays?

Mr Meaningful reappeared, as Simon tried to work out what to say.

Anna, I have thought of you all summer long. Without you the hot months were as empty as the clear sky, my days were midsummer long, my soul was as blue as the sea at Swanage.

At least Mr Meaningful knew bathos. However, the voice of Mr Meaningful also rendered Simon immobile. *I am like a tall tree, rooted in your love.* While he remained rooted to the parquet floor, rather like a small tree, he watched Anna dance. It was lovely. She had rhythm, she flowed with the music. *Heaven Must be Missing an Angel,* indeed. She tossed back her long hair, and smiled at her friends. She was wearing a dress, something he rarely saw her in, a Laura Ashley, blue with a floral pattern. She had black espadrilles on her feet. He didn't want to go over to her now, not now, he didn't want to miss these moments, her fluidity, her grace, her face so open and happy, her smile so wide. Did anybody else see this, he wondered. How could Mark see her like this, lost in the music as she now was, free in a way he'd never seen her before, and not love her too? It wasn't wild abandonment, it was controlled, but joyous.

The song was coming to an end, and Anna fell forward into Joan's arms, laughing. Simon thought he saw Joan whisper something in Anna's ear, and, in the gap between the song ending and the next one starting, Anna glanced over at Simon, and then looked away.

Did she see me? Simon wondered. *She didn't acknowledge me.*

Simon felt Mark's hand on his back, a gentle shove. But Simon was suddenly unsure of himself. The Bee Gees were singing *You Should Be Dancing*, and although Anna was dancing, it had none of the joie de vivre that he'd seen before. He felt Mark's hand again. He began to walk towards Anna. Joan glanced at him. He didn't really know Joan, had only seen her with Anna a couple of times, but did know she lived wherever Anna lived, in Truckshill or Marshfield; they'd been friends for years. Just as his own friends had done, Joan had left Anna and Simon alone before the summer, left them to flirt and laugh together. Simon had thought Joan on their side, as it were. So when she glanced at him, didn't smile, and looked back at Anna, Simon knew there must be something wrong, that something was different. Joan had... oh, what was the word that had once been used, that old-fashioned phrase... She had *cut* him. That was it. Simon stopped for a moment, and looked over his shoulder for Mark, but he had gone somewhere.

Simon swallowed, took a deep breath, and carried on through the bodies that boogied on the dance floor. It seemed a long walk, and still Anna had not looked toward him, instead was looking intently, Simon thought, at nothing, at some small space in front of her, some square of air that was, at this moment, intensely interesting. When Simon finally stood by her side, she continued dancing. She looked up at him then, and briefly acknowledged him with a nod. But she didn't smile at him as she had done last Wednesday. Without that smile, he felt adrift, as if what he was about to say was meaningless. *There is no meaning without your smile*, Mr Meaningful said. It was the last thing Mr Meaningful was ever to say.

Simon leaned in towards Anna, tried not to shout over the music.

"Can you come outside with me? We need to talk."

Anna turned to him.

"What?"

Simon leaned in again. "We need to talk."

"Why? What about?"

Still Anna danced.

"What you said at the Summer Ball..."

"What?"

"At the Summer Ball... You ran your fingers through my hair..."

"What did I say?"

"You ran your fingers through my hair," Simon continued, "and said I was really nice."

"I said you were what?"

"You said I was really nice. And I've..."

"I said you were really nice?"

"Yes, you said..."

"What?"

"You said I was really nice, and Anna..."

"I must have been drunk."

You should be dancing, yeah.

"What?"

Anna stopped dancing, and looked up at him, without that longed for smile. "I must have been drunk."

Anna began dancing again. And Simon knew he had been cut again. He walked away, confused. Where was Mark? He needed a drink. He looked around the room, but couldn't see Mark anywhere. He went to the bar, and bought a Britvic orange and vodka with the last of his money, and swallowed it down quickly.

Simon finally found Mark outside the common room, in the still, heavy air, looking up into the sky, smoking a cigarette. He nodded at Simon.

"How did it go?"

"Weirdly."

"What do you mean?"

Simon told Mark how he had been cut by Joan, and what Anna had said.

"That is *truly* weird, man," Mark said.

Simon smiled. "Weirder than a hitman?"

"Indeed. How do you feel?"

"Like I've been living under an illusion for three months. False hopes. That's it. It's all over. We should go."

"Not yet. Let's have another drink. You stay here. I'll get you one."

Simon sat down on the paving stones by the common room, and leaned against the wall. He hoped Anna would come out to find him, say it was all a terrible mistake. But he knew she wouldn't. Not now.

When Molly reached Copsehill, she was perspiring slightly. She was fit, but the walk up the road seemed even longer and steeper in the dark, and the night was still and close. She could see the shapes of a few people standing in the road. A torch briefly illuminated her, and then Gaz and Nick.

"Ah, Nick and young Molly Shepherd." It was Patterson's gentle lilt. "Come and join us."

Molly couldn't see who *us* was, but she, Nick and Gaz walked over and joined Patterson.

"Nick, we don't see you here much anymore," Patterson said. "Oh, and young Gaz. I think I've only seen you here once."

"We're not as dedicated as you," Nick said.

A very diplomatic answer, Molly noted.

"And Molly," Patterson continued. "Is this your first skywatch?"

"Yes. I'm taking your advice, Richard. I'm looking for Peta in the places she loved best."

"Very wise," Patterson said. "And you might see something while you're here."

Molly doubted it. "Yes, you never know." She looked up. Broken cloud slid across the black sky. Stars shone brightly. "It's a good night for it."

"Yes it is," Patterson said. "And there's a satellite," he added. He pointed to the sky.

Molly followed his finger. She could see the light sedately drifting across the sky. She had seen satellites before. They varied in brightness, speed, and direction. She knew the public had access to some information about satellite passes – some newspapers listed the brighter and more noticeable satellites, and Whittaker's Almanac collated information on passes that would occur during the upcoming year. However, there were the satellites the general public knew about – the scientific satellites, the telecommunications satellites, the manned space stations and orbiters – and then there were those they didn't know about – the spy satellites, the military satellites, and the secret orbiters. And some of the things that Patterson and his fellow skywatchers called satellites were detritus of the space age – boosters and casings – and in no published tables of satellite passes. The sedately moving, steady silver light was no doubt familiar to Patterson and the other skywatchers. But there were large satellites out there made up of brightly reflective solar collectors and dark panels, spinning through the night sky, that appeared to flash, and tumbling space debris that reflected light randomly and followed paths that diverged from the common trajectories.

Molly silently wished Patterson luck in sorting out the alien spaceships from the satellites, as well as from the U2s, Blackbirds, and Canberras. She looked into the darkness over Salisbury Plain. And sorting *them* from whatever the military were doing over *there*. Molly wouldn't believe she were witnessing alien intelligences until one landed an obviously alien craft on Copsehill, then got out and shook them all warmly by the hand.

A voice came from the dark; one of the skywatchers. "That satellite – I think it's Ariel 5." The voice had a hint of an accent.

"Thanks, Kurt," Nick called back. He lowered his voice. "That's Kurt. He's Dutch. He seems to be a walking compendium of satellite orbits."

Molly nodded. "He must read the Daily Mail every day." She tried to make out Kurt as best she could in the dark. "A ufologist from the Netherlands," she said, quietly. "Is this unusual?"

"Oh, no," Patterson said. "Visitors from all over the globes seek out our humble hill. Copsehill is like... an international temple at which earnest seekers after truth seek a momentary encounter with the ineffable..."

As he spoke, Patterson's voice had become slower, lower, relaxing, confident... The man was a natural storyteller, a hypnotist.

"He's actually a local," Nick said. "He's been living around here for five years. He lives with his girlfriend, Cathy, down Westfield Road. He likes the West Country, though. Before he moved here, he lived in Plymouth and Cheltenham."

"Really?" Molly said. "He sounds like an interesting guy."

"He is, in small doses," Nick said.

"He does talk a lot of hippie, New Age twaddle," Gaz added.

"I'm sure he does," Molly said. She liked Gaz's bluntness.

She looked over at Kurt again. He had lit a cigarette, but still remained a dark shape. She returned to looking at the sky, and listened to the ufologists talk about the wonders they had seen or read about while they waited for another wonder to occur. She had been lucky. She had turned up a foreign national on her first foray to Copsehill: a foreign national who also appeared to find Cheltenham, Plymouth, and Dereham interesting. She would have to talk to Edge.

Simon had his eyes closed.

"It's thundering," Mark said.

Simon opened his eyes. "Is it?"

"It is."

133

As if to confirm Mark's announcement, the sky lit with distant, electric-blue sheet lightning.

"It's miles away at the moment," Mark said. "But it looks like it's heading our way. Are you ready to go?"

"I suppose so," Simon said. He could see no reason to stay. If they stayed, he might bump into the new Anna, the Anna he didn't know, the Anna who would no longer talk to him, would snub him, cut him, ignore him, pass him by without a word...

Mark fetched their helmets and leather jackets. As they rode slowly back to Dereham, the lightning became more intense, changed from a blue glow that lit the whole sky to discrete strokes of lightning that danced around the clouds, and sometimes forked to the ground near to them. Simon could hear no thunder, with the motorbike growling and the wind rushing around the edges of his visor. And then it rained. Mark slowed to a crawl as the visibility decreased. The lightning again lit the whole sky, each stroke diffused and diffracted by the wall of rain. As they neared Dereham, the rain began to ease, and by the time they reached the outskirts of town, Simon could see stars through breaks in the cloud. The sky was still lit by the lightning, but Simon knew that it was behind him now. In Bath Road, at the bottom of the town, they rode through a flood that had spread across the road and pavements, and could see water gushing from a manhole cover. Mark rode slowly, but still a bow wave crept across Simon's baseball boots. His feet were soaked. They rode up into the High Street, through the Market Place, along Town Road, heading towards the crossroads where they would turn into Goldfinch Drive. Mark was dodging large puddles that crept towards the centre of the road, and had indicated to turn right, when Simon noticed two figures sitting on a low road sign. He patted Mark's shoulder, and pointed past his helmet to Gaz and Nick. Mark nodded, and signalled left instead.

Simon sighed. He knew, now, that he'd have to recount the whole sorry tale of this evening's experience to Nick and Gaz.

Nick would be sympathetic, and Gaz would take the piss. Really, the best part of the whole evening had been the thunderstorm.

Mark rode the bike on to the pavement. Simon jumped off the bike while Mark kicked the stand down. Simon's feet squelched as he walked over to Gaz and Nick. He imagined water squeezing through the riveted breather holes on the side of his baseball boots. His trousers were soaked, too, all the way up to his thighs. At least his leather jacket had kept his torso dry. Still, around his neck, he felt damp. The ends of his long hair, where it had escaped the helmet, were also wet.

The sign on which Gaz and Nick sat said Beech Tree Road; the road had been named in honour of the mature beech that still stood on this patch of green left by the construction company, and hung heavy branches over Nick and Gaz. This patch of green, Nick once said, having paced out its dimensions many times while waiting for the others, had been left only because the plot had been too small to build a house on. The beech tree owed its continued existence to the vagaries of developers. And, as the estate had developed, all of its streets had been named after trees. Nick's parents had been among the first to move into the estate, and had a house close to the top of Beech Tree Road. Directly opposite Beech Tree Road was Goldfinch Drive, the road that led into the estate in which Gaz and Simon lived. All of the streets on that estate were named after birds. Gaz lived in Curlew Way, while Simon lived in Magpie Road. The roads to the two estates formed a crossroads with Barton Road; Mark lived with his parents in a detached house, further along that road as it headed out of town.

The crossroads was an obvious place to finish their evenings. Each could then go their separate way home. On the other hand, if the night looked like it might carry on until the morning, somebody's house was close enough for coffee. That house was often Nick's. His parents seemed so laid back and understanding, Simon never quite understood why Nick was so desperate to get as far away from them and this town as possible.

Nick was older than Simon, and perhaps age had something to do with it. Simon knew that Nick felt he was stagnating here, that he wasn't moving through life, only floating in a still, scummy pond.

Mark joined them, having ensured his motorbike was stable, and took his helmet off.

"You looked like a pair of fucking aliens with those helmets on," Gaz said.

"Very wet aliens," Nick noted. "Did you see Anna?"

Simon looked at the pavement, interested for a moment in a puddle of water that reflected streetlights. "Yes," he finally said. "And it all went horribly, horribly wrong."

"How so?"

"The thing is," Simon said, "this morning I thought I'd done something wrong. I don't know what. It's just this feeling I have. Did I say something? Did I do something? Something, you know, annoying? Offensive? But I only saw her for five minutes the other day. And we mainly talked about Kit Kat."

"Relationships are shit," Gaz said.

"How would you know?" Mark said. "You've never had one."

"I watch you guys fucking them up. Then I know."

The wind shook the trees. Simon was feeling cold now that he was standing still. He had just been numb on the bike.

"Perhaps it was something you did before the summer holidays," Nick said.

"Well, I did think about that on the way back here. But if I *have* done something, why was she all friendly to me last week? And why would she invite me to the Ball? And then I wonder, why did she make a date with me, anyway, just to act all weird?"

"So she could do it in front of her friends," Gaz said. "And make you look about this big." The size Gaz indicated with his thumb and forefinger looked very small indeed. "I tell you, relationships are shit."

Simon bent his head back and looked at the sky. The stars were shining brilliantly in the gaps between the clouds. "I do wonder, though, if Joan is involved, somehow. She's Anna's best friend. They'll have spent all summer together. Did I do something to upset Joan?"

They were quiet for a few moments, as nobody had an answer. Simon began to shiver, and folded his arms across himself, pulling the leather jacket closer against his body.

Mark looked at Simon. "Let's go back to mine for coffee."

Nick and Gaz stood. Nick looked down and straightened his scarf, patting it flat against his stomach. A pair of headlights approached along the main road. Although the road carried traffic between the Midlands and the south coast, it could be quiet on a Saturday evening.

"Look at that," Gaz said. "You don't see many of them."

"See many of what?" Nick said.

"The NSU Ro80."

Gaz didn't know as much about cars as Mark did, but he knew more than Nick and Simon.

Nick stopped fussing with his scarf, and looked up. "The *what?*"

"NSU Ro80," Gaz replied.

"That was it!" Nick said excitedly, turning his head to follow the wedge-shaped car that had now passed by them.

"That was what?" Simon said.

"NSU Ro80! That was what the hit man said. That was what he was boasting about in the car. He had an NSU Ro80. No wonder I forgot. It sounds like a disease. Or a cure for a disease. Shit!" Nick exclaimed. "I wonder if that was him?"

"Twice in a week? Seems a bit unlikely."

"Oh well, at least I know what the car is."

"Are you going to the police now?" Mark stared at the receding tail-lights of the distant car. "Did you get the registration number?"

"No," Nick said.

"Colour?"

"Not under the streetlights. It was kind of green-y. Kind of blue-y. Could have been either. Might have been silver. I'm not sure." The tail-lights disappeared around the lazy curve into Town Road. "Shit! Shit!" Nick exclaimed again.

Simon, who had also been watching the car as it drove into the town centre, looked at Nick. He was standing on the balls of his feet, almost as if wanted to run into town after the car. "Calm down, Nick. We don't know if it's the same car." He laughed. "We don't even know whether he really is a hitman or a nutter."

"It's Chrissie," Mark said.

"What?" Nick said.

"Down the road," Mark nodded back along the main road. "It's Chrissie."

There was a figure in the distance, unmistakably female. But only Mark, Simon thought, would have been able to discern Chrissie's silhouette from this distance. Simon would never have recognised her. Now Mark had pointed out who it was, it was obvious – the short-stepped walk, the open shoulders, her long, straight, black hair falling like a cape behind her.

Mark looked at his watch. "Eleven-thirty. Pubs must have kicked out."

Simon remembered what Mark had told him earlier. "But wasn't she with Jake tonight?"

"She was, she was," Mark murmured. "And what's she doing up this end of town, anyway?"

Chrissie lived on the west side of town. Simon knew that she only ventured east when she wanted to see Mark. And, usually, she only wanted to find Mark when she needed something. At this time of night, that would be consolation.

As she came closer, she smiled at Mark. When she reached him, she put her arms around him, and then moved one hand up to hold the back of his neck softly. It seemed intimate. Almost too intimate, considering Chrissie's relationship with Jake.

"Hello, Mark," she said quietly.

After a few moments she released him, and turned to the others.

"Hello, chaps," she said, with a brightness that Simon could see was forced.

"Where's Jake?" Mark asked.

Mark knew, as well as Simon did, why Chrissie would be at this end of town. She knew that, after the pubs closed, Mark could often be found chewing the fat with his friends at this street sign.

Chrissie sighed. "Oh, we argued again, and I stormed out of the pub."

Simon wondered whether Gaz would venture his observation that relationships were shit. He didn't.

"And what did you argue about this time?" Mark said.

"Well, he got chatting to Danny, and Danny asked him if he wanted to come back to his place for some blow, and Jake said yes. But I wanted him to come back to my place tonight. So we started arguing. He said I was no fun, that I always wanted him to do what I wanted. So I stormed off. I've been wandering for a while."

"Are you pissed?" Mark wondered.

"No. Why would you say that?"

"Your arguments are always worse when you're pissed."

"Well, Jake might be..."

"No, you're just as bad. You let your mouth run off when you've had a few."

Mark and Chrissie were not unlike a bickering couple, Simon thought. As if they'd been married two years and Mark could no longer tolerate her drinking that had seemed such fun before, and yet they soldiered on regardless. Simon briefly imagined Mark and Chrissie at the altar in St Peter's church in the town centre. Because, of course, Mark would want to marry Chrissie. That much seemed obvious. *He'd marry her without even going out with her. Courting her.* He wanted to be with her that badly. *But I suppose he has* courted *her.* He had spent two years paying court to her. *But he definitely hasn't stepped out with her.*

"You look cold," Mark said to Chrissie.

"I am a bit," Chrissie replied.

Mark looked at Chrissie sympathetically. "We were just going to mine for a coffee. Do you want to come?"

"Yes, please."

Simon knew what Mark was thinking. *Now he doesn't want us there, of course. But we will go. We always do. It's not as if we're actually playing gooseberry.* Simon also knew that Chrissie liked to have him or Nick around. Chrissie had told him so one day. If there was somebody else with Mark, he was less likely to embarrass her or himself with endearments and entreaties. Before she had told Simon this, he had thought it best to leave Mark and Chrissie to whatever it was they did. But now Simon thought it gallant to accompany her. *I'm her chaperone.*

"I'd love a cuppa," Nick said.

"Not me," Gaz said. "I've got to get up in the morning."

Of course, he didn't have to get up at all, and all but Chrissie knew it. Gaz was just saving himself from listening to any of that relationship shit. And they also knew that.

"I'll see you all tomorrow, or something," Gaz said in a vague way. The others said goodbye to him, and he ambled across the road to Goldfinch Drive. Simon watched his dark shape mooching up the street towards his home. It was early for Gaz; early for all of them. They would have undoubtedly ended up in somebody's kitchen, at some point tonight. They always did on a Saturday. What would Gaz do instead? *Move his piles of coins around. Feel their weight in his hands.*

"I'll go and get the kettle on," Mark said.

He pulled on his helmet, clambered back on his Honda, kicked the engine over, and heeled the kickstand up. He blipped the throttle, and rode off the pavement, splashing into the puddles by the kerb and then down Barton Road. Within a hundred yards or so, Mark was indicating to turn into the driveway to his parents' house. Mark always remembered to indicate.

*

Simon sipped his tea. He sat at the table in the dining room with Mark, Nick and Chrissie. Mark and Chrissie were talking about Jake, while Nick listened. Simon wasn't interested. His mind was still on Anna. He had been cut, and he didn't know why. He was taken with a passing whim to look up the word *cut*. In fact, he had read about it here, at Mark's house, he remembered, in *Brewer's Dictionary of Phrase and Fable*. He knew the reference books were kept on the shelves in this room. He stood and scanned them. He found the *Brewer's*, then sat back down. Nick caught his eye and raised an eyebrow. But Chrissie was in full flow, saying how Jake was a pig, and how she sometimes felt like an accessory to his life, and Nick didn't say anything. Simon found the entry for "To cut", and read it. He found that the *cut direct* was to stare somebody in the face and pretend not to know them. The *cut indirect* was to look another way and pretend not to see an acquaintance. He had suffered a cut indirect from Anna, and a cut direct from Joan.

Hah! The next time I see Anna I'll practice the cut sublime. He would admire "the top of some tall edifice or the clouds of heaven" until she had passed by. *How lovely.* As for Joan, she would get the *cut infernal*. He would pretend to tie the laces on his baseball boots when he next saw her. He closed the book, and pushed it one side. He had to do something when he saw them again at college, on Monday or Tuesday, whichever day it would be that their paths would inevitably cross. *I've been cut! I'll cut them back!* Except he knew he wouldn't. He'd just mope around the corridors, avoiding Anna, unable to cope with this strange new world in which they couldn't talk. Because he wouldn't be able to talk to her. It would be impossible. *What would I say?* He tried to imagine himself apologising for what he'd said, that it didn't matter that she had been drunk and hadn't fancied him at all, that he felt a bit of a fool for supposing she had, and hey, we'll let bygones be bygones and get back to some serious flirting. That wasn't going to happen. For a start, it would involve a speech, and Mr Meaningful had now absented himself. Also, it wasn't in his nature. The scenarios he created in his head always fell apart when confronted with reality. The ability of such scenarios to explode into fragments had been amply demonstrated tonight. He wasn't minded again attempt bringing fantasy and reality together.

"Sometimes, I hate Jake," Simon heard Chrissie say, bringing him out of his reverie.

"Oh, surely not," Mark said. "Hate's too strong a word."

I'm not going to hate Anna, Simon thought. Not ever. *I don't know what happened, really. I don't know what it's all about.* Perhaps Joan had said something. Perhaps he had said something. None of it mattered really.

"I love him, and then I hate him. He can be really nice to me, and then forget about me in an instant, if something more exciting or more interesting comes up. Then I feel like I'm not interesting. Or exciting."

There was silence around the table for a moment. That Mark could avoid blurting out *But I love you Chrissie! You'll never be an accessory to me!* impressed Simon. Because that was what Mark wanted to say. Always. But he never did. Instead, he carried on providing a shoulder to cry on, carried on helping Chrissie and Jake stay together. It wasn't even as though Jake was a friend of anybody within their social groups. The only person he knew relatively well was Danny, Mark's friend in Honeyhouse, who was a mate from school. Jake's social group contained people who were vaguely associated with Simon's friends and the Honeyhouse gang. But they were slowly drifting further away. In that group, most of them worked, most of them were staying in town, not moving off to university or polytechnic. Some of them were already in serious relationships. They listened to the same kinds of music, smoked dope, had long hair, and in that way were similar to Simon's friends and acquaintances. They weren't smooths. They didn't go to *The Swan*, after all. But they didn't read, spent a lot of time drinking, and were into football. Not that there was anything wrong with those things. But it meant the two groups had very little in common. Simon could pass the time of day easily enough with Jake, had done so many times. But he couldn't imagine being at Jake's drinking tea and talking as he did with Nick and Mark, and even Gaz.

"It's not fair," Chrissie said. She said it so petulantly that it brought Simon back to the present again. "The only reason Danny was talking to Jake was because Imogen and James, and Kate and Stuart had gone to Bristol to see a band, and Steve and John have already gone off to Uni. So just because Danny was feeling a bit lonely, I ended up feeling lonely instead."

"Which band?" Nick asked. "Nobody told us about any gigs."

"Oh, Manfred Mann's Earth Band, at the Colston Hall. Does it matter?" Chrissie said petulantly.

"It might have done. If it had been a band I liked, I might have felt ostracised," Nick said.

"Cut," Simon added.

Nick looked at Simon and raised a quizzical eyebrow again. "But as it was the Manfreds..." He shrugged his shoulders. "Who cares?"

"Well, Danny didn't have to monopolise Jake just because he was lonely," Chrissie said.

"You should have flirted with somebody," Nick said. "Then Jake might have taken some notice of you."

Chrissie thought for a moment. "Yes, where were you Mark, when I needed you?"

"Helping Simon with Anna. Not that I did."

"Nobody could have done," Simon replied. "I've been living in a fantasy world for six months."

"And at least you don't have to do that, live in a fantasy world," Mark pointed out to Chrissie. "You've got a real live boyfriend." He laughed. "Not imaginary partners like we have most of the time."

Simon knew why Mark laughed. Because everybody, including Chrissie, was aware that Chrissie was Mark's imaginary partner. Mark showed no embarrassment at being trapped in this verbal and emotional paradox, though obviously conscious of what he had said. He carried on smoothly. "You can go to Jake any time and get hugs and kisses and comfort."

"And you can get your nimbles gandered," Nick said, and Simon giggled.

Chrissie raised an eyebrow. "I can get my what... what?"

"Ignore them," Mark said. "They are but *children*."

Nick's comment effectively silenced Chrissie for a moment. The silence threatened to last as Chrissie continued to eye Nick suspiciously, but Simon finally broke it. "What did you guys do without us?" he asked.

"Ah, well, thereby hangs a tale," Nick said. "There was an attractive woman in the Lion who was, I think, looking for you. She wanted to go to Copsehill and was looking for an escort. In the end, she settled for me and Gaz."

Simon was confused. It must have shown.

"Molly, the spy woman," Mark explained.

"Yes," Nick continued. "She seemed most disappointed that you had a date."

"But it turns out that you've been spurned and rejected by Anna anyway," Mark said. "So you might as well give Molly one."

Chrissie snorted. "He'll never give anybody one. He's too shy."

"Why did she want to go to Copsehill" Mark asked.

"Who knows. Something about her sister, I think."

"Were there many people there tonight?"

"God, yes, there were loads of loons there looking for aliens," Nick said. "So I suppose some people must still believe in it."

"I still buy the local UFO mag," Simon said. "And there's usually a local sighting in there, among all the other tosh."

"Tosh it most certainly is," Mark said. "Crap. Balderdash. Twaddle. I can't believe people think there's anything in it. We walk around those hills as often as anybody, and we've never seen a thing."

Simon recalled the skywatches he had gone to with Mark and the Honeyhouse gang. Nick had gone a few times too. Gaz had only gone once. Well, only once before tonight. Skywatching obviously had a certain glamour when it involved the intriguing new arrival in town. Skywatching was mainly, though, a Honey-house thing. James and Imogen and Stuart and Kate still went on skywatches, even while becoming more sceptical about UFOs.

"The skywatches were fun, though, weren't they?" Simon said.

"If James brought along his Martell, entertainment was guaranteed," Mark noted.

"Did you hear about the night James' cup of Martell caught on fire?" Simon said.

Mark laughed. "Yes. Something about exploding kerbstones and greatcoats aflame."

"That would have been a skywatch worth going too."

Nick looked at Simon. "So why do you still buy the mags?"

"Oh, I don't know. Habit?" Simon shrugged. "Because, I suppose, I still have some small hope that we're all wrong and something will turn up."

"Unlikely," Mark said.

"I know. The chances are vanishingly small. I don't *really* think anybody sees anything. The only things ever described in the *UFO Journal* are lights in the sky."

"Excuse me," said Chrissie. "Can I just butt in?"

"Of course," said Mark. "Butt away."

"Molly the *Spy Woman?*"

"Oh yes," said Mark. "She's Simon's new girlfriend."

Simon felt himself blush.

"She's good looking," Mark continued. "But probably madder than Nick's hitman."

Chrissie looked puzzled. "Nick's *hitman?* " Chrissie said. "A hitman? What hitman?"

Nick told Chrissie about his ride home from Bath.

"He was pulling your leg," she said.

"Perhaps he was," Nick said.

It did all sound a bit daft, Simon thought. But then what had happened between him and Anna tonight had also been daft, but nonetheless real.

"Well," Nick said. "Lying loon, deadly hitman, or whatever. " now know what car he drives."

"Do you think it was his car?" Mark said.

"Who knows? But he was coming from the Salisbury direction. When he picked me up he said he was going to Bournemouth. So if he was coming back from there, that's the right direction."

"Perhaps he often goes there. Perhaps he has a reason to, " Simon said.

"Yeah, perhaps the international headquarters of *Hire a Hitman* are there," Mark suggested.

"Or perhaps all the criminals in the world retire to Bournemouth, so most of his hits are there," Nick said. "It would simplify his life, I imagine."

"What did he look like, your hitman?" Chrissie said.

Nick frowned, trying to remember. "Oh, chiselled cheeks, strong jaw, cold eyes."

"Like a hitman should look, then?"

"Mind you, it has been five days since I last looked into those grim, steely eyes. The more time passes, the more nondescript he gets."

"Hang on, I've still got the artist's impressions," Mark said. He left the room, and came back with the sketches he'd done.

Simon stood and went around the table to the side where Chrissie and Nick were sitting. He looked over Chrissie's shoulder at the drawings as she went through them. They were still in the order in which Mark had drawn them on the Monday evening. Chrissie looked at another one.

"Who's that, Jack Lemmon?" Chrissie asked.

Mark laughed. "That's exactly what those buggers said the other night." Chrissie came to the mad, final drawing, with its mop of curls.

"And who on Earth is that supposed to be?"

"In the end they were all just shouting out names of film stars at me as I was drawing. Somebody said Shirley Temple, so I drew in the hair."

"Well," Chrissie said, "Let's just hope Shirley Temple isn't a hitman." She pulled a face. "It sounds horrible."

"I'm sure he wasn't," Simon said. "Nick was just having his leg pulled. Like that guy I got a lift with once who swore he had a small block V8 fitted into his Ford Corsair, yet still managed to nearly kill us when overtaking a lorry so slowly he might as well have had a Ford Anglia engine in there."

"I don't know what you're talking about," Nick said. "It's all gobbledygook. Car talk."

"A bloke who picked up Simon up lied about how fast his car was," Mark translated.

"Ah, yes. I remember that story. Very *droll*."

Chrissie put Mark's drawings down on the table. She looked up at him with her head still tilted down, making her big brown eyes wider. She had nice eyes, Simon thought. But surely Mark must see through the old *big eyes* routine.

"Can you give me a lift home?" Chrissie asked Mark. "It's getting late and you don't want me walking home through all those drunks, do you?"

She hadn't needed to add the last bit, Simon knew. For surely she also knew that Mark would give her a lift if only for the five minutes with her arms around him that were guaranteed by her sitting on the pillion.

Chrissie was using him. But how deliberate was it? Didn't Mark make it easy for her to use him? *He likes it, anyway.* And perhaps she liked it, too. He gave her the attention that Jake didn't. Jake had other attributes. He was big, strong, manly, and, Simon supposed, quite handsome, in a rugged kind of way. Jake was wrong for Chrissie. Chrissie could be quite sweet. And she would realise, at some point in the future, that Jake was just a caveman who wanted her for sex and the social cachet of a pretty girl on his arm. She would be much better off with Mark, if she could only see past Jake's animal charms. Although there was, perhaps, something too cloying about Mark's obsession. Perhaps she would never be able to get beyond that, would always be tempted, instead, to use her charms on Mark to get the things she wanted from him, without ever having to move the relationship forward from their dependency on each other. *Let's face it, they never argue.* They bickered, but it was always forgotten when Chrissie needed a lift or a shoulder. *But then they never have sex or even kiss.* Simon remembered the hand she had earlier so softly placed on Mark's neck. Such moments were the only degree of intimacy she ever afforded Mark. Those moments must be powerful – like lightning illuminating his world and running through him. Could he live for those moments? Were they worth everything else? *To feel a hand so lightly on his neck?*

It had been a good day, the hitman thought. He'd seen his son, and Peter had been happy, playing with the Scalectrix he'd bought. He poured himself a brandy, and put Tchaikovsky's first piano concerto on the record deck. He turned the volume down, as it was after twelve at night.

Only one thing had ruined the day for him. He sank onto the sofa and thought about the problem that had nagged him all the way home. Had it been the fucking freak he'd picked up during the week he'd seen again tonight? And if it was, had the freak made the car? It was the right place. He'd dropped the guy at that spot last Monday. What was his name? *Nick, that was it.* It had never really struck him that he might see Nick again. In all his years of picking up hitchers and dropping them off in different parts of the country, he'd never seen the same one twice. But, of course, to get to Bournemouth from here he had to drive through Dereham, so there was always a chance he'd see Nick. Had Nick seen him? Nick had been talking to a friend, and that friend had shown interest in his car. *And why not. It's rare!* But Nick hadn't shown any interest. At least, not until he'd passed. He'd looked in his mirror and seen Nick stand up. He thought perhaps Nick was looking at him, staring right at the back of his head. *Oh, so what?* As always, the freak can't have collected his wits enough to have memorised his registration when he got out of the car. *They never do... Otherwise I would have had a copper at the door long ago.* And if Nick didn't have the registration, then seeing two NSUs in one week could just be a coincidence.

Perhaps he should stop gambling with the hitchers, though. He was beginning to realise it wasn't simple fun any longer. The more he picked up, the more the chances increased that something would happen. He might pick up another Nick, but one with more nous. Someone who did believe him and did take his registration. There was always also a chance that somebody might recognise him. He had lived in Dereham with Peta. He had gone to the pubs, and talked to some of those UFO nutters. Yes, he had to stop picking up hitchhikers around Dereham. If somebody recognised him, or made the car, then it could all go wrong. He didn't want it to go wrong. He wanted to see his son grow up. He loved his son.

Another thing he had noticed tonight was that Nick was tall. *Either that or his mate is a midget.* He hadn't been aware of that the other day, in the car. It was unlikely, though, that Nick would fight. He would lie down on the pavement and say *Don't hit me, man, I'm a pacifist.* Yes, he would stop picking up hitchers. Driving down through Bath and then Dereham was the easiest way to get to Bournemouth. He didn't really want to wiggle all over the countryside through Swindon and Devizes and all that shit. Straight to Bath, down to Salisbury, then Bournemouth. Simple. Nick wouldn't do anything, he probably remembered nothing, didn't care, hadn't believed him. Any trouble from the freak was highly unlikely, as it always had been. He had nothing to worry about.

He patted his belly. He'd been doing it a lot lately. So, he was putting on some weight. And he hadn't started exercising again, like he had promised himself he would. Even out of shape, though, he was sure he could take out that lanky streak of piss, Nick, if he had to.

12

Simon had managed to negotiate Monday morning without bumping into Anna. But now it was lunchtime. So now, of course, she walked into the refectory, glanced at Simon, and quickly looked away. She was with Joan, who also looked at him. There was a light smile playing about Joan's lips, and her look lingered on him for a moment before she turned away. Simon took another bite out of his cheese roll, although he had suddenly lost his appetite. So, it starts, he thought. He had expected Anna's reaction, but that knowledge had not lessened the impact of that brief, cold glance. And what was that look Joan had given him? *Curious.*

"Are we expecting the lovely Anna to join us?" Warren asked.

"No, not really," Simon mumbled.

Warren looked at him. "What do you mean, man? You two are love's young dream." He laughed. "Invite her over!"

Simon put the half-eaten cheese roll down on the plain white plate in front of him. "I can't."

"But it's Anna! I thought you two were..." Warren paused, looked over at Anna, than back at Simon. "Didn't you see her Saturday night?"

"Yes, I did. That's why she won't be sitting with us."

Warren watched Anna walk to an empty table with Joan. He turned back to Simon. "What's going on?"

Simon allowed himself a brief glance Anna. "I wish I knew." His eyes met hers for a brief moment before she looked down at the cup of tea in front of her. To see her sitting there actually hurt him, to his surprise. There was an unexpected, never before experienced, tightness in his chest, in his stomach.

Warren spoke again. "Why didn't you say anything this morning? I asked you how the weekend went, and you said it was fine. Okay, I thought your reaction was a little flat, but I just supposed – hoped, for your sake – you were shagged out after a good weekend."

"Well, it was a bad weekend."

"So you didn't get to–"

Simon interrupted him. "No, I didn't." He explained what had happened.

Warren shook his head and frowned. "Weird, man."

"Yes. Something's changed. I don't know what. I'm not wise enough."

Warren suddenly whispered out of the side of his mouth.

"Don't look now, but her mate Joan is looking at you."

Warren looked comical, and Simon couldn't help smiling; but he knew that he also smiled because the situation was absurd. "You don't need to whisper, they can't hear us from over there. And, anyway, you look completely dumb pulling that dumb face."

Simon risked another covert glance at Anna, who was now talking to Joan.

"Oh, look, they're talking about you," Warren laughed.

Warren had said it to freak Simon out. He punched Warren's arm. "Don't mess with me," he said. But he also knew Warren might be right. There's something so stupid about all this, Simon thought. He picked up his cheese roll, went to bite into it, but put it down again. *Why can't I just walk over and ask her what's wrong? Or what I did wrong?*

"Do you want me to go over and talk to her?" Warren said.

It was tempting, though she might take offence at that. "We're not fifteen anymore," Simon said, quietly.

Simon wanted so badly to look at Anna. At the same time, every object in the refectory had taken on a new interest for him. He looked everywhere, noting posters on the walls, stained cups with tea in the saucers, plates with tomato sauce smeared across them.

"Ugh," Warren suddenly said beside him, spitting tea back into his cup. "Tea leaves."

"Perhaps you should read them for me."

"Perhaps I should. I need your cup for that."

Simon carefully drank the rest of his tea, and then passed the cup to Warren, who swilled the last remaining drops around. He tilted the cup up at an angle towards Simon. Leaves had stuck to the sides of the cup.

"What do you scry, oh wise one?" Simon asked.

"I see hearts torn apart. I see a communication breakdown."

"It's always the same," Simon said grimly.

"What?" Then Warren laughed, recognising the song. "I see. Very good. But look here." He pointed at a particular pattern. "See these?" Then he turned to Simon with a serious expression. "Did I ever tell you my gran really did read the leaves?"

Simon's interest was piqued for a moment. "Did she really?"

Warren sniggered. "You are a gullible tit." He pointed at the pattern. "What do you see?"

Simon looked but could see nothing. "Very little."

"I see an... arse. That's you." Warren put the cup back down on the saucer. "Go and talk to Anna."

"I can't."

The refectory door swung open, and Jill came in. She waved at Simon and Warren. Warren waved back. She went to the counter, bought herself a cup of tea, and came over to their table.

"Can I join you guys?" she asked.

"Of course you can, my dear," Warren said.

She smiled across at Simon, and then pouted. "You didn't wave at me, *again*."

"He has a lot on his mind, *again*," Warren said.

"Really? Now what?"

"Nothing important," Simon said.

"How *is* my sweater coming on?" Jill asked. "I've heard so little about it."

Simon felt uncertain how to proceed. Yet Jill was looking at him encouragingly. Her eyes twinkled merrily. "I'm working on it."

"Do hurry, I wouldn't want to get cold."

"Oh," Simon said, "I'll make sure you don't get cold. I'm working on something I can give you."

Jill smiled and looked at Warren. "Oh, isn't he *bold*? Don't you think he is? He wants to give me something, something to warm me up."

Warren glared at Simon. "I can't think what he's talking about."

Jill leaned across to Warren, but turned her head to Simon. "I can't either, to be honest. I like to imagine it, though. I lie in my bed sometimes, thinking about all the things Simon could possibly give me."

"I could give you all kinds of things," Simon said, not really realising what he was saying, and yet knowing that there were kinds of other meanings floating around the words he spoke so glibly.

He glanced across at Anna. Of course, *now* Anna was looking across at their table. So was Joan. Joan said something to Anna, and then shot a glance at Simon.

Simon retreated into himself, forgot about Jill and Warren for now. He returned to the internal world where he fretted about Anna, wondered about the cut, attempted to retrace a route through words, spoken over weeks and months, that might lead him back to the insult he felt he must have uttered.

Minutes passed, Simon didn't know how many. He could hear Jill and Warren talking, and her cup rattling in the saucer. There was laughter next to him, and laughter at Anna's table.

Jill distracted him from his thoughts by standing. "Simon. I'm still waiting. Let me know when you can give me what I desire." She looked down at him. "Poor boy. You'll be okay." She said goodbye then, ruffling Simon's hair as she walked away.

Simon looked at Anna, hoped she hadn't seen Jill touch him, but of course she had. She was looking directly at him, straight into his eyes, and for a moment he felt the old connection with her, and his heart momentarily leaped. She continued only to stare, however, and he now thought he could see something else in her eyes – hurt, perhaps, or sadness. He didn't know what it was, but there was something.

He looked away, but he knew the chairs he could hear scraping backwards were those of Anna and Joan. *What were they thinking?* Simon wondered. He heard the door open and then slowly close. He wanted to look up, but wouldn't. Absurdly, he wanted to go over to the table at which Anna and Joan had been sitting, grab Anna's cup and bring it over to Warren so that he could divine something in the leaves, even though he couldn't really read them.

Simon wondered – worried, really – what Anna had thought. *I hardly said a word to Jill.* What had Joan whispered to Anna? Why was Joan smiling at him? *What's it all about?* He remembered something. Early in the summer term, when he and Anna had first started hanging out with each other, he had found her in the restaurant sitting with Joan. He and Anna had started talking, joking around. Then Anna had said to Joan, "Isn't he lovely?" Joan had frowned. "Well, I think he is," Anna had said. *Why hadn't I realised then how we had felt about each other?* Then Anna had hit him on the head with the copy of *Great Expectations* she was carrying, and favoured him with a bright smile. Joan had stood up. "We've got to go, Anna," she had said. Anna stood, and touched his cheek. "See you later," she said, her eyes sparkling. Simon had looked at Joan as they left. She had been frowning at him.

Warren nudged him. "We'd better get going."

"If we must," Simon muttered. He really had more important things to think about than whatever lecture was next in his timetable. What *was* next. He'd forgotten.

Nick sipped at half a shandy. It was all he could afford. Mark came through the door into The White Lion's saloon bar. He signed to Nick, asking if he wanted a drink. Nick shook his head. Mark brought his drink over to the table.

"Lunch-time drinking," Mark said. "How decadent."

"How's work?" Nick asked.

"I'm making money, that's all I care about. I'm beginning to realise that Mondays are always grim."

Nick laughed. "You've only been there two weeks!"

Mark shrugged. "I've been a student for years. I'm used to a life of indolence. And I don't really want to be a clerk. Apart from that it's fine."

"I can guess what you want to be."

"Rock star or artist. That's me. I can see it now. The glamour, the girls, the excess."

Nick thought that Mark would actually be happiest marrying Chrissie, settling down in a nice semi-detached house in Dereham, and living the suburban dream, the kind of life portrayed in a gentle BBC sitcom. But he didn't say so. "How *is* Honeyhouse?" he asked instead.

"Well, floundering, I suppose. We haven't had a full band practice for a couple of weeks. John hasn't been back from Birmingham. Danny and I have messed around a little, but Steve didn't want to do anything without John there."

"Do you want to keep the band going?"

"Of course I do." Mark fiddled with a beermat, putting it on the edge of the table, flipping it up and catching it. "It's been a part of my life for so long. It was me, John and Steve that started the whole thing, remember?"

Nick did remember, although he knew that it had actually been John and Steve who had started the band, back when they were thirteen years old and could play no instruments. Mark had been the first member to join the band who could play an instrument. Nick had to admit that it would be odd *not* to have Dereham's premiere – *only* – prog-folk-rock band to listen to and talk about. There were other local bands, of course, but they played covers at discos and weddings. Honeyhouse played all-original material that ensured they were usually booed off stage at discos, and were never invited to play at weddings. Apart from girls, Honeyhouse was the other constant topic of conversation – what gigs were coming up (few), what equipment they should buy (that they couldn't afford anyway), which member was currently the worst and dragging the band down, and so should be offloaded in favour of some other up and coming musician they'd seen recently in a local covers band, and so on. If Steve the drummer was currently out of favour, they wondered how much a drum machine would cost. It was a bitchy little world, Honeyhouse, because it was a small community. Nick could see the band imploding over the next few months.

"But you've always got your art," Nick said.

Mark frowned. "Well yes, but I think I need to branch out a bit, don't you?"

Nick shrugged. He knew what Mark meant. "Chrissie won't sit for you forever, that's for sure. The drawings you do of Simon doing his tai chi are ... well, fantastic. I really like them."

"Thanks. When I'm drawing something, it always feels good, but afterwards, when I look back at what I've done, it never seems good enough, you know?"

"Why?"

"I can't help comparing it to everything else I've seen. Not just famous artists, you know, but even the amateurs I see in galleries in Bath, or the students I was with at college. Everybody seems better."

"Do you feel the same in the band?"

"Yes."

"So nothing you ever do is good enough?"

"No."

"Man. That is some self-esteem problem you have there."

"It's not just me. Ask James how he feels about his own lyrics. Ask Steve or Danny how well they play. We compare ourselves with others and find ourselves wanting."

"So you can never be good enough?"

"No. Not around here. If we did do anything good, well..."

"What?"

"It would be *all right*, it would be *okay*."

"What do you mean?"

Mark looked directly at Nick, his face serious. "What do you think of Honeyhouse?"

Nick looked down. When he looked back up, he gave Mark a tight-lipped smile. "I get your point. They're *all right*. They're *okay*."

"That's it, you see. Could you actually know how good the band is, how good I am? What I do is part of your world. You've been watching me draw for years, you've been listening to Honeyhouse for years. In all that time, we've got better, I know we have, because I know the work that goes into it, the learning the craft. But you can't see it, because it's just part of the background. I've always drawn, the band has always been there."

"So what would it take? How would you know?"

"When somebody buys a painting or a drawing. When somebody books the band who isn't some local who knows a friend of a friend."

"I do think you're good."

"But you're my friend. I expect you to say that."

"Is it cheapened because of that?"

"No. But it's still the praise of a friend. I want it, of course I do. But I need somebody from outside of us–" Mark indicated the saloon bar with his hand. "Somebody outside of these groups of friends we've grown up with, to say something nice, to validate what I do. And I know that's what the band want, even if they can't... uh... *articulate* it. I can feel it. If the band dissolves, it'll be because of that, not because of distance or time."

"So what can you do?"

"Keep at it, for as long as it feels good. Wait. Hope."

Hope, Nick wondered. *Is that all they could do?* Yet wasn't he waiting, hoping, too? Waiting and hoping for something that would come along and take him away from this dull town and his monotonous existence here. If he was waiting for anything, it was some inspiration, some clue as to what he should do with his life to make it meaningful, so that it wouldn't follow the patterns he foresaw - feared - in his future.

"Can't you force it in some way?" Nick said. "Make something happen?"

"That's what managers are for, I suppose. We need a manager."

"And you?"

"An agent or something. Somebody to give me direction. I don't know how to break into the art world."

"We've set up the exhibition. We've framed some of your work. We're trying. But after that, you need to make it happen."

"I know. But there's all the other..." Mark waved his hands around. "*Stuff*, always getting in the way."

"Like?"

"Work. Girlfriends."

Nick raised an eyebrow.

Mark sighed. "You know what I mean. In my case, thinking about Chrissie." He took out his cigarettes, lit one. He breathed out the smoke. "She takes a lot of... thought."

"It isn't going to happen."

"I know."

Nick heard the door to the bar open, and looked up. Molly waved to him, and walked to the bar. She was still here then. He wondered if she'd found that elusive something she was searching for - a presence, a trail, a ghost.

13

There had been no sighting of Anna yesterday, and neither had there been today, for which Simon was grateful in a way he could never have imagined possible three weeks ago. He wondered if this was one of her days out. He hoped it was. And yet, Simon found himself worrying about Anna. If she wasn't here, where was she? What was she doing? Was she flirting with somebody else? Was he even now in the process of losing her forever? Today was Wednesday; half way through a week, which would soon be over. Misery week.

Warren was sitting quietly next to Simon, sipping his tea, watching the comings and goings in the refectory. He finally spoke. "I had that tit of a bus driver again this morning."

Simon was thrown for a moment. "Bus driver? What *are* you on about?"

"That git who made us walk down the front to show our passes, remember? Then he made me fall over."

"Centrifugal force and gravity made that happen, surely?"

"No, it was the tit of a bus driver."

"Or was it centripetal force?"

"No, it was the tit of a bus driver."

"Because people do often confuse the two. Even now, I'm wont to get my fugals and petals all a-dither."

Warren sighed theatrically. "Look, I couldn't give a toss about your petals or your fugals. It was the bus driver."

"So, what did you do when you confronted the rapscallion? Did you biff him around the ear? Did you slap his cheek with your pass and call him out?"

"No."

"No? So what you're saying is that you meekly sat down at the back of the bus? Without even passing a choice remark?"

Warren shrugged. "Well, what could I do? But I will get even with him one day, you mark my words. The tit."

"I mark them well."

Warren whispered. "Aha. This will brighten my day. Look who just came through the door."

Simon did look over. Jill was holding the door open for two students on their way out of the refectory. As she made her way to the counter, she smiled at Simon and Warren.

"Do you think she'll come and talk to us?" Warren asked, eagerly.

He didn't have to wait long to find out. There was no queue, and Jill's tea was soon poured and paid for. She turned and walked towards Simon and Warren.

"You're in luck," Simon said.

Jill sat down, placed her cup gently on the table. "How are my boys today?"

"We're fine," Warren said, "Aren't we Si?"

"Yes, we're fine. Warren is a bit muddled about centrifugal and centripetal forces, but other than that, we're good."

"Aha! Centrifugal and centripetal forces. I see."

"Well," Warren began, "they are two easily confused forces that..."

Jill held up her hands. "Woah there, boy! You don't think for a moment I really care, do you? I was just being polite."

She probably knew what they were anyway, Simon thought.

"What I really want to know is-" Jill continued

"Yes?" Warren said. "We're ready to help you with anything."

Jill turned her blue eyes on Simon. A smile played on her full lips. "Did you finish my jumper?"

That tit of a bus driver, centripetal and centrifugal forces, Anna, and now a jumper that he was supposed to have finished - Simon was being continually confounded today. He quickly slung a net across his mind and trawled memories. *Anna. Jill. Confusion. Joan smiling. Wondering why. Wool-gathering? Ah, yes. Make me a jumper.* "The cable knit," Simon said, "is a new technique to me. Luckily, my mum is an excellent knitter, and attempted to demonstrate the technique. However, I purled when I should have knit-stitched and instead of a jumper I had only a very long piece of unravelled wool."

Jill laughed. "An unravelling disaster." She put a hand on Simon's arm. "You take your time. I'm sure it'll be worth it in the end."

"Knit-stitched?" Warren wondered. "Is that even a word?"

"It is now," Simon said.

"And what else could it be?" Jill noted. "Either, *I have done a knit-stitch*, or *I have knit-stitched*. Really, Warren, you don't know much do you?"

"Knitting isn't my scene," Warren said.

"Then *you*," Jill said, her eyes mischievous, "won't get the chance to wrap something warm around me." She touched Simon's arm again. "Unlike Simon here."

"Oh, but I've got all kinds of things I can wrap around you," Warren said. The attempted flirt clunked, even to Simon's badly attuned ear.

Jill deftly deflected Warren's comment. "But I don't know if they'd be the kinds of things I *want* wrapped around me. At least I know Simon will have something I *do* want."

Simon smiled, although he felt perplexed. He knew he should be feeling something other than perplexed, but he wasn't sure what it was he should be feeling. There was something here, in what Jill was saying, that awoke some unexorcised ghosts in dark corners of his mind. Because hadn't Anna once said, when he had mentioned he had a double bed, that perhaps they should test it for squeaks? And the other day, when she had the Kit Kat, and he had said "Can I have a bit," she had said, "What, here in the corridor?" Simon had thought she was being cheeky. *Suck it*, Anna had said, *don't chew it*. And there had been the same mischievous look in Anna's eyes as there now was in Jill's.

"Wool-gathering again?" Jill asked.

Simon spoke slowly, softly, without really knowing why. "Yes. After all, I have to find enough to warmly wrap you in."

"I look forward to it. Knit quick." There was a moment's pause while Jill looked at Simon, the playful smile still on her lips.

The silence was broken by Warren. "Can I say something?"

"By all means," Jill said, "but I expect it to be devastatingly witty. So. Go ahead."

Warren looked at Jill, then at the table. "Uh, that's a lot of pressure. I was just going to ask where you hang out in the evenings."

"In my cave," Jill replied.

Shit. Simon was thinking. *Shit. Shit.* Because, at last, he had realised one thing. *Shit.* He realised that he was being flirted with *right now.* Anna had flirted with him for months, and he had been too dense to see it, too naïve to understand it, to unsure of himself, had still thought himself too unattractive for a girl as cute as Anna. He realised now that Anna had not found him unattractive, and neither was he currently unattractive. Jill was flirting with him. She found him attractive. He remembered his dalliance with Julie during the summer. She, too, had found him attractive. *Anna was flirting with me all the time. Me!* He had an urge to put his head dramatically in his hands, which he resisted.

Simon returned his attention to Warren and Jill. She was telling Warren that she went to the pubs in the villages around Southleigh, and sometimes came into town with her girlfriends. Simon knew for which fish Warren was angling: her status – whether she had a boyfriend or not. Simon listened. She did not, she said, currently have a boyfriend. Warren would be pleased.

Jill picked up her cup, looked at Simon across the top of the rim as she tilted it back and drank the last drops of her tea, her cornflower-blue eyes wide, still smiling at him. She clanked the cup back into the saucer. "Right, guys, I'm off. You know where to find me in the evenings now. If I don't see you there, I'll see you here." She touched Simon's arm one final time as she stood. "And don't you forget my jumper. Remember the knit stitch this time." She gave a merry little laugh. "Although, if it unravels again, perhaps you should just find me and ravel me in wool."

She left the refectory without a backward glance.

Warren was the first to speak. "Well, apart from her unhealthy obsession with knitting, I think I'm in there."

Simon was surprised. "What? Why do you think that?" *Is he blind? Deaf? Insensitive?*

"She told me she didn't have a boyfriend, and what pubs she goes to, and everything. It's obvious, isn't it?"

Simon had a moment of doubt. *Perhaps it is obvious.* He wondered if, having been so dumb to Anna's flirting, he was now over-compensating, and reading too much into what Jill was saying. *But it can't be. It can't be. I can't be such a dunce twice over.* He thought he knew.

"I shall get myself to some of those pubs this weekend," Warren said.

"Don't go by bus," Simon said.

Simon chewed his lip. Warren was, he thought, going to be disappointed. *She was flirting with me. Wasn't she? Wasn't she?*

The pubs had closed. Chrissie and Nick were sitting on the sign at the top of Beech Tree Road. Mark was standing, happy that he'd been able to spend an evening in the pub with Chrissie. They were going to Mark's house for coffee, but had decided to wait here for a while, to stay out in the fresh air for a little longer. A cool wind shook the leaves on the beech tree. Mark looked at Chrissie, trying not to admire her. He of course admired her, but he knew that if allowed for a moment a soppy look to cross his face, Chrissie would most likely ask Nick to walk her home. He didn't want that to happen. He wanted to drink in Chrissie's presence for as long as he could. He wondered where Jake was. Mark hadn't really listened when Chrissie had told him. He tended to blank out Jake as an irrelevance. He didn't want to ask Chrissie now, as that might suggest that he hadn't been listening to her earlier. He had listened to her sweet voice most of the evening, until the dread word *Jake* had come up, and then he had switched the Jake filter on, smiled at her, and had heard very little until her Jake moment had passed. He had to be careful with the Jake filter, however. If she frowned, there was a possibility she was having problems with Jake, in which case Mark knew he should be caring and attentive, and would switch the Jake filter off. If she looked carefree, he would leave it on and only allow through words that needed a response. He was only happy discussing Jake if the conversation could be reduced to the words *Yes* and *No*.

"What happened to Shirley Temple?" Chrissie asked Nick.

"Haven't given it much thought, really," Nick said. "I mostly worry about what I'm going to do with my life."

"What *are* you going to do with your life?" Mark said.

"I want to be an eternal student. That's all I know"

A strand of Chrissie's dark hair blew across her face. Mark ached to reach out and brush it away. Chrissie brushed away the hair herself. "I wouldn't want to be a student any longer," Chrissie said. "I want to earn money. Lots of it."

"Perhaps you should marry Gaz," Nick said.

"Why, does he want lots of it too?"

"Not only lots. Lots *and* lots. Lots squared."

"Perhaps I should marry him, then," Chrissie laughed.

Mark smiled too, but still found himself, to his consternation, obscurely worried that Chrissie might indeed dump Jake and run off with Gaz at the first opportunity. That would be too much to bear, he thought. He changed the subject, even though he knew that Chrissie would never run off with Gaz. And then, oddly, before he could stop himself, he found himself talking about Gaz.

"What is Gaz up to? I haven't seen him for a couple of days."

Nick shrugged. "I'm not sure. He's keeping himself to himself. He keeps saying he wants to go to The Swan. Perhaps he *fancies* somebody down there."

"He never *fancies* anybody, does he?" Mark said.

"Well, perhaps he *does* now."

"Hey," Chrissie smiled, "he can't do that, he's my intended."

Mark felt the need to change the subject again. "Shirley Temple must have *lots* of money, if he can run one of those NSUs. They're temperamental."

"Well, if he is a hitman, I'd expect him to be well off," Chrissie said.

"They break down a lot. You have to change the engine every five hundred miles or something."

"Don't talk wet. That's *ridiculous*. Why would you have to do that?"

"It's one of those Wankels."

"I beg your pardon?"

"A Wankel. A rotary engine."

"What difference does that make?"

Mark knew what a Wankel rotary engine was, and how it worked. Having got on to the topic, however, he had no urge to pursue it, for fear of boring Chrissie. He suspected that cars and engines were topics with which Jake already bored Chrissie. "Trust me," he said, "I *know* about these things."

Mark wished he hadn't emphasised that *know*. Emphasising words was something that he, Gaz, Simon and Nick had jokingly started doing a year or two back, and now they couldn't stop themselves. By emphasising that particular "know", however, Mark had demonstrated that, just like Jake, he was a car-bore. "They break down a lot," he continued. "They look good, very modern and gleaming, and all that, but you often have to rebuild the engine."

"I didn't know you knew so much about cars," Chrissie said.

Damn, Mark thought. She had noticed he was a car-bore. "Oh, I read about it while I was waiting somewhere, in a magazine in the dentist's waiting room, or somewhere like that. I'm not *that* interested in cars," Mark lied.

He wondered what Nick would say. But Nick merely looked at him, lifted an eyebrow, and winked.

Chrissie gave a small shudder. "I still think it's awful. A hitman on the loose. And he drives through Dereham."

"If he *is* a hitman," Nick noted. "He might just be a nutter. That's what I think."

"A really *rather* well-off nutter," Mark said.

Chrissie shivered again.

"Still thinking about the nutter?" Mark asked.

"No, I'm just cold."

"Let's go and have a cuppa," Nick said.

When a smiling Chrissie accusingly waved a car magazine at Mark as he brought the mugs of tea into the dining room, he was grateful that his parents had gone to bed. "Oh, that. That's my father's," he lied.

Nick winked at Mark again.

"I saw that," Chrissie said.

"Something in my eye. A *mote* or something," Nick said.

"No, honestly, it's Dad's."

Mark didn't want to lie to Chrissie. It was all pointless, anyway. She'd never leave Jake for him. *So why lie?* It was, he acknowledged to himself, again, as he had done so often, hopeless. Yet, he never gave up hope, hadn't given up hope for two years. He couldn't imagine, now, what it would be like to live without this hope, this pathetic hope. Yet, there was a certain pleasure in that hope. They all knew, by now, what had happened between Simon and Anna at the Fresher's Ball. Mark knew he didn't want his hope taken away, ever. *If Chrissie ever goes out with me, I'll stop buying car magazines. If Chrissie ever goes out with me, I'll have no need for car magazines, anyway.* He'd be happy in a Mini Traveller if he could have Chrissie. Yet he recalled what she had said. *She wanted money. Lots of it.* He was earning money now. He would get a small pay rise after his probation period. *In six months, I'll be making more than Jake.* He wasn't sure he had the temperament to stay, though. He knew what he really wanted. He wanted to be an artist or a rock star. Those were the things he had dreamed about, for years now.

Everybody wants to be a rock star. At least, that's how it seemed. Although, of course, not everybody worked at it. Everybody wanted to be a rock star if it meant no work. Mark knew that it took work, just as his art took work. He no longer believed in genius. He believed in graft and craft.

Would Chrissie want a struggling artist as a boyfriend or husband? He didn't know. *Should I care?* She was never going to be his, anyway. She probably would prefer Gaz, if it came to it. He could feel himself at the edge of the dark chasm he sometimes felt was the natural corollary of a life buoyed only by hope. He looked at Chrissie now. She had started talking to Nick about Jake. Mark switched off, nodding occasionally when he thought a remark merited it. He watched Chrissie instead. Her long black hair was parted in the middle, her eyebrows shaped as if she were in a constant state of surprise. Her nose was straight and small. Her brown eyes watched Nick as he talked. She was always attentive, he realised, she always looked at the person speaking to her, not afraid to make eye contact. It was very inclusive. Her eyes invited intimacy. She began to speak. Mark didn't listen to what she was talking about; it was still Jake, he guessed. Instead, he simply watched her speak, her bow-mouth lips moving, always ready to smile. Her voice was soft, sweet. His heart ached.

He sipped his tea. Craft and graft. He would keep at it, at the music, at the painting and drawing, because nothing apart, from Chrissie, made him happier. He often wished, now that he *was* working, that he'd stayed on the dole. He could have practiced his bass and his acoustic guitar playing, and spent his days drawing and painting. That's what he wanted to do, and he wished he'd had the courage to follow those instincts. Yet his parents expected him to work now, to pay for his keep, as they put it. If he had gone to university to study architecture, they would have supported him. But he hadn't, and now had to pay the price, which was paying his way.

Chrissie had stopped talking, and was fiddling with her mug.

"More tea?" Mark asked.

"Yes, please," Chrissie said. "Do you still have any of that Earl Grey?"

"Yes, I think so. And Assam, and Lady Grey, and Lapsang Souchong."

"Isn't Lapsang Souchong," Nick said, "that strange infusion that steams the essence of boiled bacon and tastes like old ashes of burnt liver?"

Mark laughed. "Yes, that's the one."

"I don't like the sound of that," Chrissie smiled. "I'll stick to the Earl Grey, I think."

"I'll make a fresh pot," Mark said.

"Thank you," Chrissie said, and looked up at him from beneath her long lashes. He felt his heart lurch again. He would pick fresh, dew-glittered leaves from Ceylon, if she asked.

The hitman sat in the living-room of his town house in Cheltenham, a glass of Merlot beside him, Mozart on the Linn Sondek. He still felt relaxed after the joint earlier. He'd had word, through an intermediary, that the client had been pleased with his last hit. So the fucker should be, he thought. A nice clean headshot. *Nobody saw me. Nobody even knew I was there. In and out like a ghost in the daylight.* There had been something in the papers about it. He always checked, wanted to know if the police had inadvertently let something slip. The only thing they *had* let slip was that they thought it might have been a professional job. Good, he thought. If they think it's a professional job, they know the mark was dirty, and realise the chances of finding me are slim. They wouldn't bother with anything except a token investigation.

The only thing that had taken him slightly aback was that in one paper he'd looked at, there had been a picture of the grieving widow and her son. The grieving widow didn't bother him. There was often a price to be paid for shacking up with a criminal. The son bothered him – about the same age as his own, and similar-looking, too. Even though he only saw his own son once a week, he hated the idea that his son might be left father-less. It was always a risk in this line of work.

He should visit Peter again, soon. The Cow set no restrictions on his visits. She was too scared of him. She had no need to be. She was the mother of his son. He would have time enough to see the kid. He had no contract to execute at the moment. Another one would turn up, he knew it. He'd been paid handsomely for the last one. He wouldn't have to worry about money for a little while. He thought about the cheeky, shy smile on his son's face when he walked through the door. He loved his son.

14

That evening, home from work, after he'd eaten the meal cooked by his mother, after he'd listened to the mundane chatter around the dining table, Gaz had retired to his bedroom, played the Mahavishnu Orchestra's *Birds of Fire* at a volume that was sure to soon bring a rebuke from one of the parents, and taken the ear studs out of the pocket of the coat that was hanging on the back of the door. The studs were still attached to the plastic backing, just as he had found them on the rotating dispenser on the counter of that dumb hippie shop in the Market Place. He didn't need studs; his ears weren't pierced. They were most likely cheap tat. Anybody unfortunate enough to wear them would soon find their turning green. None of his immediate friends wore earrings. Only Danny and Steve in the band had pierced ears, as far as he could remember. *That Imogen wears earrings.* It would seem odd, though, to give the studs to her, no matter how much he secretly fancied her. *She's a classy bird, anyway.* James doubtless bought her *real* gold earrings. Gaz thought about giving the studs to Chrissie, but Mark would misinterpret the gesture. *And anyway, her earlobes would probably turn green.* He toyed for a moment with the idea of giving them to her anyway, just so he could watch her ears become gangrenous, and see the horror on Mark's face.

I could sell them. But he hadn't yet sold the aftershave. He still hadn't visited The Swan. He always seemed to be with Nick, or Mark, or Simon, and they didn't really like The Swan. He'd have to pop in there for a pint by himself one night. *I keep saying that.* He fiddled with the butterflies on the back of the black plastic mount. He wouldn't get much for the studs, anyway. He looked at the price printed on a small label. One pound fifty. He knelt down on the brown carpet, fished around under his bed, and found the aftershave. He put the bottle on his bed, and the studs next to them. He was rather pleased with himself. More pleased than if he had managed to scrape an A grade at in his exams. This was better, he thought. He was really challenging himself, at last. He didn't have much so far, only the aftershave, the studs, the vodka, and a few other trifles. Yet after obtaining each of them, he had felt a sense of achievement. Such was his lack of guilt, he wondered if this was his true vocation. There was still the problem of what he would do with it all. Sell it, he supposed, to Dodgy Len, or Greaser. He'd get down to The Swan soon. He looked at his two prizes again. *I won't get much for them.* Perhaps he should wait until he had a few more things. Sell it all as a job lot.

He looked under the bed again, and found a box with a few paperbacks in it, the books he kept meaning to take to a second-hand bookshop but never did. He put the books back on a shelf, and put the things he'd stolen in the box. Then he decided to put a couple of the books back in the box, in case one of his parents nosed around; though what they would be doing looking under the bed he couldn't imagine. He slid the box back under the bed, over the remarkably dust-free brown carpet, and wondered what he could lift next. He could go back to the hippie shop, but that had been too easy. He wanted to step up the challenge. Stealing the aftershave had been more challenging than lifting the studs. He also, he realised, wanted to try his hand in all the shops. Then he thought, *All of them?* Would that include the shops with women's clothes? *Yes, all of them.* Lifting something in a woman's clothes shop would add a certain spice to proceedings. *Would Dodgy Len or Greaser buy women's clothes?* Gaz guessed they would. They would probably buy anything they could sell on again. *No questions asked.* They would want to make a profit, though, so Gaz's cut would be small.

Does it really matter though? He thought about the box under his bed, imagined the prizes that it contained. *It's the challenge, isn't it?* He stood up, and walked over to the record player, which was on a chest of drawers next to a small table. The first side of the album had long finished. He flipped the record over, and set the needle carefully in the groove. He sat on the rickety wooden chair by the table on which his chessboard rested. He lifted a neatly stacked pile of ten pence pieces between his thumb and forefinger, just a few millimetres above the table, then slowly let the coins fall, reforming the shining column. Yes, he wanted to make money, and, as he had told Nick, he wanted to make a lot of it. His ill-gotten gains, as his mother would undoubtedly call them, would add a few more ten pence pieces to this pile. Yet he knew it was the challenge of stealing that thrilled him now. Any money he made as a result was only a useful by-product.

He rested his chin on his arms on the table for a moment, his eyes level with his columns of coins. Then he sat up and reached into his trouser pockets. He brought out a handful of change. He looked at the coins in his hand, counting quickly. He had collected more ten pence pieces over the last few days. He added three to an unfinished stack, out ten of them, and carefully made a new stack of coins, which he placed next to the others, on a black square this time. He put his chin on his arms again, and looked at the coins. *How pretty they look.*

The pubs had now closed, and Gaz and Nick were sitting on the Beech Tree Grove sign. Mark and Simon were standing. The streetlight that stood at the junction bathed them in its sodium glow. Gaz had intended going to The Swan alone tonight, already had the bottle of aftershave and the cheap earrings in the pockets of his coat. Then Simon had knocked at the door, and said he was going to The White Lion. Gaz had tried to convince him to go to The Swan, but Simon had grimaced and said he wasn't going to that lair of smooths and wide-boys. Simon had already phoned Mark, who was waiting to meet them at the bottom of Goldfinch Drive. They had then walked down Beech Tree Grove and picked up Nick. Gaz had known he could never convince all three of them to go to The Swan, and didn't mention it again. He had been tempted to give Mark the earrings, to give to Chrissie. That was the only sensible thing to do with them, really. They were cheap tat and Dodgy Len wouldn't buy them anyway. Gaz was reluctant, however, to hand them over. He could have told Mark that they were something that his sister Laura had bought but had decided she didn't like. Mark would have no reason to be suspicious, no reason to wonder why Gaz was carrying earrings around in his jacket pocket. Still, Gaz kept his hand tight around them.

Simon was talking about some Jill girl he'd just met. Gaz wasn't sure what was going on. He hadn't seen the others for a couple of days, but it felt like a week. Where had this Jill sprung from? Whatever was happening with Jill was connected to Anna somehow . Simon was allowing more of that relationship shit to clog up his mind and addle his brain. Hadn't he had enough of that with Anna? Simon was now saying that he hadn't yet sorted out his feelings about Anna. Poor fool, Gaz thought. Why did he need this Jill woman? If the conversation continued in this vein, Mark would start banging on about Chrissie. Gaz clutched at the cold, black plastic in his pocket. It seemed an emblem of stability.

Nick had the right idea. He had picked up Heather in the park one hot day during the summer. They had had their fun for a few weeks, and then they had split. *That's the way to do it.* Although Gaz knew he lacked experience in this area. He had yet to have fun of that nature for anything approaching a few weeks. He had managed the odd grope and snog with willing drunken participants at parties, and had once gone out with one girl for almost a week. There was plenty of time for that nonsense, he thought. He knew that he would have children one day, although he didn't really know why he wanted them. In his unformed future, he could see those children, and the BMW, and the pretty wife, and the large, detached house. He didn't quite understand how he'd arrived at a position where he could imagine these things, not when he'd spent his adolescence hanging around with Mark, Si and Nick, and by association with those hippies in Honeyhouse. Nick wanted to be an academic, Mark, an architect, an artist, a rock star, and Simon... Well, nobody knew what Simon wanted to be, but marriage, children, mortgage, and a detached house were almost certainly not on *his* agenda.

Gaz was, he supposed, his parent's child. His family had been, still were, well off when compared to other families. Simon and Nick came from working class backgrounds, Mark lower-middle class. Gaz's family were middle class, aspiring to upper middle class, to the upper middle income bracket, but his father and mother had never quite broken the bonds that had tied them so firmly to the middle-middle class. He had known their frustrations as he had grown up, heard them talk about the car that wasn't quite good enough, the restaurants they couldn't quite afford to eat at, the holidays they couldn't quite pay for. He suspected he would live out his parents' dreams for them, that he was, in a way, being groomed for that life. Yet he hadn't rebelled at this. Now James, Mark's friend, the lyricist for Honeyhouse, *he* was upper middle-class. *He* was rebelling, smoking weed, drinking too much, reading Marx and Marcuse, rambling on about conditioning and proles and the iniquities of the class system. Yet, Gaz suspected, James could *afford* to be rebellious, with his handsome pocket money and his Saturday job at Benson's, the local department store. Gaz had never been particularly rebellious. He was scruffy, sure enough, but weren't they all? His dark wavy hair reached past his collar, but was not as long as Simon's luxuriant, shiny fair locks. He listened to music his parents considered odd, and he liked a drink. He wasn't into drugs, though, he wasn't into sleeping around, and he wasn't into all that New Age hippie shit mumbo jumbo that lurked around the fringes of Simon and Mark.

Yet, he was a thief. Was this his rebellion? He flicked at the corner of the black plastic earring holder in his pocket with his thumb. Were these purloined trinkets the symbol of his difference, a means of creating a more exciting route, different to the path laid out for him?

"So she wants you to wrap something warm around her?" Nick asked Simon.

"That's what she said," Simon replied.

"Well, I don't think you're reading too much into it," Nick said. "Too little, I'd say."

"Sounds like you're in there," Mark noted.

Simon was biting a fingernail. "But I don't know if I want to be in there. It's only a few days since Anna rejected me."

"Oh, for fuck's sake," Gaz interjected. "Get over it. Bang this Jill girl. Get it out of your system."

"Oh, I say, steady on," Mark laughed.

Gaz kicked at a stone beside his shoe. "Well, we've had six months of him going on about bloody Anna. Next he'll be going on about this Jill for weeks on end." He paused, scowling. "I don't think I could put up with more of your pathetic bleating."

Nick looked closely at Simon. "You *do* look like a sheep."

There was silence. Then Simon said, "I promise not to bleat. I'm just confused."

Gaz was as surprised at what he was saying as the others. "Look, just shag yourself stupid. It sounds like she's up for it. Wrap something warm around her. Ravel her in that bloody wool if she wants you to. Just get on with it."

"Well, I..." Simon began, and then petered out.

His outburst, Gaz realised, had only succeeded in making Simon more confused. Gaz gave a sardonic little laugh. "Don't listen to me, Si. What do I know about women?"

"Nothing," Nick said. "So shut up."

Gaz looked at his watch in the streetlight. "Oh well, time I was going. Some of us have to work."

"Me too," Mark said. "I have a meeting in the morning."

"How very important that sounds," Nick said.

"My first meeting, and I'm sure it's very important if I've been invited."

Nick looked at Simon. "Tea?"

"Yes, thanks," Simon said.

"See you guys," Gaz said.

They said goodbye to each other, then Mark began the walk down Barton Road to his parents' house, and Gaz crossed the road to Goldfinch Drive. He glanced over his shoulder. Nick and Simon were slowly ambling down Beech Tree Avenue. They would, no doubt, entertain themselves by talking about relationship shit until two in the morning. He tightly grasped the plastic square in his pocket, until the he felt the sharp corner of it digging into his palm. Then he squeezed a bit harder.

There was a knock at the front door. If it had been a few moments later, the hitman might not have heard it; he had been about to put the *1812 Overture* on the Linn Sondek, and he was in the mood to listen to it loud. He opened the door to a courier, who handed him an envelope. Only one of his clients knew his address, one he trusted. Normally, he picked up instructions from a PO Box in town. He signed the receipt on the clipboard the courier had thrust in front of him, and then closed the door. Some of the sparkle had gone out of the morning, so when he finally placed the disc on the record player, and set the expensive stylus in the groove, he left the volume of the amplifier as it had been the night before, when he had been listening to Bach cantatas.

There appeared to be little in the envelope. The plan would, he surmised, be simple. He tore away the gummed-down flap, and slid out a few typewritten sheets. He was surprised at the name he found there. *Tim Manley*. That somebody would want to hit a Manley Boy wasn't in itself surprising. The Manley Boys were notorious in London, and he'd heard they'd been putting themselves about a bit lately, muscling in on rackets strictly in the domain of others and, in the process, roughing up a few gangsters they shouldn't have roughed up. The surprise was that the hit was on *Tim Manley*. Now, if it had been Tom Manley, that would have made sense. Tim and Tom, the Manley Boys. Tom was the mad one, the bad one. Tim was the brains, the quiet one, the one who planned and schemed. Tom was all fists and knives and razors, a bad-tempered psychopath. Yet, perhaps it did make sense. If Tim was the brains, if you were to take out those brains what would remain? The Manley Boys would be leaderless, directionless. Tom Manley would undoubtedly take over, but Tom didn't have Tim's intelligence, his finesse, his strategy, his cunning. If he took out Tim, the Manley Boys would no longer be big players, would fall back, on security and running errands, and performing grisly jobs for some other mob that wanted to keep its hands clean.

He would do the hit, of course. He didn't like to let this client down, and the money for doing it would provide a fillip to his already brimming bank balance. He wanted to buy his son something. Only one thing troubled him about this hit, and that was his tenuous connection to the Manley Boys. He had lived in London a few years back, and had worked as a bouncer at a club whose owner had once run with the Manleys. The club owner had gone straight, and had paid off the loan the Manleys had given him to set up the club. It was from that club he had stolen the stash and escaped to Dereham, had run away with Peta to a new life together, as she saw it. Poor Peta.

He doubted Len Stone would ever connect him to a hit on Tim Manley. Still, it was a small detail that could lead to complications. He needed to be careful. He was confident that the job would run smoothly. They always did. He looked at the typewritten sheets again. The information provided was sparse, but everything he needed to know was there. For some reason, the hit had to happen as soon as possible; this weekend would be best. Tim Manley would be in Bournemouth in a few days' time. His client knew where Manley would be staying and the pubs and clubs he frequented.

The urgency of the job bothered Archie. Still, it should be easy enough. The notes indicated that Manley liked to walk alone at night, without his security. He had to decide on a method. Blasting Manley with a rifle on a beach in Bournemouth would be risky. It also offended his sensibilities. After all, his *son* lived there. He realised with a smile that, after he'd done what needed doing, he would be able to pop around and see his son.

15

It was a wet Friday night, and Mark was back in The White Lion, waiting for Nick and Gaz. Now he was working he found himself grateful for weekends in a way. He'd looked forward to them when at school, true enough, but this was different. In comparison, the school day had been short. At college, he had bunked off whenever he fancied. He wondered if that was why he had failed his A-level Art. He had found the practical side, the painting and drawing, easy and had perhaps missed more lessons than he should have. He'd skipped all the theoretical, academic stuff. He hadn't thought it important. Art, the one thing he loved outside the band, possibly even more than the band, the one thing he thought himself good at, had been the one thing at which he had failed. It still riled him.

He nursed a vodka and ginger, making it last. He'd arrived at the Lion early, keen to get out after his week of work. There were few people in the bar. Many of the people he knew had now started at polytechnic or university. Chrissie was sitting at a table with Jake. He gave them a wave, but wasn't in the mood for chatting with Jake, nor to be with Chrissie while Jake pawed her. James, Imogen and Stuart arrived later, and they came and sat with him.

"Mark, darling," Imogen said. "How's things?"

"No sign of my band mates, then?" Mark said.

"I don't think we'll see much of them for a few weeks," Imogen replied.

"So. No rehearsals for a while?"

Imogen shook her head. "No. But they'll be back."

"How can you be sure? They might cheat on me with other musicians."

Stuart smiled. "I'm sure you'll take them back even if they do. They'll say it didn't mean anything, and you'll understand."

Mark sniggered. "Well, yeah... As long as they don't tell me they hooked up with someone with better fingering techniques."

Stuart and Imogen laughed, and then Stuart said, "No, they'll be back, I'm sure. It's Steve and John's band. I don't think they'd know how to play with anybody else. You've been doing this for, what, three years now?"

"Longer," Mark said. "Steve and John messed about for a couple of years, then I joined, then Danny joined later." Mark sighed. "I miss playing, though."

"Hey," Imogen said. "Why don't you jam with Stuart and me while you're waiting?"

Mark knew Stuart and Imogen wrote songs together. Stuart played guitar, and Imogen sang, though they never performed their songs live. They were both nervous about performing on stage. Stuart and Imo had joined Honeyhouse on stage a couple of times, but both had been so freaked out they had left after a couple of gigs. Stuart was pretty good, though, a rhythm guitarist rather than a lead. Mark also knew that Imogen could sing. Imogen's voice was good, clear and strong. Steve and John continued to talk her into joining Honeyhouse, but she wouldn't do it. She'd be a fantastic frontman for the band. She was tall, and beautiful, with a mess of hennaed curls.

"You could play bass or guitar," Imogen said.

Stuart nodded. "Depending on the song."

It was a good idea, Mark thought. "It *would* keep my hand in between rehearsals."

"Come and join us," James said. "Join us in our... private sessions."

Mark smiled. "Oh? I thought we were going to make music."

They all laughed. James sipped his brandy. "It'd be cool. You're a bit folkie too, aren't you? You write all the AGD songs for Honeyhouse, don't you?"

"And the E-minor A-minor D-minor ones."

"Great," James said. "We jam most weekends. Come around this Sunday."

"Okay, I will. What time?"

"In the afternoon, after two."

The door to the bar opened and Nick came in. He brought a drink and joined Mark and the others at the table.

"No sign of Gaz?' Nick said.

"I thought he was coming down with you?' Mark said.

"He said he was coming down with you."

"What is that boy up to?"

"Oh, I saw Gaz earlier," Imogen said. "I'm sure it was him. He was heading towards The Swan."

Nick looked at Mark. "He keeps going on about The Swan, have you noticed?"

"Nick thought he fancied somebody down there," Mark said.

Imogen laughed. "Gaz? He seems so... I don't know. Not *gay*. Just... sexless."

Mark wasn't sure what Imogen meant. "Really?"

"Yes, he seems so... ah...I can't express it."

"How do you know he's not gay?' Nick asked.

Mark noted the word. It was, he thought, a ... what you call it... A neologism. Two years ago, they would all have been saying queer, or homo, or bent. Now they were saying *gay*. He'd better start using it.

"Oh, I don't know," Imogen said. "I might be wrong. I always think I can tell. I've usually been right."

"Oh? Who's *gay* around here, then?' Mark said, trying out the word for the first time.

"Nobody we know," Imogen replied. "There was one at college, you won't know him. And there are two, I think, at Uni." Imogen had started university, like her other friends, but, as she was at Bath, she had decided to live at home for a while.

"So what about Gaz?' Mark asked.

"I don't think he is. He gives me a ... look, sometimes. But he just doesn't seem interested, for some reason." She looked at James. "Not that I want him to be, of course, lambiekins."

Mark smiled at Imogen's description of James as *lambiekins*. They were all used to it, but it still seemed an odd description. James had a shaggy mop of dark hair and a beard. He was more like an old goat. Still, Mark thought, I wonder what I'd call Chrissie. My little love? My dolphin of delight? My pussikins?

"Of course, I've seen him snogging," Mark said. "At parties."

"Yeah, but usually when he's drunk," Nick pointed out.

"And when the girl's drunk, too," Imogen laughed.

"Anyway," Nick said. "I think he's up to something. He's being *most* furtive."

James smiled. "Perhaps he's finally realised he hates you both. That would be understandable."

Nick punched James's arm. Mark hadn't noticed anything different about Gaz. "He's always been a bit aloof, secretive, distant... and... well, you know... Gaz. Blunt but loveable. He's been like that ever since we've known him." Yet, he did wonder, since he mainly had eyes only for Chrissie, whether he would have noticed a change in Gaz in the last year.

"I still think he's up to something," Nick said. "I mean, *The Swan*. It's just not our kind of place."

"I don't know, it might be Gaz's, after all," Stuart said. "Let's face it, on the scale of beardy weirdness, James is top freak, then it runs down the scale of weirdness through Honeyhouse, then Simon, you, and then Mark. Gaz is only just above Jake and Chrissie."

Mark looked over momentarily at Chrissie, and wished he hadn't. She was kissing Jake.

"Where's Simon?' Imogen asked.

"Good point. Where *is* Simon?' Nick said.

"I thought *you* were phoning him," Mark said.

"I thought *you* were!"

"Honestly, you two couldn't organise a piss up in a brewery," Stuart said. "First you lose Gaz, now Simon."

"Oh, I'll phone him," Nick said. He stood up, and made his way to the payphone.

"I saw Si doing his tai chi in the town park the other day," Imogen said. "It looked cool."

"He's good. He good at kung fu, too," Mark said.

"You should know after what he did to you at the party."

"Yeah, yeah," Mark said grudgingly. He had ended up on his back after Simon had broken up a fight between him and Jake.

James drained off the last of his brandy. "Right," he said to Mark. "We're off back to my place to listen to some music. Do you two want to come?"

"No, not at the moment thanks. I need a few more drinks."

"Okay. Come around Sunday, and bring a guitar or two."

Imogen kissed Mark on the cheek, and then they left. Nick returned. "Hey, was it something I said?"

"No, they've gone back to James's. He probably needs a joint. What news on Simon?"

"He said he was actually waiting for Gaz to call. So we all got our wires crossed, it seems. He'll be along in a while."

They sipped at their drinks quietly for a few moments, before Nick spoke. "What are you doing with your weekend?"

"Some drawing I expect. I might go around James's Sunday and jam with Stu and Imo. You?"

"Nothing much. Haven't really thought about it. The usual, I suppose. Read, watch a bit of telly, and then come down here."

"I was thinking of riding down to the coast tomorrow and doing some drawing down there. Fancy it? The weather's supposed to be good, better than tonight at least. And the beaches will be pretty much empty."

"Where were you thinking of going?"

"Oh, I don't know. Poole? Weymouth? Bournemouth?"

It was a nice morning, Nick noted. The sky was pale blue, and tufted cumulus drifted slowly across it. There was an autumnal haziness to the day, as if the previous night's rain had turned to mist briefly before dawn and now thinly lingered. He climbed onto the back of Mark's Honda CB250 and flipped his visor down. He patted Mark's shoulder, then reached behind and gripped the chrome supports for the top box. Mark pulled away gently.

Dereham was about fifty miles from the nearest beach, and they had their favoured destinations – Swanage, Poole, Lyme Regis, Weymouth, Lymington. In the end, Mark had decided on Bournemouth. Nick wasn't fussed. Whichever beach he went to, Mark had a choice of two routes, and both were pleasant rides. They headed towards Salisbury. The wind was cool, but not cold; a lovely day for travelling on the motorbike. They wound along the road known locally as Death Valley, hugging the downs, folds and hangings, and then skirted Salisbury before heading down into Hampshire, towards Fordingbridge, through tunnels of trees. Nick watched tree trunks flow past him and then felt the Honda begin to slow. He turned his attention back to the road. There was a garage ahead of them. Mark turned the bike into the forecourt. Nick dismounted when Mark did, flipped up his visor and did some stretches.

Mark flipped up his visor in turn. "Are you okay?"

"Yes. My back and legs are stiff, that's all," Nick said.

Nick moved around, shaking the tension out of his arms. After a few minutes, Mark tapped him on the shoulder and asked if he wanted anything. Nick shook his head. He walked slowly back to the bike, and sat on it, side-saddle, while he waited for Mark, stretching his legs out in front of him as far as he could without slipping off the bike. He noticed, out of the corner of his eye, a car pull onto the forecourt. He wondered if the driver would want to use the pump in front of the bike, but the car drove over to the other row of pumps. Nick didn't need to move, and continued to look at the trees opposite the garage. He felt relaxed, as he always did when he got out of Dereham. He moved his shoulders, releasing some of the tension.

Mark returned and stood next to him, looking in the opposite direction, across the forecourt. "Don't turn around," Mark said quietly, folding notes and putting them back into his wallet. "There's a familiar car in the garage."

"Oh?" Nick said. "Who is it?" He thought it must be Jake, who his own car.

"Not so much who, as what," Mark said. His voice was still quiet. "It's an NSU Ro80."

Nick began to turn, but Mark stopped him with a gentle touch on the arm. "Flip your visor down, at least," Mark whispered.

Nick did, then stood and turned to look at the car. The driver's back was to them. Nick thought it might be the hitman, but couldn't be sure. Mark tapped Nick's shoulder, and indicated that he should get on the bike. Nick climbed onto the pillion, and gripped the supports of the top box again. Mark climbed on, inserted the key into the ignition, and then kicked the engine over. The engine didn't start. Nick saw the man walking to the kiosk, his back towards them. Mark tried to start the bike again, with the same result. Nick glanced over Mark's shoulder. The ignition wasn't on. The man came out of the kiosk. Nick could see his face now. It was the hitman. Or the crazy man. Mark now switched the ignition on, and stood on the kick-start. The engine roared into life. The hitman glanced up at them as he put his wallet into the inner pocket of his suit jacket. Mark gently pulled away. Nick stole a glance at the hitman, knowing his eyes were hidden behind the tinted visor of Mark's spare helmet. It was definitely him. As they drew level with him, the hitman looked at them again. Then Mark pulled onto the Bournemouth road and gunned the engine, forcing Nick backwards against the top box. Nick wondered why Mark was suddenly in a hurry. Mark continued to ride fast for a few miles, and then began to slow. A layby sign flashed past them. Nick realised Mark was going to pull into the layby.

Mark kicked the main stand down. Nick helped rock the bike onto the stand with his legs, but remained on the pillion. Mark got off the bike and flipped his visor up. Nick pushed his visor up, too. "What are you playing at?" he asked.

"Put your visor back down," Mark said. "I'll tell you in a minute."

Mark bent down beside the bike and began to fiddle with the engine. He was simply turning the fuel stopcock on and off as far as Nick could make out. A couple of minutes later, the NSU sped past them. Mark stood, and tapped Nick's helmet. Nick flipped his visor up again.

"Was that Shirley Temple?' Mark asked.

"Yes, that was him," Nick said.

"He looks nothing like fucking Lee Marvin!"

Nick smiled. "Nor Clint. Oh, well. What are we going to do now?"

Mark smiled. "Follow him." He flipped his visor back down, and got back on the bike.

As they pulled out onto the road, Nick wondered if this was good idea. Shirley Temple might be a madman, or a hitman. Was it a good idea to follow a hitman? Or to follow a madman, for that matter. After a few minutes, Nick could see the NSU some distance down the road in front of them. Mark slowed so they could keep the NSU in view. Sometimes they lost sight of it around bends, but when they came to a straight, they would see it again, half a mile or so in front of them. Nick felt sure they appeared innocuous, that they would go unnoticed at this distance, that the hitman would just think them a couple of day-trippers enjoying a relaxed cruise down to the coast. And that was, after all, what they were supposed to be doing. They passed Ringwood, and turned onto the Bournemouth road. As they neared Bournemouth, the traffic became heavier, and the NSU slowed. Mark was slowing too, maintaining his distance; but as the traffic increased, Nick could see they were closing on the hitman. After a few more miles, Mark turned left, towards Christchurch. They stopped by the side of the road, dismounted, and took their helmets off.

Mark lit a cigarette. "I didn't think it would be a good idea to follow him any further."

Nick was stretching again. "Very wise."

"Where do you think he was going?"

"Somewhere in Bournemouth... or Poole, I suppose."

Mark breathed out cigarette smoke. "Yeah. It would have been fun to see what he was up to."

"I'm not sure I want to know what he's up to."

"Well, if he's a nutter, nothing. But if he *is* a hitman..."

"I think we should leave it for other people to sort that out. I'm no hero."

"Fair enough," Mark said.

Nick laughed. "Oh, I see what you're up to. You just want Chrissie to think *you're* a hero, don't you."

"Well, it might help her see past the handsome Jake."

"If you're dead, she won't see you at all."

16

It had been a week since the disaster with Anna. Simon had met Gaz, Nick and Mark down the pub during the week, as usual. He had seen Anna in the refectory and the corridors at college a couple more times, and had been cut again and again. Joan had smiled at him, with that irritating, supercilious smile. She knew something, Simon was sure. Nobody had seen an NSU Ro80 when they gathered at the crossroads to chase the day's end. Chrissie hadn't fallen out with Jake again, so Mark's nape had remained untouched all week. Gaz had used the words *shit*, *fuck*, and *bollocks* a lot. Nobody had mentioned his piles of money, although all were sure that such piles were being modified and manipulated.

It was a sunny Saturday afternoon. Simon was reading Colin Wilson's *The Philosopher's Stone*, and listening to Streetwalkers' *Red Card*, when he heard the phone ring. Simon's mother called to him. "Si. It's for you. It's Warren."

Warren didn't phone that often. Simon picked up the handset. "Hello. This is an unpleasant surprise."

"Fancy a night out in Southleigh?' Warren said.

"Now what could entice me to go to Southleigh?' Simon said. He knew why Warren wanted to go there.

"Oh, come on, man. I want to see Jill, and my friends around here are such plebs. They'll be drooling all over her. At least Anna messed you up. You'll be no competition."

"Yes, I should be able to keep my drool under control. Unless I fall asleep listening to you."

"So, what do you say?"

Mark and Nick had gone to Bournemouth, and Simon had no idea what time they'd be back. "Yeah, all right, you're on."

Warren arranged with Simon a pub in which they would meet at eight. At least, Simon thought, I can ramble about Anna to Warren. Gaz would only insist that it was pointless relationship shit. *Anyway, he's been keen to go down The Swan for the last week. This is his chance.* Simon phoned Gaz, anyway, and asked if he wanted to come over to Southleigh. Gaz said no, as Simon had expected. They arranged to meet up on Sunday. Nick was right; Gaz had been behaving rather mysteriously of late. Simon wondered if Gaz fancied somebody down The Swan. He did know Gaz fancied that girl who worked in Boots. Janet, that was her name. Gaz had snogged her at a party last Christmas. *Does she go down The Swan? She seems like a Swan kind of girl.* Perhaps Gaz wanted some of that relationship shit for himself, after all.

Warren was already sitting at a small table in The Vine Tree when Simon arrived. The bus had been running late. The pub was still quiet, although Simon knew that it would fill up and become noisier as the night wore on. There was no sign of Jill. Simon wondered if this was a wild goose chase. "You do realise," Simon said to Warren, "that we could spend all night going to different pubs and miss Jill each time. Or she might've decided to stay in tonight and wash her hair. Which she probably would if she knew you were out and about."

"Yeah, right. Actually, she does know I'm out and about. I phoned her after I phoned you. She fancies me, I tell you."

"I didn't know you knew her number. I didn't even know you knew her surname."

"She told me the other day."

"I don't remember."

"You were wool-gathering, as she likes to say."

"Did you tell her I'd be here?"

"Yeah. It didn't put her off. Oddly." Warren lit a cigarette. "I hope I don't bump into any of my other friends. They'll cramp my style."

"Oh yeah, right, your *style*. I look forward to a demonstration of your *style*."

Simon sipped his drink while Warren leaned back, smiling, and then blew smoke rings. He sat up, the smile wider, his eyes wide. "Bloody brilliant," Warren muttered. Simon turned round. Jill had just walked through the door, alone. "She's by herself, see," Warren said. "She *wants* me."

Perhaps she did, after all, Simon thought. Warren stood and walked over to Jill, led her to the bar where he bought her a drink. Simon looked at his half-empty glass, and thought it would have been nice if Warren had also bought a drink for him. But Warren was, after all, very excited; he could be excused for forgetting to buy his friend a drink. When Jill and Warren returned to the table, Simon noted that, though she sat down – by necessity at the small round table – between the two of them, she did move her chair slightly towards him. Warren still smiled, and looked at her with glittering eyes; he appeared not to have noticed this small and subtle movement.

"It's good to see you," Warren said to Jill.

"Well, I was surprised you phoned. Very bold of you, I must say. Still, it makes a change from going out with the girls." Jill turned to Simon. "And I was pleased to hear he was bringing you along. How's my sweater?"

"Not finished yet," Simon said. "I asked mum if she could knit it for me instead – she would be much faster, you know – but she said if a girl wanted to be wrapped in something of mine, it would be better if I created it myself."

"Your mother is very wise," Jill said.

Warren was frowning now. "You're not talking about the bloody knitting again, are you? When will you ever give up with that?" Warren was already feeling left out.

"I will give up when it's completed, or when it fails to be completed," Jill said. "If its realisation never appears likely, then I shall... Have my answer..."

"There *is* no wool anyway," Warren said. "I don't know what you're talking about, really."

Jill's smile was gentle. "The wool is, of course, imaginary, as is the sweater. The production of the sweater is a metaphor. Simon can yet knit me what I require."

"You've done A-level English, haven't you," Warren said.

"Indeed, young man."

"Young? I'm eighteen, how old are you?"

"Twenty-two."

"What! You're old!' Warren laughed. "I could be your toy boy."

Jill was flustered in a way Simon hadn't seen her before. "You could be. Perhaps, if you... well..."

"If I what?' Warren asked.

"We'll come to that another time," Jill said.

She's trying not to hurt Warren's feelings, Simon thought. She's trying to bring him down to Earth gently. *But then what does she want? Why is she here?* She could simply want to be their friends. They got on well when they met up at college. Simon wondered if this was the way men and women became friends, now they were older. There are, after all, the girls you grow up with, the ones who are around all the time, who become friends through proximity and time. Then there are those you meet when you're older, the ones with whom the initial stages of a friendship must inevitably be fraught – are they potential girlfriends, or possibly only girl *friends*? Simon reviewed the girls he'd known. There were the ones he'd grown up with through school, the Wendys and Sarahs and Julies and Joannas, some of whom he'd fancied, many of whom were now friends. Then there were the Imogens and Annas, the ones he'd discovered at sixth-form college, the ones he'd fancied, had chatted to, chatted around, chatted up. Imogen had gone out with James. And Anna? She had been a possibility, and now was gone. She had been a friend, but was now distant. *Is this how it is now? Potential girlfriends, girlfriends, or nothing?* Yet Imogen was still a friend, even though she was now with James and all potentiality had disappeared. It was possible, then, to be friends, to find a friend, a new *girl* friend. So perhaps Jill just wanted to be friends with two boys who amused her. *But then, Nick does think she's flirting with me.*

Jill touched his arm. "More wool?"

"Yes, I'm afraid so. It takes a lot to card and ... whatever else you do to wool."

"Felt."

"Yes, felt."

Warren lit another cigarette. "If you're twenty-two," he said to Jill, "why are you still at college? Shouldn't you be at Uni or something?"

"I decided not to go."

"Why not?"

"I didn't think I needed it. I liked the idea of earning some money. I'd been at college for three years, anyway."

"Ah," said Warren, "were you like poor Si? Did you have to re-sit some O-levels?"

Again, Jill was unsure of herself. She paused before she spoke, looked down at her drink. When she did speak, Simon could see why she had composed herself. "Um, no, actually. I don't like to... boast... but I took four A-levels, English as you astutely noted, and Maths, Sociology and Art. Then, well, it was suggested I try S-level Maths and English. So I took another year doing those."

Warren looked amazed. "And you passed them all?"

"Well, yes, of course." She said it with the air of somebody who never thought for a moment that she would fail at anything.

"I feel humble in your presence," Simon said.

"No need for that," Jill said. "I'm just a product of my middle-class background... And my simply amazing brain, of course."

"So what have you been doing with the past two years?' Warren said.

"Two?"

"Well, yes, if you started your A-levels at eighteen, you would've finished the S-levels. That's three academic years. And you're twenty-two now, so–"

"Ah, I see. Well, contrary to your name, and also paradoxically, you've made an unwarranted assumption."

Simon interrupted her. "Surely, to be contrary to his name, what he said would be *un-warrened*, in which case he hasn't dug himself into a hole."

"Ah, yes, good point, young man." Jill smiled. "He has, indeed, un-warrened, even, you could say, un-sett himself." She began laughing. "Dis-tunnelled, un-mined, anti-holed...' She paused.

"Non-dug, de-sunk," Simon continued. "Un-trenched, back-shafted..."

"Sounds a bit rude, that one," Jill said.

Simon began to laugh. "Anti-bored, de-routed, non-drilled, un-cored, de-reamed... uh...' He too was running out of ideas.

Jill's eyes twinkled. "Generally, you might, say, uncut, unsliced, unlifted, or, or in any other way disturbed in any cutting, boring, digging or,' She was finding it hard to continue with a straight face. "Or otherwise mechanical or manual lifting action applied to any sod, turf, soil, humus, rock... or, uh, any other part of the...' She waved her hands around vaguely, "Lithosphere and the layers above it however they may be... constituted." She looked at Simon, and sipped her drink.

"Indeed," Simon said. "You took the words right out of my mouth."

Jill spat the drink back into her glass and laughed.

"What the bloody hell are you two on about?' Warren said.

"Oh, Simon caught me making an arse of myself in an ungainly pun... Now where was I? Ah, yes. Anyway. I took a year out, so I didn't start college until I was nineteen. I therefore left last year. Since then, I've been out of work."

Warren was fidgeting, Simon noticed. He'd hardly had a chance to speak since Jill had arrived, and looked ready to burst with pent-up flirtiness. "So why are you back at college?' Warren finally asked. "To do chemistry? Physics? Become a rocket scientist?"

"No, to learn shorthand and typing. I'm doing a secretarial course."

"That seems rather... humble...' Simon said.

"We all have to start somewhere."

Simon stood. He'd give Warren a chance to chat-up Jill. "I'm going for a slash," he said.

Jill looked up at him as he stood. "What colourful language you use," she said. "Slash." She laughed. "Oh, and backshafting, of course."

While Simon urinated, and stared blankly at the nothing – a black zed-shaped crack – on the something – a white tile – in front of him, he considered Jill. He found her, he had to admit, rather exciting. He liked talking with her. She was playful, like Anna. Not as good looking as Anna. Taller, though. Nice eyes. Striking eyes. She was clever. Intimidatingly bright, in fact. He felt rather disloyal thinking about Jill in this way. He still hadn't got over Anna; it had only been a week or so since she'd first cut him. Though nothing had ever happened between them, she was bound up in his nervous system – her look, her smile, her mannerisms, her way of talking, were all still there within him.

As he came out of the toilet, back into the smoky fug of the bar, he looked around quickly. Then his heart fluttered. He recognised Anna's long, wavy brown hair, even though her back was towards him. He didn't dare look again. He focused on Jill and Warren at the table in the corner, barely visible through backs and heads and shoulders and beer glasses. He wanted this walk to end quickly now, he wanted to sit down, anonymous, hidden by the crowd, knowing that his back would be towards Anna when he did so, and her back towards him. The walk could not pass quickly enough, however. He had to pause and say excuse me, sidle and wheedle his way through the crush. His blood and face burned. His stomach felt light. Ignoring Anna all the time was so damned hard. He *wanted* to talk to her, he *wanted* to turn back, sit down next to her, and talk nonsense with her again. Yet he also knew that he didn't want to be cold-shouldered, stone-walled, ignored and made to feel small. He didn't want the cut direct again.

Warren was talking to Jill. She was smiling; that was something. Warren at last had the chance for an extended flirt. Simon could ignore them when he sat down. Jill might think it weird, but Warren would understand. Well, he would if he'd noticed Anna's arrival. But Warren only had eyes for Jill. Warren was looking at her now, intently, smiling, lighting a cigarette. Jill turned to Simon as he sat down. "So you're back, Zorro," she said.

Simon was thrown momentarily; it didn't connect with what he'd been thinking. "Pardon?"

Jill mimed a sword-stroke, cutting a zed in the air. "You went for a slash, Zorro. I expect Warren will find your mark on the wall."

Simon remembered the cracked tile. "Funnily enough, he might well do."

"How did you know that's what we do when we piss?" Warren said to Jill.

"She knows everything, you dunce," Simon smiled. "After all, she has four A-levels and two S-levels."

"Quite right," Jill said. Then she laughed. "Piss art was on the syllabus. Isn't it on yours?"

"Must be an S-level thing," Warren said. "Right, who's for a drink? What will you have, Jill?"

Jill stood before Warren could. "It's my round. I wheedled money from my parents for tonight."

Warren asked if she could afford a vodka and coke for him. Jill nodded. Simon eyed Warren, wondering if he was aiming to get merry, then asked for a lemonade, lime, soda water and ice.

"I can afford a proper drink for you as well," Jill said.

"No, that's what I drink. I don't like alcohol much. I don't like the aftertaste. I can taste the alcohol."

"You're weird," Warren said.

Jill rubbed the top of Simon's head. "But sweet." She went to the bar.

Warren leaned over the table. "Did you see who came in?"

Simon knew who he talking about. "I noticed her on the way back from the bog. I don't know if she saw me."

"That Joan's with her."

Simon groaned. "Fuck, no. Not Joan."

"Yep, and unfortunately for you, Joan is facing this way. She knows you're here. And by now, so does Anna I guess."

Simon wanted to turn around and look, but resisted.

"Uh-oh," Warren said. "Joan has noticed me looking at her... Now she's leaning across to Anna... still looking this way...' Warren was quiet for a moment.

"Now what?' Simon could feel the pull to look over his shoulder, as if Anna had a fish-hook in his mouth and was trying to reel him in.

"Now... they look like they're having a hushed conversation. You know, like, their heads are down, they're leaning in towards each other, and Joan's talking, and Anna's fiddling with a beer mat... and... You know, I can't hear what they're saying, but I bet they're talking about you."

Jill returned with the drinks, and placed them on the table. "Some bastard pinched my arse while I crushed up against the bar. Bloody cheek."

Simon smiled. "He must have pinched it quite hard then."

Jill frowned. "What? Oh no, he's got a bloody cheek. As I'm you sure you understand, I don't have a bloody cheek." She paused. "I hate it when men do that. It's so bloody aggressive and territorial."

"I could check whether you've got a bloody cheek," Warren said.

Warren was looking from Jill to Simon, smiling. Simon frowned. Didn't Warren realise that was the wrong flirt at the wrong time? Jill also frowned at him. "See, that's what I mean."

Warren's smile had turned from amused to mischievous. Simon knew what was coming. "Oh, come on," Warren said. "It's not that bad. It's just a bit of fun. It's just a way for us males to pick out the females we're interested in."

"But what," Jill said, firmly, "if I'm not interested in the pincher, the fondler? What if I think he's an ugly fuck?"

"Well, you don't have to respond, do you? But at least you know the guy is interested."

"I would rather *not* have an assault upon me to show interest. The guy could talk to me. Amuse me. Dazzle me. This is my body, Warren. It's not here to be shared without my consent, I'm not here to be touched up for a laugh. You know, the guy who pinched me never had a hope in hell of interesting me. So he's got a free feel. He knows what my arse feels like."

"So what? In that crush, anybody around you would have known what your arms or legs feel like."

"I put myself there. I accept the contact for what it is... Now here's the thing. When I'm up there, struggling to get you a drink, do you think I'm standing there with a male body pressed against me, thinking, hmm, *hot*, I can feel his steely shanks through his denims?"

"Well, I don't know, you might–"

"Don't be stupid, Warren."

Simon noticed that Jill was using Warren's name, a sure sign of irritation. She continued. "They're just bodies. They mean nothing. I feel nothing. The contact is devoid of meaning." She paused, leaned back against her chair, and pushed her glasses back up her nose. "If I went out with you, would you enjoy that memory? Would you like to remember that guy, the guy who fondled my arse? Would you be jealous? Could you imagine him boasting to his friends about how he got to touch up the tall blonde? *Your* tall blonde? Or would it be all right with you?"

"No, well, I–"

"No, of course it wouldn't be okay. You'd get up and punch him I expect, for invading what you would feel to be *your* property. Well... this isn't yours or any other man's property, *this*–' Jill indicated her body by moving her hands down beside her, towards her waist. "This is *my* property. I shall give it to whomever I deem worthy of my love and trust, or my affection and attention."

And that person, Simon now knew, wasn't going to be Warren. But would Warren see that?

"Okay," Warren said. "I see where you're coming from... I apologise for being me... and a man."

The apology was hollow. Warren had pinched a girl's behind, on more than one occasion, and Simon knew it. It amused Warren, and he would doubtless do it again. Simon had never done and would never do such a thing. He agreed with Jill, although he had never articulated it in the way she had. It was, Simon thought, about respect.

Jill sighed. "And now I need to make the mark of Zorro, and I have to go back through that crowd." She eyed the route to the toilets. "And somewhere in that crowd is a man who thinks he has now branded me, who thinks he in some small way owns me." She paused. "I'll punch his fucking lights out if he tries it again." She stood with determination, pushed her chair back, and began muscling her way through the crowd.

"Do you think," Warren said, "Jill might be one of those feminists?"

"She might well be," Simon said. "There's nothing wrong with that."

"And do you think I'm in with a chance?" Warren laughed, self-deprecatingly.

Simon smiled in return. "Honestly, Warren old bean, you *never* stood a chance."

"Oh well. I'll give you an update on Anna instead."

Simon had forgotten about Anna. Warren had now returned him to reality. "She still has her back towards you," Warren said. "But Joan's looking over here again. She looks over here a lot."

"How do you know?"

"I kept one eye on their table while Jill was ... ranting. It's almost as if Joan fancies you." Warren sat forward. "Hey, you don't think..."

Simon had never given Warren's implied question a thought; but he did now. "I don't think... Are you saying...? No... *Joan* fancies me?' Simon fiddled with a beer mat. "You think she's been putting Anna off somehow, so she can benefit?"

"Perhaps. You say Joan smiles at you mysteriously, and you don't understand it."

"Well, yes, but I always thought she was smiling because she knew something, because, you know, Anna had told her something and because she knew what was happening and I didn't, and felt kind of smug about it."

"Consider this, then, instead. She smiles at you because she fancies you. And just as you didn't recognise the signals with Anna, got them all mixed up somehow, now you're not recognising a signal from Joan."

"No, no. That can't be right. Joan always seemed ... amused that Anna fancied me. As if she thought I was too... I don't know, unattractive, dull, stupid, whatever... to be with Anna." Simon felt the tug again of the fishhook in his mouth. He refused to turn. "What's happening over there now?"

"I can't see. There's too many bodies in the way." Warren lit a cigarette, breathed out smoke that was soon lost in the ever-present blue haze that lingered in the bar. "Relationships, eh? Bloody complicated."

Fucking relationship shit, as Gaz would say. Could Warren be right? It seemed implausible that Warren could be right about anything to do with relationships, but perhaps, this once, he was.

Jill returned to the table. "Sorry, that took a bit longer than expected. I stopped and said hello to Anna."

"You said hello to Anna?' Simon said.

"Yes, Anna. I know her sister." Jill smiled. "Anna's the pretty girl over there, with her back to us. "

Warren blew a smoke ring. He smiled knowingly. "Oh, he knows who Anna is."

Jill nodded. "Well, I had worked that out, actually. I was teasing. Her friend Joan wanted to know why we were here. She seemed most interested."

"Do you know Joan?' Simon said.

"No, not really. I know she's Anna's friend. She used to be at Anna's house sometimes when I went around to see her sister."

Warren leaned forward. "Tell me more. Such as... What's Anna's sister like?"

Jill laughed. "Out of your league, Warren."

Warren turned to Simon. "Perhaps you should start chasing Anna's sister instead."

Jill flashed her cornflower blue eyes over the top of her glasses at Simon. "Oh no, he doesn't want to do that, let me assure you both."

Warren looked at Simon, and winked. Simon didn't know why Warren was winking. He knows something I don't, Simon thought. *What have I missed?* Simon had seen Jill look at him, but hadn't really heard what she'd said. Warren had, it seemed. Simon had been thinking about Anna. All the talk of Anna and her sister had clouded his mind. Jill could have said that she fancied him for all he knew. He now suddenly felt doubly befuddled. Had Jill said something important? Was that why Warren was winking at him? *I am such a blockhead. I'll never get a girlfriend at this rate. I'm always missing signals.* Somebody dropped a glass behind him. It shattered on the wooden floor. The drinkers behind him were quiet for a moment, and then started laughing and hooting. Simon turned to look. Instead, he saw Anna and Joan stand and then head towards the door. For a change, Joan didn't grace him with the smile he thought supercilious or knowing, but which Warren thought meant something else. She never looked at him at all.

But Anna did. For the first time since the night of the Fresher's Ball, Simon found himself looking into Anna's eyes. There was something in her look that Simon strove to under-stand, but, for a moment, he had felt the connection with her again. Then she looked away, and went through the door, leaving him to wonder what that brief look had meant. He was sure it meant something, that he was supposed to read something into it. Yet he had failed to immediately understand that look. He had failed to find a key to the text.

Simon turned back to the table, and found Jill and Warren looking at him. "They've gone, then?' Warren said.

"Yes, they've gone," Simon said. He felt close to asking Warren about *that* look, and what it meant, but knew he'd receive no help whatsoever. He wanted to say something to somebody. It seemed inappropriate somehow to talk to Jill about it. He wished he could talk to Nick. Perhaps he could, later on. Nick and Mark would be back from Bournemouth by now, and were most likely down the Lion.

Jill laid her hand on Simon's forearm, and rubbed it gently. "Don't you worry about them. You've a jumper to knit me."

"Your round," Warren said. Then he winked again.

Molly thought she had better go to Copsehill again. She went down to the saloon bar of The White Lion, but her new friends weren't there to accompany her. She didn't really want to go to the hill alone and listen to all the nonsense. Yet if she wanted to stay in Dereham, she had to do some work to keep Edge happy. She had told Edge about Kurt the Dutchman, and he had said he would look into it. He had also congratulated her, and encouraged her to return to the hill in a way that made it obvious that he expect it, as it was her job now.

She went back to her room, and flicked through *Panlyrae: A Message for Mankind*. So much new age twaddle, she thought. It was intriguing that an ordinary guy, a farmer from California, should think he was communing with aliens. Why a farmer? Why not a politician, scientist, or world leader? Patterson would have an answer to that, she thought. Something like... The aliens are too wise to provide politicians or scientists knowledge that could give them power. But then Molly couldn't help thinking: God moves in mysterious ways, just like aliens. She could see little difference. She had been brought up a Catholic, but was now agnostic, if not an atheist. Still, she remembered enough about her religious upbringing to see similarities. She thought that if ufology were to one day become a religion, then books like this would fit into its Old Testament, and people like this contactee, this Ed Freeman, would be revered as prophets. The language was vague, the prophecies inaccurate or located so far in the future that by the time the dates came, they would be forgotten. Any advice or encouragement was simply that proffered by hippies and by religions throughout the ages. Be nice to each other. Do unto others as they would do to you. Don't mess the planet up. War is bad. Watch out for those nuclear bombs...

Molly sighed, and put the book down. She left the room and headed down the stairs towards the bar, hoping that, by now, somebody she knew would be there. She'd even take Gaz if he was willing to come. She didn't fancy him, but she liked his gruff no-nonsense approach. There was nobody there she knew. She looked at her watch. It was nine o'clock. Pam was behind the bar. She brought Molly her vodka and coke.

"Do you think Simon or Nick will be in tonight?" Molly said.

Pam wiped the counter with a damp rag. The saloon was quiet this early on a Sunday evening, and the counter didn't really need wiping. "Well... possibly, I suppose. But Simon's a student, you know, and Nick's not working, so really, I think they rely on Gaz and Mark. They both got jobs, so I don't see them so often on a Sunday now."

"Thanks, Pam."

"Why are you after those two?"

"Somebody to walk to Copsehill with."

"Well, Richard will be up there tonight. You won't be alone. I overheard him yesterday saying that if it was dry he'd be paying a visit. Well, really, he's up there most dry nights, so that's no surprise. Have you met Richard?"

"Yes, I've met him, my sister knew him."

"Oh, of course she did." Pam paused and looked at Molly. "Well, you'll know that Richard is harmless... He just has a bee in his bonnet about his flying saucers."

"Yes, I know. That is some big bee."

"And he'll buzz at you all night, if you're unlucky."

"That why I was rather hoping Simon or Nick might be around."

Pam laughed, and walked off to serve some customers.

Molly looked at her watch again. If nobody came, she decided, she would leave at ten. Near her, at the end of the bar, was a *Wiltshire Times* from the previous Friday. She slid it towards her and began scanning the stories, the usual mixture of council doings, traffic accidents, projected enterprises and enterprising projects. On page eight, a small story, obviously one of Richard Patterson's, caught her interest.

Car Engine Cut Dead

Major Arthur Downing, of Trowbridge, was surprised when, with no warning at all, his car stuttered to a halt on the road between Dereham and Burnt Norton. He had been travelling at forty-five miles per hour when the engine died, the headlights faded away and the lights on the instrument panel fizzled out.

Mystified, he got out of his car and went around to the bonnet with the torch from his glove compartment. Then he noticed an amber light above him. He shone his torch towards it, but the moment the beam touched this mysterious glowing jewel, he became aware of a rolling motion beneath him. He leaned forward onto the bonnet. The whole car seemed to be vibrating.

Major Downing is a hardened veteran of war-time campaigns, and fought with a beach-landing group attached to the Brigade of Guards in the Middle East and Europe. He is not easily frightened. But when the car started to vibrate, he wanted, he said, to "get the hell away'. The air also began to vibrate, and he heard a whining and crackling. It was not loud, but seemed to fill the darkness all around him. "There was a definite impression," he said, "of something pressing down on me with force. It was odd, uncanny."

As suddenly as it had started, the noise and vibration ceased. Major Downing looked up, but the amber light had gone. He jumped into his car again, and to his surprise, it started at the first turn of the key. He was grateful that it did so, as he had been feeling vulnerable on that isolated stretch of country road. "I would still like to know what it was," the Major said. So would many of us in Dereham, Major. And so the Dereham mystery continues to provoke and mystify, after nearly five years.

It was an odd tale, certainly, but correlation is not causation, she thought. Just because the torch beam hit the amber object and everything began vibrating, did *not* mean the amber object was the cause of the vibration. She took a sip of her vodka and coke. The door to the bar opened. She looked up, hoping it was Simon or Nick, but it was only that smooth-looking bloke who was the boyfriend of that girl Mark fancied. What was her name... Chrissie? The man smiled, but she didn't return it. She liked Mark, and she didn't like the man's smile.

The newspaper article gave no indication of the weather conditions. If there had been broken cloud, couldn't the amber light have simply been a star? Could the car have been vibrating because of the wind? Why did the car engine cut out? Well, cars could be unreliable, she thought. She looked at her watch. It was quarter to nine. She finished her drink, then went back to her room, and put on another sweater. She had only brought with her the leather jacket, and the nights were getting cooler. On her way out, she popped her head around the door of the saloon bar, but there was still no sign of Simon or Nick.

When Molly arrived at Copsehill, a small group had already assembled, and in the middle of them was a tall figure that could only be Patterson. She walked over and said hello to them. The night was breezy; broken cloud, reflecting the orange streetlights of Dereham, slid quickly across the sky. Her eyes were drawn first to one, and then to another bright star. She asked the assembled group what the brighter of the two stars was.

"That's no star, that's a planet."

Molly recognised the voice. It was Kurt's. "I'll guess it's Jupiter then," she said. "It's a bit late for Venus."

"Very good," Kurt said.

Molly looked around. "That bright one, close to the horizon, what's that?"

"That's Aldebaran," Kurt said. "Fourteenth brightest star in the sky."

"Oh, really," Molly said. "What are the others?"

"Sirius is first, of course. Then Canopus, then Alpha Centauri."

"This is our friend Kurt," Patterson said. "He's a walking planetarium."

"I prefer to think of myself as a stellarium," Kurt said. "I don't just know the planets." She could hear the smile in his voice as he said it; also an element of pride.

Molly needed to hear him talk some more. "I'm Molly," she said. "Pleased to meet you. Surely Jupiter is brightest?"

"No, no. Jupiter is a planet. I was talking only about stars."

"I see, I see," Molly said. "My friend Nick, he said you knew all the satellites, as well. We were up here the other night."

"Most of them," Kurt said. He laughed. "But not all, of course. I don't know the secret ones. And people mistake debris for satellites." She noticed the reference to the *secret ones*. Most people forgot about the secret ones, or didn't even know they existed.

"Really? What kind of debris?"

"Stuff jettisoned from space craft." The "stuff" he pronounced *shtuff*. "Boosters and casings, that kind of thing."

Patterson spoke. "Karl is a *very* handy person to have around," he said. "He helps keep our feet on the ground."

Molly wondered what Patterson did when Kurt wasn't around. Floated off to fantastical realms, she supposed. But then, Kurt could just lie. Even if he knew all the satellites, planets and stars, he could simply commit a sin of omission, and forget to tell Patterson and the other skywatchers that something at which they were looking was a mundane satellite. In fact, if Kurt were to be on the hill during a sighting and failed to provide a mundane explanation of it, that alone would surely multiply the sense of wonder for Patterson and his friends.

"Where are you from?" Molly asked Kurt.

"Utrecht."

Molly didn't know enough about Utrecht to test his knowledge, to catch him out. "So why are you here, in Dereham?"

"I came over to see your prehistoric sites, you know. Stonehenge, Avebury." *Shtonehenge*.

"Yes, I know. Don't you have your own stones to explore in Holland?"

"We do, but not as famous. Your West Country, it is famous everywhere. Stonehenge, Glastonbury, Avebury, burial mounds everywhere. I love it."

"Have you always lived here?"

"No. I lived in Plymouth, so I could explore Cornwall and Dartmoor for a while. Then I moved to Cirencester ... You have Roman there, and also in Gloucester... And so much prehistory around. Barrows and crosses, and hill forts. You'd be surprised what you can find there."

Molly didn't think she would be. GCHQ, that was why Kurt had been there, she was sure. But was he really Kurt, or was he somebody else? The accent was good, and at the moment she had no reason to doubt he was who he said he was. Perhaps he was, after all, only a stoned hippie come to connect with the ley lines. Ah, but places he had lived were too... suspicious. Plymouth and the docks, Cirencester and GCHQ, and now here, on the edge of the Plain.

A bright light flared in the distance. There was an intake of breath from a couple next to Patterson. "No," he said. "No. What you're seeing there is a car. The headlights have merged to become one bright light. A comes over the top of the ridge there, east of Southleigh. It must be five or six miles away. It often catches out newcomers." Patterson benevolently and warmly drew the couple into his social embrace. "I hope you'll come here often enough that you'll learn all the pitfalls of skywatching from our little hill. Given time, you'll see one of our flying friends. Everybody does, in the end."

I'm sure they did, Molly thought, if they wanted it enough.

Patterson began to regale the couple with a story about the last UFO he had seen. Molly watched the sky, and looked around the landscape in the dark, at the distant streetlights and houselights. The cloud had thinned, and only the occasional cumulus scurried across the sky. The stars shone brightly despite the moonlight. A meteor burned across the sky, a thin silver line that lingered for a moment and then dissipated. She had been the only one to see it. Patterson was still talking to the couple, his voice low, relaxing, authoritative. She saw another meteor, shorter in duration this time, its tail dull, over in a flash. Again, nobody mentioned it. She saw a light in the distance, shining white, brightening as it came out of the mistiness closer to the horizon. It looked like a satellite, although it was very white indeed. A voice she didn't recognise called everybody's attention to it. Patterson stopped talking, and they all watched. Molly was aware that she was part of a group, in sympathy, all watching this thing - whatever it was - as one.

The light moved slowly, in a straight line, heading towards the zenith. "Do you know it?" Patterson said. He was speaking to Kurt, of course.

Molly glanced across. Kurt looked at his watch, then back to the sky. "No, Richard, this one I don't know."

Molly lifted her eyes to the sky again, and followed the light. Just over halfway across the sky, the light suddenly vanished. There were gasps from the small crowd, and then, just as suddenly, the light flared again, before it sped across the star-studded dome above her and then vanished in an eye-blink. Excited chatter began. What had they seen?

"It was one of our visitors," Patterson said.

"This is so exciting," the male half of the couple said. "Who'd have thought we'd see a flying saucer on our first visit to Dereham?"

"Sometimes, visitors are so blessed," Patterson said. Molly noted the quasi-religious phrase, and the hint that the blessed couple were thus important, special, tied now into the events at Dereham.

"It felt so... friendly," the female half of the blessed couple said. "So full of... I don't know... joy... Like a dance, a dance of the spirit..."

Molly looked down and smiled. That had been a dull dance, she thought. *She probably has* Jonathan Livingstone Seagull *and* Be Here Now *and* Steppenwolf *on her shelves at home.*

The group began to talk about the light they had seen. Kurt didn't take part, she noticed. He listened. Molly considered the sighting. It was only a light in the sky, and really, you couldn't know anything other than that. Alien spaceship, or some kind of secret airplane, or... something else. You couldn't tell. Listening to the skywatchers, she realised that it was from such inconclusive evidence that webs of fancy were built. Molly continued to listen, as did Kurt. Patterson began reminiscing about similar things he had seen. The only odd thing about the sighting, Molly thought, was that the object had suddenly become visible again, and then accelerated across the sky before abruptly disappearing. Before that, the light had looked exactly like a satellite, although perhaps a little brighter than those she had seen before. If it was a satellite, Kurt claimed not to know its identity; but who knew what game he might be playing. Molly wondered how much longer she should stay. Nearly everybody here seemed to be a genuine skywatcher. Kurt, however, she suspected – of what, she wasn't yet sure.

*

The bell behind the bar rang for time. "We'll have to get a move on if we want to catch the train," Simon said.

"We've got ten minutes," Warren said. "Plenty of time."

"Why don't you come back to my house?' Jill said.

"Where is it again?' Warren asked.

"Foxton, remember? I've told you at least once. Do you know it? It about two miles out of town."

Simon knew it, even if Warren didn't. It was a pleasant little village between Southleigh and Dereham. It was the kind of place middle-class people lived. It was like Burnt Ashton to the north of Dereham, where Imogen and Jake lived. Yet, it was different to the other villages around Southleigh and Dereham – Downham, Chaldon, Upton, Northleigh, in any of which Anna might live. Those villages were a mixture of classes, poor and rich, farmers and lawyers, doctors and mechanics. Foxton, like Burnt Ashton, was quiet in the daytime, as everybody headed off to Bath, Bristol and Salisbury to their jobs. Foxton won Best Kept Village awards, had a pleasant village green, and a good primary school.

"Won't your parents mind?' Warren said.

"No, they won't mind. When you live in a village, you get used to friends staying over. There's a spare bed, and one of you can kip on the sofa. They might mind if one of you tried sneaking into my bedroom, and I might mind if *one* of you tried sneaking into my bedroom."

It struck Simon that perhaps Anna *did* live in Foxton. "Uh, Jill. Does, uh, Anna live there?"

"No, she doesn't, don't worry, and neither does Joan. She lives in Downham. Don't you know that?"

"No. I know very little about her, I suppose. It might amuse you to know that my friend Mark and I spent some time cruising around the villages last summer, trying to find her. He brought me over on his motorbike. We couldn't find her in the telephone book."

"Why couldn't you find her in the book? I've phoned her

sister, Angela, often enough. Unless they're ex-directory... No...
no, they're not, I had to look the number up once, when I lost
it."

"Well, I don't know. We looked but couldn't find her."

"Did you spell her surname right?"

"How hard can it be? She wrote it on my trousers." Simon
spelled it out. "L-E S-L-E-Y."

Jill laughed. "Well, I assumed you might have forgotten the S
at the end, rather than actually spelling the whole thing wrong.
Try E-D-W-A-R-D-S. Lesley is her–"

"So it is her sodding middle name! I did wonder, when I
couldn't find her in the phone book."

It was Warren's turn to laugh. "What the hell did you two ever
talk about?"

"Oh, I don't know," Simon said. "Nonsense. Frivolities. That's
why it was fun."

"It's about time," Jill said, "you told me what you and Anna
were up to."

Molly had been watching the sky for a while, looking for
shooting stars, and listening to Patterson. She thought she
might as well head back to the Lion; she might catch Simon
and Nick there, although it was getting close to last orders. Just
as she was about to say goodbye to Patterson, she noticed the
headlights of a car heading along the road to Copsehill. A
couple of minutes later, it arrived. Even before the driver had
switched off the engine and headlights, doors opened and the
passengers tumbled out. Excited voices overlapped each other.
Then, a woman's voice said, "Richard, is that you?"

"Yes. Is that Mary?"

"Yes, it is. I'm with Mike and the others."

A young woman passed Molly. Between the blue afterimages
from the headlights, Molly made out a young woman with a
mop of curly hair, dressed in hippie garb. Her friends followed.
They made for Patterson and gathered around him. Molly was

near to Mary; she could smell patchouli, possibly weed. Pot-smoking was of no concern to Molly – she had smoked a few joints herself over the years.

"Did you see it?" Mary asked. There was excitement in her voice.

"The light? Yes, we saw it. Where were you?"

"The other side of Derebury Hill," one of Mary's friends said. "At the layby below Manton Down."

"I know it," Patterson said.

"Well," Mary said, "We'd just started walking up the footpath from the layby to the top of Manton Down, when Tom said he thought he could hear something..."

"Yes," another voice said, which Molly guessed would be Tom. "Something the other side of the hedge, footsteps or something in the fields. It seemed to be following us up the path, you know, but... On the other side of the hedge..."

"It was spooky," Mary continued, wresting the narrative back from Tom. She was used to being the centre of attention, Molly could tell. "I thought I heard voices... Quiet, you know, like whispering..."

"Could you hear what the voices said?" one of Patterson's group asked.

"No," Mary said. "They were too quiet. I'm sure it was voices though. You know, the same way they sound when it's in a neighbour's garden... a few houses down... You know it's people talking, but you can't hear what they're saying."

Molly wondered if Mary really could be sure the sounds she heard were those of voices. The sounds might have been the wind through the hedgerow; she wondered what sounds rabbits made at night, or how sheep sounded when chewing grass. She had no idea, and wondered if Mary could really distinguish all the sounds of the night.

"Did anybody see... a figure? An entity?" Patterson asked.

Tom spoke again. "I might have seen something. A head, eyes, through a gap in the hedge." Tom looked at Mary. She nodded.

There was a faint smile on Mary's lips; encouragement for Tom. He seemed to need little encouraging: there was a boy head-over-heels.

"And then the light flew over," Mary said. "We all stopped to look at it. And when it disappeared, I went all... dizzy. And the voices seemed to stop. And then it flared up again, and everything was quiet. I couldn't hear the voices anymore."

"Interesting," Patterson said.

"We thought," Mike began shyly, "that the aliens might have teleported... back to the ship..."

"That's just what I was thinking," Patterson said.

"We spent a while searching the fields for ... well, something, but then we thought we should come here and see what you knew."

Everybody began talking again, about the voices, and the light. Jan still said nothing, but listened. Molly decided she'd had enough excitement for one night, and she felt cold. She said goodnight, and began walking back down Lavington Road, into town. Walking soon warmed her up. She unzipped her leather jacket. She couldn't deny that what had seen had been slightly odd. The light had disappeared, and then reappeared. Mary and her friends were excited about something. All of these occurrences had become intertwined, and tied everybody on the hill together. Even she had felt the urge to belong. Peta had felt like this, Molly realised. And because of the abuse Peta had suffered as a child, and the loneliness she had felt as a teenager, that desire to be part of the group would have been keen; she would have wanted to be excited and to share with them. She would have felt all of this more strongly than Molly had.

Molly looked at her watch. The sudden arrival of the car, and the stories of its occupants, had delayed her departure. If Simon and Nick had been in the pub, they would have gone by now. She walked slowly back to town, imagining how Peta must have enjoyed life here, even with that bastard Archie. Peta would have felt welcomed; and she would have had something to give back in return – her warmth, her kindness, and her smile. Molly missed Peta's smile. She wondered if she would find it in the town if she stayed long enough. She walked beneath the avenue of trees near Red Post Farm. The leaves chuckled gently in the wind. She should talk to Edge about the UFO – and about Kurt. A photograph of Kurt would help. She wondered if Simon or Nick had a camera. She should talk to them about the UFO. Edge might be in intelligence, but when it came to flying saucers, the locals had the experience.

It had taken an hour to walk to Foxton. Simon had described his platonic relationship with Anna. Warren had interjected amusing and sarcastic comments. Jill had explained what she knew about Anna and Joan. Then Simon had rounded off the story with the sorry tale of his rejection at the Fresher's Ball.

"And you think Joan has something to do with it?' Jill said.

"Yes, I do, but I don't know what," Simon said.

"I think Joan fancies him," Warren said. "It would explain everything."

Jill laughed. "It seems like a lot of girls fancy you."

Simon sighed. "Yes, but I never seem to realise it. It always takes other people to point it out to me."

"Well, we'll see if that's *invariably* the case."

They had arrived at Jill's parents' house. It was, as Simon had expected it to be, a large and undoubtedly expensive stone-built house, that had once been a manse or rectory. Jill opened the gate, and a cat slinked out of the hedge that bounded the garden. It regarded Simon's baseball boots warily as it tried to reach Jill's legs.

Jill bent down, clicking her fingers and making noises to attract the cat. "Come here, Tabby, come on." They stopped walking. The cat sidled over to Jill, wound its way between her legs, and then Jill picked it up.

Warren stroked the cat's head. "Tabby? Funny name for a tortoiseshell."

"Her full name is Tabitha. She's our second cat. Mum named the first one, and I was allowed to choose the name for this beauty. The minute I saw she was a tortoiseshell, I knew I had to name her Tabitha. I knew she'd be called Tabby all the time, you see. I liked a good paradox, even then."

"How old were you?" Warren said.

"Eleven."

"Bit of a smartarse kid, then?"

Jill rubbed her cheek on Tabitha's head, and smiled. "Oh yes, I certainly was."

Tabitha wriggled, and Jill allowed the cat to jump down on the path. Jill opened the front door, and the cat followed, brave now between the alien legs behind Jill into the hallway. Tabitha miaowed, and skittered through an open door into a dark room on the left. Simon presumed that it was the kitchen, or, at least, led to the kitchen. Tabitha had caught the scent of something good. Jill opened a door on the right, and led Warren and Simon into the lounge, where her parents were still awake, reading, listening to what sounded to Simon like Radio 3. Jill introduced them. Her father stood and shook their hands. Simon wondered if Warren found that as peculiar as he did. No friend's father had ever stood and shook his hand before. Jill's father was, Simon supposed, *proper*. And, of course, Simon realised, he and Warren were no longer simply teenage students. They were at that crux point between teenage and adulthood; they were, to all intents and purposes, adults who could now drink and vote. Simon supposed he would have to get used to what he still regarded as adults and respectable people shaking his hand. Jill asked her parents if it would be all right for Warren and Simon to stay the night. Her parents said that of course it would be. Jill led Warren and Simon to the kitchen, where she made coffee. They sat around the small table and talked.

An hour later, Jill's parents went to bed. Jill said she'd be back in a minute and disappeared to her bedroom. When she returned, she said, "Let's take a stroll around the garden."

Jill led them through the back door of the kitchen, and into the large garden. They walked down a path, under the moonlight. At the end of the path was a low wall; here, they looked out over a field. Jill climbed up and sat on the wall. Simon and Warren followed, and then they all sat on the wall. Jill took a small tin out of her pocket, and some Rizlas. "Could I have one of your cigarettes, please, Warren?" Jill asked.

"I thought you didn't smoke," Warren said.

Jill shook the tin in front of Warren's eyes. "Grass."

She expertly rolled a joint, and lit it up. After a couple of tokes, she offered it to Simon. Simon shook his head. He didn't smoke dope. Simon wasn't surprised when Warren took the offered joint and drew deeply on it. Warren smoked grass, but only if offered to him by somebody else – he couldn't afford to buy it. He handed the joint back to Jill, and then hopped down into the field and sat on the grass, his back against the stone wall.

"Nice night," Jill said.

Simon looked at the sky above him. It was the same as it had been all day, except a waxing moon had replaced the sun. Small cumulus drifted across the bright stars. Jill patted his knee. "I shouldn't worry about Anna. Something will happen. I'm sure of it."

"Oh, I'm not. I have no idea what's going on. It still seems so freaky at the moment."

"Well, forget about her for tonight. Relax in this bucolic field with me. Although there is no *boukolos* about tonight. Actually, there are no bovine, either."

"You're losing me," Simon said.

Jill laughed. "Sorry, I'm rambling." She offered the joint to Warren, who took two more drags and then closed his eyes before handing the joint back to her.

Jill looked down at Warren. "I think we're going to lose him soon."

"Well, he did have a few to drink tonight," Simon said.

"Yes, he did. I suspect he was trying to get me drunk."

"Aren't you?"

"A bit squiffy, I suppose, but I didn't keep up with Warren despite his best efforts." Jill looked at Warren. "Well, when I've finished this joint, we'll get Warren inside the house. Then you can play Scrabble with me."

"Fair enough."

Jill sucked on the joint, and blew a sweet-smelling cloud into the still air.

She leaned down towards Warren again to offer the joint, but he'd crashed out. "Pathetic," she said. She turned to Simon instead. "Do you love Anna?"

"Love might be too strong. We never got together. I fancied her, yes, and I made efforts to find her over the summer."

"But you didn't know her very well."

Simon shrugged. "I knew her well enough."

"You didn't know her surname, and you didn't know where she lived. It's all very romantic, I'm sure, but it's not *real*, is it?"

"Not real? It seemed real enough last term."

Jill turned to him, and held out her hand, ready for Simon to shake it. Simon was perplexed, but did so. "Hi," Jill said. "My name is Jill Smith. Jill Mary Smith. My surname is bland, but I am not. As you can see, I live here in this pleasant middle-class village, with middle-class parents, who have encouraged my education and support me in whatever I want to do next. They wouldn't like to know that I smoke dope, but I do. They probably have their suspicions, though, and my smoking it here on this wall and keeping it hidden in a tin under my bed under my old dolls is all part of the game. I don't really know what I want to do with my life, but I do want to earn money for a while. Perhaps I'll go to Uni after a couple of years, perhaps not. I listen to all kinds of music, including classical and jazz. I like reading, and music. I play the piano passingly well. I have a sister who is younger than me, her name is Beth. You've met the cat, Tabitha. I want to learn to drive, and that's one reason why I want to earn money. I dye my hair blonde, as I believe it suits me. I like Laura Ashley, Indian sandals, and kaftans. In the summer, I tend not to wear a bra." She laughed. "An interesting tit-bit for you there. Talking of breasts, my favourite food is chicken. I've had four boyfriends, and slept with one of them. They don't hang around, though, as I tend to intimidate them. I don't know why. I think of myself as intelligent and attractive, and have no problems with self-confidence or self-esteem, as I'm sure you've gathered by now. I hate football, but find watching cricket oddly soothing, though I'm not sure I understand all the rules. I listen to it on the television while I read. My favourite author is J D Salinger. However, I read all kinds of things. My favourite films are *M.A.S.H* and *One Flew Over the Cuckoo's Nest*. I have a bad temper." She paused, stubbed out the joint, then stood and ground it into the damp grass beneath the wall. "Now, tell me what you know about Anna."

"Uh." Simon was nonplussed. "She's cute and funny."

"Like me, then. Except you now know something about me. I'm *real*, with a *real* life. Not an anima figure."

Jill bent down and shook Warren. Warren woke with some incoherent mumblings. When he realised who was waking him, he said, "Oh, hello darling, fancy meeting you here."

"Don't you *darling* me," Jill said. "Time for you to go and crash out. Unless you fancy playing Scrabble.

"No, Scrabble, boring," Warren mumbled. "Need kip, was all comfy until you woke me. Need piss too."

"I'll show you where the bathroom is. Follow me." Jill climbed over the wall. Simon turned and slid off the wall onto the path. Warren clumsily clambered over the wall and stood unsteadily in the garden. The three of them walked slowly back to the house, Jill leading the way. When they entered the house, Simon asked if he could phone his parents. Jill looked at Warren, who unsteadily leaned against a kitchen worktop, his eyes half-closed, smiling beatifically. Jill put the kettle on, and then took Warren's hand. "Come along, young man."

"Are you taking me to bed?' Warren mumbled.

"Yes, where you shall sleep alone. Try not to puke on the carpet, my parents will not be amused. If you feel, you know, that way inclined, I advise a straight-fingered jab to the tonsils while in the toilet."

"Night, mate," Warren said to Simon as he trailed Jill up the stairs. "See you in the morning." He bestowed a sleepy wink on Simon, although his right eye barely opened again at the completion of the gesture. After talking to his father, Simon went back to the kitchen and sat at the small pine table.

Jill soon returned, carrying the Scrabble box. "You set it up while I make the coffee."

By the time Jill sat down at the table Simon had set the game up. The board was open, and the tile racks on the proper sides of the board. Simon held out the bag of tiles to her. "Choose a letter." Jill removed out a tile. Simon put his hand into the bag, stirred the tiles around and chose one.

"I'll show you mine if you show me yours," Jill said.

Simon looked at the tile in his hand and held it up between his fingers. "U," he said.

"And so it should be," Jill said. She held her tile up to Simon, and smiled. "Snap. *U* too. Right back at you."

"We'd better choose again."

"No, instead you should contemplate the coincidence of us both selecting that most euphonious letter, while you go first. You're the guest."

"Oh, okay, since you put it that way."

Simon selected his seven tiles, then Jill hers. "I'm very good, you know," Jill said.

"I'm sure you are." Simon concentrated on his letters. Then he wondered what Jill had meant about contemplating the coincidence of euphonious letters. Simon could see various opening words, including *vole*.

"I've got rubbish letters," Jill said. "Too many vowels."

She moved her letters around, setting them clacking on the

plastic rack. "See, take a look at this." She turned the rack around.

Simon put his hands in front of his eyes. "No, don't show me, it'll make it too easy."

"Well, in some ways it might," Jill said. "But you still won't beat me at Scrabble."

Simon opened his fingers and glanced quickly at the smiling Jill, and then at the rack of tiles. *uneedme*.

"Peekaboo," Jill said, then turned the rack back towards her.

She was right, Simon, thought, she did have a lot of Es. She at least though had the words *dune, dene, mend, mud, deem*, and, obviously, *need*. Simon put down the word *vole*. Jill reached over and transposed the *l* and *v*. "Better, don't you think?"

"It doesn't get me any more points."

"It does on my private scorecard."

Simon shook his head, smiling. Jill was being mysterious and cryptic, but he thought that she was probably slightly stoned. She put down her letters, and made *need* and *loved*.

"Hey, you wouldn't have got that with *vole*."

"Don't worry about that. It's what you notice as the game progresses that's important."

What is she on about? Simon wondered. *Never play Scrabble with somebody who's stoned.* Then he remembered the tiles she had shown him. *uneedme*. Love. Need. Loved. U and U.

"You'd have got more points for *deem*," Simon said.

"Not on my private scorecard, I wouldn't."

She sipped her coffee, and looked across the top of her mug, again favouring him with her big, smiling, cornflower blue eyes.

It was two in the morning, and Jill had, of course, won at Scrabble. She'd had two seven-letter words, and beaten Simon by 75 points. She had now gone to make another coffee. He had been thinking about college. When his course finished, his involvement with Anna would also finish, as would all the hopes he'd ever had of something happening between them. He imagined that she would be permanently etched in his memory, whatever happened in the future. What had happened – the nothing that had happened – had been intense. The door to the lounge opened, and he was brought out of his empty reverie by a shape that was tall and blonde, bringing him back to this present.

Jill smiled at him as she handed him his mug. The mug had a big red heart on it. "Ah. Still wool-gathering, of course." She sat next to him on the settee, close, her thigh against his.

"I wonder how Warren is?' Simon said.

"Dreaming of revenge, I should think."

"Why?"

Simon noticed a momentary furtive look cross Jill's face. "He's had his Anna moment, you might say."

Simon was puzzled. "Now you've confused me."

"Well, imagine I was Anna, and he was you, then..."

"No, I can't do that, it's too... weird. Spell it out for me."

Jill leaned in towards Simon, putting a hand on his leg as she did so. "He asked me out. I rebuffed him."

Simon was unsure why she felt the need to whisper, as if it were some secret. "When did he ask you out?"

"Tonight. While you were making the mark of Zorro.

Simon was surprised. There had been instances earlier in the evening when he and Warren had been alone. But Warren had said nothing. Simon remembered that, after he had been cut by Anna, he hadn't mentioned anything about it until Warren had asked how the date had gone. Simon understood how Warren must feel. He must be as disappointed as Simon had once had felt. "I thought it was obvious along that you didn't want to go out with him."

"Well, I thought so too."

"You dazzled us with your charm."

"Nice to know I have some."

Simon fiddled with the teaspoon in the saucer. "Of course you do. Don't be so... modest." He laughed. "It doesn't become you."

She held her mug in front of her face, and looked at Simon over the top of it. Her eyes seemed to contain caution, rather than the twinkle with which she usually favoured him. Simon waited for her to speak again. Her hands curled around the mug. Simon had noticed before that her fingers were long, delicate; he imagined she could play the piano more than passingly well. She smiled at him, and then looked down. Her blonde hair fell forward, masking her face for a moment. "The chances are, Warren is dreaming a lexicon, containing words like *cheat*, *disloyal*, *cuckold*, and phrases like *back-stabber* and *fickle friend*." She smiled at him, but the smile was thin.

"Why? Why would he be doing that?"

"Well, I told him none of this was your fault, and that you were so dense you probably didn't know what was happening... What had happened."

Simon was bewildered. Jill was talking in riddles, making no sense. Why was he dense? And what had it to do with Warren? "What *has* happened?"

Simon was surprised by a laugh.

"You see," Jill said. "I told him you were dense. How many signals can I give you, Si?"

"Signals? What signals?"

Jill laughed again. "You need me. I am real. Love and need."

Simon remembered the Scrabble game. "Yes, you were good at Scrabble, but you cheated by changing my *vole* to *love*."

"You needed love, Si. You still do. Mine."

Simon realised that Jill was trying to tell him something, and that *something* was now so obvious he didn't wonder she had called him dense. Nick had told him, Mark had told him, and even Gaz had told him about Jill, but still he'd found it too unlikely to contemplate. He leaned back into the cushions on the sofa. He imagined there was surprise on his face. "Warren is pissed off because you fancy *me*. How did he know?

"When he asked to go out with me, I didn't say, *no, I fancy Si*. He just knew. Just like you know... now. *Finally*."

"Yes, now."

Jill took her hand from his thigh, and took his free hand. "So what do you say, Si?"

He thought of Anna, and the way she had cut him. And then, following instantly from the feeling that arose in his chest at that thought, he remembered Anna as she had been before the summer, the Anna with whom he had laughed and joked. But, since then – and it was limned in his memory – he had been cut. He looked at Jill. She, too, was funny. She was bright. She was pretty, tall, and kind of sexy. He was eighteen. Was he really going to continue to fret over Anna, when Anna would be out of his life forever when they reached next year's summer break? Did he want to turn into Mark, forever locked in adoration of something he couldn't have, forever missing opportunities for love and fun and excitement?

Jill put her mug on the floor, then sat up and looked at Simon. "What's it to be, Si?' Jill spoke quietly. "Reality or fantasy? Me or a dream? Jill Mary Smith, or Anna Who?"

Anna *was* pretty. Petite. How she and Simon had laughed together in the spring, and revelled in each other's company. At least, he had revelled in hers. The events this term had made him unsure whether she had ever revelled in his. And now there was Jill. What she had said was true; she *was* real. He had found out more about her in two weeks than he had in four months with Anna. He hated to think it, to compare them in this way. He had no doubt that Anna was prettier than Jill. Yet, he did find Jill interesting, and exciting. Jill had a certain sultriness. She amused him, as Anna once had. He admired her intelligence. He had admired her legs more than once. He liked the way her eyes smiled at him. Why not, he thought, go with this reality? It was exciting in its own way. Nothing was going to happen between him and Anna. He could see nothing, between now and the end of their time at Southleigh College, but a continuing exchange of looks, glances, and meetings of eyes that he wouldn't understand, and which would never be translated for him by the only person who could translate them.

Jill still held his hand gently. She had been looking around the room, but not at him, allowing him to think. He didn't quite know what he was doing yet. Still, he put his empty coffee cup on the table next to the settee, and put his forefinger under Jill's chin, turned her head gently towards him and tilted her face up. Following impulse only, allowing thought to fly his sleepy head, he leaned into Jill and put his lips gently on hers. He had partly surprised himself, and drew back slightly and looked into her blue eyes. There was something in those blue eyes, a smiling sparkle that made him smile in return and kiss her again, longer this time, mouths opening and tongues touching. He stopped kissing for a moment and again moved his head back far enough to see those eyes. "It looks like it's you." He smiled, and kissed her again, urgently, his hands in her hair, sliding across her cheeks to her neck, shoulders and arms. Slowly, together, they sank into the cushions of the settee.

The hitman was paddling in the sea, a mile or so along the beach from Bournemouth, at two-thirty in the morning. Tim Manley liked a walk after he came back from the pub, or the night club, or wherever he had been, and he particularly liked to stroll along the beach from his hotel towards Canford Cliffs and then back again. The beach was deserted this late on a September night, but Manley never walked with a bodyguard. The hitman wasn't surprised. Manley would think himself hard, a person not to be messed with. Up against most lads out in Bournemouth tonight, Manley would be right. The hitman had followed Manley in the street earlier today, and Manley had the look of a proper hard man. He had the walk, the swagger. He was not as mad and bad as his brother Tom, but still, you would know not to mess with him if you met him in the dark. Unfortunately for Tim Manley he was about to meet somebody as hard as he was. Manley was also a homosexual, which was why the hitman was paddling in the water in a dress suit, as if he had had just come back from some swanky night club, and had, like Manley, fancied a stroll along the beach.

He had waited here since midnight. He was cold now. The breeze off the sea was cool. He would have already left, had the notes provided by the client not told him that Manley would certainly be here, that he passed by here every night, alone, whether he picked up somebody that night or not. The notes had been vague about the time, however. The hitman pulled the jacket of his dress suit tight around him, and folded his arms across it. He looked at the moon, and tried not to shiver. Small cumulus occasionally drifted across the sky. Today had been a pleasant day, one of few such days since the end of summer, and the night of the thunderstorms. Tomorrow was set fair, and he would see his son. He was looking forward to it. It would have been nice to see Peter today, but he had needed to work out the lie of the land instead.

He had brought to Bournemouth with him the tools of his trade: the knives, the guns, the garrottes. He had, in the pocket of his suit, a flick knife, but he didn't intend using this to kill Manley. He thought it always best to make the death look natural, if possible. As well as the knife, he had with him a quart of brandy. Manley was partial, so he had learned from his notes, to brandy. Waves slid coldly around his ankle. He was patient, used to waiting in this game. If only he didn't feel so cold. He was losing heat out of his feet, he realised, so moved backwards out of the water. At that moment, a larger wave washed around his standing ankle, and the foot he had raised met a small ridge of sand. He fell down on his behind in the cool water. He cursed under his breath. Then he heard laughter, and a voice behind him. "Let me help you, sir."

A hand reached out to pull him up. He grabbed it, was pulled up, and found himself face to face with Tim Manley. He couldn't help but admire the stealth with which Manley must have moved. But then the waves had been washing around him. Water always did make a good cover for other sounds. And he hadn't looked along the beach for a little while.

"Thank you," he said. This was the moment, he thought, to offer Manley a drink. It would be natural. He wanted Manley to drink as much as possible. He could make Manley drink, of course, but he didn't want to, as too much of it would dribble over his suit and shirt. That might look suspicious, later, after Manley had been found.

"Drink?"

"What's your poison?" Manley said.

The hitman took the quart bottle from his jacket pocket. "A small but warm bottle of Martell." He handed the bottle to Manley. Manley unscrewed the top and took a swig, then handed the bottle back to him.

"What are you doing out here at this time of night?" Manley said.

"I've been out clubbing. My... friend... we... fell out. So I came down here to get some air." Then the hitman put the bottle to his mouth, but kept his lips closed. It was easy to pretend to drink in the dark. He offered the bottle back to Manley, who took another large swig.

"Where is your... friend?" Manley said.

The hitman walked back up the beach, away from the sea, and sat on the cold sand. "He went back to our hotel room. I expect he's asleep by now. He didn't appear too troubled by what happened... between us."

"Oh dear, it was nothing... serious, I hope?"

"No, I think we shall... kiss and make up."

"Is he... bona... then, in that way?"

He knew enough Polari to understand. It might be homosexual cant, but it was also thieving cant and fairground cant. He'd picked up some of it over the years. He offered the bottle to Manley again. When he took the bottle back, he held it up to the moon, could see that nearly a third of the brandy had been drunk already, and none of it by him. Manley would soon be feeling the effects of it, on top of whatever else he had already drunk tonight.

"He's usually a bona omi, but tonight he got a bit jealous... This other omi came and chatted to me, you know... I was just looking at him, but..."

"You and your friend, are you... exclusive?"

"He thinks we are, but..."

"Not you?"

"Well..."

The hitman felt Manley's hand on his knee. Whatever was going to happen would have to happen soon, otherwise Manley would take things too far and then... Well, then things would move apace anyway, but he would rather he was in control of events. He passed the bottle to Manley. "This should help warm you up," he said. "Take a big swig if you like. I've got another one in my other pocket."

"I do like a good brandy," Manley said.

The hitman was gratified to see Manley pull hard from the bottle. When he took the bottle back, he stood quickly, and walked down to the sea's edge. He looked back at Manley. "Come over here and get your shoes and socks off," he said. "Get your lallies in the water."

"You're on," Manley said. When he stood, he wobbled. "Fuck me," he said, and fell down onto the sand again. He tried again. Slowly, clumsily, and with a great deal of effort, he stood, brushed down his trousers, and made his way towards the hitman. "I've had a few tonight already," Manley said. "This walk was supposed to clear my head."

"Don't worry, you'll feel peaceful soon," the hitman said, quietly.

Manley put an arm around his shoulders. "Is that a promise?"

"Oh yes." The hitman looked around him. The dark beach appeared to be empty. The roads were quiet. There was nobody around as far he could tell. Now would be a good time to do it. He passed the bottle to Manley one last time. "Not much left in there. You finish it off while I open the other one."

Manley did. The hitman could feel Manley swaying next to him. He shrugged off Manley's arm and walked further out into the sea.

Manley laughed. "Hey, where are you going?"

"I'm feeling a bit crazy," he said. "Aren't you?"

"But your suit, sir!"

"Oh, fuck the suit." He adopted what he thought was a reasonable come-hither look. "Why don't you come over here? What's your name?"

"Tim. I'm Tim. Tim Manley."

"I know that name don't I?"

"Perhaps. I'm notorious, ain't I?' Manley slurred his words now.

"How notorious? Why don't you come here and show me how notorious you can be."

Manley came over, obviously finding it hard to stand against the waves, laughing as he staggered. The hitman tried to make his response to Manley's embrace as natural as possible, as if hugging a man was something he often did. He rested his head on Manley's shoulder and took one last look around. He could see nobody – no people and no cars. The lights in the windows of the houses and hotels were mostly off, and where they were not, the windows were empty. Manley kissed his neck. "What's your name?"

The hitman whispered it into Manley's ear.

Manley turned his head then, drunk, confused, and looked into the hitman's eyes. "Haven't have I heard that name before?"

"Oh, you won't have heard..."

"Shush." Manley drunkenly put his fingers to his lips. "Archie. Archie Conn. I've heard... I've heard of you, ain't I? I've... Oh, yes, dear old Len. You.. you were... you were..." Manley frowned in the moonlight. "You were fucking trouble..." Then his eyes went wide. "Archibald Franklin fuckin' Conn!"

Death

17

Shit. I should have been more careful. Archie felt a wave rising behind him.

"What the fuck are you...' Manley began, but as the wave rose between them Archie launched himself forward, taking Manley with him. Manley was beneath him when they crashed into the water. Manley's mouth was open, as if he had been about to say something, or to curse or shout, but nothing ever came out. His open mouth went beneath the water. Archie's head also went into the cool sea. He took his arms from behind Manley's back and placed them over Manley's face. Archie came up for air. Manley didn't. His arms and legs thrashed in the water. He was strong, and fit. But Archie was stronger, fitter, younger, and, most importantly, on top. Manley managed to get his head above the water just once, and Archie felt fists beating against his back and waist. Archie forced the head beneath the water again, and shrugged off the blows. Those blows were, anyway, becoming feeble. Finally, they stopped; and then the thrashing ceased. Archie had been keeping one eye on the beach and seafront as he drowned his victim. A car had passed along the road, but the driver would never have seen him, out here in the dark water.

Archie continued to sit on the dead body for a little while longer, just to be sure. The empty brandy bottle floated in the water beside them. Archie grabbed it, and put it in Tim Manley's jacket pocket. Manley's head bobbed in the waves, the nose sometimes breaking the water, his hair waving like seaweed. Archie bent down, looked closely at Manley's face. It showed some contusions, but Archie wasn't overly concerned. A coroner would think Manley a drunk who had fallen over once or twice, and then finally fallen into the sea. The important point, and what Archie was most pleased about, was that he hadn't needed to use the knife. He just wished he hadn't used his real name. That had been stupid. Manley was dead now, so couldn't talk – but what if he had managed to get away? The wind caught Archie, and he shivered. He grabbed the scruff of Manley's jacket, and began to swim out to sea. Archie was a strong swimmer, and knew he could tow Manley a good quarter of a mile or so.

When Archie reached the sand again, he was exhausted, and not entirely sure where he was. He had drifted with the currents while he'd been swimming. He rested for a few moments, before lifting himself up, and identified landmarks – a hotel, the pier, streetlamps. He knew now where he was. He stood on tired legs, and made his way down the beach, towards the dry clothes he had hidden in a bag in a waste-bin. He passed the spot where he had met Manley. He looked around, but could see nothing incriminating. A good night's work, he thought. Tonight he would drive over to Poole, sleep in his car, and then come back tomorrow to see Peter.

A motorbike revved its engine on one of the dark streets. It reminded him of something, something he'd been thinking about earlier in the day. He rubbed a sandy hand over his face. He felt tired. Then he remembered. He'd been wondering why the motorbike he'd seen yesterday – at the garage, and then in the lay-by – had seemed so familiar. And then he remembered Nick and his friends.

18

Gaz sat with Simon and Mark in Lord Parks' Room in the Wool Hall, where Mark's drawings were on display. There were only three other people in the small room, quietly viewing the pictures. Another week had gone by. Little had happened. They had all met up a couple of times at The White Lion for a drink. Simon had continued to suffer the thousand small cuts applied by Anna and Joan, but, now he had kissed Jill, and thought he no longer cared. Nick had whined about living in Dereham. Chrissie had used Mark. Gaz had stolen a small transistor radio from Currys, and one or two small items from other shops. Their lives appeared to be following the usual grooves.

Gaz drank a mug of tea Mark had made him. The fee they had paid for the room at least covered unlimited cups of tea. Gaz glanced around the walls. The pictures Simon and Nick had managed to frame looked good, but nobody had bought one yet. Mark had sold two unframed drawings, both of them the scribbled abstracts of Simon doing his tai chi. Mark had taken photographs of his pictures on the wall, and of some of the visitors - quite a few of Chrissie, naturally, when she had shown her support.

Simon broke the silence. "Anna gave me a look yesterday," he said. "It seemed to say quite a lot. It was such a breakthrough that I had to smile at her. And she smiled back." Simon frowned, and then blew over his own mug of tea.

"I don't know why you're worrying about her," Gaz said. "Bang Jill. She wants you."

Mark snorted. "Always blunt and to the point, Gaz."

It was Saturday again, a week since Simon had stayed over at Jill's. Gaz had unfortunately, he thought, been present when

Simon had described to Nick what had happened during his visit to Southleigh, the puzzling Scrabble game, the kissing. Nick hadn't been surprised. Jill's intentions had been obvious to him, if not to Simon. So, Jill fancied Simon. Gaz didn't understand it. The boy appeared to be a sex-god. Rather than revelling in it, Simon appeared to be even more confused than when he'd only had Anna to worry about, the poor boy. And then, from what Simon said, perhaps this Joan fancied him as well. Yet the person he wanted to fancy him did not, it seemed. He had Jill, though. She was pretty, Simon said, she was bright and funny. Gaz was fed up with hearing about relationship shit. All they seemed to talk about was women and Nick's frustration at being stuck in town. "Look, Anna doesn't want you," Gaz said. "So forget about her. Bang Jill, for god's sake."

One of the visitors to the room, a woman, turned and looked at Gaz.

"I would," Simon said. "But..."

"But what? If you're not careful, you'll turn into Mark, always dreaming about what he can't have."

Mark laughed. "That *is* a danger."

Gaz sighed theatrically. "Yeah, tell him what *you* were doing last night."

Mark narrowed his eyes at Gaz, and then looked at Simon. "Talking to Chrissie, of course. Being her counsellor, giving her a shoulder to cry on, because she'd had another row with Jake."

"You see," Gaz said. "He still *wants* Chrissie, still *yearns* for her. After two years! How long will you be whining about Anna? You'll be just the like him, you'll see. "

Simon looked down at his half-empty mug. "I like Jill, I really do. But... Anna has been... well, looking at me... a lot over the last week. At first, when she, you know, cut me, she wouldn't look at me at all. When she looked at me in The Vine Tree last week, there was... Something..."

"Are you sure you're not just imagining it?' Mark said. "Still hoping?"

234

Simon shook his head. "No, I don't think so. When she looked at me yesterday it seemed so... meaningful."

Gaz's laugh was sarcastic. "You *are* beginning to sound like Mark."

"I don't want to be like Mark," Simon said. He looked at Mark. "Sorry."

Mark shrugged. "I know how pathetic I am."

Simon sipped his tea. "Oh, I don't know. Perhaps I should forget about Anna. I do have Jill. After all, Anna could have said something if she wanted, she could have apologised for cutting me, you know, could've come over and talked to me again, just like she always did? I would have forgotten her snub."

Mark smiled knowingly. "So what about Joan?"

"Yeah," Simon said. "That's a conundrum in itself. I'm sure Joan is at the root of it, whatever *it* is. What she wants, why she's doing it, I don't know."

Gaz swigged at his tea, and clattered the mug back onto the table. "Bloody relationships. Who needs 'em."

The same woman looked across again, disapproval on her face, and then walked out.

Simon looked across at Mark and raised an eyebrow. "Well, somebody spends a lot of time wanting to go down The Swan, that den of smooths and spivs. And, we can only think of one reason why that should be."

Gaz looked from Simon to Mark. He was amused, but didn't show it. "Oh, yes? And what would that be?"

"Well, Janet, we thought."

"That slag? You must be joking."

"Now, now," Mark said. "That's not the way to talk about your true love."

"Hah!" A wry smile played on Gaz's lips.

"We thought you'd say something like that, to be honest," Simon said. "We thought you'd call her some name or other. We knew you'd put her down. You are, after all, Gaz."

Mark laughed. "We think that's how you'd display your love."

Gaz held back sly laughter. "Hah!" he said again. "And why Janet? Why not Wendy, or Julie, or..."

"Well," Simon said. "Julie is out of your league."

"And out of yours, it seems," Gaz said.

"You did, of course, snog Janet at the party at Mark's last Christmas. And you did talk about her for a couple of days afterwards. Which for you is quite something."

"Well, yeah, she is cute. But... a relationship? Come on, I see you and Mark making tits of yourself and think, *there but for the grace of God...*"

Mark surveyed the now empty room, and then said. "But the evidence continues to pile up. We know Janet likes The Swan. Stuart told me that it's her favourite drinking hole. I also had a chat with Imogen last weekend. She saw you going into The Swan on Saturday." Mark looked at Gaz triumphantly. "Worm your way out of that."

"Well, what can I say?' Gaz said. He knew there was a small smile on his lips, and he knew Simon would notice. He knew, though, that they would never guess what was happening.

Simon had noticed the smile, but misconstrued it. "Before you do try to worm your way out of it, I'll add one more piece of incriminating evidence. Who did I see coming out of Top Shop last Saturday? And who claimed to be buying a present for his sister? You foxed me at the time, but I've since confirmed with my learned friend Lord Nick that Laura's birthday is indeed in July. So why were you in Top Shop? We put it to you, Gary Robinson, that you *were* shopping for a present, but in truth, you were shopping for a present for your beloved, Janet. How do you answer that?"

Gaz rattled his mug on the table. "I'm empty."

"Don't change the subject," Mark said.

Gaz smiled down at his mug. He was a silent for a few moments. Finally, he said, "Yes, okay, you've got me bang to rights. I fancy Janet, okay?"

"Splendid!' Mark said. "And how long has this been going on?"

"Oh, a few weeks." Gaz said.

"Why haven't you said anything?"

"Well, we're still at the flirting stage. It's been nine months since Christmas, and we were both drunk then, so we're just getting to know each other again, really."

"Bring her up the Lion sometime," Mark said.

"Or you could come down The Swan."

"The Swan? You're joking, right?' Mark had always felt as strongly about The Swan as Nick. Simon didn't care so much.

"Well, Janet thinks the Lion is a den of drug-taking hippies who listen to weird music. Which it is."

"Oh well, I'm sure we'll all meet up at a party."

"I'm sure we will." Gaz looked at Mark and Simon, favouring them with what he thought an amused but mysterious look. Mark ignored him and began counting the small amount of money in the Tupperware container that served as his till. Simon smiled as if he knew something. Yet what could he know? "Right," Gaz said. "I'm off to do something more useful with my life." He stood.

"We'll miss your optimistic chit-chat," Mark said.

Gaz nodded at the money in the container. "Don't forget, ten per cent of that is mine. Because I won't." He turned to go. Molly Shepherd entered the room. "Hi," Gaz said as he passed her. He wondered if Molly too fancied Simon.

Molly was drinking tea with Simon and Mark when Nick entered Lord Parks' Room. She saw him glance quickly around the room he had helped set up yesterday.

"I see one of the framed drawings has gone," Nick said.

Molly bent down and picked up one of Mark's drawings from beside her chair. She held it up to Nick.

"Ah, the missing picture," he said. "You bought one, then."

Molly held it out at arm's length and looked at it. "Yes. Mark's good." She looked at Simon. "And it will remind me of this handsome fellah." She tousled Simon's hair. Simon blushed.

Nick smiled at Simon. "You really are rolling in it at the moment, aren't you?" he said.

Simon blushed again.

Nick sat on the edge of the table at which Molly and the others sat, being careful not to crease the smaller drawings there. He was carrying a newspaper.

"Do you want a cuppa?" Mark said.

Nick shook his head. "Have you seen this?" He unfolded the newspaper. *Manley Boy Found Dead* the headline shrieked.

"No," Mark said. "So a gangster's dead? And?"

Molly leaned forward a little, attempting to scan the print. "Which Manley?"

"What?" Nick said. "Oh, I don't know." He turned the paper towards him. "Um. Blah blah blah, London crime-lord Tim Manley."

"Shame it wasn't Tom," Molly said.

Mark looked at her. "You know them?"

"Only in a roundabout way. They're the Sweeney's territory, not mine."

"Because you're a spy," Simon said.

Molly nodded enthusiastically, a mischievous twinkle in her eye. "Yes, that's right, because I'm a spy." She looked at Nick. "How did he die?"

Nick scanned the newspaper article again. "It doesn't really say. They think he drowned. But foul play hasn't been ruled out."

"They'll probably never know."

"Will they care?" Simon asked.

"Yes, of course. One thing leads to another. If somebody killed him, then it was most likely gang-related. If it was, chances are a hitman was involved. If there was, then, well, if you can take down the hitman, he'll probably blab, and that will lead to somebody else. They won't find the hitman. They're usually good, and whoever it was, he's made it look like a drowning. When did they find him?"

"Thursday," Nick said.

"All bloated like a... bloater, I expect."

"But that's not the important point," Nick said. "Not for us anyway." He looked at Mark. "Guess where he was found."

Mark shrugged. "No idea, although I suppose this impinges on our lives in some oblique way."

"More than bloody oblique. Positively squiffy in its angular displacement. *Bournemouth*."

"Bournemouth?"

"Yeah, Bournemouth."

"Shit," Mark muttered.

Molly wondered at the relevance of Bournemouth. It obviously had significance to Mark and Nick. "Why does it matter so much to you where he was found?"

Nick explained how he had met a hitman, and how he and Mark had, the previous Saturday, followed a car they thought belonged to this hitman.

"Curious," Molly said. "But that proves nothing. It could be just a coincidence. He might be, as you said, a nutter."

"Yes, I know. Still, it's... rather... odd, isn't it?"

"I suppose it could be seen that way. This is rather an odd little town in many ways."

Nick ran his fingers through his short hair. "Yes, I suppose it is. Flying saucers, hitmen..." He looked at Molly and smiled. "Spies."

"What can we do, anyway?" Mark said.

Nick shrugged.

"I'd keep your noses out of it, if I were you," Molly said. "You don't know what you're getting involved with."

"I'm just inquisitive," Mark said.

Molly sipped at her tea. "Fair enough."

The door to the room opened, and Kurt came in with a woman.

"Ah, our Dutch skywatcher," Molly said quietly. "Who's that with him? His girlfriend?"

"Yes, that's Cathy," Nick replied. "Why do you want to know?"

"I'm just inquisitive, too."

Kurt walked around the room, studying each of Mark's pictures. Molly had already noted Mark's camera on the table in front of her. She assumed that Mark would already have set the shutter speed of the camera and the aperture of the lens to the values required for the room. She picked up the camera, feigning interest. "Oh, a Nikon F. These are expensive, aren't they?"

"Well, yes. But that one is very old, early sixties I think. Plus, I know the guy who runs the camera shop in town. He let me have it relatively cheap. Shame the lenses are so expensive."

Kurt was walking across to the table to look at the unframed pictures. Molly raised the camera to her eye, said "Hello, Kurt," and took a photo, quickly. She then slowed down, remembered she had to focus, felt for the knurling on the lens barrel, and focused on Kurt. She took two more photos. She smiled at his girlfriend, and then took two photographs of Cathy, just in case she wasn't simply some woman Kurt had picked up in his travels. The smile Kurt returned after he realised what Molly had done was forced. He didn't like to be photographed.

"Just some candids to mark this exhibition," Molly said, breezily, and forcing a smile that she knew would be most ingenuous and convincing.

"Oh, wow," Cathy said, "I must see them when they're developed." She smiled and looked at Molly. "You're new here aren't you? I haven't seen you before."

Interesting, thought Molly - straight in with a pertinent question. She wondered then if Kurt and Cathy were a team.

"Oh, I've been around and about," Molly said. She put her arm around Simon. "But mainly, I'm Simon's new girlfriend." Molly kissed Simon on the cheek. Molly was pleasantly surprised when he kissed her back, and said, "Aww, thanks, lovely."

"That's sweet," Cathy said. "I don't blame you. Simon has always been a good looking boy."

"Oh, I know," Molly said.

Kurt picked up one of Mark's drawings and bought it. "I like to support the local artists," he said. "Remember to let us see the snaps from the exhibition." *Schnaps.*

Kurt and Cathy walked across to the walls to look at a few more of Mark's framed pictures.

Mark whispered. "What the bloody hell was that about? You've wasted a load of my film on that hippie."

"Don't worry," Molly said quietly. "I can get the roll developed for free."

Mark brightened. "Oh, okay. If you could get some ten by eights of Cathy for my ... err... private collection, that would be... nice."

"I'm sure I can get some copies made."

Mark reached under some of the paper scattered around the desk and brought out two more rolls of film. "Can you do get these developed, too?"

Molly sighed theatrically. "I suppose so. But I need that roll of film out of your camera now."

"But," Mark spluttered, there's twenty frames still on this one."

"You're getting two and a half rolls of film developed for free, and some lovely eight by tens of Cathy. Stop complaining."

Nick leaned over and also spoke quietly. "But to get back to Mark's original question... what the bloody buggering hell was that about?"

"If I told you, I'd have to kill you. All of you."

"Well, all of them except me, surely" Simon said. He looked at Molly seriously. "Because, after all... You *love* me."

Molly laughed. "You *are* a lovely boy. I'll save *you*."

"Was that some of that spy stuff?" Nick said. "Is that why you're here?"

Molly looked innocent. "Whoever said I was a spy? I'm just looking for my sister."

"Yeah, yeah," Simon said.

Molly swigged down the last of her tea and grimaced, "Ugh, cold." She stood up. "Right. I'm off for a walk up Copsehill. I'm rather enjoying my holiday. I can see why my sister liked it so much here." As she stood, she picked up her picture. "Can I leave this here with you boys?" Mark nodded, and took the picture from her. "I'll get your photos to you, Mark. I'll see you guys soon."

She turned at the sound of expensive shoes on the polished wooden floor of the room. A short, portly man had just entered, and was looking around him. He wore a blue, almost black, suit over a velvet waistcoat, and a fedora. His shoes were leather. He smiled at Molly, and then walked across to a wall where he began to examine each of Mark's pictures.

Molly realised that, in all the excitement, she had forgotten to talk to the boys about the UFO she'd seen at the weekend. Oh, well, she was certain to catch them in the Lion soon.

Gaz walked up Goldfinch Road, which was quiet at this time on a Saturday afternoon. He wondered if Simon and Mark were talking about him and Janet. How happy they would be that he'd finally found a girlfriend. Except, of course, he hadn't. Janet was okay, he'd chatted to her in The Swan last weekend. He hadn't visited The Swan to chat up Janet, of course, that was simply a by-product of his being there. He'd lifted a woman's blouse from Top Shop. He had it securely hidden under his coat when he'd bumped into Simon last week. Having nicked it, he now wondered how much Greaser or Dodgy Len would give him for it. This was good, fashionable stuff, something they'd be able to sell on. The top had been labelled in the store at nearly five quid. Gaz had left the tag on it, to prove its worth. Greaser said he'd give two quid for it, Dodgy Len said two pounds fifty. Gaz let Dodgy Len have it, and then brought them both a drink out of the money. Gaz had then, buoyed by his success, began to chat up Janet. It might be fun to go out with Janet. She wasn't bad looking, and was different to the girls in The White Lion. Still, if Nick and Simon wanted to believe that he was visiting The Swan to see Janet, it would avoid any awkward questions. It was true that she was unlikely to visit The

White Lion, so Gaz could easily explain her absence. There were no parties on the horizon, and not likely to be until Christmas. He had just over two months in which he could either go out with Janet for real, or sadly end his invented relationship with her.

There was one thing that troubled him. He still hadn't tried to offload the earrings, the aftershave, the vodka, and all the other things he had acquired. He still kept them in the box under the bed, covered with books. In the last couple of weeks, he had added more trinkets and trophies of his activities – his successes, as he liked to think of them. There was a tennis racket from the sports shop hidden at the back of his wardrobe, a plate from one of the antique shops, and a book from the bookshop. He might read the book himself, he couldn't imagine Dodgy Len or Greaser would be the least interested. He'd stolen, anyway, a sci-fi book he might be interested in, Frank Herbert's *The Eyes of Heisenberg*. He was stealing stuff that couldn't easily be sold. He was stealing for the challenge. Stealing the tennis racket and getting it out of the shop had not been easy.

Gaz reached his home, and went to his bedroom. He had added another two stacks of ten pence pieces to his silver columns. Ten columns now occupied ten squares on the chess board. How quickly, it seemed, he had saved this money, just from bits and pieces of change he hadn't missed. How long would it take to cover the whole chess board? Sixty-four pounds, he thought. Sixty-four whole pounds. What could he do with that? Buy Janet a drink, he supposed, if he ever did really fancy her. Perhaps, though, he should put it in a bank, where it could make him more money. He picked up one of the columns of coins, and slid the silver ten pence pieces from hand to hand. He enjoyed the feel of money. He wanted to make money. So why, then, was he loathe to sell the stuff he was nicking? Because they *were* trophies, he supposed. They were symbols, as real as driving licences and exam certificates, of success. *Real success*. He had to gamble on nobody noticing what he was doing, he had to use dexterity and cunning and skill to hide what he lifted. He had to accept risk, and apply craft. The things in the box beneath the bed were markers of his abilities.

He wished he could talk to Nick, or Mark, or Simon about what he was doing, and the sense of pride he felt. But that would be madness. They might understand, but they would see it as wrong; well, Simon and Mark would. Nick might not care, but would still caution him strongly about the dangers of being caught. And that was a danger. Gaz knew he'd lose his job if he were ever caught and prosecuted. He was only a clerk, but he was working in a bank. What kind of bank employs a thief? If he lost his job he'd make no money, and the piles of coins on his chessboard would begin to disappear. His imagined future would also vanish, as the road leading to it was torn up

It was the first time Gaz had ever really contemplated the dangers of what he was doing. He knew the dangers of being caught, had felt the immediate thrill of apprehension, and that was part of the buzz, the reason why he did it. He realised now, though, that the consequences of being caught would not only be immediate, but would also run off into the future, and affect all his plans. He again looked at the stacks of coins on his chessboard. He had felt proud of them, admired them as representatives of his ambition. He imagined the board bare; it was... depressing, disappointing. Yet this was the risk. Could he imagine stopping the shoplifting? Not quite yet. The challenge was still there. The thrill was still there. The pull of it remained, for now, stronger than his fear of seeing the chessboard empty.

Perhaps if he were to go out with Janet, he might find something as exciting as shoplifting – sex, perhaps. If he'd carried on with his education, gone on to do a degree, that might have provided an intellectual satisfaction as fulfilling as the excitement of his petty thieving. However, his A-level results had been average, and no degree course had ever interested him. And Janet? Perhaps she could provide something, a spark, intrigue, sex. Yet he couldn't imagine marrying her, and his imagined future always involved a beautiful wife to sit beside him in his BMW. While Janet's body was fulsome and offered undoubted sexual promise, he didn't see the point of involving himself with somebody who would not become the dazzling creature he imagined on the soft leather upholstery.

The coins were still rattling slowly between his fingers, from palm to palm. He was risking too much, he decided. He would lift something one more time, to confirm to himself his skill, and then stop. He could stop easily, he was sure. It wasn't like Mark's smoking, it wasn't an addiction. Perhaps, though, he thought, he should steal two more items. *One as a prize, a reminder of my talents, and one I can sell-on to Len or Greaser.* He felt the need to prove he had an eye for the sellable goods. So, only two more items. *And then I'll stop.*

19

Nick had arrived at The White Lion after Mark, who'd finished his first drink, and bought himself another and one for Nick. It was only seven o'clock. Mark wondered if work was driving him to drink. "I hate work." he said, "I bitterly resent being educated to lounge about at college and enjoy myself, only to find I have to go out and earn a living."

"It'll make a man of you," Nick said.

Mark frowned. "I'm not sure I want to be a man if this is what it takes."

"You made money from the sale," Nick said. "That must have made you feel good. How much was it in the end?"

"Twenty quid."

"Two of which you owe Gaz."

"Of course. He won't let me forget. And a fiver for you and Si. For the time and effort. And the wood and glass."

"Oh, don't worry about that. The picture glass had been in the garage for ages, I don't know why Dad kept it. As for the wood... well, there's always wood."

Nick picked up the newspaper he had brought to the pub with him. "More news on Manley." He folded the newspaper over, and handed it to Mark. He pointed at the article Mark should read. Mark quickly scanned the article. The article went into more detail about the Manley Boys. The papers had been reporting on their criminal activities for years, but the police had never been able to pin anything on them. One newspaper, possibly the *News of the World*, Mark recalled, had often made fun of the ineptitude of the police. Hadn't everybody known what kind of people the Manley Boys were? Hadn't the news-papers discovered evidence of their wrong-doings? Why couldn't the police? He found what had obviously piqued Nick's interest; the newspaper and the police were now calling Manley's death a gangland killing.

"What do you think?" Nick said.

Mark handed the newspaper back to Nick. "Like Molly said, it could be a coincidence."

"A pretty big one."

Mark hadn't seen Molly in the bar for a couple of days. He wondered if she'd returned to London. Simon came into the bar. Simon signalled to Mark, asking whether he and Nick needed drinks. Mark shook his head, and then said to Nick, "And you're sure it was him we saw?"

"Kind of," Nick said.

"Kind of?"

"Well, he did have his back to us most of the time. And then we left pretty quickly."

Simon came over and sat down with them. Mark was thinking about the hitman. Nick had seemed so sure about him the previous weekend. Now he doubted himself. Why? Mark was going to say something, but Nick spoke first. "Somebody smells of *girl*. What is it? Charlie? Tramp? Havoc?"

"It's bloody havoc, to be sure," Simon said.

Mark sniffed. Simon did smell of perfume. Mark thought it was Tramp; Chrissie wore it a lot. "Is that Jill's?"

Simon smiled and sipped his drink, then said, "No, it's mine."

"Don't give me that. You've been kissing Jill."

"Okay, I confess. I met her in the park, you know the one, over the road from the college–"

"The one where you used to meet Anna," Mark pointed out.

"Yeah, well... So I finished at half four, and Jill was there."

"And then?" Nick said. "Give us the juicy details."

"Just some kissing. And some hugging. Then she said what she said the other night, you know... *This is real. Did you ever do this with Anna?*"

"You didn't, did you?" Mark said.

"You know I didn't. The thing with Anna wasn't like that... it was like... oh, you know." Simon smiled. "Anyway, then I wanted her to do it again. And she did. And we did. So, we spent an hour kissing in the park. It was... nice."

"And Anna?' Nick said.

"That's why I said it is bloody havoc. Jill knows about Anna. Turns out she's a friend of Anna's sister. Jill says she doesn't care, that she knows that the thing with Anna was... *not real*, as she keeps saying."

"And you fancy Jill?"

"Yes. I do." Simon sighed. "Look, I know it's going to be all confusing, but Anna doesn't want me, and Jill does. I do like Jill. I'll soon be nineteen. I'm not going to chase Anna forever. We'll all part ways next year, anyway. We'll go off to study somewhere else, possibly miles away. I'll might never her again after next June. I might not see Jill after next June, who knows? So, I've decided. For now, I'm going to enjoy Jill."

"Hoo-bloody-ray," Mark said. "When will we meet her?"

"Oh, I'm sure she'll be over here soon enough. You'll like her."

There was silence for a while as they reflectively sipped their drinks. Mark was pleased for the still-smiling Simon. He'd been worried that the *Anna-thing* might turn into something similar to his *Chrissie-thing*, and he wouldn't wish that on Simon. One hopelessly-in-love fool was quite enough. Now, if only Nick could find somebody. Mark had rather hoped, during the summer, that Nick would stay with Heather. He liked Heather, and thought that she and Nick made a good couple. Nick had been determined that it would only be a summer fling, and Heather had seemed of the same mind. She, too, had gone off to Uni now, up to Leeds, so she was rarely seen in Dereham. Rain battered the window of The White Lion. The nights were drawing in; October was just around the corner. It was a good night to be in the pub. Nick showed the article in the newspaper to Simon.

Mark looked at Simon. "Nick's unsure whether the guy we saw on the way down to Bournemouth was the hitman."

"Is that really so surprising?' Simon said. He looked at Nick. "When you first told us about the hitman, you said you found it difficult to remember his face. We ended up with somebody who looked like a cross between Shirley Temple and Lee Van Cleef."

"Clint Eastwood."

"Hank Marvin," Mark said.

Simon and Nick burst out laughing. Mark wondered what they were laughing about.

"Hank Marvin," Simon said, and laughed again.

Mark laughed too. "Did I say Hank Marvin? I mean Lee Marvin. No wonder my drawing was so confused, it probably had features from Hank."

"So what are you going to do?' Simon said.

Nick shrugged, and sipped his bitter. "I don't know. What can we do?"

"Go to the police," Simon suggested.

"I've thought about it. If he is a hitman, I'm pretty sure he left no evidence. We don't know his name, anyway. We do know he drives an NSU. I'm pretty sure he'd have a clean criminal record, or at least nothing that would suggest his current occupation."

"How do you know?"

"I've thought about. I imagined what I'd do if I were a hitman. I'd want to keep myself clean, out of the spotlight. He might have some old convictions for petty stuff, but nothing serious."

Mark wondered what they could do. "There must be some way we can prove something?"

Nick leaned back in his chair and ran his fingers through his short, spiky, brown hair. "I don't know."

"You could follow him again," Simon said.

Nick frowned. "It seems... foolhardy, if he is what he says he is."

"But then, at least, you'd know."

"I'm not sure I want to."

Mark had some sympathy with Nick's reluctance, but there was also truth in what Simon was saying. They were the only people who could make the connection between the Manley killing and the hitman. "We should do something," he said.

"Okay," Nick said. "But what?"

"Follow him again," Simon said. "Try to find out where he lives. Once you know that, you can suss out others thing, perhaps."

Mark smiled. "Has snogging Jill excited your brain?"

"Possibly," Simon conceded. "And other... things."

Nick still looked uncertain, Mark noted. "What can go wrong?' he said. "Nothing happened when we followed him the other day."

"I can imagine lots of things going wrong," Nick said. "Then I see guns, and knives, and me lying by the side of the road."

"But he doesn't know our names. He knows we live in Dereham, but that's it." Mark was finding the idea of following the hitman again seductive. It would be... interesting. He would have something interesting to tell Chrissie. Perhaps Chrissie would regard him more favourably. He would have done something... noble? Heroic? Daring? Whatever it was, it would be more than that stay-at-home layabout Jake ever did. "Look, we know that Shirley Temple is heading towards Bournemouth. When we see his car one night... Perhaps we should follow him. It wouldn't take five minutes to walk to my house and jump on the bike. We could catch up with him near Salisbury."

"That's true," Nick said. "We could do it. He wouldn't see us get on the bike... We'd just be a couple of unknown bikers that appeared somewhere around Salisbury."

"Are you going to do it then?' Simon said.

Nick smiled grimly. "Yes, okay, let's do it. Let's find out who this bugger is."

"Far out!' Simon said.

Mark was pleased. He had become even more convinced while they were talking that this was just the kind of experience that would make him more daring and dashing in Chrissie's eyes.

Molly pushed the door to the saloon bar open. She glanced around quickly and was pleased to see Mark, Nick and Simon sitting at their usual table. There was no sign of the Honeyhouse gang. She wondered where Gaz was. She asked them if they wanted a drink. She went to the bar, where Pam was serving this evening, and ordered.

Pam busied herself behind the bar, pulling pints and taking the lids from Britvic bottles. "How much longer are you staying, Molly?"

"I don't know, I haven't thought about it, really. Why, do you need my room."

"Oh, no, don't worry about that, love. It's nice to have some female company here, and, anyway, at this time of year, we're usually quiet. I was just being nosy." Pam smiled. It was a warm smile, genuine, inviting. "I mean, you were here to find your sister, I thought. Have you found anything?"

"I was... I am. I've discovered some things. For example, I think I've found out why she liked being here. A walk around the hills is very lovely. And the view from Copsehill is very... scenic. And there's something relaxing about the town, you know?"

"Don't tell, Richard that, or he'll be talking about atmospheres and trying to convince you it's all because of our friendly space brothers."

"You don't believe in any of that then?"

"I don't know, dear. Still, you don't need to know about atmospheres and aliens to realise this town is ... special. The hills embrace us all. The trees and copses rustle and whisper."

"My, Pam, you *are* lyrical this evening."

Pam handed Molly the last of the drinks. "Well... You do get to like it here. I mean, look at you... You're getting all comfortable and in no hurry to leave."

"Well, I have found some other things to do while I'm here."

"And you've been making eyes at Simon, I've noticed."

Molly almost blushed. She hadn't realised she had been that obvious. "He's a nice young lad, but I don't have time to follow that up. Besides, he's besotted with some other girl."

Pam laughed lightly. "He's only eighteen, love, and you'd turn anybody's head."

"Thanks. But like I say, I don't have the time for... a dalliance... this holiday."

She took the drinks on a tray over to the table, and sat down next to Simon. She looked at him thoughtfully and smiled, she hoped, enigmatically.

Simon laughed and kissed her on the cheek. "I know you're not my girlfriend really, but is it okay if I steal a kiss occasionally?"

Molly sighed. "I suppose so."

Mark lit a cigarette, and then said, "What about me?"

"No hope," Molly laughed.

Mark smiled in return. "I thought not."

"How was Copsehill?" Nick asked.

"It was delightful," Molly said. "It was a lovely afternoon on Saturday. There was nobody else there. I know it's not far from town, but it felt very peaceful, you know?"

"Oh yes," Nick said. "I know. That peace around the copse is the one thing I'll miss when I go."

"Isn't that worth staying for?"

"No. I have to go... somewhere."

"Well, you never know what might turn up," Molly said.

Mark took the cigarette from his mouth, and politely blew the blue smoke into the already smoky air above their heads. "Did you see anything? We have to ask. It's like a ritual."

"No, I didn't," Molly said. "Oh, except a stonechat, perhaps. Do you get them around here?"

"Yes," Nick said. "Sometimes. You see them quite often further out in the Plain."

"Anyway, I didn't see a UFO or any aliens. Though I might have done, last weekend. I haven't had a chance to talk to you about it."

She explained what she had seen, and how the girl Mary and her friends claimed they had seen aliens.

"Ah," Simon said. "Mary. She's just a little... excitable. Prone to flights of fancy."

"She fancied you," Nick said.

"She didn't," Simon said.

"She *did*."

"She *didn't*."

Mark drew on his cigarette, blew the smoke out, and looked at Simon. "Simon. This is my serious face, okay?"

"Okay.

"You are improbably dense."

"Oh."

"Now, go on with your story, Molly," Mark said.

She recounted what Mary had said.

"So she never *saw* an alien," Nick said.

"No. And I must admit, I thought she might well have heard sheep, or rabbits. What noises do rabbits make, anyway?"

Mark barked like a seal, laughed, and stubbed his cigarette into the scratched ashtray with the large 6X in the middle.

"That means we have no idea," Nick said. "However, you're surely right and it was nothing out of the ordinary. They *saw* nothing. Everything else is just supposition."

"But what about the UFO? When it disappeared and then reappeared, that was a bit... freaky."

"Explain what you saw again," Mark said.

Molly did so.

Mark looked at her thoughtfully. "Did you see anything else that night?"

"Oh, some meteorites. About three I think."

"Ah. Interesting." Mark lit another cigarette as he pondered.

"There might have been a meteor shower," Simon said. "If you saw that many so easily."

"Good point," Nick said.

"Aha!" Mark exclaimed, puffing out smoke. "So, you could have seen a satellite going into eclipse..."

"Eclipse?" Molly said.

"Yes, it passes into the shadow of the Earth from your viewpoint, and essentially seems to disappear." Mark said. "So, the satellite goes into eclipse, and disappears. And then, a few moments later, a meteor appears at roughly the same point, and your mind makes a connection."

"A connection that's not actually there," Nick emphasised. "It's what James and Stuart have noticed, when we talk about skywatches with them... How quickly people make connections between things that are unconnected, and kind of... weave it into a tapestry, to make sense of what they've seen."

"Yes," Mark added. "The shooting star you saw only has to be in roughly the same place, and heading in the same direction. You wouldn't be able to keep the exact details of where the satellite was and where it was heading once it had disappeared. So when the meteor appeared at roughly the same place, going in roughly the same direction, it provided a... a.. what?" He waved a hand around. "A cue? A solution?"

"It ties the pattern up," Simon said.

That did make sense, Molly noted. "One thing though, Kurt was there. He said he didn't know what satellite it was. And, you know, Nick said Kurt knows everything."

Mark sucked on his cigarette. "Hah! He *thinks* he knows everything."

"He could make it all up," Simon said. "Nobody would know. I bet nobody checks the next day."

That was true. She hadn't. "Well, thanks, lads. That kind of clears up that mystery." She took a sip of her vodka and coke. "Now, what about Kurt?"

Mark ground out his cigarette in the tin ashtray. "What about him?"

"Well, what is he? He looks like a hippie, but he's never in here."

"He doesn't really do pubs much," Simon said. "I think he's your classic pot head."

"He goes down the Swan sometimes," Nick said. "That used to

be the equivalent of this bar. So the older hippies, and the bikers, that's the pub they use. And–" he leaned in and spoke quietly. "Frankly, you're more like to meet a dealer there than here."

"What's the deal with Cathy?" Molly said. "How long have they been together?"

Simon laughed. "We don't know everything about them."

Nick looked at Molly with a raised eyebrow and a smile. "What's all this about. Do you have suspicions about our Dutch friend?"

Molly rocked forward on her stool. "Let's just I'm intrigued."

"Why?" Mark wondered. "A dopey pot-head in Dereham is hardly mysterious."

"Just think where he's lived."

"Where has he lived?" Simon said.

"Devon," Nick said. "Up near Cirencester, and then here."

"Right," Molly said. "Not just Devon. Plymouth. Devonport. Royal Navy. What do you know about Cirencester?"

There were shrugs and frowns around the table.

"GCHQ is near Cirencester. Have you heard of it?"

There were more shrugs, and a shake of the head.

"It's where signal intelligence arrives and is analysed."

"Okay, but why here?" Simon said. "Why sleepy old Dereham?"

"You *are* on the edge of the Plain. You don't have to go far to see tanks, helicopters, artillery, men in uniform. You could overhear things. Even up at Copsehill, in amongst the skywatchers..."

"Was that why you took his photo yesterday?" Nick said. "Are you sending the photos to... somebody?"

"You are a spy, after all," Simon said.

"So I am. That's why somebody is *already* developing Mark's photos. In London."

Mark shook his head, disbelievingly. "How did you manage that?"

"Motorcycle courier. Now, what about Cathy?"

"I've known Kurt and Cathy the longest," Nick said. "And they've been a couple since they've lived here. From what he's told me, she's been with him pretty much since he moved here."

"Do you think he's really Dutch?" Molly asked.

"How the fuck would I know?" Nick said. "He sounds Dutch to me. Does he sound Dutch to you?"

"Yes, I suppose he does." Molly smiled. "Oh well, enough of that." She realised she was going to get no more information from these lads. And, anyway, Chrissie had come into the bar, alone, and Mark's attention would soon wander. The girl looked miserable. Molly assumed there was boyfriend trouble, and that Mark's shoulder was about to be cried on. She said goodnight to the boys and went back to her room. She rang Edge, but he wasn't at the office. She left a message with a duty operator.

Kurt made her suspicious. Hippies usually hung around Totnes or Glastonbury. They didn't by chance end up in militarily sensitive areas. And if, as Nick thought, Kurt and Cathy had been together for years, there was a chance that she too was... whatever Kurt was.

20

On Tuesday evening, in the park, Simon kissed Jill again. That night, Gaz, Mark, Nick and Simon mooched about the Beech Tree Grove sign. Gaz had, by now, heard about the plan, and said they were completely fucking mad. They didn't see the hitman. On Wednesday, Jill and Simon hugged and kissed in the park, Gaz decided he might make a move on Janet, as it would provide back-up for the story he had concocted, and went to the Swan. Later that night, Mark and Nick sat on the Beech Tree Grove sign, but didn't see the hitman. On Thursday evening, it rained heavily. Simon went over to Jill's house in Foxton, where he kissed, stroked, and hugged her. The next day, Mark told Simon that it had rained far too hard for him and Nick to sit on the Beech Tree Grove sign. On Friday night, Jill came over to Dereham. They all went to The White Lion. Afterwards, Simon inducted Jill into the subtle art of mooching around the Beech Tree Grove sign. Simon had already told her about the hitman, and their plan, and she had said she hoped he really was a nutter. Now, though, she put her arms around Simon and kissed him, right there, at the crossroads, by the Beech Tree Grove sign. Simon was amazed that Gaz made no comment at all, about relationships, relationship shit, or anything else. What Gaz did finally say, and what finally interrupted Simon's kiss, was "Tally-ho. Action stations. Act as normal as you can."

Simon glanced over at Gaz, who was looking down Town Road. There could be only one meaning to what he'd said. They all understood. Simon turned back to Jill. "What's normal for you?"

Jill smiled and pushed Simon's long fair hair away from his face and reached up to kiss him.

Mark and Nick continued their conversation about UFOs, and whether they existed, and whether Dereham really was being visited by alien spaceships. Simon heard the NSU pass by them. He and Jill stopped kissing, and he looked over at Mark.

"Here we go, then," Mark said.

Nick stood. "Yes, here we go."

"Are you up for it?"

"As ready as I'll ever be." Nick seemed eager to start now he'd committed himself.

Mark held him back. "Wait a minute."

The tail lights disappeared around a corner in Barton Road, heading out of town, on towards Salisbury.

"Good luck, men," Gaz said.

Mark and Nick hurried off down Barton Road, towards Mark's house, to don their leathers and mount the Honda.

"I wonder what they'll learn," Simon mused.

Jill put her arms around Simon again. "Now they've gone, do we have to continue standing here? Is there some ritual that must be duly fulfilled before we can continue with the rest of the night?"

Simon loved the way Jill talked. "We'll go back to my place for coffee."

They crossed the road, and began to walk up Goldfinch Drive. Gaz tagged along behind them.

"Do you think this is sensible?" Jill asked.

"Drinking coffee after the pub?" Simon said. "Of course it is."

"No, Nick and Mark following the hitman, if he is a hitman."

"Well, it can't do any harm. It's dark, and the hitman will never recognise them."

"Whose idea was it? Mark's? He seems really into it."

Simon thought back to the night in The White Lion. "Uh. No, actually. It was my idea."

Gaz piped up from behind them. "Of course, Mark likes the idea. He wants to impress Chrissie."

Simon hadn't thought of that.

"And, of course," Gaz continued, "it's no skin off Si's nose, as he was never going to be following the hitman, anyway"

Simon hadn't thought of that either. It had been an easy thing to suggest; after all, he wasn't putting himself in danger. But was there any danger? It seemed to be a bit of a lark, really. A lark with a frisson of danger, but a danger that was remote, nebulous, and unlikely. The hitman was almost certainly, as they always said, a nutter. It was only a coincidence, Simon believed, that the gangster – what was his name, Tim Manley? – had been killed in Bournemouth. Molly the spy had said so, as well. And she *was* a spy; she should know. The hitman was always heading towards Bournemouth. He obviously lived there, or had friends or family there. Would he hit somebody on his own doorstep?

"Who's Chrissie?" Jill said.

Simon turned to Gaz. "Did we just spend an entire evening in the pub with Mark without Chrissie's name coming up *once*?"

"Yes, I believe we did," Gaz said. "I think he was dazzled by Jill."

Jill laughed. "Who wouldn't be?"

"Not me," Gaz said. Then he added quickly, "No offence. I have my eye on somebody else."

Simon wondered if he really did. For somebody who supposedly fancied Janet, he mentioned her very little. He went to The Swan rarely. Gaz was such a mystery. Simon had known him for over five years, and still there was something mysterious about him. In fact, he had grown more mysterious as he had grown older. Simon had met Gaz at a kick-about with other friends in the town park. They had only been thirteen, and Gaz had then been a typical boy of that age – into music and sport – but slightly taciturn, and already given to monosyllabic replies. Now, however, Gaz was keeping secrets, Simon knew it. What the nature of those secrets was, he had no idea. Janet could be a front. Mark wanted to believe that Gaz was at last chasing a girl, and even Nick, normally more worldly than the other three given his extra two years, seemed to think Gaz was having secret tryst with Janet. Simon wasn't so sure. Gaz's current interest in Janet seemed to have come from nowhere. Apart from their Christmas party snog, neither had seemed interested in the other. Simon didn't know Janet well, but enough to say hello to her in the street, and to pass the time of day with her if they were waiting together somewhere. She had never asked about Gaz. Perhaps he should ask her.

"Chrissie is Mark's paramour," Simon said.

Jill frowned. "Is she married?"

"No, why?"

"Paramour most often refers to an illicit lover, the other party in an adulterous affair."

"I suppose it's kind of adulterous, in that she has a boyfriend, Jake."

"Although lover is stretching the definition of that word a bit," Gaz added.

"So she's kind of illicit, but not a lover," Jill said. "Not much of a paramour really."

"Well, okay," Simon said. "Mark fancies the pants off her, and has done for two years, but has never done anything with her."

Jill smiled. "Sounds like somebody I know."

"Oh, yeah, but I've got you now. Mark will always love Chrissie, and die a bachelor."

Gaz shook his head. "Sad bastard." He looked at Jill. "Are you staying with Simon tonight?"

"Yes, in his bed. But not with him in it, unfortunately."

Simon's heart fluttered at the unspoken promise. "Mum would have a fit if she found us in bed together," he said. "I'll be sleeping on the sofa."

"Will your parents be awake?' Jill said.

"For a little while, perhaps," Simon said. "They'll go to bed soon enough, though."

"Good. We can snuggle up on the settee and watch a movie or something."

"That would be nice."

"Just as well I'm leaving you here then," Gaz said. "I wouldn't want to see that."

They stopped walking. Jill turned to Gaz. "It was nice meeting you," she said, and kissed him on the cheek.

"You too," Gaz replied. "We'll meet again."

Gaz turned into Curlew Way. Simon took Jill's hand, and led her towards Magpie Road. They walked in silence for a minute or so, and then Jill said, "How much further?'

"We turn just there." Simon pointed to the junction. "Then it's a couple of houses down the road."

Jill stopped Simon walking. She moved close, and put her arms around him. Simon looked down into her eyes. Streetlights glittered there. She seemed so much taller than Anna. He banished the thought. He didn't like to think of Anna when he was with Jill, and especially didn't like to compare them. "I think you should kiss me now," Jill said. "We don't know how long your parents will stay up."

"That's true. You really are very clever."

"I certainly am. And I'll teach you everything I know." Jill reached up to kiss Simon. Simon backed away slightly.

"Everything?"

"Absolutely. In fact, absolutely everything. You'll enjoy learning it, too. Now, fold around me like a warm woollen wrap, and kiss me."

Simon sighed theatrically. "Oh, well. If I must."

They kissed deeply and passionately. Thrills ran all through Simon's body. It felt good to do this. Mark didn't know what he was missing because of his deeply entrenched and misguided commitment to Chrissie. Jill and Simon stopped kissing, and for a moment Simon looked into her smiling eyes, and smiled back at her, happily. Perhaps, he thought, Mark would become Chrissie's hero. She would dump Jake, and then Mark would be happy too.

Alternatively, the nutter would be a hitman, something would go wrong, and Mark would be dead before ever kissing *anybody* again. Whose dumb idea had it been to chase the car? *His.* Simon's smile fell for a moment.

It was nearly midnight. Archie was going to stay the night in Bournemouth, at The Cow's house. He had made the decision very late. He looked forward to seeing Peter's face in the morning. It was something he missed, now that he no longer shared a house with The Cow. He wanted to see Peter, and, he supposed he was bored. The Cow would be in bed when he arrived, but he had a key.

The roads were quiet. Most people were too pissed to drive at this time on a Friday, Archie thought. He looked in his mirror. There was a single headlight following him, some distance away. The only heavy traffic he had seen had been around the cities, Bath and Salisbury. Nick and his mates had been sitting at the top of that road in Dereham. They always seemed to be there. Archie thought back to when he had been younger. He supposed sitting around on street-signs, after the pub, was a way to delay the inevitable. They were all still young, and still lived with their parents. They could swear and smoke while they were outside. No doubt, they would go back to somebody's house for coffee later, when it got colder. There had been a new person there tonight, he had noticed. He felt proud that he *had* noticed; he was still observant, he was still aware of his surroundings, of differences, of possible dangers. A tall, leggy blonde. He smiled to himself. Perhaps that's why he had noticed. Perhaps he wouldn't have noticed if it had been another guy. Perhaps he wasn't quite as observant and alert as he thought, and had merely responded to a particular stimulus. She'd been wrapped around the kid with the long fair hair, the one he thought of as Hippie Boy. He knew Nick's name, of course, he never forgot a name. Then there was Hippie Boy, Biker Boy, and Combat Jacket. And now he could add Blondie. Blondie and Hippie Boy. She looked okay. Hippie Boy was lucky.

Archie leaned over to the car radio, and switched it on. He found Radio 3. He thought he recognised Bartok. He looked in the rear view mirror again. The single headlight was still there, some distance from him. He'd first noticed that light just outside Salisbury. Well, he assumed it was the same light. He hadn't been looking in his mirror all the time, and this might be a different motorbike altogether. The bike behind him didn't appear to be in a hurry, which was slightly odd, Archie thought. After all, bikers always seemed to be keen on speed. Perhaps the rider was drunk. Pity the poor pillion passenger if that were true. But, then, perhaps the passenger was also drunk. It was that time of night. Archie flowed the car around bends, and lost sight of the headlight behind him. His mind wandered back to the blonde he had seen wrapped around Hippie Boy. Archie hadn't had a serious relationship since his marriage to The Cow had broken down. He'd had a couple of one-night stands, and a fling that lasted a few weeks. Of course, eventually, any girlfriend would want to know what he did for a living, and look what had happened with The Cow. She tolerated his visits to see Peter, but her eyes were always wary when he was around. She never asked the question that he knew was foremost in her mind. *Had he killed anybody recently?* Their conversations were bland. He could never ask her how work was going because it would only invite the reciprocal question, the question he couldn't answer. They talked about Peter, the weather, films, and television. But never jobs.

The news about Tim Manley was out, and The Cow always read the newspapers; she took the posh ones on Sundays. She'd know by now that Manley was dead, and where he'd died. She would suspect who had done it, and she would be right. Archie imagined that the conversation with her this weekend would be even blander than usual. She was the only person who could tie him to Manley, but he knew she'd say nothing, to preserve his relationship with Peter. He was still very satisfied with how he had handled Manley. The reports in the papers had suggested the possibility of a gangland killing. In the better papers, however, the type The Cow chose to read, the possibility of an accident hadn't been ruled out. The empty brandy bottle that Archie had placed in Manley's pocket had been found, just as he'd intended. The autopsy would find high levels of alcohol in his blood. Bruising to the face could have been caused by anything. Manley had been in the sea a few days before a dog walker found him. A doctor would be unable to ascertain the time of death. His paymaster had been pleased, had paid up quickly and congratulated him on a job well done,. There was no need to work for the rest year. A hit on a Manley Boy was worth a lot of money.

He thought again about Hippie Boy and Blondie. That was one thing he missed. *Money can't buy me love.* It could buy him a hooker, but he didn't want that, even though he knew the sort of people who could provide him with beautiful, high-class hookers if asked. In fact, if he asked, his client would provide access to a friendly and amenable escort for a few months, although that would entail a cut in his pay packet. Blondie had wrapped herself tight into Hippie boy as they kissed. He had looked in his mirror as he had passed, and Combat Jacket was looking at the car. Nick and Biker Boy had stood up. Going for a coffee somewhere, back to one of their houses, to watch a film on television, listen to some music, or something. He almost envied them. Young and carefree. And Blondie. He had noticed one new thing tonight – he wouldn't like to get into an argument about Blondie with Hippie Boy. Hippie he might be, but there was something about him that Archie knew well; Hippie Boy had seemed broad across the shoulders, but also looked light on his feet, like he could move.

Archie now followed the streets into Bournemouth. A few drunks wandered home, but the pavements were otherwise empty. A couple of bobbies patrolled the streets. The night and streetlights flowed past the car. He glanced up in the mirror again. The single headlight was still there, closer now he was in town. He yawned. He liked to arrive at The Cow's late; it meant less interaction with her. Peter would be in bed now, but he wanted to be there in the morning, when his son awoke. He had seen Peter last week, after the hit, but that had only been for the afternoon. At least he was still at liberty to see Peter. There was no chance, he thought, of being nicked for doing Manley. He was home clear on that one. It felt good. He remembered being on the beach, after the job had been done. He had felt confident and cool.

Yet, now, he remembered something that had happened the night he had killed Manley. It was nothing serious, simply a false note in the calm. The roads had been quiet, like tonight. But there had been a motorbike. Why had that seemed so important last week? He had forgotten it since. More came back to him now. A bike had gunned its engine on the empty streets, and that had somehow connected back to the motorbike he had seen in the garage last week.

He retraced that path. The rider had such trouble starting the bike, he remembered. Then, a few miles down the road, he had seen it parked up in a layby, where the rider had been fiddling with the engine. And that was the bike that had ended up following him to Bournemouth. And again, tonight, a motor-bike followed him. Last week, the bike had turned off, taken the Christchurch road. Tonight, however, the motorbike had followed him all the way into town. It was quite a coincidence, wasn't it, that a motorbike would twice follow him into town, always remaining a careful distance behind him. Who had a bike and would follow him? And why? It made no sense. He pulled into the street where The Cow lived. Archie watched the bike carry on down the road. A biker, following him? Who could it be? The group of figures he saw at the crossroads flashed into his mind. Of course. Biker Boy and Nick. Surely, they wouldn't be that dumb.

Archie was suspicious by nature. Before he had become a killer he had been a simple thief, a conman, and a fraudster. He had become accustomed to watching, to being patient, to checking out the lie of the land. He parked by the kerb outside The Cow's house. Her lights were still on. She was expecting him. He remained in the car. He looked in the rear view mirror, back up the road towards the junction bathed in amber street-light. He caught sight of himself in the mirror. He was, he knew, good looking. He'd been a thief, a charmer, a chancer. Now he was a hitman. Archie the murderer. Deadly. Didn't Nick and Biker Boy realise that? Unless Nick hadn't believed him. It was something he hadn't really considered when he was playing his games with hitchhikers. Perhaps they just thought he was a crazy man. Well, perhaps they were right. He was, he supposed, what psychiatrists called a sociopath. A psycho. He pushed his fingers through his hair. He didn't like to think like this. Killing had only come after his relatively unsuccessful career as conman and thief had played out to its pathetic conclusion. He'd been trained to kill in the Army. Killing came naturally to him, and, it turned out, meant nothing to him. He liked to think that circumstances had made a killer of him, that the unfairness of the world had forced him into the first murders.

A few minutes later, a motorbike passed the junction, slowly. The head of the pillion passenger turned to look down the street, the street where his child lived. He couldn't be sure, but he intuitively felt that this this to be the bike that had followed him last week. Otherwise, why would it slow up, why would the pillion passenger look down this street? The guy on the pillion seemed tall, hunched up on the bike, similar to the one he had seen on the pillion last Saturday.

Tall, lanky. A streak of piss. It was Nick, Archie was certain.

Molly was lying on her bed in her room in The White Lion. She was reading Patterson's latest edition of the *UFO Newsletter*, which she'd picked up from the bookshop in the Market Place. Although it had happened less than a week ago, the UFO sighting at Copsehill, and Mary's encounter with aliens had made the front page. But then, Patterson only had to type the story onto the stencils for a mimeo or Roneo duplicator, and he could be printing within an hour. He had undoubtedly spent an evening collating his stories, laying out and typing up his stencils, hand-cranking the duplicator, and then stapling the whole lot together. She imagined some of the other skywatchers would have helped. They would have drunk tea, eaten cakes and biscuits, and swapped UFO stories. She imagined it would be fun, a communal activity that brought them all together and reinforced their beliefs in the things they talked about. It would strengthen their trust in and empathy with each other.

Patterson had made a meal of the sighting at Copsehill. Three closely-typed pages described the incidents, the reactions of the witnesses, and correlated the events with past Dereham sightings and sightings from all over the world. Patterson suggested reasons why the aliens would visit Dereham, linking the sightings to local archaeological sites and folkloric sprites. The article was an inspired mixture of fact, speculation, fiction, delusion, and desire.

The phone rang, startling her. She looked at the clock. It was gone midnight. It could only be one person. She picked up the receiver. "Hello?"

"Did I wake you, lassie?" Edge said.

"No."

He laughed. "That's a shame."

"Why are you ringing me at this time of night?"

"I bring you interesting news."

"Are you still in the office?"

"Aye. I've been chasing this all week, and today we began to get closer. The photographs you sent... Well, we drew a blank for a couple of days, you know? Nobody here knew anything. I tried a couple of contacts at Six, but they couldn't put a name to the face. Then Liz Carter came into the office a couple of days ago and saw the photos of Cathy. I'd been a fool, you know, concentrating on the photos of Kurt. Liz recognised Cathy, but couldn't place her at first. Cathy had grown her hair, and there was hippie garb, right? But then the face clicked. Cathy Davidson had started at Five at the same time as Liz Carter. I didn't meet her. She was downstairs, and only here a month or two before she changed track, and was shipped out to GCHQ."

Molly shook her head. "So it's Cathy that's the spy? One of ours on the hills?"

"Ach, if only things were so simple in this business. Miss Davidson turned out to be... lacking in discipline, let's say. She had the brains for the kind of analysis they do at Signals, that's for sure. Liz says Davidson can be dauntingly brilliant. But, as I say, she lacked discipline. Word got back to personnel that Davidson liked a drink. She also liked to talk in the local pubs about how brilliant she was, and where she worked. Nobody in our business likes that kind of talk. So she was quickly... uh, *let go*... before she could do any real damage."

"How did she take it?"

"Not well, by all accounts. I handed over the task of following these leads to Liz, she's good at this stuff, you know. Well, people at GCHQ who were friends with Davidson said she took it really badly, an insult to her, and a slight upon her character. So we think she was turned. Not that she knew much, but you know how it is. Any information is... information."

"It is that. And so she was picked up by Kurt? And Kurt is?"

"That is what Liz has been working on. And finally, tonight, she got the answers we needed. Now obviously, Davidson was ripe for picking, but only somebody from a foreign agency would want to pick her. And all week, we've been thinking, Russia, East Germany, Poland, all the obvious places... So, it was back to Six, but nobody could help. The face meant nothing, and no connection could be made through Davidson. Liz went as far up the chain as Pritchard, but he knew nothing, either. Then she had an idea."

Edge let the tease hang. It was an opportunity for her to respond, she knew. "Which was?"

"You remember the unfortunate chain of incidents a couple of years back, in which we lost some of our best people?"

She knew. Harry had died then. And Edge's friend, Morrow. Liz Carter and Len Stone had been injured. It had been a complicated few months. She missed Harry. And Peta.

"Yes," she said slowly, softly. "I remember. Of course."

"Well, you weren't around then, but some of the operatives being used by the Yank were mercenaries. And a couple of them were ex-SIS."

Molly knew about the Yank. Harry had told her some of what had happened. She had discovered the rest when she joined Five. She had forgotten about the mercenaries.

"So, Liz checked out them out. The first guy, Freddy Barnes, he knew nothing. But the second, Brian Britten, he recognised Kurt straight away. He had dealings with him ten years ago."

Again, Edge let the words hang for a moment, encouraging a response from Molly. "Come on, Mick. Cut to the chase."

"Okay. Here it is. Your Kurt is in fact Dieter Köhler."

"So he's HVA?"

"No, he's BND."

"On our side, then."

"You'd think, wouldn't you?"

Molly knew better. "There are no sides."

"No. There's only information and advantage."

"So, what do I do?"

"First, find out why he's here. Then tell him to go boil his head. You know I don't like unauthorised operations on my turf. I don't like any operations on my turf that aren't mine."

"When shall I do it?"

"Whenever you like. But do it on the hill. Let Dieter see who you work for, but nobody else. Make sure you're overheard, though, when you identify Köhler. Let's see if we spook anybody else."

"And Cathy?"

"Take her to one side, and explain her foolishness. Point out that organisations like Special Branch or the Sweeney like a hard-drinking big-mouth. Tell her that unless she finds gainful employ in another branch of the security services, we'll be watching her."

"What was she doing?"

"Nothing much. She was Kurt's doxy. She used her looks to get people talking. She did some watching, we think. She was, we assume, paid by our friends the Germans. She's basically harmless. She wanted some measure of revenge, and to prove herself."

There was a pause. "Did you get the big prints done for my friend Mark?"

Edge laughed. "Aye, I did that. She's a fine-looking woman, that's for sure. All the prints are on their way back to you. Give the big prints your friend, show the others to Dieter and Cathy, so that they know we know."

"Anything else?"

"Not that I can think of. What have you been up to? Ready to come back yet?"

"Soon, I think. I'll sort out this business with Dieter, and see who else I can flush. Otherwise, I'm just flirting with boys and reading about UFOs. Richard Patterson is very excited by his latest story."

"Oh yes," Edge said. "That other thing you asked about. That UFO. It was a satellite. It's no wonder Dieter didn't know it. It's a new one. Very hush hush. The Yanks put it up there. Pritchard let it slip when Liz was explaining what the Kurt story was all about."

"Patterson will be disappointed."

"You can't tell him."

"Oh, Mick. He needs to know."

"I know one or two spooks on both sides of the pond who are grateful for the efforts of the likes of Patterson. The waters are nicely muddied."

"Can I use my discretion?"

There's was a moment's silence at the end of the phone. Edge was thinking. Finally, he sighed. "Aye. Go on. I understand you want to help these people. But be careful."

21

Archie had reversed the NSU between two cars in what he had seen from the road sign was Malthouse Road. The two cars in front of him would be enough to conceal him. Nick wouldn't expect to see the NSU parked in a small street in Dereham. Archie thought himself adequately concealed. He looked down towards the junction, where Malthouse Road joined Town Road, the street that ran into the centre of Dereham. It was Saturday night, the night when most people went out on the piss. If Nick had been out with his mates to the pub, he would need to walk along Town Road to get back to the crossroads where he and his mates congregated. Archie didn't know what he was going to do yet. He wasn't sure what he would do if Nick didn't appear, or was with one or more of his mates. A knife might be needed. He had one in the case on the seat next to him. He'd prefer not to use it, though. He wanted to frighten Nick, not kill him. He still had his ethics. Nick needed a warning, that was all. When Nick realised how serious the situation could become – was becoming – Archie was sure he'd back off. Archie had concluded that for Nick, Hippie Boy, Combat Jacket, and particularly Biker Boy, following him, trying to work out what he was doing, had become a kind of exciting game, a bit like the Famous Five, wizard pranks, bottles of ginger beer, and dastardly spies uncovered. Archie intended to show Nick that what he was becoming involved in was nothing like the Famous Five and wizard pranks.

Archie hoped to catch Nick alone. Then he'd have no need for a knife. If Nick wasn't alone – if he was with either Combat Jacket or Biker Boy – he'd take the knife, if only because then he'd be able to control the situation. There was no reason to use it on any of them. Just show it. If Nick was with Hippie Boy, he'd give it a miss and come back tomorrow. Archie was wary of Hippie Boy. There was something about him. And when it came to a job - and this was a job, however small - he followed his intuition. Intuition, he thought, had developed in the time of men with clubs and tigers. If there was a smell you didn't recognise, a sound you couldn't place, a colour where it shouldn't be, or a rock that had moved, then you ran to safety. You couldn't remember the subtle clues, so you called it intuition. There were subtle clues in Hippie Boy. The build, the lightness on his feet. No, if Hippie boy were there, he would give it a miss. If there were three of them, he would also give it a miss. There was time enough. That the police had not already knocked at Archie's door could only mean that Nick was uncertain whether he and Biker Boy had followed the right car, or still didn't know what to do with whatever information they had discovered that night. If the circumstances weren't right tonight, Archie had decided, he would keep coming back until they were.

He lit a cigarette. Something by Beethoven played on Radio 3. The Pastoral, he thought - he wasn't keen on Beethoven, it all tended to sound the same to him. He looked at his watch. It was ten past eleven. The pubs would soon be kicking out. He reached over to turn the radio down. He didn't want the sound booming out through the doors and attracting attention. He wondered how much longer the Beethoven would go on, and hoped it would be followed by Bach or Mozart. He stubbed his cigarette out, carefully trying not to drop ash on the upholstery. He caught sight of a figure out of the corner of his eye. walking along the pavement of the main road. He looked up. It was Nick, and he was alone. Archie waited until Nick had passed the entrance to the junction before getting out of the NSU. He didn't need to follow Nick immediately. He already had a plan. Near the crossroads where he had dropped Nick was the gateway to a large house. Barton House, he remembered it was called. The gateway was closed by locked wooden gates. Barton

House had been converted to offices, and these were approached through Beech Tree Grove. The layout of the town was coming back to him, even though it was four years since he had lived here. The gates were set about ten yards back from the road. He would drag Nick into this gloomy gateway. They wouldn't be completely hidden, but neither would they be obvious. Anyway, Archie hoped no violence would ensue. He only intended giving Nick a slap if necessary. Once Nick understood the seriousness of the game he was playing, he would learn to forget about Archie.

Archie closed the car door quietly, and walked slowly down to the main road. He saw a road sign opposite. Barton Road. Of course. Town Road led to Barton Road, and Barton Road led out of town through the small hamlet of Barton. Nick was fifty yards or so ahead of him. Archie stayed on the right-hand pavement, and followed Nick, walking quietly. Even if Nick turned, Archie thought it unlikely he'd be recognised in the dark at this distance. Archie looked behind him. There was nobody around. The pubs wouldn't kick out for another ten minutes, he supposed. Plenty of time to get done what needed doing. A few cars passed him. Another fifty yards, and Archie began to walk faster, catching up now with Nick. The gateway was only twenty yards away. Archie crossed the road, and hurried after Nick for a few yards. He wanted to time it right. He wanted little fuss. He slowed as some cars passed. He didn't really care if there were cars around – what he was about to do would look like drunken horseplay – but there was no point in taking risks. The road was quiet again. The cars that had passed him were now only red tail-lights trailing down Barton Road. One more glance around, and Archie was ready. They reached the gateway. Archie jogged forward and tapped Nick on the shoulder. "Excuse me, mate."

Nick turned. For a moment, his face was pleasantly blank, the look of somebody about to be asked for a light, or directions, or something.

"Boo!' Archie said.

Nick's face changed in an instant.

"Hello, Nicky boy!" Archie grabbed Nick's arm and spun him into the gateway where tall trees blocked the light from the street.

"Ah, the hitman," Nick said.

Archie remembered this – that when he'd told Nick that he was a hitman, last month, on the journey from Bath, Nick had been cool, he hadn't freaked, he hadn't asked a lot of dumb questions. After the initial surprise, Nick looked cool again.

"Yes, it's me," Archie said.

"You really don't look like Shirley Temple at all," Nick said.

Archie wondered what Nick was on about, but wouldn't ask. Anything Nick said was irrelevant at this moment. The important thing was to immediately stamp his authority on the situation.

"Now, listen to me, Nick. I am, whatever you may have thought after you got out of my car, a hitman. I realise that you might have thought me a nutter. However, let's be clear about this. I *am* a killer. I *do* kill people for money. I wouldn't kill you for money. There are, however, circumstances in which I *would* kill you. It would be to your benefit, and that of your family and friends, if you understand *now*, that this isn't a game, this isn't an adventure or some interesting story you can tell your mates down the pub. You followed me, on your mate's motorbike, and by doing so you entered *my* world. My world is, by necessity, brutal. It lives by codes and ethics outside of your world. Now, what I've said should be enough to keep you quiet. However, I suspect it won't be."

"I know you killed Tim Manley," Nick replied. "So do my friends. You'd have to kill us all."

"You only suspect I killed Tim Manley."

"Did you?"

"Of course I didn't," Archie said. He knew they both knew it to be a lie, but Archie wasn't so stupid or so proud as to implicate himself. "However, I do realise that is precisely why you followed me the second time."

"Second time?" Nick said. His look of innocence was almost convincing.

"The first time, well, you could have been any bikers taking a trip down to the coast. Well done, you weren't *too* obvious. And that was a smart move, turning off for Christchurch. However, the second time... Well, that was pushing your luck too far. What are the chances that, within a few days, two motorbike riders follow me all the way into Bournemouth, hanging back half a mile while they did so? A bit of a coincidence, wouldn't you say? And who do we know who has a motorbike? Your friend... Biker Boy. What's his name?"

"Biker Boy will do," Nick said.

Archie favoured Nick with his warm smile, the smile that he had used to good effect back in the simple days when he had only been a conman. "You're not dumb, are you, Nick."

"I like to think not."

"So, if you aren't dumb, you'll recognise the truth in what I am about to say. I am *deadly*. I won't hesitate to kill you if I believe you're about to affect my life." Archie paused, moved closer to Nick. Archie was shorter, but was broader. He knew how to look mean, how not to blink, how to keep an impassive face. He looked into Nick's eyes. "You see, Nick, I'm older than you. I'm a family man. I have a son. I will do whatever I can to give that child the best. Barring unfortunate incidents, I intend to be around for that child until he has reached adulthood. Then... then I don't care what happens, really. Until that time, however, I am his devoted father. Do you understand? I want to be *there* for him. Anybody who gets in the way of my paternal instinct will inevitably give way before me. Do you get my drift?"

"Of course. But if you didn't kill Tim Manley, who did? You talk about coincidences, and you say you're a killer. Tim Manley was killed in Bournemouth. You visit Bournemouth often, as far as I can work out. The police would be very interested in that coincidence, don't you think?"

"Yet, you won't go to the police. It would be madness for you to go to the police."

"Are you going to kill me?' Nick asked.

Nick was definitely cool, Archie thought, very cool. "No. It's against my ethics. So far, you haven't affected my family or me. So you're safe, for the moment."

"But if you aren't going to kill me, what's to stop me going to the police?"

"Two things. If you continue to insist that you *will* go to the police after I leave you tonight, I will give you a slapping. A sort of lesson in the pain you will feel if you continue with this pursuit of me. Secondly, if I do go inside because of you, I already have a hitman lined up to do a job on you. Call it insurance."

Archie didn't, in fact, have a hitman lined up. He wouldn't want news of this little problem to spread. However, if Nick didn't give him what he wanted tonight, then a contract *would* go out in the morning. "So. What's it to be, Nick?' Archie saw the defiance in Nick's eyes. He knew then that Nick would need some roughing up.

Nick's eyes narrowed. "At the moment, I'm tempted by the police. You're bullying me, and I don't like bullies."

"I'm not a bully. I'm probably a sociopath." The smile Archie gave Nick was a sad one. He knew that what he had said was true. And he now had to hit Nick, who was on the face of it a nice enough lad. Archie punched Nick hard in the jaw. Nick staggered but didn't fall.

"What will this achieve?' Nick said, rubbing his face. "If you don't kill me, I'll go to the police."

Archie hit Nick again. "You won't. Because in the morning you'll remember this pain, and trust me, it won't feel good. And then you'll remember what I've already told you. There *is* a contract out on you. If I go down, so do you."

Archie didn't understand why Nick wasn't fighting back. He supposed the first punch had been so unexpected, Nick was still battling to get his wits together. Perhaps Nick didn't fancy it. Fine. The sooner he felt enough pain, the sooner he would forget all this stuff about the police.

Archie drew his fist back again, thinking to go for the solar plexus this time, just below the sternum. Nick was already flinching. Archie let his fist go, but was surprised to find that his arm had stopped moving, and that he was instead being spun around. He found himself face to face with Hippie Boy. Combat Jacket was standing uncertainly behind him. There was a frown on Hippie Boy's face. "Who the fuck are you?' Hippie Boy said.

Archie didn't answer, but danced away from him, and then aimed a right hook at his jaw. It didn't connect. Hippie Boy had bobbed slightly to the left, and trapped Archie's arm as his fist passed into a vacant space. Archie was surprised, caught motionless for a moment.

"I can't say I like you much," Hippie Boy said.

Archie felt a sharp pain in the bridge of his nose, and then he felt nothing else.

Gaz looked down at the crumpled figure on the floor, then at Nick. "Have you been flirting with other men's girlfriends again?"

Nick was still rubbing his jaw. "No. That's the hitman."

"Now he tells me," Simon said. He was rubbing his forehead. "Shit, that hurt. I never want to do that again."

"Are you sure it's him?' Gaz said.

"Absolutely. He told me often enough before he began hitting me."

Gaz went down on his haunches, and looked closely at the hitman's face. "He looks absolutely *nothing* like Shirley fucking Temple."

"We should go to the police," Simon said.

"I know, we should," Nick said. "The thing is... He said there's a contract out on me."

Gaz looked up at Nick. "You're joking. Why would he do that?"

"Insurance, he said. "He has a son. He doesn't want to be put away. And I have information that could put him away. So he's taken out a contract on me. If he goes down, I'm dead."

"Fuck," Gaz said.

Simon still rubbed his forehead. "It might not be true. He might still be a nutter, living out some Walter Mitty fantasy."

"That may be true, but imagine the consequences if it's not. What if the nutter really is a hitman? One dumb move from me, and I'm *dead*." Nick paused, and also looked down at the hitman. "Perhaps I'm dead already." He looked up at Simon. "Perhaps we all are."

"Well, look on the bright side," Gaz said. "I won't be. I'm nothing to do with this."

"Aren't you? Don't you think he might suspect you of knowing what we know? I expect he thinks Mark and I have told you everything. He'd be right, too. He's *aware* of us, you know. He has names for everyone. He called you Combat Jacket. I knew who he meant straight away. He's... *observant*."

Simon looked down at the unconscious figure. "That's the first time I've ever knocked anybody out. Well, deliberately that is. I once *stunned* a fellow student at my kung fu class."

"He'll wake up eventually," Nick said.

Simon looked concerned. "I don't want to leave the guy unconscious. He might swallow his tongue, or something. Perhaps we should get some water from one of the houses and splash it on him."

"No, we don't want to do that," Nick said.

"Why not? I don't want to leave him unconscious."

"Yes, you do."

"Why would I want to do that?"

"Because I don't want him knowing where we live. I think he knows who we are because he sees us chatting at the Beech Tree Grove sign. But he doesn't know where we live. I don't want him following one of us."

"We can't leave him here."

"We can, and we will."

Gaz certainly didn't want to be part of this madness. "He's right, Si. We need to leave him."

Gaz and Nick grabbed the hitman's collar and dragged him further into the darkness of the gateway. They manhandled him into a sitting position, and leaned him against the locked gates. The hitman groaned, but didn't come too.

"Now he looks like your average Saturday night drunk," Nick said.

Gaz kicked the hitman in the ribs. "Shit head." Gaz rather enjoyed it. He wished now he hadn't stood back when Simon had gone for the hitman.

"Hey, you boys!' Gaz turned to see a grey-haired man crossing the road towards them. The door of a house opposite the dark driveway was ajar. The man's smile was uncertain. "I saw what he was doing to you," the man said. "If I wasn't so old, I would've come an' give you a hand." The man looked at Simon. "Just as well you know how to look after yourself. Do you want me to call the police? I can back you up, it was self-defence, I saw what happened."

"No, that's all right, mate." Nick thought for a few moments. "But you can do me a couple of favours. Have you got a pen and a piece of paper?"

"Course I have, hang on." The man went back to his house.

"What are you doing?' Simon said.

Nick looked at the figure crumpled against the gate. "An assault charge will mean nothing to him. A fine, a few days in jail. So what? He'd be free again. If he's in jail for a couple days, that might... initiate the contract. We need to settle the matter now, before it gets out of hand. Before I end up, well...

Gaz heard the unspoken implication. *Before we all end up dead,* he thought.

The man soon returned with a notepad and a pen. Nick scribbled a note. He showed it to Simon and Gaz.

Don't blame Hippie Boy. You were duffing me up. He was only protecting me. He didn't know who you were.

I'll forget you, and won't go to the police, if you forget me, and forgive Hippie Boy.

Deal?

"Am I Hippie Boy?' Simon said.

"You certainly are. And Mark is Biker Boy."

"He really does know us, doesn't he?' Gaz said.

"Yes. So let's just hope this piece of paper mollifies him." Nick tore the note from the pad, and handed it to Gaz. "Stick that in his top pocket."

"Try not to kick him again," Simon said.

Gaz walked down to the gate, but could still hear Nick speaking to the man. "I want you to give us five minutes. If he hasn't come around, splash some water on his face."

"Like they do in the films. I'll enjoy that," the man said.

"I feel like I should give you a quid for your help," Nick said.

Gaz bent over the hitman. He heard the man laugh, and then say, "Oh, don't worry about it, young lad. It certainly brightened up my evening."

Gaz wondered which pocket he should put the note in. The inside pocket, he thought. *The one where the hitman keeps his wallet. That's where he's most likely to find it.* Gaz flapped open the hitman's sports jacket. Sure enough, he could see the bulge of a wallet. He bent down and slipped the note inside the pocket. The hitman's wallet felt cool and fat; made from expensive leather, and a filled with notes, Gaz supposed.

Gaz returned to Nick and Simon. Nick said goodbye to the man, and thanked him for his help. The three of them walked quickly down Town Road towards the crossroads. There would be no mooching around the Beech Tree Grove sign for any of them tonight. They said goodbye to each other perfunctorily, then Nick made his way quickly down Beech Tree Grove. Gaz and Nick crossed over to Goldfinch Drive, and hurried up the road. Gaz wanted to tell Simon that he now had his one last thing. But he knew he couldn't.

Gaz felt fulfilled now. His days of shoplifting and thieving were over. His one last thing was safely in the pocket of his combat jacket. At the junction of Curlew Way, Simon said goodnight to Gaz.

"I'll see you tomorrow," Simon said.

"You hope," Gaz laughed. "Hope your headache gets better."

Simon grimaced and walked away. Gaz felt light and happy. He walked down Curlew Way. He patted the pocket of his combat jacket, smiling to himself. His one last thing. His greatest achievement. The hitman's wallet.

22

Archie checked his nose in the mirror, again. It was bruised, but not broken. After his wash and shave, Archie made himself a coffee. He watched the kettle boiling, on the gas hob. He'd get Nick and Hippie Boy, he thought. The flame beneath the kettle was almost hypnotic, dancing blue and yellow, licking at the kettle's base. It had been a long night, and he'd found it difficult to sleep with his bruised nose. The coffee would help wake him. He imagined getting Nick first, and then Hippie Boy. He'd give Nick another slap, and then he'd break Hippie Boy's nose. No, he decided, that wasn't fair. Hippie Boy had only been protecting his mate. A slap would do, no need to break anything. Just to show them all who was boss.

He was surprised, really, that Hippie Boy had got the jump on him. He had suspected the hippie could look after himself, and he certainly was a big fuck, taller than Archie had imagined. He thought Hippie Boy must be trained in something. Nobody was that fast and on their toes unless they had a skill, a technique. Boxing? He couldn't see Hippie Boy as a boxer, he was probably against it. But what about Judo? Or kung fu? Yes, kung fu, that would be Hippie Boy's bag. *Still I should have had him.* Archie made his coffee, and then carried it to the living room. He set the mug down on the coffee table, and then patted his stomach. It felt fleshy. How many weeks had it been since he'd made that promise to himself to start exercising? He still hadn't. He must be getting old. He was approaching his forties, he realised. Perhaps it was time to get out of the game. He could always go back to the cons. Mind you, he had plenty of money in the bank. Why not live on the interest? Because, he thought, his son would soon be demanding even more money - tuition fees, for a start, and good clothes. Archie wanted only the best for Peter. Perhaps it *was* time to get out of the killing game.

He wouldn't see Peter this weekend, as he normally did. He needed to revisit Dereham. He had to catch Nick and Hippie Boy alone. He felt he should send Peter a present to make up for his absence. He would send a generous cheque to his ex-wife. She could find a present for Peter in Bournemouth. He trusted her not to spend the money on herself. She knew better. His sports jacket was on the sofa next to him, where he'd dropped it when he'd reached home last night. Archie picked up the jacket by the back of the lapel, and allowed it to twirl in front of him. It was grubby. It would need a dry clean. He reached into the inside pocket for his cheque book. When he pulled it out, a piece of paper fell onto his lap. He read it. So, Nick had accepted his advice. He wanted to protect Hippie Boy. Noble, very noble. He read the note again. He was sure this was legit. Nick was going to forget what he knew. Sensible boy.

Archie realised that he now had no need to visit Dereham, and could see Peter after all. Still, he decided to write out the cheque. A present in the middle of the week would be a nice surprise for Peter. He could go down to see him today, he thought, but decided against it. His nose was too bruised. The Cow might ask questions, and Peter might be frightened and start crying. Archie didn't want that.

Archie wrote out the cheque to his ex, and slipped it into an envelope. When he returned the chequebook to the inside pocket of his jacket, he realised something was wrong. His wallet was missing. He patted his trousers, and then looked around the sitting room. He couldn't see it. He searched the kitchen, then the bedroom, then the bathroom. He patted his pockets again. He went out to the car, and checked around and under the seats. He came back to the flat, checked everything again. He patted his pockets one more time. The wallet was definitely missing. He wondered if it had fallen out during the scuffle. If so, it would still be in the gateway on Barton Road. He sighed. He would have to drive to Dereham after all.

23

Mark had spent most of the afternoon in James' attics rooms. Stuart had also been there with Kate, who was back from university. Imogen had also been there. Steve, Danny and John were still at their respective universities, but had promised to return next week for a full Honeyhouse band practice. Mark still foresaw the band disintegrating. He hoped it wouldn't. He enjoyed these afternoon sessions, though. He and Stuart played a few standards, and wrote some new songs using James's lyrics. Stuart wasn't as good as Danny on the guitar, but he was a competent enough rhythm player. And, unknown to everybody, Mark had been practicing his dancing, when his parents and brothers were out, bouncing around the room to the funkiest records he owned. Not that he'd owned many to begin with, but he'd supplemented those few with some funky singles that James had marked down in Bentons. Mark had bought them during the week, when James wasn't working. Simon had been right. Mark did feel more confident in his bass playing, and on-beats and off-beats suggested themselves in places he'd never before considered. Even his acoustic guitar playing was benefitting from his new-found rhythmic confidence.

Mark couldn't sing as well as Imogen, Stuart and Kate, though. He could hold a note, but his singing voice had a nasal quality, like an in-tune Bob Dylan, Stuart said. Mark didn't need to sing, because when Imo, Stu and Kate sang together, it made him even more glad that he came around to jam with these people. They had worked out harmonies for some of the standards. They could do a very good *Lady Eleanor*, and Mark loved playing that one with them. They had added some new harmonies to old Honeyhouse songs, as well, but neither Mark nor James could yet convince Stu and Imo to sing in the band. Kate was up for it, Mark thought, and as a keyboard player, she would add a lot to the sound. James and Mark would suggest it. Getting keyboards together for her would be expensive though. She had some money in the bank she said, saved up from presents and pocket money and Saturday jobs and small legacies from long-gone relatives. It wouldn't yet, however, buy her a Hammond B3. There were cheaper alternatives, James said. He bought magazines about musical instruments, although he only played three chords on guitar and a bit of harmonica. He was, sure they could sort something out when the band finally got back together, after university or in the summer holidays. They did one last song, *Bridge Over Troubled Water* with a three-part harmony.

Halfway along Town Road, on the road back to his house, Mark found Chrissie walking towards him. She was crying. "Where have you been?" she sobbed. "I've been looking for you."

Mark put an arm around her. "I've been at James's. We've been having a jam. What's up?"

Chrissie leaned her head onto Mark's shoulder. "Oh, just the usual Jake shit, you know? We've been arguing again."

"What about?

"His drinking, and his dope smoking. Wanting to be one of the boys. Ignoring me."

"Yeah, the usual," Mark said. "Come on, let's go back to mine for a coffee. You can tell me all your troubles." He put an arm around her and squeezed her against him fondly. He glanced at her faun-like features. He was surprised to find her brown eyes looking at him. There was something new in them, behind the drying tears, that Mark hadn't seen there before.

Chrissie looked away, down Town Road, wiped the back of one of her delicate hands across her eyes. "Is anybody else at yours?"

Mark thought. His mother and father had gone out for a drive. Both brothers, older than him, had gone to see their girlfriends. Nobody would be back for two or three hours. "No, nobody is in. Why?"

"I wouldn't want them to see me like this. Besides..." Chrissie giggled. "I might swear a lot."

Mark and Chrissie sat at the dining table at Mark's house, drinking alcohol rather than coffee. Chrissie did swear a lot. Mark had heard her swear before, but never with such intensity, never so copiously. Jake was a shit. He was a fucking shit. His friends were wankers. They fucked with his life. Jake fucked her about, because of his fucking friends. Wanky fucking friends. Wanky shitty fucking friends. Bastards, they were, and Jake.

"And Danny?" Mark interjected at one point. Danny was the one friend Mark and Jake shared.

"No, Danny's okay." Chrissie considered for a moment. "He's one of you."

Mark didn't quite know what that meant, but nodded anyway.

"But the rest of the lazy fucks are fucking wankers. Dope-head shits who couldn't give a toss for anybody outside their little gang. He's boozing, too, you know, away from the pub. Jack Daniels. He thinks it's cool."

Mark considered the drinks he kept in his own bedroom, one of which Chrissie was drinking now, a glass of vodka, neat. He hoped he wasn't going to turn Chrissie into a wanky shitty pisshead. Chrissie looked at her glass. "Oh, I don't mean anybody with drinks at home is bad, you know. I know you've got drink in your room, and James has too. But, you know, you keep it under control."

That wasn't entirely true. James had until recently found it difficult to control his drinking. Mark didn't say anything, though. It would interrupt Chrissie's angry flow.

"Every couple of days that wanker has to get himself a new bottle of bourbon, you know, because he's getting pissed and it's so cool. And then in the evenings he's pissed *and* stoned. Honestly, it's like having to tend to a baby when he's out of it."

"Don't his parents, uh, notice?"

"Oh, Jake is hardly ever in Burnt Norton now. Will Tanner has a place in Dereham, and Jake crashes there most nights. There's a spare room, with a double bed, you know, and he could be, you know..."

Mark did know. Teetee rimpling. Gandering her nimbles. He didn't like to think about it, so he thought instead, while Chrissie looked into her half-empty glass, of the honeyed voices of Stuart, Imo, and Kate interlocking as they sang *Lady Eleanor*.

When Chrissie looked at Mark again, he saw the look he had seen earlier, the look he didn't understand. "You wouldn't do that to me, would you Mark?" she said.

Mark's heart skipped a little, just as it always did when she said something like that, or hugged him, or touched his neck with her soft hand. "Of course I wouldn't," he said. "You know my friends, you know what they're like. You'd be part of us, not on the periphery. You'd be part of my world, and part of theirs."

"That would be nice," she said, and reached over and took Mark's hand. "You've always been kind to me, Mark," she said.

"I've always wanted to help," Mark said. He had wanted more, of course, but helping was all he had been able to do.

"You understand me. You've listened."

"Yes, I do. I've tried to be there for you." Although Mark didn't understand, really. Why would she stay with somebody like Jake? He used her, she said, and treated her badly. Why put up with it all, cry on Mark's shoulder, and then return to Jake. Mark didn't understand at all. He took his hand away from Chrissie's.

Chrissie watched as Mark lit a cigarette. "Can I have one?"

Mark held the packet out to her. She smoked sometimes, not often. She never seemed to turn green on her first cigarette, though he did wonder if she would be able to handle the nicotine mixing with the vodka and anger in her bloodstream. He reached over the table and lit the cigarette for her. She smiled at him. Smoke drifted from between her lips. Her free hand took his free hand again. They smoked, holding hands, looking at each other.

"I sometimes wonder," Chrissie said, "what it would have been like if we'd got together."

Mark felt a semiquaver rest in his heart, then two quick quavers before it settled back to a steady four. "Well, you know I wanted to, but you chose Jake."

"Why, I don't know." Chrissie was speaking softly now. "He's a bit of a chump, you know. You're... much more steady..."

Mark's voice had softened too, matching hers. "Boring, perhaps?"

"Oh no," Chrissie said. "It's not that. You and your friends, you're... smarter than me, you know. Intelligent. I always feel a bit... inferior around you."

"Oh, Chrissie. You don't need to feel that. You're bright. We've just got different ideas about where we want to go in life." Mark caught himself. "Not that different, of course. We're both in Dereham, we both work. I like reading, and learning about things, you know that. You're bright too. Your interests just take you in a different direction." Then it dawned on Mark that he didn't actually know what Chrissie's interests were, or if she had any besides going out with Jake and then arguing with him. All he ever saw of Chrissie was that face, and that slight figure, all he heard about was Jake, all he had ever done with her was taken her on the back of his motorbike to meet friends of hers, or to places she had suggested, like the beach, or a pub. He had never taken her somewhere he had suggested, she only hung around with him and his friends when there was nobody else to hang around with, or when she had argued with Jake. Who was *Chrissie*, really? As he was thinking this, Chrissie stood, came around to the other side of the table, and hugged him.

"Thank you for saying that," she said. "Thank you for being there for me."

"No problem," Mark said, feeling her soft cheek against his.

"You're *so* nice."

Chrissie pulled her cheek away from his, moved her head back so she could look into his eyes. That look was there again, he noted. Then she leaned forward and pecked him on the lips. She moved her head back again, looked into his eyes for a moment, and then her lips were on his again, this time more fully. A hand touched the nape of his neck, and Mark fell into the kiss, surprised, but her lips were warm, and moist, and now her tongue was in his mouth. The kiss became more urgent, passionate, for both of them. Mark began to stand, and pulled Chrissie up with him. Their bodies pressed together. Finally, they stopped kissing, their breathing heavy.

Chrissie's skin was flushed, and she looked up at him through her dark eyelashes. "How long will the house be empty for?"

"Hours yet," Mark said.

Chrissie looked at him, her intention plain in her heavy-lidded look, and pulled Mark by the hand, towards the stairs, towards the thing Mark had so long desired.

An hour later, Chrissie was standing naked beside Mark's bed, her face different now to how it had been. Still, her small breasts arrested Mark's gaze, and the wonder of the dip of her waist was almost enough to block the words that Chrissie was muttering. The swearing had stopped some time ago, in the warmth between the sheets and their tangled limbs. They hadn't fucked. They had made love – or, at least, Mark had. But when – as Chrissie struggled into her pink tangas, slightly unsteady on her feet after one too many vodkas – her mouth had shaped the word *Jake*, something like a hand grabbed something like Mark's stomach and squeezed it. He drew his legs up beneath the sheets, wrapped his arms around the legs beneath the tight fabric, and rested his chin on his knees, looking at Chrissie.

"And so we return to Jake, in both senses of the phrase," Mark said.

Chrissie looked at him, puzzled. "What? Jake will kill me if he finds out. You won't tell him?"

"Why would I?" Mark said sadly. The sadness in his voice passed Chrissie by.

"And you won't tell your friends?"

Mark reached for a cigarette. "Of course not." He lit the cigarette, tilted his head back and blew smoke towards the ceiling, not looking at Chrissie. Fuck you, he thought, of course I'll tell my friends. Nick, Simon. Not Gaz, no. But the others, too fucking right. Not because he wanted to boast, but because he now felt terrible.

Chrissie had finally struggled back into her clothes. She sat on the bed, and rested a hand on Mark's naked arm. "I like you, Mark, I really do. But I love Jake. I know he can be a shit..."

Mark interrupted. "A wanky shitty little fuck, if I remember correctly."

"Yes, yes, I know. But I love him. I'm sorry it can't work out for us, it can't..." She stroked his hair, his face. "I know you're better a person than him, a better person than me..."

Mark said nothing.

Chrissie stood. "I've got to go, Mark. I can't stay."

"See you," Mark said, sadly.

Chrissie smiled as she opened the bedroom door. "Yes, of course you will."

Mark listened to her feet running quickly down the stairs, and then the front door quietly closing. He stubbed out the cigarette in the ashtray, and then laid back, one arm across his forehead, staring at the ceiling.

Mark ripped up a charcoal of Chrissie. It was funny, he thought. It wasn't so long ago that he'd been idly thinking what it would be like to marry her. Now, he no longer wanted to. Making love with her had been exquisite. She was still beautiful. She had, however, talked about Jake when she had no need to. She could have walked out quietly and still gone back to Jake. She had tainted *that* moment with *that* name. Had she simply left, perhaps with a smile, perhaps with a kiss and some simple platitudes about how lovely Mark had been, everything would have been all right, everything could have remained the same. Now, though, he felt differently.

Mark had seen Nick earlier for an hour. Nick had been exasperated. She was a user, he said, didn't Mark get it yet? For a moment, Mark had wanted to defend Chrissie, as always. Yet what Nick said made sense. He was her go to man, the one she always talked to when Jake messed with her head, the one who took her places, bought her things, provided a shoulder to cry on. Chrissie had used him. The sex had been more of the same. It was a tool, to bind Mark more closely to her, to make her feel better. However good that sex had been, it had only been for Chrissie's benefit, not for his.

Chrissie's glamour had been blinded him for so long. He was in thrall to her. He had given his heart to her unconditionally. She would take his love from him when she wanted it, Nick warned, to gratify herself, or to make Jake feel bad. The rest of the time he'd be out in the cold, watching Jake and Chrissie doing what they did. Now Mark had tasted that honey, Nick said, he'd want to taste it again. He'd be jealous in ways he'd never been before, because Jake would get unconditional honey, and he would get only fleeting tastes of it. Nick had laughed. "This metaphor is crap," he said. Mark agreed. Yet he understood what Nick meant. It had been difficult enough watching Jake and Chrissie together for the last two years without really understanding how it felt to be so close, so intimate with Chrissie. Now that he did know, not having those experiences would be unbearable.

Mark had returned to his house, and then his parents had come back from their day trip. He said little to them, and nothing about what had happened with Chrissie this afternoon. He had eaten with them, sandwiches and cake, and then tried to read a book, a dull book about COBOL programming. He had become bored. It was then he decided he would destroy all the pictures that had Chrissie as their subject. He'd started on the smaller ones, the ones sketched quickly in notebooks, or on the backs of cigarette packets, or on envelopes. As he made his way through the pictures, he realised how many images he had of her, how many he had tucked into drawers, into boxes under the bed, and into cupboards. The small ones, the early ones, were easy to dispose of. They were exercises. He had two framed pictures from the exhibition on his wall. Jake had never bought a picture of Chrissie. So much for Jake, and love. He would smash those, he thought. Then he changed his mind. The frames that Nick and Simon had made would come in useful. He would remove the pictures, and use them as brands to start a bonfire. He wasn't sure, though, how he would really feel as he slowly worked his way up towards the larger canvases, the larger drawings. As he ripped and shredded, wondering which he should put them on his bonfire, he heard the phone ring. After a few moments, his mother knocked on his door. The call was for him. "It's not Chrissie, is it?" Mark said.

His mother shook her head. "A man. Somebody called Mr Fredericks. Says he wants to talk to you about your pictures."

Mark followed his mother down the stairs, relieved, and picked up the phone in the hallway. "Hello, this is Mark."

"Hello, sir. My name is Michael Fredericks. Sorry to phone you on a Sunday evening, but I'm away in London next week. I'm an art dealer in Salisbury. I came to your small exhibition in Dereham a week or so ago and I was rather taken by some of your pictures, I must say. I'd like to hang them in my gallery, and see if we can sell a few."

"That sounds interesting," Mark said cautiously. He thought quickly. "Fredericks? You own the gallery near the Cathedral, don't you?"

"Yes, that's right."

"You sell interesting stuff, I've been in for a look. I can't afford to buy any of it, though."

Fredericks laughed. "You won't be able to afford any of your own works, then."

Mark was eager now. "I'd love to exhibit in your gallery. But you're not really telling me I can sell my pictures at the prices you charge, are you?"

"I certainly am."

"But you saw what I had on display. You could've bought them for the prices I was charging, and marked them up at your place."

"I have ethics, young man. I like to help new artists find an audience."

It was Mark's turn to laugh. "And make some money."

"Indeed. A man has to live."

"So what's your cut?"

"Ah, why don't I come over to see you, look at your other work, and then we can go down the pub and talk about the money. Money talk becomes so much more convivial over a good port, I think."

"Fine," Mark said. "You're on. Where are you now?"

"Salisbury. I can be with you in an hour or so."

"It'll be nice to meet you." Mark began to give Fredericks his address, but Fredericks already had it, having picked it up from the Wool Hall during the exhibition. Mark said goodbye, and then ran back to his bedroom. He'd move the pictures to the dining room. His bedroom was a mess. He looked at the box of shredded drawings of Chrissie, and the pile he still had to go through. He ripped one more for luck. He had another way of getting rid of the pictures now. Those that Fredericks didn't want he'd burn.

24

Simon's father showed Jill into the kitchen. Simon looked up from the *News of the World.*

"Your, Simon," his father said in his broad Wiltshire accent. "It's your bit of stuff." He smiled, and then left the two of them together.

Jill came up behind Simon where he sat at the small kitchen table, put her arms around his neck, and kissed the top of his head. "My hero!"

"How do you know about that?"

Jill sat on the chair next to Simon. "I saw Gaz in town. He said you were fantastic. All that kung fu has made a street fighting man out of you."

"Well, you know..."

"Don't be so humble. It sounds like you saved young Nick's neck."

"Well, I don't want to boast, but–"

"Go on, be egregious in your statements, meretricious, outspoken. Boast young man, boast."

Simon laughed, leaned over and kissed Jill quickly. "Nah, don't want to. How was Gaz?"

"He had a duplicitous look, like the cat who'd got the cream and was hiding the secret. Gaz is weird."

"Tell me about it. Where was he going?"

"To The White Lion. We're meeting him there, right?"

"Yes, and the others." Simon looked at his watch. "He's blinking early."

"Perhaps he's up to something."

"Perhaps he is. He's been looking shifty for weeks."

"Perhaps he's meeting Janet."

"I don't think it's anything to do with Janet. I don't even think he's interested in Janet."

"Really? What do you think he's up to?"

"I don't know. I just hope it's not something stupid and dangerous."

Simon watched Jill move the salt and pepper pots around on the table. She was silent for a moment, and her face, so normally open and bright, was serious, intent on the pots. She was thinking about something. "I've been talking to Anna's sister, Angie," she finally said.

"Oh yes? How is she? Angie, that is."

"Angie is fine. Anna is too." Jill looked up at Simon. "Don't pretend you're not interested."

Simon knew that he was, but couldn't bring himself to say it. He shrugged instead. Jill's gaze fell upon the salt and pepper pots again. "Angie told me that Anna's been talking about you a lot. She missed you."

Simon's heart skipped a beat. "Well, that doesn't matter. I'm with you now."

"Are you sure it doesn't matter? I know how you felt about her. Don't forget, I've known her for years, longer than you have. I *know* she's a lovely girl."

Simon tried not to let any feelings show on his face. "Are you trying to get me to like her?"

"Of course I'm not. I want you to be with me. This is real. But..."

"But what?"

"I had thought it wasn't real for both of you, that you'd both been living in some romantic fantasy dreamland before the summer. Neither of you made a move. It seemed a fair thing to think. "

"And now?"

"Now Angie's told me why Anna never made a move. Do *you* know why she never made a move?"

"She didn't fancy me. She liked being with me, she thought I was funny, but-"

"Wrong. Wrong. Wrong. She didn't make a move because *you* never made a move. She thought you didn't fancy *her*. Boys have always made a move on her, you see? We girls get used to men making a pass at us. If a man doesn't, we assume he's not interested. Do you see?"

"I think I see."

"So you were both held back by a mutual misunderstanding of the other's feelings and desires."

"Oh. So what did you tell Angie?"

"The truth. That you're shy. That you were enamoured of Anna, but didn't know how to move it forward."

"That's... That's big of you. Anna will know how I really felt now. Aren't you worried?"

"About what? I don't want to hang around with a boy whose true heart lies elsewhere, always with somebody else. So now, here's your chance. If Anna talks to you on Monday, you'll know where your true heart lies. And so will I."

Simon was confused. He had been growing more and more fond of Jill over the last few weeks. While she had not, as yet, erased his feelings for Anna, those feelings had, at least, attenuated. When he was with Jill, he rarely thought of Anna. Until this evening. Now, Anna had been placed back into the centre of his mind. She would now, he supposed, become the thought you should never think, which, once thought, becomes obdurate, and refuses to leave the mind, popping up when least expected. "Right now," he said, "I want to be here with you. I'm glad you're here." He leaned over and kissed her, his tongue gently touching hers.

Simon's dad came into the kitchen. "Do'ee want a knife and fork with that?"

Simon pulled away from Jill and laughed. "One day you and mum will go out for the evening, and then I hope to get the main course."

"I'm sure you will," Simon's dad said. He winked at Jill.

"You, Mr. Darby, are a dirty old man."

"Hey, less of the *old*, young "un." Mr Darby put the kettle on, and then left them.

"Do you really want to sleep with me?' Jill said quietly.

Simon spoke softly in return. "Of course I do. We never get a chance though."

"I've enjoyed where your hands have been, when we have the opportunity."

Simon slipped a hand along Jill's leg, under the soft cotton dress. "I've enjoyed putting my hands there." With his other hand, he reached for one of Jill's hands. "I've enjoyed your hands, too. I like the way you–"

The kettle huffed and began its shrill whistle. They both laughed. "That's ruined the magic of the moment," Jill said.

"Dad will ruin it even more in a minute."

Simon stood and turned the gas off. The whistle slowly died away. Mr Darby returned to the kitchen, and began to fuss around, making tea.

Simon sat down again, and looked at his watch. "We should go soon," he said to Jill. As he finished speaking, there was a knock at the door.

"No, don't trouble yourself, lovebirds," Mr Darby said. "I'll get "un."

Mr Darby returned with and Nick. "I found this squashed old prune on the doorstep. Belong to you, do 'e?"

Jill smiled at Mr Darby. "If he's an old prune, what does that make you? The dried-up, desiccated, dusty remains of an old prune?"

Mr Darby came over, put his arm around Jill's shoulders, and tousled her hair. He looked at Simon. "I likes 'em feisty, I likes "em feisty. Can I have this one? Go on, Si, go on."

"I don't think mum would be keen," Simon said.

Mr Darby laughed as he picked up the mugs and carried them away to the lounge. "I likes 'em feisty, so you better mind your p's and q's."

"What does that mean?' Nick said. "I've always wondered."

"I don't know," Jill said.

"You don't know?' Simon said. "You don't know. Amazing. You don't know something? Stumped at last. I'm flabbergasted."

"Come on," Nick said. "My stomach thinks my throat's been cut. Let's go and find Gaz."

"He's already down the Lion," Simon said. "Jill bumped into him on the way here."

"We'd better get down there then," Nick said. "Before he can claim he's already spent all his money waiting for us."

"Where's Mark?" Simon asked.

"He phoned me an hour or so ago. He said might meet us later. He's meeting some art dealer from Salisbury."

"What?"

"He came to the exhibition and liked what he saw. He wants to sell some of Mark's pictures."

"You two did something really good." Jill said. She smiled, and her eyes twinkled. She kissed Simon's cheek.

Simon felt good. He was happy he'd helped Mark. Jill's smile was warm, and Nick smiled too. Yet, despite all this happiness, Simon was confused by what Jill had said. Why had she told him about Anna? Why had she rekindled his confusion?

He looked at Nick again. The smile had fallen and the eyes were distant. They both knew something mad and bad had happened last night. They had each phoned the other during the day, and phoned Mark and Gaz, to check that that they were safe, that nothing had *happened*. None of them knew if the hitman would take any notice of Nick's note and leave them alone. Only time would tell.

25

Copsehill was quiet. It was a Sunday night, so Molly had been unsurprised to find only a few people on the road by the gates. Richard Patterson was there, of course. She hadn't yet seen Kurt and Cathy. Patterson said he thought he'd seen them earlier, but was vague as to the time, and whether they had been arriving or going, or leaning on a gate, or sitting on a grassy bank. Perhaps they had walked up to the copse. One of the women she had visited with Nick was on the hill, so Molly passed some time chatting to her. The topic of Peta came up, inevitably, but the woman knew no more than she did the last time Molly had talked to her. There was the really quiet guy, Billy, red-haired, round-faced, a little dumpy. He seemed to be on the hill nearly as often as Patterson. She had tried once or twice on her visits to the hill to engage him in conversation, but he mumbled and shuffled around shyly, providing only terse responses. She had given up on him, and left him to stare at the sky alone.

Molly was beginning to wish she'd hooked up with the guys at the Lion, although she'd seen Nick earlier and he seemed distracted, somehow. Perhaps he'd fallen out with his friends. Such things did happen, so she'd heard, but she had never had a group of friends close enough to fall out with. Perhaps Simon and that Jill he was dating had split up. Perhaps Nick had cuckolded Simon. Her imagination was beginning to run away with her. Something was up, she was certain. She would find out soon enough. She would be back in the Lion tomorrow, or the next day. Her time in Dereham was, though, winding down now, she could feel it. She hadn't found Peta, she hadn't found Archie, and soon Kurt would be back in West Germany. She looked around the skywatchers, at the distant lights scattered around the distant streets, across the downs and around the edge of the Plain, the car headlights on distant roads; she looked into the sky at the bright, hard stars, visible fleetingly between broken cumuli.

"Penny for them," Patterson said, beside her.

Molly sighed. "Oh, I'm going to miss all of this."

"Are you leaving us?"

"Yes, my holiday is nearly over. There are a few loose ends to tie up. But I must get back to London, back to work."

"It's been a pleasure meeting you."

"Thanks, Richard. It's been nice connecting with you, and coming up here."

"Do you believe in our flying friends yet?"

Molly smiled at Patterson. "I'm afraid not."

"Not even after the things you saw and heard last weekend?"

"No." Molly chewed her lip. Patterson seemed a gentle man, obsessed, perhaps, with his harmless if misguided beliefs, and though he was distant and detached he had been, from all she'd learned and heard, kind to Peta. "That UFO, last week," she said quietly. "It was a satellite."

"I'm sure it wasn't. Kurt had no idea what it was."

"I'm afraid Kurt doesn't know everything."

"What about the aliens Mary saw?"

"If they *were* aliens, that Mary saw them when she did was a merely a coincidence. Chances are, though, they weren't aliens."

"Have you been talking to people? Sceptics?"

"I have. Simon, Nick..."

"Both deniers, certainly. Was it from them you heard about this *satellite*? What makes them so sure?"

"From them, I learned about the power of coincidence and how the mind likes to make meanings from patterns. Although they suggested the light could have been a satellite, my confirmation didn't come from them."

"Oh? Where did it come from?"

Molly heard voices on the track down from the copse. She recognised one as Kurt's.

"Recall our first meeting, Richard. Do you remember something Nick said in passing? Something he might have joked about? Something that might have struck you as a little odd?"

Patterson stroked his chin. "I remember you talking about Archie. I remember you saying how he might be a murderer, and I remember... Oh, yes, Nick joking about you being a spy."

"That light we saw *was* a satellite. Who it belongs to, I cannot say. What it does, I cannot say. But a satellite it most assuredly is."

Kurt and Cathy had climbed over the gate that blocked that path to the copse. They stood now between Patterson and the other skywatchers, perfectly placed such that a conversation with them would be overheard by everybody. Molly moved around Patterson to meet them.

Cathy saw her first. "Hello!" She looked around. "Is Simon not with you?"

"Not tonight."

"I thought I saw him with another woman this afternoon," Kurt said, with a hint of amusement.

"Oh, you almost certainly did. He has a girlfriend, Jill. I was just joshing the other day."

"Did you get the photos developed?" Cathy asked.

"You look great. I gave the photos of *you* to Mark. He has a crush on you."

"Oh. Really?"

"Why would you do that, Molly?" Kurt said.

"You found out my name! How very... sweet!"

"And where are the other photos?"

Molly unzipped her leather jacket and pulled out a manila envelope. "Don't worry, they're here." She waved the envelope in front of the man she still thought of as Kurt. She shouldn't do it, but this was the denouement; she should be allowed some fun. Soon she would go back to London, and read reports, follow, and watch. She rarely had the chance to face up to somebody on whom she had intelligence. "I should tell you, there has been great interest in these photos."

Movement caught her eye. The few people who remained on the hill were pretending to ignore a conversation they didn't really understand. Billy, however, was wandering slowly around the back of the group, his hands pressed into his bomber jacket, his head down. Molly knew Billy was shy and awkward. He might be mildly autistic, she thought, and having difficulty with this confrontation.

Kurt too looked around to see who was moving. Then he looked back at Molly. "Who would be interested in those things?"

Billy was walking faster now, still not looking at the group.

"Many people are interested in these photos..." Molly said. Then she added, "Dieter."

Many things then happened in very quick succession. As soon as Billy heard the name Dieter, he began to run. As soon as Billy ran, Kurt ran too. Molly had no option but to zip the envelope back under her jacket and chase after both of them.

She heard Patterson say, "What on earth..." before the only sounds in the darkness were the slap of footsteps and the susurration of breath. Billy and Kurt were shapes ahead of her. Then Kurt was shouting out to Billy to stop, and then some swearing, she thought, mainly in German, and then the shapes ahead of her fell to the ground. Then Molly too was on Kurt, trying to pull him off Billy. Thirty seconds later, Cathy was pulling Molly's hair and shouting, "Get off him, bitch."

Cathy was easily dealt with. Molly, five inches taller, turned, head-butted her, and then punched her on the chin. Cathy dropped quietly to the floor. Meanwhile, Kurt and Billy were still locked together on the road, wrestling. She looked at the pair of them. Whatever Kurt was up to, he was from West Germany, and was, at least, on the side of democracy. She had no idea who Billy was. One well-aimed quick stopped his struggling. Kurt untangled himself from the unconscious Billy's arms, and sat down on the road. Molly sat down beside him. "Should I call you Dieter or Kurt?"

Even in the dark, Molly could detect Kurt's resigned smile. "In this country, I prefer Kurt."

Molly stretched out her hand to him. "Molly Shepherd," she said. "Security Service."

Kurt took her hand and shook it. "Dieter Köhler, Bundesnachrichtendienst."

The rest of the skywatchers were walking down the road towards them. How to explain all of this? She thought she should make everything official. When Patterson was close enough to hear, she said, "Richard, do you have a torch with you?"

"Yes, yes, I do."

"Could I have it, please?"

"Of course."

Molly took the proffered torch, and then removed her identity card from the inside pocket of her leather coat. She shone the torch on it and showed it to Kurt. "You know I have no power of arrest. However, we should have chat, don't you think?"

"Yes," Kurt said. "But you do need to arrest him." He nodded towards Billy.

"Local plod or Special Branch?"

"Oh, Special Branch, certainly." Jan's accent had now become more obviously German. "But you need him arrested now. Your local police can do that."

"True enough." She looked up at Patterson. "Can you or somebody get down to Red Post Farm and phone for the police?"

One of the regular skywatchers stepped forward. "I have my car here. I can drive to the police station."

"Good idea," Molly said. "Take Richard with you, they know him."

Patterson and the skywatcher walked back up the hill towards a white Hillman Avenger. Molly and Kurt stood. Kurt dragged the unconscious Billy to the side of the road, and leaned him against the bank. Molly went over to Cathy, and shook her. Cathy's eyes opened, slowly at first, and then wide. "Bitch," she said weakly, and made to flail at Molly, before falling slowly back down.

"Hello, Cathy Davidson. I'm Molly Shepherd from the Security Service. Liz Carter sends her regards."

Cathy looked around to find Kurt. He nodded at her, and she sagged, defeated. Molly put an arm around Cathy's waist and helped her up, and walked her to the bank at the side of the road. The other skywatchers moved out of the way as the white Avenger passed them.

A skywatcher spoke. It was the woman Molly had been chatting to earlier. "What should we do, Molly? Do you need our help? Do you need us as witnesses?"

Molly shook her head. "No, Sally, you can all go. The police will only move you on when they get here anyway."

The remaining male skywatcher said, "What if it gets rough again."

"It won't will it, Kurt?" Molly said. Kurt shrugged. "He knows we know who he is. He's got nowhere to run. Anyway, Kurt's on our side. If our friend Billy there wakes up, he's going to be too feeble to fight me and Kurt. So go on, push off the lot of you. Indulge in some idle speculation on the way home."

There was some nervous laughter, but the skywatchers said goodnight, and walked slowly away down the hill. Molly waited until they were out of earshot. "We've got about ten minutes before the police get here. Everybody will be arrested, of course, and I'll have to do some paperwork. Special Branch will arrive and take you all away somewhere, but you, Kurt will undoubtedly soon be out, and on your way back to Germany, and Cathy... Well, you've been a naughty girl, but I expect we'll forgive you. We know you were just grumpy with us. We have a suggestion to make. Now, tell me Kurt. What are you up to? You're on our side!"

He had been sent to England for three reasons, Kurt said. One was to find out anything he could about military hardware.

There was a feeling that, because of their position in the Second World War, West Germany was not being fully informed about American military innovations. There was some resentment, Kurt said

"So that explains your movements then," Molly said. "Plymouth, Cirencester, and then here."

"Yes. Cirencester was where I met Cathy."

Cathy laughed quietly. "And I had my own resentments, of course."

"Of course. What else?"

"Second," Kurt continued, "there were the alien contacts."

Molly groaned. "Not BND too?"

"Ja, BND too. Our Michael Schmidt is the equivalent of your Parker-Martens. He too thinks that the... contactees... might actually be talking to spacemen and might find out something important. And if the spacemen tell the British how to make a better gun, Schmidt thinks the Germans should know too."

"It's mad isn't it?" Molly said.

"Probably," Kurt said. "It's a good job for me though."

Billy groaned beside them, but remained unconscious.

"I'd imagine it would be. Have you discovered anything?"

"Well, there aren't that many real contactees – whatever a real contactee is. Many frauds, of course. The best one I saw was here."

Molly's heart suddenly filled. "Here? Who?"

"Oh, it was quite a long time ago now. Peta she was called."

"Of course," Molly said quietly. "Peta."

"You knew her?"

"She's the reason I'm here. You and Cathy are a sideshow. Peta Shepherd is my sister. I'm trying to find her."

"Have you?" Cathy said.

"I find traces of her," Molly said. "But nothing of substance. Only the skywatchers really knew her, and everything about her is wrapped in that experience. I don't believe in it, so I can't share it. It distanced her."

"We never knew her well, either," Kurt said. "It wasn't only her belief in UFOs that made her remote. She was wrapped up in that boyfriend of hers. She spent a lot of time at home, reading, I think, and looking after him."

"Archibald Franklin Conn," Molly said. "I'm looking for him, too..."

"So am I," Kurt said.

"Michael Schmidt?" Molly said.

"Yes. Daniel Parker-Martens?"

"Oh yes. It seems we're all worried that Archie found out something from Peta before he left."

"Do you think he did?"

"Well, if you're looking for him too, you'll know he appears to lead a quiet life as a respectable antique book dealer. He's not involved in the UFO scene, and though his bank balance shows large, one-off payments, we assume these are associated with the sale of interesting and rare first editions. If he'd learned about some anti-gravity device and sold it to the Yanks or Japs, I'd expect rather more money in his bank account."

"Yes. And I would expect him to be secured in a well-guarded ranch in the middle of Wyoming, not in... where is it, a town house in Cheltenham?"

"What was he like?"

Cathy spoke now. "Good looking. Obviously a bruiser. Kurt picked up information on him, stuff you'll know, ex-Army, been in security, done some petty thieving, had been ear-marked for special forces, so not somebody you'd casually pick a fight with. Full of himself. Always looking for easy money. All the ladies around here liked him, but I don't think he ever cheated on your sister. I think he liked her, as far as that went. Your sister was a pretty girl, there was no need for him to chase anybody else."

At the words "pretty girl", Molly's heart filled again, and her throat tightened.

"He was a bad man, I suppose," Cathy continued. "He should never have dumped your sister like that. The skywatchers didn't liked him, and when Peta... left us, you could tell the sky-watchers all blamed him. But..."

"But what?" Molly forced out.

"He was just a *bloke*, you know. He liked Peta, but didn't love her. Whatever it was he wanted, he wasn't getting it from her, or from this town. So he split. He might have had some trouble coming his way, too, I don't know. Men like him often do. Unfinished business, you know?"

Molly did know - Len Stone was coming, and Archie had to leave.

"Whatever it was, he didn't love Peta enough to stay here with Peta and suck up whatever he had coming, nor strong enough to take her with him, wherever he was going."

Molly could see flashing blue lights in the distance now. She turned to Kurt. "So, they'll be here soon, and we'll be separated. You know you shouldn't be working here without the authority of MI5. We have arrangements in place, as you know. You'll be rapped on the knuckles and sent home. Cathy, we're going to forget you were Kurt's accomplice. We know you had a grudge against the security services. But we strongly advise... *strongly*... that you apply to Special Branch and use that brain of yours. We'll help you."

"Can't I go to Germany with Dieter?"

Now *that* was love, Molly thought. She shrugged. "I don't know. I can't see why not. I'll talk to my boss about it."

Two police cars and an ambulance came up the hill. Molly wasn't surprised to see Patterson get out of one them. The police handcuffed the still unconscious Billy, who was then loaded into the ambulance. Kurt and Cathy were handcuffed and put into a police car. The ambulance reversed down the hill. The police car containing Kurt and Cath drove up towards the gates, executed a three point turn, and then returned. As it slowly passed Molly, she had a sudden thought, and banged on its roof. The car stopped. She opened the rear passenger door. "What was the third thing?"

"What?" Kurt said.

"You said there were three reasons you were here."

"Oh. Billy, of course. His name is Hans Gerber, and *he* is HVA. He was here, wandering around the Plain, chatting to soldiers, spying on military installations, counting armour and trucks, photographing planes and helicopters... We think he had a handler over here, somebody higher up. It was his handler we wanted."

"Oh," Molly said. "Sorry. I've ruined your operation."

Kurt shrugged, and smiled grimly. "Those are the risks in our business. We'll pass on what we know. You might get to follow it up."

"Thanks. That'll be a job for Six, really." Molly said goodbye to Kurt and Cathy, and closed the car door. The police car headed down the hill. Molly got into the other police car, which turned around, and then drove into town, leaving Patterson alone on the hill no doubt contemplating his latest news story, and whether he would be able to tell it.

As they drove under the amber streetlights, Molly knew the rest of the night was unlikely to be her own, with first the local police and then Special Branch asking questions. She thought she had at last learned something different about Peta and Archie, something not seen through the eyes of the skywatchers. She felt she had for a moment been in contact with two broken humans, Peta and Archie. She loved and missed Peta, of course – but was Archie really the bad guy, the demon, she had so often wanted him to be?

26

Molly came down from her room, and pushed through the door of the lounge bar. It was quiet at the moment. Few of the tables were occupied. But then it was Monday evening. She saw Simon's friend Gaz at the bar. Gaz, the curt, unfathomable one, with his mop of curly hair and battered combat jacket. She sat on a bar stool close to him, and thought she might start a conversation with him. He wasn't bad looking. She was in a strange town, and up for a bit of harmless flirting. She might leave soon, anyway. Patterson hadn't known much, and there were few people around who remembered Peta. Her interest in ufology had quickly formed and had as quickly faded. People talked about UFOs too much, and not enough about Peta. Her sister might have left footprints in this town, but now, after four years, those prints were fading.

Gaz rolled his pint glass between his palms, and looked vacantly at the optics in front of him. On top of the bar, between his arms, was a wallet.

"Hello, Gaz," Molly said,

He seemed surprised to hear her voice. He turned. "Oh, hello Molly." He smiled at her. "You're a nice looking bird. Any chance of a date?"

Molly laughed. "Not a hope."

"Oh well, those boots make you look a bit too tough, really."

Molly leaned closer to Gaz. "That's because I am."

"Oh, yes? Think you could beat me up?"

Molly favoured him with her cold, hard stare. "Almost certainly." She was pleased to see the cheeky grin fall from Gaz's face. His eyes returned to the wallet in front of him.

Gaz looked at her again. He sipped his beer, and then said, "What about Simon? Think you could have him?"

Simon was a big lad, there was no doubt. Gaz's eyes were mischievous. There was something he knew that should temper her reply. "Probably not," she said.

"Oh, very good. You're very... astute..."

"That's because I'm a spy."

"Yes, Simon told us. I didn't believe him."

"I don't think Simon believed me either."

"You look nothing like a spy. You're too pretty."

"How do you think Mata Hari got all those secrets?"

"You don't mean to say you–"

"No, I don't mean to say I sleep with men to get information."

"Shame. Mind you, I haven't got any information, anyway." He looked down at the wallet.

"It's quiet in here," Molly said. "I'm going to put some money in the jukebox. Anything you fancy?"

"No. No, thanks." Gaz was still looking at the wallet.

Molly walked over to the jukebox. There was an interesting selection of music on it. So, had happened on Copsehill had not been broadcast. The skywatchers were a tight-knit group. Patterson might have had some influence there. She picked two obscure singles, *Oscilloscope Traces* by The Mighty Ones, and *House on the Hill* by The Gentlemen Farmers. She had one more selection, and chose *Burlesque*, by Family. *Burlesque* came on first, and the riff crashed out of the speakers. She moved her hips slowly for a moment, and sipped at her vodka tonic. She turned to look at Gaz, who was now reading something, a piece of paper he held in his hands in front of him. Gaz looked tense as he examined that paper. Molly walked over to him quietly, alert for something. She never knew why she was alert, what had triggered the feeling. They had told her at Five she was good at reading body language. She hadn't understood what that had meant, but soon found herself reading *The Naked Ape* and understanding more. She was now a student of body language, and read any books she could find about it.

She crept up quietly behind Gaz, who now seemed lost in what he was reading. She could see that it was only a driver's license. She came closer, until she could read the name on it. Her stomach flipped.

"Archibald Franklin Fucking Conn," she said. "I thought your name was Gaz?"

Gaz came out of his reverie. "Oh, that's not me. I *am* Gaz. Archibald Franklin Conn is... well, he's a..."

"Yes?' Molly said. She was eager for more. "What is he?"

"Look, are you really a spy?"

"Would you believe me if I said yes?"

"Maybe. Maybe not."

"Yes."

Gaz shrugged. "It doesn't matter."

"Come on Gaz, tell me."

"I... I found it. In the road."

"What road? Where?"

"In... Barton Road... I found it."

This was the moment to hit him, Molly knew, right now, while he was confused, while he was lying, trying to construct a story that he hoped would make sense. She would confuse him even more, break the stories down until the truth came out. "Yes, you found it, but found it where?"

"In Barton Road, I said–"

"In the gutter or on the pavement?"

"In the gutter. I–"

"Or the hedgerow or the road? The wallet's black, how did you see it?"

"It was there, in the road, and–"

"I thought you said the gutter? How could you see it? Gutters are so dark and dirty, dried dust and weeds, how could you see it, it's so black, surely you mean the road, that would be easier to see, yes?"

"Yes, that's it, of course, in the road, that's–"

"And did you dart out in between the cars to fetch it, did you look both ways before you went, how fast did you have to run, it can be difficult picking up things in the road, I hope you were safe."

"Well, of course, I looked both ways, I found a gap, I went into the road, and then-"

"Are you sure it was the road? After all, it would be difficult in the traffic, cars running over it, it would look like a bit of tyre rubber, wouldn't it, or a bit of exhaust pipe. What made you think it was interesting, if it was in the road, it could have been a brake pad... Do you often run out into the road to check out small, dark squares? I mean, it's dangerous out there, all those cars. You must have seen it in the hedgerow, that's easy to spot, right? A black square, in among all those leaves, that would be easy, right, you'd expect to see it there, yeah?"

"Yes," Gaz, said, "the hedge, it was in the hedge."

"Top or bottom, down by the roots or caught in the branches? Was it a flat privet hedge in front of a house or a straggly old hedge around a playing field? I don't know Dereham like you, but you'd think if it was a privet, well, they grow close, don't they, all the leaves and twigs tangled together, you'd expect the wallet to be right on top, easy to see, wouldn't you, yeah?"

"Oh, I don't sodding know where I bloody well found it," Gaz finally said.

Molly had overloaded him, and it had worked. "Yes, you do know where you found it, but it wasn't in the road, or a gutter or whatever. You lifted it, didn't you?"

Gaz gave her a steady look. "Okay." He looked around at the barman. "Not here." They carried their drinks over to a small table in the corner of the bar.

When they'd seated themselves, Gaz sipped at his pint and then said, "Archibald Franklin Conn is hitman."

"Is that what he's been doing?"

"You didn't laugh."

"What?"

"You didn't laugh. A bloke you hardly know says some other bloke you don't know is a hitman. A *hitman*. Bloody hell. You don't come across one of them every day. *We* all laughed, at first."

"We?"

"All of us. Me, Simon, and Mark."

"Nick mentioned meeting a hitman at Mark's exhibition."

Molly rubbed her chin, thinking. "Is this the hitman Nick was talking about?"

"Yes. But how do you know him?"

"What?"

"You said, *Is that what he's been doing*, as if you knew him."

"I don't really know him at all."

Gaz looked at her coolly. "But you do know something."

"And so do you."

"Are you looking for him?"

"I'm looking for my sister."

"So this Conn has something to do with her?"

Molly sighed. Everything returned to Peta. "Yes, he's involved. Now tell me, what do you know?"

"You said Nick had told you about him."

"Tell me again, in your own words. How the hell did Nick meet a hitman? And why do you have his wallet"

Gaz explained everything, from Nick's first meeting with Archie, through the repeated sightings of the car, the Manley death, and Nick and Mark following Archie on the motorbike. Molly listened attentively.

"He must be a rubbish hitman, though," Gaz concluded. "Simon got him with one hit. He nutted him." He stopped talking then, and sipped at his beer.

"And the wallet?" Molly said.

"Oh! Surely you've guessed," Gaz said.

"Confirm it."

"When the hitman was unconscious last night, I couldn't resist the urge to...' He nodded at the wallet on the table in front of him. "Well, steal it."

"What did Archie look like?' Molly said.

"Shorter than Si or Nick. About the same height as me, I think. But mean looking. Tough." Gaz smiled. "Like you.

Handsome too, I suppose. Nothing like Shirley Temple." Gaz started laughing.

"Shirley Temple?"

Gaz told Molly about Mark's drawing. Everything fitted. Rough, tough, handsome Archie. Her friend Len had always said Archie was a good looking bloke. A chancer, a rogue, a conman, and now a hitman.

"Simon's a big enough lad, as I recall," Molly said. "But how could that hippie have got one over Archie?"

"Kung fu," Gaz said. "He does kung fu. He's very fast. He never boasts about it."

Of course, she thought. kung fu was sweeping the nation. Simon must be good. If he *was* good, and was living the discipline like in that TV programme, he wouldn't boast about how good he was. He'd be *quietly* good, he'd be modest. He'd only fight when necessary. It made sense.

"So Simon *would* be able to best me in a fight."

"What?"

"You asked earlier if I was hard enough to beat Simon in a fight. The answer is obviously no. Shit. Nick's lucky Simon turned up."

Gaz nodded, the swigged back some beer. "Lucky indeed. I always thought the kung fu he did was a bit..." He looked at Molly, slyly. "*Wanky.* But it came in very useful last night."

They were both quiet for a moment. Gaz broke the silence. "So what are you thinking? Are you a spy? Is there a connection here, some secret spy thing? Or is it all ... circumstantial?"

Molly studied Gaz, wondering how much she should tell him. "You've probably guessed that I've been looking for Archibald Franklin Conn."

"Yeah, I was slowly sussing that out." Gaz voiced his fears, then. "But I'm worried about this wallet," he said. "I was dumb to steal it. He's not going to like that, is he?"

"I guess not. But what can you do? You could chuck it, but that wouldn't help. I'd keep it if I were you. It could be good evidence. Why did you steal it?"

"I'm... Well, I think I'm a bit of a kleptomaniac. The wallet felt good, you know, and I could tell there was a lot of money in there."

"How much?"

"A hundred quid in notes."

"Keep that too," Molly said. "He's hardly likely to ask for it back." She waved her empty glass in front of Gaz. "You could buy me a drink with it."

"What are you going to do?"

"About what?"

"About Mr Franklin Conn."

"Funny you call him Mr Franklin Conn, while I, who hate his guts, call him Archie. But that was how we all knew him, Peta, Len, Harry, and now me. He was Archie. Always Archie."

"So... What are you going to do?"

"Call Special Branch. Now get me that drink. Vodka and coke this time."

As Gaz walked to the bar, the others arrived – Mark, Nick, Simon arrived, with a blonde girl Molly guessed must be Jill. Gaz bought drinks for them all. Molly saw that he wisely used Archie's money. They carried their drinks over and joined Molly at the table. Gaz handed her the vodka and coke.

"I told her about our adventure last night," Gaz said as he sat down.

"Well, she is a spy," Simon said. "Who better to tell?"

Jill looked around them all, puzzled. "What?"

"Prepare to get your brain even more bent out of shape, blondie," Gaz said. "She *knows* the hitman."

Nick looked over towards Molly "Personally?"

"I've never met him," Molly said. "I know people who have. My sister was one of them, of course. He is, as far as I can tell, an egocentric, selfish, self-centred bastard, who very likely drove my sister to suicide. He is Archibald Franklin Conn."

Jill looked at Molly. "How did you make the connection between Nick's hitman and this man Conn?"

Molly looked at Gaz. "I think you should ask your friend."

All eyes turned on Gaz. He blushed. He explained how he had stolen the wallet, and how Molly had seen the driving license.

The eyes staring at him had slowly grown a little wider. Mark finally said, "You bloody idiot. He's going to come back for that."

"Hey, if you hadn't wanted to be Chrissie's hero, none of this would have started."

"Yeah, well..." Mark said. "Blame Simon."

Jill interrupted the flow of tit-for-tat. "And if you and Nick hadn't followed the car the first time, if Nick had never told you about his journey, if Nick hadn't got in that car, if he'd only caught the bus. Cause without end all the way back to the prime mover! We can't untangle the web we've created."

"What?" said Gaz.

Nick laughed. "Fair point, Jill. Let's blame God."

"Especially if you don't believe in him."

There was silence around the table. Molly felt the need to add some more detail. "And *somebody* killed my boyfriend, Harry. It was a hit. My friend Len - he's one of those hippie, new age sorts, you know - well, he thought Archibald Franklin Fucking Conn killed Harry."

"How did he know?"

"He didn't know, not in the way you're thinking - there was no evidence, there were no obvious links. He just *felt* it. Len... umm... thinks of himself as spiritually advanced, in contact with... higher beings, let's say."

"Of course," Simon interjected. "Your sister was into UFOs, that's why she was here."

"Yes, and Len was the Peta's first real friend. A father figure, definitely, but a friend too. They shared... experiences together." Gaz smirked. Molly pretended not to notice. "Archie was with her in those days," she continued. "And then the story gets complicated, and involves security stuff including my boyfriend, and we can't go there. Suffice to say, Harry is dead, and I have reason to believe, on no other evidence than the wacky theories of my hippie friend, that he died at the hands of Archie Conn."

"So what will you do," Nick said.

"Nothing. Without evidence there's nothing I can do. Archie beat you up, that's all we know for certain. Even you knew he'd get nothing but a fine or a short sentence for ABH. Gaz told me about the note. I'll talk to Special Branch – this would normally be their concern – and tell them what I know. But that's all I can do. You'll just have to be careful."

Molly shrugged. "We are where we are, my new found friends." She smiled. "I'll do what I can through... uh... channels I have."

Simon smiled at Molly. "Go on, tell us. Are you really a spy?"

Molly smiled back. "And I will inform Special Branch that we might have uncovered a hitman. Sadly, they will need more evidence than duffing up Nick, but it'll be something for them. Gaz, keep the wallet on you. Keep the money, of course, but if Archie turns up looking for it, the best thing you can do is hand it over. Just say you're a kleptomaniac."

Nick looked up from his drink. "What were you doing stealing his wallet anyway?"

Gaz glanced at Molly. She remained impassive. "Well, I thought, you know," Gaz said. "Mr Franklin Conn had just done over one of my mates, and this seemed like a way to get him back. He paid for these drinks, after all."

"Oh, that's all right then," Mark laughed. He lifted his pint of lager. "Cheers, Archibald Franklin Fucking Conn." He took a large gulp.

The others also cheered Archibald Franklin Fucking Conn. They laughed, although there was something brittle about the laughter, Molly thought.

Gaz put down his glass. "And what about you, Molly-Tough-Spy-Woman?"

"Oh, I'll be around. Somebody has to watch out for you all."

Molly wanted to reassure them, to make them feel safe in the town they called home. But she didn't feel assured herself. She couldn't be everywhere. And Archie was, after all, a hitman. A military-trained professional. A sociopath. Archie *would* be back. She had to remain in Dereham now, she had to be here for the next act - to protect her new friends, and to finally meet Archibald Franklin Conn.

27

That evening, Archie parked his car in Malthouse Road, and then walked again on the main road out of town, towards the gateway of Barton House. There was nobody else on the pavements. The road was quiet. He kept his eye on the crossroads as he approached the gateway, wondering if Nick and his freaky friends would all converge on the street sign around which they so often congregated. Nobody came, and he reached the gateway unseen. He looked over the road for a moment. Was it possible that the old geezer who'd splashed water on his face had stolen his wallet? He doubted it. Evening was falling, and the gateway, shaded by trees, was dark. He looked around the tarmac on the short driveway leading to the gates, in the scrubby grass at the edge of the driveway, and kicked away the leaves that had already fallen. His wallet was nowhere to be seen.

He had thought that Nick or one of his friends would have been too sensible to steal it. One of his friends might have been tempted by the money – Combat Jacket, he looked the sort. But keeping the wallet and the driving licence would, they surely knew, be dumb. Hippie Boy might have got one over on him, but that wouldn't happen again. Archie thought that Nick had understood the danger they were all in – hence the note.

Somebody else might have taken the wallet, of course. Finders, keepers. There had been a lot of money in it. He would have taken it if he'd found it. He'd have kept the money and dumped the wallet, including the credit card. The money would have been enough for most people. He searched around the ground one last time, and then gave up. He returned to the pavement and looked down the road into town. It wouldn't hurt to check out the police station. Archie knew Dereham from his stay here, four years ago now, and trips to the town when he had been stationed at Tidworth. Pleasant people lived here, salt-of-the-earth working men and middle-class families, the kind of people who handed fat wallets into the police.

When he reached Town Road, he glanced behind him, wondering if he would see Nick, or Hippie Boy, or Combat Jacket following him. He would have liked to see Blondie, but he saw instead a woman at a distance behind him, still in Barton Road. He could see she was wearing jeans and a leather jacket. Even from this distance there was, though, something disconcerting about her. She looked somehow familiar, like somebody who shouldn't be there. He was tempted to wait for her, yet at the same time he didn't really want to bump into people who might recognise him, like Richard Patterson, or some of those crazy ufologists he and Peta used to hang around with. He entered the police station and talked to the desk sergeant, who checked the lost property, but found no wallet matching the description Archie gave. Archie provided his telephone number to the sergeant, and then walked back toward his car.

As he passed The White Lion, he glanced at the door, wondering if this was the pub favoured by Nick and his friends. It almost certainly was – when he had lived here, this pub had been the haunt of hippies and students. Should he go in and see if Nick was there? He decided against it. As he walked back up Town Road, towards Malthouse Lane and his NSU, he looked behind him again. He felt as if he was being watched, and wondered if the woman in the leather jacket was still behind him. There were only a few Sunday-night drinkers heading towards The White Lion and The Swan, a few cars with their lights on now as darkness fell.

He reached his car. He started the NSU, and slowly approached the junction of Malthouse Road and Barton Road. He edged out, and drove into Town Road, intending to turn right onto Derebury Road and cut around the top of the town, on the road that curved beneath the down that fell from Derebury Hill. Then, just as he indicated, he noticed the woman in the leather jacket and jeans leaning against the wall of one of the houses on the corner. He cancelled the indicator, driving instead slowly along Town Road. The woman was looking down at her feet, her hair falling across her face. Archie felt sure he recognised her, and in that recognition there was a frisson of fear. Why that should be, Archie didn't understand. He glanced in his rear view mirror. The woman had levered herself away from the wall after he had passed her, and was now walking into town. She had lifted her head, but it was dark, and she was becoming more distant as he drove into the Market Place. Yet, even then, there was the odd feeling of recognition, and a sensation of danger because of that face.

He drove on through Dereham, thinking about the woman, and this feeling. Once outside of town, and on the Bath Road, he put his foot down and began to speed towards his home in Cheltenham. His thoughts returned to his wallet. If somebody had nicked his wallet for the money, well, he could understand that. He'd have done the same. But what if Nick or one of the others had picked it up? They'd have his address now. What could they do with that? Come up to Cheltenham, mob-handed, and beat him up? Nick wanted to let sleeping dogs lie. Yet, his wallet *was* missing, and it had gone missing the night of the fight. Nick or one of his friends could have taken it. Who else could it have been? It would be so useful to them, a kind of insurance. They would know his name now, as well. That hadn't struck Archie before. They knew his name, they knew he lived in Cheltenham, they knew he went to Bournemouth. Peter had Archie's surname, as did The Cow. Nick wasn't dumb, he'd be able to make the connections. Archie wasn't in the telephone book, but his wife was. She had no reason to be ex-directory. Nick could, if minded, find out where Peter and The Cow lived. That information would give Nick a certain amount of traction, a lever if he needed it. And Nick now knew that Archie was a hitman. If Nick had the licence, he might think he had power over Archie, that he could use that power.

Travelling fast, enjoying the sweep of the bends even as he thought through his problems, he soon arrived at the outskirts of Bath. He knew a short cut to the A46. Before he indicated, he wondered if he should turn back to Dereham, and find Nick. That would mean adding another forty miles to his journey as he went there and back, another hour. And there was the disconcerting image of that woman. He didn't turn back, he indicated right, turned into the narrow road and skirted past the centre of Bath to the Cheltenham road. He would visit Dereham again, very soon. He would find Nick, and ask about the wallet. He must know what had happened to it, for Peter's sake – even if that meant roughing-up Nick to the point where Archie could be sure he was telling the truth.

28

Jill hadn't been at college today. Simon didn't know why. He had sat in the refectory at lunch-time with Warren, who had come to terms with Jill snubbing him. Anna had come in with Joan, and while Joan favoured Simon with her supercilious smile, Anna had caught his eye, and looked at him thoughtfully. She then smiled at him in a way she hadn't for weeks. She had stood then, and walked over to Simon's table. "What the bloody hell are we doing, Si? Can you meet me, in the park, after lectures?"

Simon looked up at her, at the oval face, the almond eyes, and something clicked into place, a piece had been fitted into the jigsaw.

Anna smiled, and walked out of the door. Joan hurried to catch up with her. The refectory was walled on the corridor side with windows full of meshed safety glass. Simon could see that Joan was talking sternly to Anna, but she was only laughing in reply. They disappeared from view. Simon smiled as he sipped at his tea, but then Warren spoke, his voice stern.

"Yes, what the fuck *are* you doing, Si? What about Jill?"

He remembered what Jill had said. "We spoke about Anna on Saturday night. Jill had been speaking to Anna's sister. It turned out that Anna liked me all along. Then Jill said something like "I don't want to hang around with a boy whose true heart lies elsewhere, always with somebody else." Then, she said, "If Anna talks to you on Monday, you'll know where your true heart lies'."

"So you know where your true heart now lies?"

Simon smiled at Warren. "I think so."

"So I can have a crack at Jill then?"

"You haven't a hope in hell of cracking that nut."

"I don't want to crack her nut."

"Yeah, well you have little chance of cracking anything else."

"I know. I'll go back to seeking revenge on that tit of a bus driver."

"You're not still thinking about that are you?"

Warren smiled conspiratorially.

After college, as arranged, Simon had met Anna in the park. They had quickly fallen back into the easy togetherness they had shared before the summer holidays. They walked around the paths and across the grass together. They laughed. Then things became serious. She *had* kissed a boy during the holidays, just as he'd kissed Julie. Those kisses hadn't meant much, she said.

Simon looked down. "But what about Jill?"

"I'm not jealous," Anna said, "I understand."

"Jill encouraged, me, you know... To talk to you."

Anna laughed. "I'm not surprised. She talked to Angie. Then to me. Did she say anything about true hearts?"

"Oh! Yes she did."

"She's very wise, Jill. I've known her years, of course, because she's Angie's friend."

They were walking beside each other, along a gravel path. Simon took Anna's hand. "We never loved each other, Jill and me. We never did."

"You never had time to. I can imagine you two might have fallen in love, though."

"But I couldn't get you out of my head."

"I couldn't get you out of mine."

"What did I do wrong? Why did you snub me, at the Fresher's Ball?"

"Oh, nothing much, you know. Ever since I've known you, I've dropped these little hints, hoping that you'd do something."

"I never spotted them. I thought you were just a cheeky girl who liked making suggestive jokes."

"After we'd been apart all summer, I hoped you'd missed me, and that when we met, you'd just... jump on me. I had all these visions..."

"Ah, so you had visions. I had Mr Meaningful."

"Who was he? Nick? Mark?"

Simon laughed. "No, he was an inner voice who constantly made-up speeches that would impress you and make *you* jump on me."

"Anyway, of course, when we met in the corridor, and you didn't jump on me, I was... kind of offended, deflated... All my fantasies during the summer had been trashed. Even my pathetic attempts at suggestive humour fell flat. I felt a bit embarrassed."

"You know, it was only when you snubbed me that the penny dropped. I realised that all the little jokes you'd made had another meaning. Sorry. I'm a bit dense when it comes to these things."

Anna squeezed his hand. "Well, we know where we are now, don't we?"

"Yes we do."

"And there was one other reason, I realised, why it was all going wrong. Have you read Lord of the Rings?"

"Yes, of course. I almost fell asleep at some points, though."

"Remember Grima Wormtongue?" Simon nodded. "Well, Joan is my wormtongue. All through the holidays, when I talked about you, Joan wound me up. She said that you'd never liked me, really. That you just wanted to be my friend. She thought you might be... gay. And, anyway, I think she was doing it for another reason."

"Oh yes?"

"Yes. I think she fancied you too, and wanted to get me out of the way first. I'm going to have to have it out with her, or she'll be wormtonguing me all year."

Simon laughed. "You know, Warren isn't usually wise in the ways of love, but he thought Joan fancied me." He laughed again. "I'm a sex-god!"

"As long as you reserve your mighty staff only for me, I can handle it."

"I look forward to it," Simon said.

They would both have to get their buses soon. They headed for the park gates. Simon now knew his true heart. "Can I kiss you?"

"Of course, you can, you idiot."

At last, they kissed. Awkwardly at first, a bit shyly. But when they finally melted into the kiss together, it felt like the most completely correct and utterly right thing Simon had ever done.

29

Archie headed back towards Dereham in his NSU Ro80. Over the preceding day, he had worked himself into a perfect state of righteous anger. Of course, Nick or one of his friends had stolen his wallet. They obviously wanted to use the driving licence in it as a lever. If he didn't get that driving licence back, he and Peter were in grave danger. If Nick didn't have it, then everything would be all right. The only way he could know for certain whether Nick, or any of his friends, had the wallet was to ask, and to get an answer in any way he could.

He couldn't help thinking that the pain he might have to inflict on Nick was wrong. Nick was just an ordinary freak, hoping to do his freaky things. Chance had put him in Archie's car. Another day, and it might have been somebody else. Another day, and Nick might have caught the bus. Another day, Archie might not have become a hitman, but might have been the salesman Nick almost certainly thought he was the first time they'd met. Another day, Archie's father might not have been a distant, soulless bastard. Another day, Archie might not have found out that his real father had been Johnny Franklin's dad. Another day, and his brother and sister, now only half-brother and half-sister, might not have been mean to him, having found out what he was. Another day, another day, another day. But out of all those other possible days, Nick had got into the rather expensive car of a hitman who liked a joke. And out of all those other possible days, Nick had tried to take him on. And now, as a consequence of all those possible days, Nick would feel pain. Poor Nick. But rather poor Nick than poor Peter. He had do this to protect himself, and by extension, his son.

Archie turned the car, for the last time he hoped, into Malthouse Road, and parked in a space between other cars. He got out of the car, went down to the junction, turned right and headed up Barton Road, towards the drive to Barton House, where he would wait, patiently, for Nick to walk in one direction or the other. Even if he had to stand here for three or four hours, he would wait. This time, he was tooled up, in case Hippie Boy or Combat Jacket were there. He wouldn't do anything to Blondie, except tell her to run. He could do what he needed to do before she could get the police, he was sure of that. But the chances were that Blondie would not be there. He guessed they went to the pub one by one to the pub, from their different houses, and only returned together to chat by the sign at the crossroads.

He reached the driveway. He looked over at the old geezer's house. The curtains were closed. He looked around one more time for the wallet. It wasn't there. He turned and moved back into the shadows, facing the road, and waited. He felt uneasy though, in the shadows. He wasn't superstitious, he didn't believe in any of that New Age shit, the spirits, the UFOs, the paranormal. But there was something creepy about being here, a sense of foreboding.

He didn't have to wait long. The lanky form of Nick appeared from behind the trees on his left, illuminated by the amber streetlights. Archie was quick this time, and had a strong forearm around Nick's neck. He dragged him quickly back into shadows.

"Where's my fucking wallet, hippie?"

Nick only gurgled. Archie released the pressure slightly.

"I don't know," Nick said, his voice quiet and hoarse.

Archie dragged Nick backwards slightly, and kicked his legs out from under him. Nick's weight fell onto his neck. Archie bent slightly with the weight, so Nick's neck wouldn't break - yet at least. "Where's my wallet?"

Nick shook his head, his breathing ragged.

Archie let Nick go, knowing he'd be weak, turned him around, and nutted him on the nose. Nick went down. "Hurts, doesn't it? Where's my wallet?"

"I don't know," Nick mumbled.

Archie kicked Nick hard in the small of the back, and then picked him up by the lapels. Nick struggled feebly, but the constriction of the blood flow at the neck had weakened him, as Archie had intended. Archie screwed Nick's lapels into one hand, then he hit Nick hard, twice in the stomach with his fist. Archie knew what he was doing. He wanted Nick conscious, but unable to shout or scream, always winded, only able to talk quietly.

Hippie Boy moved softly. Archie was impressed. He hadn't heard feet on the pavement, though he'd been listening for interruptions. "Oh no, not you again," he said.

"Ditto," Hippie Boy said.

Archie clamped his left arm tightly around Nick's neck again. With his right hand, he reached under his jacket, and took out the knife that he had sheathed there.

"I can't be arsed with any of your kung fu trickery tonight, Hippie Boy. Do you know where my wallet is?"

"No, I don't," Hippie Boy said. "And my name is Simon."

"I like Hippie Boy, it keeps it impersonal. Well, Hippie Boy, now there are two of you, I don't have time to fuck about." Archie made a small cut on Nick's face with the knife. "Where's my wallet?"

"I don't know."

What happened next brought the dark foreboding Archie had felt into relief. A ghost appeared on the pavement.

"Archibald Franklin Fucking Conn."

Now he knew why he recognised that face. Here he was in Dereham, the place where Peta had died, and here was her ghost come back to haunt him. The hair on the back of his neck stood up. For a moment, he had literally been scared stiff, and Simon had recognised that moment. How quickly he moved! Archie felt the pain as Simon did something to his hand and wrist, and the knife involuntarily fell to the ground. Archie dropped Nick, who fell heavily, and swung a wild fist at Simon, who staggered backwards. Archie took this opportunity to flee from the ghost.

He ran down Barton Road, towards the town, towards the light. Seeing Peta's face had been like something from a dream. For a moment, he had wanted to scream, but, like in a dream, nothing would come out. He heard footsteps behind him, and looked around to see that face following him. A hundred yards further on, he heard more footsteps. He knew then that Simon had recovered and joined the chase. If he ran any further into town, he would be too close to the police station. He turned off down Church Street, scattering a few pedestrians, who called out after him. Still he could hear the pursuing footsteps. He knew that, a few yards down, on the right, was a footpath through the park.

The footfalls behind him now were quieter as they ran on mud and grass, but he could hear his pursuers as they brushed past bushes and trees. God, that ghost was fit. The running had sharpened his mind. He knew now that there was no ghost. There was only Molly Shepherd, Peta's little sister. He kept running, though, because at this moment it was the only thing he knew how to do. Everything had gone wrong, everything *was* going wrong. His life, which he had seemed so perfectly designed over the last few years, was beginning to break apart.

The path through the park exited onto the Poole Road. Archie quickly negotiated the stile and ran straight into the road, where a Morris Montego skidded to a halt, blaring its horn. Molly and Simon were close behind him. Archie's breathing was laboured now. He wished he'd followed through on that resolution to get fit. He ran into the Poole Road industrial estate, and then around the back of a timber merchant. Something behind him had changed. There was only one set of footsteps pattering on the asphalt. He glanced around quickly and could only see

Molly. Where was Hippie Boy? He soon found out, as Simon appeared in front of him. Archie took a left, breathing heavily, and ran around the back of Shuttlewood House. Molly followed him. Simon had disappeared again, had obviously gone around the other side. At the back of Shuttlewood House was a high fence. Molly and Hippie Boy closed on him. He ran to the steel fire escape at the back of Shuttlewood House, and began to run up it, his feet clattering at each step. As Molly and Simon followed, the estate echoed with the singing of flat steel bells. Shuttlewood House was four stories high. Archie found himself too quickly on the wide platform at the top of the fire escape. He tried the fire door, but it had been locked from the inside. He kicked at it, hopelessly. Hippie Boy arrived on the platform first, and Archie kicked out at him in frustration. Molly then arrived, standing on a step behind and below Hippie Boy, looking at Archie cautiously.

Archie launched himself at Simon, aiming a fist at the face. Hippie Boy dodged it, and Archie's fist hit the brick wall. Archie yelled, and stumbled. Simon grabbed Archie's head and banged it into the same wall. Archie staggered backwards, as if rebounding from the impact. Simon grabbed him before he could tumble backwards over the guard-rail, and kneed him in the stomach. Archie curled up, gasping for breath, and sank down onto the grey metal. Simon was about to hit Archie again, but Molly grabbed his arm. "Enough, Simon. He'll be no trouble for a while."

Archie manoeuvred himself into a sitting position against the guard-rail. Simon. What a perfectly pleasant name. He touched his forehead and felt the blood welling in the graze. A bruise was developing. His right-hand throbbed. He tried to open the still balled fist. Only three fingers responded. The knuckle of the first finger was damaged, and the thumb broken. He looked at Simon. "You're good. You should try my line of work."

Simon said nothing. Archie turned to Molly. "Hello, Molly. Nice to meet you. At last."

Molly sighed. "You know, I'd like to say the same, but I've hated you for years."

Archie laughed weakly. "Me? What have I done?"

"The ironic thing is, you don't know what you've done to me."

"Peta?"

"Of course, Peta. She was broken, Archie. Abused by her father, homeless, on the streets. She wanted love, she wanted trust. She thought she had it with you."

"How do you know? She never talked to you the whole time she was here. She kept saying she would, that she'd find you, bring you here, but she never did." Archie could see pain in Molly's eyes.

"Did she? Did she say that?"

"Yes, she did." Archie reached up and wiped a palm across his forehead. The blood from the graze had reached his eyebrows. He looked at the blood on his hand and glanced up at Simon, who stood with his arms folded, looking at Archie impassively.

"But though she said it, she never did. She was... a bit of a bird-brain, don't you think? A dreamer. She believed in the fucking UFOs, she believed in spirits, and she believed she wanted you to come down here and live with her. A romantic."

"You brought her down to this town and then just abandoned her. She became depressed, she..."

Archie held up his good hand. "Yes, yes, I know. Don't think I haven't thought about that, Molly. I'm not totally devoid of feeling, despite my... profession." Not totally devoid, no, Archie thought. But he didn't have much feeling in his stores, and he knew it. He had some for Peta, a small amount, but never enough to stop him moving on, or, in Peta's case, running away, running away from the consequences of his life and leaving Peta behind, alone. He had heard about Peta's death four years ago, a chance meeting with somebody from Dereham. It had saddened him, perhaps the only genuine feeling he had felt in all this time, apart from his love for Peter. Even he, as hard and cold as he was, knew why he had named his son so.

Molly spoke again, softly. "I kind of forgave you for that. It wasn't your fault that Peta was so... broken... so weak. I know couples break up, move on. I regretted that you had left her so... abruptly, not thinking about her weaknesses. But..." Molly looked down at her Dr Martens. She appeared to be remembering something equally as painful. Her mouth pulled into a tight line, and her eyes were closed. "Do you remember of your first love, Archie?"

Archie thought for a moment, back to the days before he had tried to shut away feelings, back to when he was seventeen and living in Wales. Bright summer days walking in the countryside with... what was her name? "Kind of."

"I remember mine clearly, like a slideshow, like a tape-recording, sharper, in focus, because my time with him was so short." She stopped talking quietly at her boots, and looked at Archie, a cold, hard stare. "Do you remember Colin?"

Archie's heart skipped a beat. "Of course I do. He lived with Peta and me in the house in Dereham. What's he go to do..."

"Do you know what happened to him?"

Honesty could only go so far. "No. I moved out, Colin stayed in Dereham. I never knew what happened after that."

"Well, Colin - whose real name was Harry, by the way - is dead."

"Really? That's a shame. He was a nice lad."

"Indeed he was, Archie. He was my boyfriend for a couple of months before he died. I was young, only eighteen, and fell in love quickly. I hoped it might develop into something serious, like you do at that age. But then he died."

"I'm sorry to hear that," Archie said.

"Are you? Because, you know, he was killed by a hitman."

Hippie Boy still stood impassively, watching Archie. It would be difficult to make a move, any move, while Hippie Boy was there. If it were only Hippie Boy, he'd try and take him on, even with his damaged hand. Hippie Boy was good, Archie knew that, but how hard was he? How far would he go? He looked back at Molly. She was an unknown; that was a problem. She was taller than Peta. She looked about five foot eight, trim and muscled, like she worked out. He wondered what she did, where she worked. Because when he looked at her, he could see a hardness in her that Hippie Boy didn't have. He suspected she might go where Hippie Boy couldn't. Right here, right now, she was, perhaps, his greatest enemy.

Molly spoke again. "I think you killed Harry."

Archie said nothing.

"I think you killed Harry, and then turned your gun on your paymaster, Colonel Skinner, and a mercenary named Oldrey. You attempted to kill Michael Edge, but he was, unknown to you, wearing a bulletproof jacket. You then turned your gun on Len Stone. Does any of this sound familiar to you, Archie?"

Hippie Boy now looked a little less impassive. He turned to Molly. "Fucking hell," he said.

"Oh yes, Simon," Molly said, still looking at Archie. "It was a bloodbath."

Archie shrugged. He wouldn't implicate himself.

"Nobody knows who did it, Archie. You were good. However, Len is sure it was you, even if he didn't see you."

Archie smiled ruefully. "Len always was full of weird ideas."

Molly returned his smile "So am I. I know you killed Harry. I've always known. I've been keeping my eye on you. I came to this town looking for Peta. Instead I found Simon and his friends. And through them, I found you. Archibald Franklin Fucking Conn."

"A strange series of coincidences."

"Peta always thought this town was magical."

"So what happens now?"

"I can never prove you killed Harry. However, I will cut you in whatever ways I can. So your performances in Dereham have been most useful. What you did to Nick today? GBH. And you have previous, don't you? You're going down. I don't know how long for, but you are." Molly looked at Simon. "He attacked Nick before tonight, didn't he?"

"Yes," Simon said. "Most severely."

"So there you are. ABH, GBH. I *will* make it look like attempted murder if I can."

"Uh, there's the contract on Nick," Simon said.

"There's no contract on Nick, is there," Molly said to Archie.

Archie said nothing.

"Oh, sod it, Archie. Simon and his mates will just come under my protection. They will get new identities, new jobs, new lives. You'll never know where they are. Now tell me about that contract."

She could take them into her protection? Just who the hell was Molly Shepherd? "Okay, there is no contract. I told Nick that to shut him up."

"Of course there isn't," Molly said. "Because you couldn't let word of this little local difficulty get out. If you couldn't handle a bunch of hippies, that would affect your reputation, wouldn't it?"

Archie slowly pulled himself up. Molly kicked his legs away, and he fell onto the base of his spine.

Archie yelped. "Fuck, that hurt!"

"How many years will he get?" Simon said.

"I don't know. As many as I can."

Archie didn't want to go down. He had Peter to protect, and how could he do that from a prison cell? Perhaps Nick would seek revenge for the cut Archie had given him. Nick didn't seem the violent sort, but Archie knew how people could be turned. It had happened to him. Peter would have money, always, he could arrange that. He'd always accepted that his job might land him in jail one day. But this? This was an injustice. He didn't know who Molly worked for. He had studied her during their conversation, and knew she wasn't somebody to be messed with. Security services? Mercenary? Manley Boy security? She did know Len Stone, after all. There was something about her, though, something he recognised after his dealings with the underworld. Would she turn a blind eye if a bitter and twisted

Nick went to Bournemouth and cut-up his son in revenge? And she too held a grudge against him. Could she resist hurting his son in revenge for what he had done to Harry?

Anger began to boil in Archie. He needed to protect Peter, he wanted to take revenge on Nick and Molly for crimes they hadn't even yet contemplated. He would save Peter. Without thinking, he sprang from his sitting position towards Molly. She was the dangerous one here. She was the one with authority, the one with connections. If he could push her over the steel railing she leaned against, he would only then have to worry about Simon. But, again, Hippie Boy was too quick. All he felt was a nudge against his shoulder that deflected him from Molly.

His own impetus took him over the guard-rail and into the night air, where his arms and legs flailed for a second, trying to find something solid, something to hold onto, before he realised what had happened. And then he felt at peace. Images of Peta and Peter flitted across his mind. He need worry no more about anything, he need no longer contemplate the cold deadness inside him through dark, lonely nights in his opulent house in Cheltenham. He would, though, miss Poulenc and Prokofiev and all the others.

30

Simon looked down at the unnaturally bent body in the empty car park beside Shuttlewood House. Dark liquid pooled around the head. He didn't feel sick. He didn't feel much emotion at all, at this moment, although his body burned with adrenaline.

"You have to go," Molly said. "You have to go *now*."

He looked down at Archie's body again. "But what about..."

"If you stay here, questions *will* be asked. You and your friends are not liars. Whatever Archie did, you have committed GBH on him and manslaughter. If you end up in the dock, I can't guarantee a good brief wouldn't get you to say what actually happened here, and make it look as though we killed a perfectly innocent man."

"But he was a hitman."

"We have no evidence of that, Simon. All we have is that he twice attacked Nick, and that he attacked you. I only need a couple of truths from you. About everything else, you must remain silent. I want one lie from you, and if you have any sense, you will maintain it. *You were never here*, you understand? You protected Nick, I arrived on the scene, and I chased Archie here. I alone. Have you got that?"

Simon nodded.

"Good. Now you need to get back to Nick, while I work out... what happened."

Simon ran down the fire escape, leaving Molly at the top, leaning over the rail, looking down at Archie's body.

Simon found Nick, sitting now in the shaded gateway.

"You look pale," Nick said.

"You look like shit," Simon said. "Should I call somebody? An ambulance? The police?"

"They're on their way. The old man across the road has saved the day again. He was letting his cat out for the night, and heard me moaning."

Simon told Nick some of what happened. "You do understand, Nick. I'm not telling you everything. There were certain details we must keep secret, that we can't even tell Gaz and Mark.

An ambulance arrived, and a police car. The police asked perfunctory questions, and then Simon rode with Nick in the ambulance to the Royal United Hospital. Simon provided Nick with more detail about what had happened in the Poole Road Industrial Estate.

Simon stayed with Nick at the hospital for the first few hours. When the police arrived, Nick kept to the story Simon had told him.

After the police had gone, Nick sighed. "I feel... aggrieved. There's been no justice. The hitman is dead, but he'll never be held to account for the deaths he's caused, the shit he caused us."

Nick was right, Simon thought. Nobody would ever know what Archibald Franklin Conn had been, what he had done. Perhaps only Molly would ever know everything, could tally up Archie's sins and provided a reckoner. Simon was suddenly struck by something else. He still didn't know whether Molly really was a spy.

Nick lay in his bed in hospital, nursing two broken ribs, and a cracked vertebra. He had been here for two days now. Nurses and doctors periodically came to check if he was okay. Simon, Gaz and Mark had been in to visit, and his parents. He'd had a surprise visit from Jill, who had told him about her split with Simon. A policeman sat outside the private room. That made him feel secure, although if what Molly Shepherd had said was true, he had no need to worry. He had received a letter from her this morning. After talking to the police, she had returned to London. She had written the letter just before leaving The White Lion, in which she explained how Archie had fallen, and how everything she was now doing was to protect Simon.

Intriguingly, she also suggested a way out of Dereham for Nick. He could, she suggested, join the Security Service. He had shown intelligence and resourcefulness when tracking down Archie, and fortitude in the face of his violence. They needed agents. She could sponsor him. Agents were recruited this way, she said. Suitable candidates were identified, and then there were meetings back at the office. So she *was* a spy. He would have to tell Simon.

London would be good, Nick thought. Perhaps he would work in the field. It appealed to the romantic in him. Travelling, meeting new people, and then coming back to Wiltshire for holidays and to meet up with the lads.

Molly had liked Dereham, she said. She would miss it when she returned to London. Once the Archie mess had been sorted out, she would be back, this time to concentrate on the people she'd come to know and like. There was a P.S. *I even liked Gaz.* Nick had laughed at that.

Gaz had been in to see Nick, and apologised for stealing the wallet, the action from which so much had flowed. Nick had told Gaz not to worry; everything had started when he had accepted the lift from Archie. Gaz told him about the shoplifting. He was going to stop, he said. The episode with Archie had scared him. Nick told him to give it all to a charity shop. They would never know it had been nicked, and at least it would do some good.

Now, Nick lay back in his bed, contemplating the offer from Molly, at last seeing a way out of Dereham clear before him.

Simon met up with Jill at the Vine Tree in Southleigh. He still liked her, and didn't want to tell her about what had happened with Anna. But he did, he had to admit to himself, love Anna. He and Anna were getting to know each other, properly, at last. It was becoming *real*.

Simon and Jill sat at the table they had sat at only a few weeks ago. Jill sipped her drink and smiled at him with the amused cornflower blue eyes Simon had found so attractive. "Don't worry," she said. "I already know. Angie told me."

"I'm sorry. I didn't want you to find out from Anna's sister. But with all the shit that's happened since the other night... I've been trying to find time to see you, but with Nick in hospital, police to talk to, parents to placate, Gaz to sort out... you know..."

"Yes, I know. I always worried about Anna. I liked you Si, I liked you a lot. But Anna was always there, however much you tried to put her in the background."

"Yes, I know. Look, I really liked you, too. In other circumstances, you know..."

Jill shrugged, but smiled. "At least we hadn't fallen in love with each other. That *would* have been a nightmare. Go and love Anna, Si. She's a lovely girl. Not as bright and good-looking as me, of course..."

"Of course," Simon said. "Who could be?"

Jill sighed. "I shall have to give myself to somebody more worthy."

Simon smiled. "Warren?"

"You're joking. I did think, maybe... uh... how about Nick?"

"That would be cool. We could still hang out."

"How would Anna take it?"

"She'd be fine. She likes you, she knows you better than she knows me, I think."

Jill smiled mischievously. "Not in every way."

Simon blushed a little. "Well, no, not in every way. Not yet."

The next day, Gaz took all that he had stolen to a charity shop, having removed the price tags, and roughed up a couple of items to look used. On Mark's advice, he met up with Jake and gave him the bottle of vodka. Jake asked why he was doing this. Gaz told the truth. "I don't drink vodka. Mark said you might like it."

Jake looked at Gaz suspiciously. "What do you want for it?"

"Nothing," Gaz said.

Jake smiled, and put it into his coat pocket.

Simon met Gaz, Mark and Molly in The White Lion that evening. Anna sat next to him, holding his hand. Mark had a copy of The Western Daily Press with him. The police had finally released the story of Archie's death. They all read the story in turn. Simon found it strange to read about an event that had happened four days ago, an event that, as shocking as it was, he was already beginning to move into the past. He thought he might feel bad about what had happened. But he didn't. He had been protecting Nick and Molly, and ultimately all his friends. He didn't feel good about it. It was something that had simply happened. He knew he would do it again, but hoped he would never have to. Molly Shepherd's name was mentioned, but his name was not. The paper never said if Molly was a spy. There was no picture of her, as might be expected in a newspaper, with a caption reading *Molly Shepherd, 22*. There was a photograph of Archie, however.

Anna leaned in, to look more closely at the grainy photograph. "Mark was right. He looks nothing like Clint Eastwood."

"He looks nothing like Shirley Temple, either." Gaz said.

They all laughed, although the laughter of Simon, Gaz and Mark was perhaps a little uneasy.

"I have some happier news," Mark said. "Fredericks wants to buy more of my drawings. He's arranged an exhibition in London."

"Wow!" said Anna. "That *is* cool."

"Who is Fredericks?" Simon asked.

"When we were at the exhibition at the Wool Hall," Mark said, "do you remember a short bloke in a suit and a white fedora?"

Simon thought back to that day. "Yes, yes I do."

"*That* is Fredericks."

"What's his cut?" Gaz said.

"Uh... Twenty per cent."

"Shit," Gaz said. "I should have asked for more."

On the Saturday, Danny, Steve and John returned for the long promised Honeyhouse band practice, much to Mark's relief. James and Mark had asked Stuart, Imogen and Kate to come along to the practice and add whatever they could to the sound. They added harmonies to some Honeyhouse songs, shyly and awkwardly at first, but became more confident. Mark, also more confident in his bass playing since he had started dancing, walked as far in front of the band as his lead would allow. He turned and faced the band, and listened as he continued to play. Stuart, Imogen and Kate were singing strongly. Their harmonies were having an effect on the rest of the band. Steve, Danny and John were glancing at each other, nodding, smiling. He hoped that this version of Honeyhouse could stay together, somehow, through the next three years. With these voices, and the songs they were writing now, Mark thought they might have a chance.

At the pub that night, Mark asked Simon if he wanted to go to Bournemouth on Sunday. "It'll be like a closing," Mark said.

Simon considered for a moment. "Yeah, okay. We can draw a line in the sand."

Mark wondered what Simon's part in the whole affair had really been. He couldn't imagine Molly Shepherd, however tough she was, taking on the hitman by herself. *Had Simon done a Charlie?* The full story would come out in time, he supposed. There was no point in pushing it, and he had no intention of doing so.

Mark and Simon spent a pleasant afternoon in Bournemouth, walking along the beach, and looking in the shops. They didn't talk about Archibald Franklin Fucking Conn, nor about what had happened over the preceding couple of months. They talked about music, and Anna and Jill, and Chrissie. Simon bought himself an army surplus shoulder bag from a hippie shop. He thought about buying a wooden flute, and asked if he could join Honeyhouse with it. Mark laughed. Simon really wanted to buy it to feel like Caine from *Kung Fu*. But his pragmatic side warned him that he might appear pretentious. He looked in a hippie mirror on the wall of the hippie shop. He was thinking about cutting his hair really short. Anna had said she wouldn't mind. He'd recently recognised his freakiness as a form of uniform against which he was rebelling. He had bought himself some black Doc Martens, like Molly's. His hair got in his eyes, in his mouth, and in his food; and he hated getting his hair in his food. And it *was* 1976, man.

Mark bought pasties and pies from a pastry shop near the sea front, and he sat with Simon on a bench looking out over the sea. The beach and roads were quiet. The day was bright, and warmer than they'd expected. Simon felt hot in his jacket. He looked around. A girl carrying an A3 drawing pad arrested his gaze. Her jeans had been hand-bleached. One bleached patch looked like the figure of a man, others like spikey leaves. She was wearing a jersey. Simon wondered if she was as hot as he was. She might have droplets of sweat running down her, inside her jersey, just as he had inside his shirt under the jacket.

Her jeans, patterned with her handiwork, were very tight, almost as if she had painted the patterns on her legs. He looked at the jeans more closely, as if he needed to confirm to himself that they were fabric, and not painted skin. He glanced at Mark. He was looking, too.

"Go and talk to her," Simon said.

"Oh, I don't know," Mark said.

"Not every woman will be Chrissie," Simon said. "Remember, this trip is supposed to be about closure. You could do with some closure yourself. Look, she's got a Rowney pad under her arm! She's your kind of woman. Tell her about the exhibition in London. She'll genuflect."

"Well, that would be something." Mark stood, and straightened his Belstaff. "Well, here goes nothing."

"*Per adua ad astra.*"

"Too bloody right."

Simon, Anna, Gaz, and Mark were in The White Lion again that night, with all of Honeyhouse. Simon was surprised when the door opened, and Warren came in. He was more regularly seen in The Swan. He bought a drink from the bar, a short of some description, and came and sat with Simon and the others. He drank the clear liquid down quickly, and laughed. "You should see something," he said.

Simon frowned. "What's that?"

"You have to see it."

"Oh, come on, Warren, what is it?"

"No, you have to see it. You'll like it. It's a surprise."

Simon was in a good mood after his day in Bournemouth. The sea breeze had been cleansing, if nothing else. "Okay, I'm up for it."

Mark was also in a good mood. He'd wangled a date with the arty Bournemouth girl. "I'm up for it, too."

"Oh well, count me in, then," Gaz said. "Although I expect it's a pointless shitty waste of time."

Warren scuttled towards the door, still smiling. Simon, Anna, Mark and Gaz stood, ready to follow. Then everybody at the Honeyhouse table also stood.

"If you lot are intrigued, so are we," James said.

Danny called out over the seated patrons: "If anybody uses these tables or touches our drinks before we get back, Simon will kill you."

For a moment, a dark shadow crossed Simon's heart. But at that moment, Anna squeezed his hand, not knowing about the dark shadow, and the shadow passed.

Warren was waiting for them, bouncing on his soles, eager. He smiled as the others trooped down the steps of The White Lion. "The more the merrier!"

"I think Warren's pissed," Anna said.

"Undoubtedly," Simon agreed.

Warren led the laughing and chatting group of friends down through the Market Place and the High Street, and then turned into Station Road. They were heading for the station. Simon noticed an orange glow. In the distance, he could hear a siren.

Soon, they could see the source of the glow. Every night, the Southleigh to Dereham bus, after its last run at eight o'clock, was parked-up near the station. The bus was on fire. Orange flames danced around the green metal bodywork. Some of the windows had already popped out. One of the tyres was burning.

"Cool," Anna said.

"Holy shit," Simon said.

Warren laughed. "That'll teach that tit of a bus driver."